THE GEMS

M. C. JETER

M. C. JETER BOOKS, LLC

ISBNs: 979-8-9883732-7-8 (paperback), 979-8-9883732-5-4 (ebook)

Edited by J. Berry Editorial

Cover artist and illustrations by K. Yan

Proofread by T. A. Jeter

1st edition 2023

To my 4th grade teacher Mrs. Piazza,
for being my inspiration to
start writing.

CONTENTS

Beginning Author's Note

Dear Reader,

Thank you so much for choosing to read this novel. I'm so happy you've decided to embark on Ruby's adventure to save the world.

Although *The Gems* is a fantasy novel with romance and action sprinkled in, the story deals with references to sexual assault (graphic), trauma, torture, and death.

Pieces of Ruby's life reflect some of my own experiences, but she is the strong woman I wish I was more like. Although at times impulsive, Ruby is loving, intelligent, and resilient. She may fall, but she does what she can to get back up again, seeking change and justice whether it be directly or indirectly.

Her story is one filled with power, love, strength, and family, and I sincerely hope that you enjoy it!

~ M. C. Jeter

Content Warning

THE FOLLOWING SUBJECTS APPEAR IN THE GEMS:

- Blood and Gore
- Death
- Generational Trauma
- Guns
- Mental Illness
- Murder
- Sexual Assault (Graphic)
- Sexually Explicit Scenes
- Suicide Ideation
- Swearing
- Torture

- Violence

CHAPTER 1

*O*verwhelmed by the smell of smoke clogging my lungs and burning my throat, I squeeze my eyes shut, tears of pain streaming down my face. Wails and gurgles fill the cluttered meadow, but I can't identify where they're coming from.

"Shh, it will be okay, my little Ruby," a woman's voice echoes. I feel hands gently touching my body, wrapping me in something soft. The wailing is louder now, and my face is damp with moisture. Jumping, I realize where the sound is coming from: me. The shadowy figure that the woman's voice belongs to comes closer. I blink away the ash and tears until the face comes into focus. She's pretty. Her face mirrors what I assume mine looks like: dirty and slick with sweat.

It's hot. Suffocatingly hot. I pull at the blanket, reaching for the woman. There's a call from somewhere far off. The woman turns her head. No, look at me again. As if reading my thoughts, she turns back. Although her face is filled with fear and her brows are furrowed with stress, her presence is a cool breeze of solace in the sweltering heat. She looks as if she wants to pick me up, but then she's tugged away, disappearing into the smoke. The soft fabric has me wrapped in a cocoon, trapping me in a tight bundle. I stop crying as the shadow returns.

"Help me! I'm stuck!" I try to say, but it comes out in babbles and screeches. When the shadow gets closer, its arms are broader, head larger, chest wider. This shadow is different, towering over me like a predator to its prey. Struggling, I try *to wriggle away, fear bubbling in my stomach as it reaches out its arms. My efforts are useless. The shadow reeks of hot leather and wine as it presses down onto me, crushing my lungs and small arms.*

I scream.

I wake up in a pool of sweat, trying to gather my bearings. My limbs are like blocks of cement, too heavy to move. My eyes are fixated on a shadow in front of me. Like the one from my dream, it's holding me down. My lungs burn, barely taking in any air as I focus on the figure. Tears and sweat mix as they run down my face.

Help me! I think in a panic. *Let me go!* I try to move my arm to shove the figure off me, but I have no luck. My throat constricts as I feel the pressure on me increase, pressing me onto the bed, immobilizing me. Another tear falls. Another drip of sweat. *Is it trying to choke me?*

I hear the calls of the mourning doves, cooing at the breaking of dawn. Light trickles into my room, creating an eerie luminescence. As the room brightens, the shadow seems to ease its grip on me. I focus all my attention on moving my arm. *Just a finger, that's all I need.* Through gritted teeth and a wave of panic, there's a twitch. My pinkie. The weight on me lifts, and hope surges through my body. Another twitch and air flows into my lungs. More light, less weight; I can move.

My movements are slow and groggy, but the shadow is almost gone. I inch my hips to the edge of my bed, blinking rapidly.

Deep breaths.

After several minutes of minimal movement, the pressure that was overtaking me fizzles, dissipating into the stale morning air of my room.

It's the fifth time I've had a nightmare in the past couple of months, the second time of sleep paralysis. They seem so real . . . so true. So . . . terrifying. I shake myself awake, feeling returning to my limbs. After I'm able to stand without falling, I stumble into my bathroom. My heart is pounding in my chest as I lean against the counter, head down. *Relax, Ruby, it's over.* I look up slowly, bringing my eyes to my reflection. The strands of my dark red hair that escaped my bonnet are stuck to my face, slick with sweat. I strip off my clothes, slap on my shower cap, and step into the cold water, letting it blast against my bare back. I shiver, scrubbing at my skin so hard I'm surprised it doesn't tear. It's a failed attempt at washing away the nerves of last night's dream and the sleep paralysis.

Whatever, I think, brushing off the anxiety I know will bubble in my gut if I continue that train of thought. Wrapping myself in my ruby red towel, I step out of the shower. After brushing my teeth and washing my face, I put on my favorite red plaid skirt and white dress shirt. I grab my favorite pink tie and put it on, along with my knee-high red socks. I walk over to my dresser mirror and yank off my shower cap and bonnet. My hair bounces to my shoulders as I let out a sigh. Tapping my finger on my cheek, I stare at my reflection. *What to do . . . what to do?* It's nearly time for me to take my twists out, but I think they can last for one more day. I grab my hair and hold it in two space buns. *No, maybe pigtails?* I move my hands. *Definitely not. I could braid them?* I start to braid one side but barely make it halfway. *No, I'm too lazy for that.* Throwing one hand up, I grip all my hair, holding it atop my head. With a curt nod, I'm satisfied. This will do.

I reach for my bottle of moisturizer and squirt generous amounts in my hands. I lather my twists in it, running my fingers from my roots to my split ends. When I'm done, I grab my satin ribbon and bend over, letting my hair fall in front of my face. I wrap the ribbon around it tightly. When I throw my head back, the updo is nearly perfect. I pull at my hair to make sure all the twists made it in, as well as pull a couple twists out in the front. *There.*

I grab my glasses and check myself out again. *Damn, I look even better when I'm not blurry.* After slipping on my high-top Converse, I lace them up tightly, grab my backpack, and run down two flights of stairs to the kitchen to make breakfast for everyone. I live with my stepmother, Lisa and three step siblings: Maria, Jack, and Paris. Since Paris started school at Dartmouth this fall, she's become happily irrelevant in my life. After my adopted dad died, Lisa made me take cooking lessons when I was around ten, and now I'm a borderline professional.

I always thought of her as a trophy wife to my dad. She never cooked or cleaned. All she would do was sit around, look pretty, watch her kids, and love him. So, while he was alive, he would cook, clean, and run errands. He absolutely worshipped her. With him gone now, those chores fell to me. My phone buzzes and when I see the message, I sigh.

Lisa: Ruby. Jack has a book report today. Breakfast should be filling, but light.

I don't think Lisa ever learned to cook, or that she ever wanted to. Until I could cook a decent breakfast, lunch, and dinner, she would always order in or buy "food-in-five-minutes" stuff for Jack and Maria. She refused to hire anyone either, saying that she "values her privacy" and doesn't want anyone else in the house. Thus, I have to make all the meals, as well as do all the other chores. Although never explicitly stated, it's giving "house slave."

That was never her intention though—at least I don't think it was. I walk past the fridge, a picture of Lisa and Terry's wedding grabbing my attention. As an Asian American, I'm sure she's had her own handfuls of microaggressions and racist encounters. I've even heard her speak actively against recent racist events, so I strongly doubt she's discriminatory. She just doesn't like *me*.

I take out flour, eggs, and the water pitcher to make a runny batter. After finely chopping scallions, I add them to the batter along with ground pepper. While making the egg and scallion crepes, the aroma of the cooking scallions dance in my nostrils. After making four servings, I plate them, placing all but mine on the table. Lisa had once said, and I quote "True families eat together, and, yet, you still eat with us." Ever since that moment, I've always prepared meals before the others come into the room and leave as soon as I can.

I shovel down my food, barely having enough time to enjoy the flavor, and head straight to the garage, get on my bike, and ride to school.

I pedal through my sizeable community called Owl Estate, passing the typical white, rich, suburban houses with mowed lawns, multiple garages, stone exterior accents, and basketball hoops in the driveways. Trees sprinkle the neighborhood, dense in more places than others.

When I pass Schwartz Road, I crane my neck to see the end of the street. The biggest house in Owl Estate . . . at least that's what I was told, lies maybe a mile east. I haven't seen it myself. It's deep in the forest and from the street, all you can see is the end of the driveway and the house's mailbox. Rumor has it the owner of the house murdered her entire family, froze them, and has been living off their corpses for several years. It sounds like a load of crap to me. Panting, I pedal until I see Lynn High School and my three best friends waiting for me by the bike rack: Moonstone, Jordyn, and Camy.

Moon's hair is in her iconic white braids, the sun casting a golden aura around her melanated skin. Her goddess-like features have always been something I've admired: full lips, sparkling brown eyes, long lashes. She says something to Camy, making Camy and Jordyn laugh. Camy's short auburn curls bounce as she giggles, and Jordyn's upturned button nose scrunches. Both of the fair-skinned girls' cheeks are rouge, hot from the September heat. As I get closer, Jordyn looks toward me, giving me a friendly wave.

"Ruby, you made it in time again, and with two minutes to spare!" Camy says, amazed.

"Well, yah, I'm just *that* good," I reply, smiling broadly as I lock up my bike.

"Come on! Let's go or we'll be late!" Moon ushers us with her hands as she heads toward the building. We get to our lockers just as the warning bell rings. Mine is right between Camy's and . . . Zach's. His arm is outstretched as he leans against the lockers, eyebrows furrowed. When he sees me looking, he smiles, and I smile back. Bundles of butterflies erupt in my stomach. Some seem to fly in my throat, and I clear it, watching him walk into the classroom. I place my backpack inside and take out my books before heading into the same classroom for homeroom. We sit in alphabetical order, so I take my seat in between Zach and Camy.

Lynn High is like the standard high school, grades nine through twelve, and I plan to make every moment of my last year worth it. As much as I love school, I can't wait to graduate. My grades are off the charts as well as my test scores. I know I can get into any college I want. I've started a handful of supplemental essays over the summer, but as for my personal statement, I have no idea what to write, and the longer it takes me to figure it out, the more anxious I get.

"Hello, class. We have a new student joining us for the rest of this school year, Ani Joel," says Ms. Sanders, my homeroom teacher. "Ani, you will sit between

Zach and Ruby." Smiling, I raise my hand and gesture for her to take the now empty seat between Zach and me. She stares at me as she walks over and takes her seat, never straying her gaze.

She's absolutely gorgeous. Her wavy, long, jet-black hair just reaches past her shoulders. The wig is expertly applied, her baby hairs in delicate swoops. Her large, rounded box-like glasses sit atop her nose, and her lips are glossed. She's wearing an oversized navy sweatshirt and shorts. The sweatshirt is so long though, you can barely tell she's wearing anything underneath. Her features are soft, but her eyes hold an intensity. She drops her bag on the desk and plops into her seat. As I'm about to open my mouth to introduce myself, she digs her phone out of her bag and texts with urgency. I begin to pull away but decide not to. Attending a PWI (predominantly white institution), Black faces aren't all that common. I tap her on the shoulder.

Holding out my hand, I introduce myself. She stares at it, then me, then my hand again. I notice a smile tugging at her lips. She starts to say something, but then her phone buzzes. The smile vanishes as she looks down at it.

"Excuse me," she says as she pushes out of her seat and scurries to Ms. Sanders, whispers into her ear, and then ducks out of the door.

"Well, that was friendly," says Zach as he watches everyone stand to say the pledge.

"I'll say," I whisper, staying seated as well. There are a handful of other people sitting, too, but the majority of the class is on their feet, reciting the words engraved into their heads from kindergarten. *I pledge allegiance . . .* is definitely American propaganda. Of course, I didn't always think so. I was an obedient little girl, pledging my allegiance to the flag. The flag that wronged my people in so many ways. And not just my people, every marginalized community. When realization struck—well, the realization was Moon telling me why she stopped reciting the pledge—I stopped standing. When the overhead speaker clicks off, everyone files out of the room for first period, but I hold back outside the door, waiting on Moon. We don't have the same homeroom, so we always meet outside mine.

"We have a new senior," I say once I see her, and we walk to our next class.

"So . . . what are they like? Nice? Cool? Could be our new friend? Tell me all of the tea!" blurts Moon.

"*LOL*, her name is Ani. She didn't even say hi to me, so . . . I mean, I introduced myself! It was kinda rude, not gonna lie . . ." I trail off, thinking of the conversation we had minutes before. *Well, more like lack thereof.*

"Well, where is she from? You did ask, right?"

"Yeah."

"So, are you going to tell me?"

"I dunno, fam."

"So . . . you're not going to tell me."

"No, I don't know. She didn't say anything." I dodge a person who's staring at their phone. "She's pretty though, like, *really* pretty. She's Black too!"

"Yesss, we need more melanin in this hellhole," Moon says as she flips her white braids over her shoulder. I smile. We walk into the choir room and Ani is there, standing with Mrs. Beachler.

"Daannng, you wasn't lying," she whispers into my ear.

Ani and Mrs. Beachler talk a little before she comes to take the seat to my right. Mrs. Beachler explains that instead of teaching us new music today, she will be having us get in groups of five to practice sight reading before singing the piece to the class. Moon, Kylie, Jordyn, and I quickly form a group, Ani striding over to be our fifth.

"Okay, I have no clue what sight reading even is. This is my first year doing any music," says Ani.

"It's not that bad. Sight reading is just reading a piece of music that you have never seen before and trying to sing it how it is supposed to go. Don't worry, you will get the hang of it," encourages Moon.

"If you say so," Ani responds skeptically. We start going through the music. I expected Moon and me to carry the whole group, but everyone is doing well. For not taking a music class ever, Ani is surprisingly good too.

"You're really good at this Ani," I say, smiling.

"Thanks," she responds. After we finish sight reading and perform it, the rest of class is a study hall. I take out my book and begin reading. I feel Ani's stare.

"Ruby," whispers Ani, as she scoots to sit across from me.

"Yes?" I respond, slightly irritated, closing my book on the best scene.

"Does something about me seem . . . familiar to you?" she whispers so softly I have to strain to hear her.

"Um, no? Not really," I say hesitantly, a little creeped out by the question.

"Oh. LOL, okay. Never mind then. I just feel like I should know you from somewhere," she says, disappointment creeping into her whispers. To be honest, she *does* look slightly familiar, but I just can't place her face.

"Yeah . . . I don't know what to tell you, fam," I say, shrugging. She looks at me, a small smile on her lips.

"Mmph," she huffs sweetly, winking and moving away from me to go talk to Moon.

She's . . . a character, I think, settling back into my book.

Ani happens to be in every single one of my morning classes. During study hall, which has everyone from my homeroom, Camy and I try to do our homework, but we get distracted easily.

"C'mon, Ruby, let's go save Ani from the claws of the creature . . . Zach," she says, heading over to them. "Hey, Ani, come hang with us, you do not want to get the Zachys! You'll get it if you touch him!"

I stare at Camy to avoid eye contact with Zach, trying not to laugh at the same time. We came up with that in elementary school and now, it's a running joke between the two of us.

"And what exactly are the 'Zachys'? Do I have some kind of disease that I don't know about?" Zach asks, feigning fear. I can't help it; I have to get in on this.

"It's called 'Zacooties' and they are *really* contagious. The Zacooties give you the Zachys. I think you have to be quarantined. Be gone with you, and your sickness as well. We refuse to be infected," I say to him dramatically, my voice full of confidence as I playfully shoo him away.

"You refuse?" asks Zach.

"Refuse!" I repeat, turning from him and walking away.

"Is that so?" he says, coming up from behind me and trapping me in a hug. I yelp.

"*No*! Must . . . not . . . be . . . infected!" I say, struggling in his grasp.

"Well, now you are," he responds, his lips brushing my lobe as he whispers in my ear. A bundle of butterflies swirl in my stomach. When he lets me go, I fall on the ground. Camy laughs, moving to help me, but I hold a hand up, telling her to stay.

"No! Not you, Camy. I'm now infected. I can't let you be too!" I yell over-dramatically, putting my hand up to my forehead as if I'm faint.

"Here, I'll help Ruby, since we're both *infected*." Before I can say anything, Zach pulls me to my feet. I'm standing right in front of him, and all time stops. His hands are in mine, and I am looking into his eyes. Sometimes, I forget how pretty he is. His smile seems to lighten the room, and I can't help but glance at his lips. His eyes carry a playful twinkle, the irises nearly matching his chocolate skin. The sun is doing him many favors right now.

"What's going on over here?" asks Ms. Sanders, walking back into the room. I pull away from Zach and tuck a twist behind my ear.

"Nothing, Ms. Sanders. I just fell and Zach was helping me up, that's all," I mutter, moving to my desk and sitting down, Camy and Ani close on my tail.

"Okay . . . well keep it down in here, please. This *is* study hall," Ms. Sanders replies, returning to her desk. We sit down, giggling quietly, before working on homework. It's an efficient study hall; I finish all my homework for the day. When the bell rings, I stack up my books, tell Camy I'll see her at lunch, then dip out into the hall to wait for Moon. I smile when I see her, looping my arm with hers before heading to the lunchroom.

When we come across an intersection of hallways, I pause, asking her, "Which way do you want to go?"

"Why do we always do this?" She chuckles, placing her hands on her hips and leaning on her back leg. "Which way do *you* want to go?" She asks.

"I want to go whichever way you want to go," I respond. Ever since I can remember, Moon and I could never agree on which path to take anywhere. So much so, it's become a running joke of ours. Whenever we come to a fork in our path, we always ask the other to decide our route to our destination.

"You're the strong one," she says.

"So you think. Just pick a way so we can go to lunch. I'm not picking." And to prove my point, I sit smack dab in the middle of the hallway, receiving odd looks from passersby. I know I'm just wasting time at this point, but I don't care.

"Okay, fine! Get up. Let's go left." She laughs. I stand, and we walk down the hall.

I take my seat with Moonstone, and we eat our lunch as Camy comes to sit with us.

"Hey, guys. Ani didn't have a place to sit, and I knew that we had an extra seat. So, is it okay that she sits here?"

"Of course," says Moon. Ani takes the empty seat across from me, and immediately takes out her calculus homework, pointing out a problem.

"Ruby, can you help me solve this problem? I have absolutely no clue how to do it, and we have that quiz Monday. And I am freaking out."

"Sure, you probably won't have to take it since you're new though," I reply, showing her the steps to solve the problem. But she's still confused. Moon tries to show her but Ani still doesn't understand. We discuss more about the homework, then decide a group study session on Saturday would be the best. Moon and I are pretty confident in our skills, but if Ani wants to do well on this quiz Monday, she'll need our help.

The only class Ani and I don't have together is band. She isn't as bad as I originally thought, just a little weird. In the downtime that we had in our shared classes, she opened up more about herself. She's from Alaska and moved here because of her mother's job promotion. We talked about colleges we want to apply to and what we want our majors to be. When she said aerospace engineering, my eyebrows shot through my twists.

"Whatcha thinking about?" Moon asks as she crouches next to me, dropping her bags on the floor.

"Nothing much. Did you know Ani and I had all the same classes today?" I ask her, taking out my flute and putting it together.

"That's cool!" she says, putting together her piccolo. "Have you learned anything else about her?"

I nod, pushing myself off the ground just as Moon does. We walk toward the door, mixing in with the sousaphones and snares as we all head outside. The regular band sessions won't start for another couple of months. Until then, it's marching season, and our practices are outside.

"Yeah, she wants to go to MIT or Georgia Tech. And as an *aerospace engineer!*" We walk toward the football stadium, seeing our director already at the top of the bleachers.

"Damn, she gotta know math for that though," Moon says, then she quickly clamps a hand over her mouth. "That was insensitive. I'm sorry. Pretend like I didn't say that." Her eyes are bulging out of her head, and I chuckle.

"Relax, Moon, it's just me." I've known Moon basically my whole life. Terry and her parents were good friends from college, so we had a lot of playdates before he died. She's the first friend I ever made. "Anyway, you do have a point. But we'll help her Saturday."

"Yes, we will." When we make it to the field, the blow of a whistle hushes my fellow band mates.

"We're going to do a full run-through of the show today!" Mrs. Patrick, our band director, speaks through a megaphone. "I need to see what areas we need to work on before the game Friday." After a quick warm-up, we rush off the field to our designated spots, preparing to march on as if it were our halftime show. With the click of the drums, I mentally count inside my head, marking time. On twenty-nine, I step off the sideline, rolling my feet so my toes point to the sky with each step. After all the clicks have sounded, Mrs. Patrick blows her whistle in a series of short tweets, signaling the band to play the Motown themed show. As I'm marching and playing, the percussion and brass drown out the small notes of my flute, making my sound invisible to everyone.

After band rehearsal, Moon and I grab our things, making our way to the front of the school to meet up with Camy, Jordyn, and, now, Ani. After saying our goodbyes, Moon and Camy head to Camy's car, and Jordyn walks to her own. I walk to the bike rack, and I'm surprised to see that Ani does as well.

"So, you were adopted?" asks Ani, as she falls in step with me. My head whips in her direction, and I scrunch my eyebrows.

"Yeah . . . who told you?"

"Uh . . . Moon," she responds, tugging at the end of her sweatshirt.

"Okay . . ." I trail off, looking away. *Why would Moon do that?*

"It doesn't make sense, though. You were adopted, so why do you have a stepmother?" Ani asks. Damn, this girl was here for five seconds and she knows a concerning amount about me already.

"It's a long, confusing story," I say, trying to dismiss the conversation, but Ani persists.

"I've got time."

I explain all that I know briefly. How my birth parents died in a plane crash, but I somehow survived. How I was put in a private adoption center, and my adopted dad, Terry, adopted me immediately after. Then, my adopted mom, Dove, died in a car accident a few weeks after I was adopted. So Lisa became my stepmom when Terry married her when I was seven. Three years later, he died in his sleep.

"Wow," Ani says with a look of pity on her face. "Was Moon adopted also?"

"Yes, her parents died in the same plane mine did, apparently. We were both put into the same center too," I add, matter-of-factly. "She was there longer than I was, though."

"So you guys have known each other, like forever?" Ani asks, leaning over her bike handle.

"Yeah. Terry knew the couple who adopted Moon, so we would see each other often when we were little . . . Wanna ride home together?" I ask, changing the conversation as I unlock my bike.

"Sure, why not?" We exchange addresses quickly, and it turns out she lives in Owl Court, too. As we pedal off of school property, unease for the newcomer rushes my veins. Sharing my history is not something I do often, but her prying couldn't be ignored. To my surprise, opening up to her felt easy, despite her weird mannerisms and strange persistence. There's just something about her, quirks and all, that has me curious.

CHAPTER 2

I run upstairs to take off my backpack and shoes before heading to the bathroom to pee and wash my hands. I dash back downstairs to warm up the beef stew I made yesterday. I heat the stew in a metal pot until the thick aroma of hot beef and carrots dances through the kitchen.

I scoop the stew into five different bowls, all porcelain, except for my paper one. After placing the four porcelain bowls on the counter, I put a plastic spoon in mine. Leaving my bowl by the door to the garage, I go back upstairs to change into some cute jean shorts and a white tank top, then go down the stairs again and out through the garage, bowl in hand. I slip on my red Rollerblades and skate to Perkin Place. As I'm skating, I dig into my bowl of stew. Its deliciousness warms me inside, and when I finish, I throw the bowl away in the first garbage can I see. I skate fast, and after passing three houses, I skate up the fourth driveway.

"You're late," states Zach as I skate up his driveway.

"I am *sooo* sorry," I say sarcastically as I pull off my skates. "I had some things I had to do. You know, patience is a virtue, one which you clearly don't have."

"Shut up," Zach scoffs. "Did you bring your tennis shoes?" he asks, watching me tug off my skates.

"Nope. I'm going to use Terra's." I skip to his garage and open the door. "Hi, Mrs. Klight," I announce, walking into the mudroom and putting on Terra's sneakers. Zach's mom is the definition of a goddess. The mudroom is right across from the kitchen where she's stirring a pot. Her hair is in a short 'fro, and she's wearing diamond-studded hoops. Her skin is absolutely flawless, not a single blemish in sight. She looks up at me and smiles. The smile seems to lighten the room, and even myself. Her eyes are filled with so much love, it causes my heart to flutter, only making her more beautiful. She isn't just a MILF (mom I'd like to fuck) but a MILHDRM (mom I'd like to have divorced and remarried to me). It isn't a real saying, but it should be.

"Hi, Ruby, how are you?" asks Mrs. Klight as I walk toward her.

"Great, whatcha cookin'?" I ask politely.

"Spaghetti."

"It smells very good; can I get a taste?"

"Sure, but then go outside and have fun before you have to start heading back."

"Thank you." She grabs a spoon from a drawer and dips it into the sauce. When I put it in my mouth, my eyes widen, and I do a little dance. "Yum, this is really good."

"Thank you, Ruby. Aren't you just the sweetest."

"I only speak the truth," I say, opening the garage door and heading back outside. Mrs. Klight is the mom I wish I had. She has always welcomed me into her home, and for that, I will forever be grateful. I hope she sees me as her surrogate daughter, because she's been more of a mother to me than Lisa ever has.

"You ready to play?"

"Oh, you know it," I reply to Zach, as I steal the basketball from under his arm and make a basket.

"We didn't start yet. That doesn't count."

"Fine. But I'll win anyway." We play five rounds of one-on-one, and I win three of them. "Like I told you," I say, out of breath, "I always win."

"Okay . . . you win, but I'll beat you tomorrow," he pants out.

"Yah, okay, you keep dreaming," I mock, heading into his garage and opening his freezer. I pull out two Popsicles.

"It's how you just walk into my house like it is your own, for me," Zach says.

"You know you love me," I purr, blowing him a kiss. "This is like my second home," I add sincerely as I hold out the Popsicles. "I basically live here. I'm here, like, every day. Which one do you want?"

"What are the flavors?"

"Orange and grape."

As soon as he says 'orange,' I smile mischievously. Slowly, I open the popsicle and hand it to him. Right as he's about to take it from me, I pull it back, sticking it in my mouth with a satisfying slurp. His face twists with irritation before he grabs my hand, snatching the ice treat from my mouth and bringing it to his. He licks it obnoxiously, still holding my hand that's holding the Popsicle stick. I gag.

"You're nasty." I cringe, pulling my hand away in disgust, but he just shrugs. The smug look on his face sends a surge of confidence through me. I march up to him, rip the Popsicle from his mouth, and stick it in mine. The weird texture of warm saliva and melted Popsicle makes my stomach turn, but I ignore it. The look on Zach's face makes it all worth it.

Sliding the Popsicle out of my mouth, I smirk, then turn and run toward his backyard. I can hear his feet pounding the September grass behind me and I toss the grape Popsicle back toward him. Zach ignores it, his focus on the chase. I grin and run a little more before I get a horribly terrific idea. I throw the orange popsicle up into the air and do a front handspring, and immediately after, a roundoff. I look up into the sky and see the Popsicle falling right over me. Once it's above my head, I reach up and grab it. I manage to wrap my hand around the stick, but just barely. *Damn, I can't believe I pulled that off.*

I turn to see Zach gaping at me. I smile shyly and feel my face heating up. I cover my blushing by sticking out my tongue. Well, it's not like he would see the red in my cheeks anyway. He shakes his head and looks down. Honestly, I didn't think I would be walking away looking like a badass. When he finally looks back up again, he's grinning. I run again and can hear him panting, right on my tail. I climb up my favorite tree in his backyard as quickly as a squirrel and sit on the branch that looks into Zach's window. I finally relax and eat the slightly melted

Popsicle. The tree shakes as he makes his way to the branch, significantly less elegantly than me. I scoot over to give him room, and he snatches the Popsicle from my hand and finishes it off. We sit in peaceful silence, staring into his bedroom window across from the tree. I lean my head on his shoulder casually, swinging my legs in the wind.

"Remember," Zach starts, "when we used to come up here as kids?" I lift my head up, laughing, before nudging him playfully.

"Yeah, and then you busted your butt falling—"

"Hey! It wasn't my fault. The branch broke . . ."

"You couldn't . . . sit right . . . for days!" I cackle between words, gasping for air. We spend the next thirty minutes reminiscing on old times. Zach reminds me of my stalker phase, and I cringe. In middle school, I used to climb up this tree every morning, leaving seconds after his alarm. When he caught me one day in eighth grade, I died of embarrassment. I swear my soul left my body, because even it couldn't tolerate me. For revenge, I bring up the time in sixth grade when he forgot to take his Lactaid pill. Mr. Crocker wouldn't let him use the restroom, and Zach stunk up the entire classroom. In response, he shoves me gently, and I don't hide my grin. When I see the streetlights come on, I sigh, gesturing toward them.

"Hey, Zach . . . I have to go now." He nods in understanding but refuses to let me ride home alone, which is ridiculous. I've done so every other time. I don't know why he's making such a big deal out of it today.

He moves down the tree, and I follow him. He holds out his hand for me, and I take it as he helps me down the last few branches. When I'm finally on the ground, Zach's still holding my hand. *Will he let go?* He doesn't, and I make no gesture for him to. So we walk on the soft grass to his garage, just like that. He lets go of my hand and goes to find his Rollerblades and to tell his mom he's dropping me off. As I slip on my Rollerblades, I can't help but think of his soft, warm hands. *Why did he hold my hand for that long?* I mean, I'm not complaining but . . .

"I'll take Terra's shoes," Zach says, holding out his hands for his younger sisters' shoes. I place the sneakers in his hand and lace up my blades. When he comes back, his skates are on, and he's ready to go. We skate side by side, in a peaceful silence until we reach my house.

"Well, here is my stop," I intone, slowly skating to my garage.

"So you live here? It is a beautiful home," declares Zach, gazing at the cream-colored house. "I can't believe I've never been to your house before." I give an awkward laugh. *Yah, that's because I've never really wanted you to come here.*

"Thanks, but it doesn't feel like a real home. A prison would be more accurate," I add, placing my skates in my spot in the garage. "Well, a comfortable prison, I guess." Zach places his skates next to mine. When we walk back out, I make a left, heading for my backyard.

"Where are you going?" he asks, confused about why I'm not entering through the garage.

"My room. I'll get in trouble if I enter through one of the doors this late, so it's better this way," I confess, climbing the tree that leads to my bedroom window. Zach climbs after me.

"You don't have to come up here. You aren't wearing any shoes, and you could rip a hole in your socks and cut yourself," I note, worried for Zach's well-being. For his well-being *and* that Lisa might walk in and see him and all Hell will break loose.

"You could too," he says, eyeing my shoeless feet. *He got me there.*

"Touché," I reply when I reach the branch that leads to my room.

"So, this is how you got so damn good at climbing trees." He chuckles. "You live in the attic?" he asks, noticing that my room is on the highest floor. I nod.

"More like a guest suite, but sure." I open my window and bend into my room. I take off my socks before walking to the door and flicking on the lights. My blue covers on my bed are folded nicely, and I am silently thanking God I cleaned my room. I crumple my socks into a ball and throw them in my hamper. "Take off your socks if you want to come in. I don't want you trailing dirt," I say to Zach, as I duck under a small doorway that leads to Snowball's room.

"Wow, your room is really nice," Zach says. As I stroke the bunny's soft white fur, I watch him walk around, admiring my furniture, or should I say lack thereof. Entering from my window, my bed lies directly on the left. The mattress sits in a king-sized frame made of whitewashed wood, giving an almost "princessy" feel. On the wall across from the window are two sets of stained wood drawers, the entrance to my closet, my bathroom, and Snowball's room. There's nothing against the far-right wall besides a bunch of boxes. "Hey, Ruby, what's this over here?" I follow the sound of Zach's voice until I see him in the corner of the room with the cardboard boxes. He's rummaging through them, eager to know what's inside.

"I dunno. I don't usually go over there," I say, placing Snowball on the carpet and heading over to Zach. "Some of it is stuff that belonged to my parents that was found in the crash. When I was adopted, they got me and the boxes. I was a packaged deal," I admit, chuckling as I open a box labeled *jewelry* and find stacks of old jewelry boxes. "But some of it is my adopted parents' stuff too. I was going to go through it all one day. I just haven't set a date yet."

"You ever wonder about your birth parents?" Zach asks, head in a box. I let out a huff.

"I mean, of course. But they're dead." I pull out one of the jewelry boxes. This one is covered in emerald green velvet. "It's not like I can ever talk to them. Anyway, I kinda like to fantasize about who they might have been. I'm not sure if I want to find out, though."

"Why?" comes Zach's muffled voice. "If I were adopted, I'd want to know what my birth parents were like." A weird feeling zips through my body as I trace the gold engravings on the velvet jewelry box.

"Well, that's you," I say, my voice slightly hard. "My focuses are school, my chores, and sneaking in fun when I can. My birth parents are dead," I answer with a shrug as I open the box. "I can try to find out about them when I have the time, and the resources."

"That makes sense." Zach's head pops out of one of the boxes. "You know I didn't mean anything by what I said. Right?" I sigh.

To be honest, of course I've wondered about my birth family and what my life would have been like if it weren't for that stupid plane crash. I think about it a lot. But it's not like knowing would change anything. I need to focus on my future, not my past.

"I know you didn't mean anything by it," I say, picking through the jewelry. My eyes land on something that makes my lips part: a beautiful ruby necklace. "Wow, look at this, Zach! Isn't it gorgeous?" I hold it up against the light. The necklace has five rubies on it. One in the middle and two on each side, progressively getting smaller. The rubies are linked together by a Figaro gold chain. "I can't tell if the gems are real or not, but if so, this must be worth, like, hundreds of dollars," I say, feeling every ruby, afraid it will break from my touch. The necklace isn't incredibly heavy, but a comfortable weight in my hand. The gems also aren't large. In theory, I could casually wear this necklace every day.

"And look, there are earrings to go with it," comments Zach, holding up a pair of ruby studs. I didn't notice them under the necklace. I take the earrings and walk from him to my dresser and look at myself in the mirror.

"Zach, can you please help me put this necklace on?" I ask as I put in the studs.

"Sure," he responds, coming up behind me. "A ruby for a Ruby." He chuckles as he clasps the necklace around my neck and hesitantly lays his hands on my shoulders. A comforting sigh slips through my lips. I turn my neck so I can look into his eyes, and he looks down into mine. I smile and he smiles back, causing heat to bloom in all the crevices of my body. His eyes hold a deep look, and he licks his lips unconsciously. He leans in closer, and my stomach fills with frantic butterflies. *I've never kissed anyone before; will I be good? Crap, are my lips chapped?* I subtly rub my lips together, and the dry, dead skin gets caught on each other, gently scratching my lip. *Oh. My. God. Wait, what if this isn't even what I think it is?* But this is Zach. Zach, who I've known since forever. Zach, who will call me "Crusty Rusty" if our lips end up colliding. I peek up at his eyes. Relieved that they're closed, I wet my lips, rubbing them together in a frenzy until the chap is nearly gone. There is no way my first kiss with him will be bad. I think of what he may taste like, and tingles shiver down my spine. Our lips are inches apart when Jack barges in.

"Ruby, I want—Ruby!" he interrupts himself, gasping. "You have a *boy* in your room." He clamps a hand over his mouth, dark brown eyes wide in disbelief. We jump apart. "Mommy! Ruby has a boy in her room!" Jack yells, running down the steps. I freeze. This is bad, really, really bad.

"He made that sound like it was a bad thing," says Zach as he lays his arm over my shoulders. I shrink away. This *is* a bad thing. I've never been allowed to have people over. Of course, I sneak them through the window, but we've never been caught. I'm usually listening intently for footsteps and creaking stairs, but Zach was distracting.

"Zach, you need to go," I muster, avoiding his eyes.

"Why?" he asks. "What can your step brother do?"

"Please go," I plead, hearing the steps of Lisa's house heels coming up the stairs. He sees the panic in my eyes and takes a step back.

"I don't want to leave you . . . Can I just hide?" he asks. The footsteps are louder now.

"Sure. Yes . . . just get out of sight." Zach dives behind the boxes and watches from afar.

"What is going on here?" demands Lisa as she steps into my room. "I specifically gave you this room so I wouldn't have to see you all day. And yet, your brother has screamed to the whole entire *neighborhood* that there is a boy in here." Lisa looks around my room. "I don't see a boy." Her figure towers over me in my room, and I feel so small. Her jet-black hair is in a braid that reminds me of Elsa from *Frozen*. Her lips are pursed in a thin line, and her eyes are shooting daggers at me. She would be pretty if . . . Well, she *is* pretty. A scary, slit-your-throat type of pretty. One that makes you not want to get on her bad side like how, unfortunately, I seem to always be. Her hand goes to rest on her hip, her plum purple robe moving elegantly with the movement.

"There was a boy, Mommy, honest!" cries Jack from behind Lisa's legs. Her eyes dart down to my necklace. She marches over to me and clutches the largest ruby, pulling me close to her.

"Where did you get this?" she asks, fire in her eyes. "Did you steal this from my room?" she asks tightly.

"I found it in my mother's jewelry box," I say, letting the accusation go. "It was with the things that came with me when I was adopted." She slides her hands across each ruby, eyeing it hungrily. A chill runs up my spine.

"Oh, did you?" she asks as she clamps her hand around the largest ruby and rips it from my body. The chain pulls apart as it tears across my neck.

"Hey!" I yell, bringing my hand to the spot that's burning at the back of my neck. My skin is raw. I reach for my necklace, but she's too quick. "Please," I beg, "that was my mother's!"

"And she is dead, Ruby." I suck in a sharp breath. "I'll just hold this for you. You don't deserve something as priceless as this." She puts it into her robe pocket, turns, and walks toward the door. "Anyway, I *am* your mother now," she adds, twisting back to me, a smirk freely on her face. "Come, Jack." Jack sticks his tongue out at me and laughs before he leaves my room.

"There really was a boy, Mommy. I swear," I barely hear the ten-year-old say before they're both out of earshot. I walk over to the stairwell door, wanting to slam it. But I don't. I close it softly. Frustrated and embarrassed, tears well up in my eyes. *Zach watched that all go down.* I lean my forehead on the door and breathe. I refuse to let my tears fall. I walk over to Zach's hiding spot and climb over the boxes. He's facing me, and I can see the pity in his eyes. I hate it. I sit down and pull my knees to my chest. I know he's looking at me, but I don't meet his gaze. We sit like that in silence for I don't know how long, with him staring intensely at me and me staring intensely at the carpet. I don't notice him moving closer to me until he grabs my shoulders, and I meet his eyes.

"Are you okay?" he asks.

"I'm fine," I reply softly. His eyes are hard.

"Ruby, you are not fine."

"I'm *fine*," I repeat, and I mean it. This isn't anything new to me, only him.

"Well, good," he resigns, letting my shoulders go and moving back to sit across from me, "because we have to get that necklace back," he adds heroically.

"What? No, we can't. I'll never see it again. Well . . . I'll never see it on *me* again," I admit, tears threatening to fall. One slips, and I wipe it away furiously, angry at myself for showing weakness. "I don't even know why I'm crying anyway. We just found the stupid thing." But I do. Yes, I am frustrated. Yes, I am embarrassed. But the necklace felt like it belonged with *me*. When I was wearing it, I sensed a connection with the life I was supposed to have, and without it, I feel empty. It's the missing piece I didn't even know was lost. Zach doesn't notice my tears, though; he's on his phone, dialing a number.

"Hello . . . Hi, Mama, Can I sleep over at Ruby's house? Yea . . . No. What? Why would I . . .? Okay . . . love you. Good night." He hangs up and looks at me. A weird expression is on his face, probably from whatever his mom said. But then, it's quickly replaced with a grin.

"Oh no," I say as I gently massage my temple, but he spies my grin anyway. "I don't like that look."

"Okay, here's the plan."

CHAPTER 3

We creep down the stairs, Zach right on my tail. Once we are down one flight, I point to the door at the end of the hall.

"That's her room," I say quietly as we tiptoe toward it. I open the door slightly, and it creaks. Zach parts his lips as if he is about to say something, but I shush him, putting my finger over his mouth. A warm, wet feeling glides up my finger, and I yank my hand away, rubbing Zach's spit on my shorts. He lets out a silent huff of laughter, and I push his face away.

Spreading out across the room, we let our phones light the way so we don't trip over clothes and shoes. Lisa's room is the second largest bedroom in the house, and it's cluttered with her clothes.

I'm rustling through her dresser when I hear Zach whisper. "Found it." I scurry to where he is beside the bed and look at where he is pointing. The necklace is around her neck. *My* necklace is around her neck. "Is she a light or heavy sleeper?"

"Heavy," I whisper. Zach nods.

"Good." He leans over Lisa and unclips the necklace, clutching it tightly. We head for the door when she rustles. Our eyes meet, mine wide with fear, before we scatter. He half runs, half tiptoes to the bathroom, and I go to the walk-in closet. *Some luck I have.* I just make it behind a wall of clothes when a yawning Lisa walks in. From my hiding spot, all I can see are her legs. I see her clothes drop, first her sweatpants, then her thong, her shirt, and her 36C size bra. Her feet walk out the door. *Shower time, I assume.*

I turn, looking for Zach, but remember he hid in the bathroom. The bathroom that Lisa is heading for right now. I say a silent prayer for him, then untangle myself from the hanging clothes. I leave the closet and wait for him by the door. After a few minutes, the bathroom door creaks open, and Zach steps out behind a blanket of steam. The moonlight shines on his handsome face, and the look he has is priceless. I try to hold back a laugh, but a few giggles escape. After we leave the room, I let my laughter loose.

"I don't know why you're laughing, Ruby," he says quietly as we walk down the hall. "Your stepmom has some pretty nice titties." I cringe.

"Thanks, I always wanted to know," I mumble sarcastically. He sticks his tongue out and wiggles it at me, which makes me cringe even more. We tiptoe back up the stairs toward my room. When we make it, I run and flop on my bed, smiling broadly. "We did it," I say happily. Zach scratches his head.

"Yeah, we did," he adds with a small smile. "Hey . . . if I am sleeping over—?" Zach begins.

"Yeah, sorry," I interrupt as I roll off my bed. I bend down and pull out the drawer under my bed for the trundle mattress. I pat the covers gently. "Here's where you're gonna sleep," I say, standing up and walking over to him.

"Sweet. Thanks," he says. "Let me put the necklace on you," he urges, holding it up.

"Sure," I reply as I turn my back to him.

"Damn, a chain got pulled out," he huffs. "It must have been loose and unlinked when I held it." I turn back to face him and see the broken necklace in his hand.

"Here, give it," I demand. He places the necklace in my extended palm. I hold it up to find the loose chain. I re-link it around the intact chain, bring it to my mouth, and bite down hard, closing the open chain with my teeth. It takes a couple of bites before it's secure. Zach chuckles as I hand it back to him. "Good as new."

"Ruby, I can literally see the imprints of your teeth on—" Zach starts.

"Good enough as new." I turn away from him and face my bed. He chuckles.

"Close your eyes," he says, and I silently obey. The necklace touches my neck, and the feeling from an hour earlier returns. I let out a small sigh of relief. "There." I open my eyes and turn to stare at myself in the mirror. I walk closer while rubbing my hand along the largest ruby. It's about the size of a large bread crumb. Zach walks up behind me and puts his chin on my head. "Perfect," he says, admiring where the necklace rests on my clavicle. We stay like that for a few seconds before he turns me around to face him. I stare back at him, at his waves and his sparkling brown eyes.

"Thank you," I mumble.

"Ruby," he whispers, "there's something I need to tell you." The intensity in his eyes makes me nervous. So nervous I don't want to hear what he has to say. "Ruby, I really like . . ."

No. He better not say he really likes me. Do I like him? Does he like me? If so, that will ruin our friendship. I can't be here right now. This is not happening. I wish I could just disappear. Sink into some invisible world and pretend like this never happened. I don't want him to like me because I might kinda like him too. Do I reject him? My mind is racing, spilling all my thoughts, feelings, and emotions so much that I don't notice the shift in the atmosphere.

"Ruby?" he whispers urgently. *Oh my God, did he just say that he liked me and I missed it? Stupid, stupid, stupid . . .* He yanks his hands off my shoulders and backs away, his eyes filled with fear. *Crap, did I break his heart?* "Where did you go?" he gasps, looking around the room urgently. *Ah, I see. Smart . . . smart . . . he's lightening the mood.*

"Nowhere, LOL. I'm here. Sorry, I got into my head a bit . . ." I laugh awkwardly and let my words trail off. "I kinda missed what you said, ahem." I look down and tug at another escaped curl. When I let go, it bounces back. I reach to grab it again. Welp, this sucks. "Sorry," I say, as I hesitantly place my hand on his shoulder. He jumps back in fear. "What?" I ask, worried. I don't really cuss, but this feels like one of those *shit-shit-shit-shit* moments.

"Ruby . . . Ruby, I can't see you," he says, frightened. My face twists in confusion.

"But I'm right here," I attest, touching his arm. He tenses. "Ruby . . . You're-you're invisible."

CHAPTER 4

"What?" I ask again, concern filling my body.

"L-look in the mirror," he stammers. I turn to face the mirror, and as I do, I can't help but think this is all some weird joke to kill the tension. But when I look, I don't see my mahogany curls or big glasses. I don't see *me*. "Ruby, what did you do? I'm kinda freaking out."

"I-I don't know," I reply. I hold my hand up to the mirror but see no movement. I look down at myself and see nothing there, either. I suck in a breath. *Well, at least he doesn't hate me.* But I don't know if this is much better.

"What did you do? Right before I started freaking out, did you do something?" I shake my head. We're in silence for a little while longer before I feel like an idiot. He can't see me.

"Zach, I don't . . ."

"Think, Ruby, think," he says. He keeps backing away, heading toward the window.

"Are . . . are you going to leave?" I ask, taken aback.

"Listen, Ruby . . ."

"I don't know what the heck is going on and you're just gonna leave me like this? I'm scared too, y'know," I bellow, starting to panic.

"I know, Ruby. I'm not gonna leave. This is just . . . a precaution."

"A precaution?"

"I don't know what's happening. You don't know what's happening. We don't know what *else* could happen," he explains. Fear shoots through my body, and the panic inside seems to increase. "Now, *think,* Ruby. 'Cause I know there's no way in hell I did this."

"Well, I know there's—" I start, but he interrupts me.

"If you didn't do it, who did, Ruby?" he asks. I pause, surprised at his tone. "We don't know what the fuck is happening, and I'm not trying to point any fingers, I swear," he says, holding his arms up in innocence. "But last I checked, we're the only two people up here, and people don't just disappear." I tense. "So you're really gonna have to use that big brain of yours Rubes, 'cause this shit just don't make sense." Zach is pacing now. He's parallel to the wall with the window but within arm's length, just in case. *Just in case. For what? I don't know.*

"Okay," I say softly, thinking back. He was standing close to me, wanting to tell me something. That's when I started to overthink and freak out. I was thinking so many things I can't even remember—I just don't understand why I can't see myself. Why I'm literally *invisible.* I want it to stop. *Is this some stupid joke that the universe has for me? Making the invisible girl truly invisible.* As soon as I think that, I cringe. *Ugh. I'm not some "pick me" girl. I'm just out here living my life.* "Zach, I dunno . . ."

"Ruby, I can see you again!" he announces, interrupting me, his tone full of relief. I turn back to the mirror and see my reflection.

"Thank God!" I say as I hold my face. Everything is just as it was. I quickly turn to face Zach, and he takes a step back.

"Were you able to do this before?" he asks, keeping his distance from me.

"Do you think if I did this before I woulda freaked out like that?" I ask, irritated. When I see his face, I let out a sigh. "I mean, I remember wanting to be invisible a bazillion times, during presentations and when I embarrass myself. But doesn't everybody? *This* is new for me," I say, wrapping my arms around my torso.

"You wanted to be invisible just now?" Zach asks, confused. He takes a hesitant step forward.

"Well, yes . . . no . . . maybe?" I admit as I feel my face heat up for the umpteenth time today.

"Try it again," suggests Zach, as he inches toward me cautiously.

"What? Why?"

"Why not?" he encourages. "We gotta know what's happening, right?"

"I guess." I awkwardly shift from side to side. "It just feels stupid." I sigh, uncertain of what will occur with my next words. "I want to be invisible." A sense of heat runs through my body that I hadn't noticed before. It's a warm kind of fire that goes from my toes to my ears. It feels like I'm blushing all over my body. Not a bad blush, but something more comforting. Like the feeling of drinking hot cocoa on a frosty day, how it warms you up inside. I turn to the mirror. Invisible. My eyebrows shoot up to my baby hairs. He was right. Zach is *right*. Dang, I usually hate when he's right, but I'll give him this one. "I don't want to be invisible anymore," I announce, and watch my body form from thin air.

"Damn, Ruby, this is amazing," Zach says as he paces around the room eagerly, seemingly no longer afraid of me. "You have accomplished what scientists all over the nation, no, all over the *world* have been trying to figure out." He walks toward me and grabs onto my shoulders. "We put this on TikTok, and we'll be viral in seconds. You'll be on the news! I'm talking Channel 5, 6, 7, 8, 9—"

"No! I do not want to be like some guinea pig for scientists," I say, pushing him off. "Black people have been that for way too long. Respectfully, I'm not tryna be like that. This stays between us!" I add, walking over to sit on the end of my bed. "Anyway, I don't even know how this happened," I murmur as I fidget with the center stone on my necklace. "My necklace!" I say the exact moment Zach says, "Your necklace!" We laugh as I push myself off the bed. "It's the only new thing in my life. And even though it doesn't make sense, nothing does right now." I unclasp the necklace and hand it to Zach. Immediately, I feel like a part of me was taken away, and I know it's because of the necklace.

"The earrings, too, Ruby." *Right.* I take off the studs, feeling even more empty as I place them on my dresser. Then, I take a step back. "I want to be invisible." Nothing happens. "We were right. It is the necklace!" I say.

"Let me try," says Zach as he puts the necklace on himself. "Make me invisible!" he declares with confidence, but nothing happens. *If it worked on me, it should work on him too.* Zach looks upset, but then his face brightens. "I know how it works!" he yells while doing a happy dance.

"How?"

"What is your name?"

"Zach, you know my name. What does it have to do—?"

"Work with me, please. *What* is your *name?*" I roll my eyes.

"Ruby," I say, crossing my arms. This is going nowhere.

"And what gemstone is the necklace?"

"Zach, it's a ru—" I tighten my lips into a line. I'm such an idiot. Zach grins. "Okay, great, but it still doesn't make any sense, Zach. My name is Ruby. So what? The necklace just *knows* that? This isn't some fantasy novel where anything and everything goes." I cross my arms over my chest.

"Ruby, I know you're the one who usually has the plan here, but it's okay. This guy," Zach says, pointing his thumbs at his chest, "has got a plan." I roll my eyes for the second time.

"Well, spit it out, Mr. Has a Plan," I assert, tapping my toe.

"Just think! We found your ruby necklace over there," Zach reminds me, pointing to the boxes. "So maybe we can find more just like it! I am talking blue stone, pink stone, gem the mem stone, the whole enchilada!" A smile creeps onto my face, and I nod, agreeing with him.

"Zach, please never utter that sentence again. But I think you're on to something," I concede. Coincidentally, birthstones have been my life. They have a beauty in them that just gives me a feeling of belonging. I'm always on those "what your birthday means about you" sites. Zach is already at the boxes, pulling out another jewelry box. He dumps it all over the carpet.

"You start looking through those while I find more," Zach says, submerging himself into the sea of cardboard boxes. I walk to my white writing desk adjacent to my bed and pull out my field journal on gemstones. It's brown and worn. The journal will tear with the smallest pull, so I hold it precisely in my palms. Inside is a small magnifying glass and a green mechanical pencil. I walk over to the pile of jewelry on the floor, lie on my stomach, push up my glasses, and get to work.

"Did you find any more necklaces?" he asks me. So far, I have gone through three boxes and found much more birthstone jewelry.

"Not just necklaces, bracelets and earrings too!" I hold up a tanzanite bracelet, opal studs, and a moonstone necklace.

"Wow, that easy, huh?"

"Well, not exactly." I adjust my glasses and look up at him. "I had to get my journal so I could identify which ones were real or not a gem at all," I state matter-of-factly. "But look at this," I add, holding up a small tiara. "This is a citrine tiara. That gem in the middle right there . . ." I say, pointing at it. "That's citrine, November's birthstone." I feel myself geeking out. "Did you know that some months have more than one birthstone?" I put the tiara in the pile with the other birthstones and place the nonspecial necklaces back into their boxes. "The stupid economy is why. Some stones are more expensive than others, so they wanted to provide more affordable options. The other stone for November is topaz." I smile at Zach. "However, ironically, blue topaz is also considered one of the stones for December." I feel myself rambling. In fact, I *know* I'm rambling. There's a weird look on Zach's face, a look that makes me feel squishy inside. "Sorry, I got a little excited."

"You did? I couldn't tell," Zach says with a smile. "It was cute." At that, I look down, twiddling the costume jewelry between my fingers. Suddenly, a wave of fatigue comes over me. I yawn.

"Maybe we should get some sleep. I mean, it is a school night," says Zach as he watches me yawn.

"Yah, good idea. It is like, two thirty," I say, standing up and walking to my dresser, putting the birthstone jewelry on top of it, and pulling out my pajama pants. I turn to face Zach. "Close your eyes, please," I announce. He looks at me, confused. "I want to change into my pj's," I assert, getting annoyed.

"Just change right now. I mean, you've known me since first grade. We've practically taken baths together. Why would I care? And you could just change in your bathroom. It's not like you are *actually* going to change in front of me," he says, challenging me. *Man, can he be bold.* I smile.

"We did not take baths together, number one, and number two, this is pathetic. *You're* just trying to get *me* to change in front of *you*."

"That is exactly what I'm trying to do."

"Why? Were Lisa's boobs not good enough for you?" I ask, crossing my arms over my chest.

"No. No, they were not." The confidence I had gained disappears quickly. I struggle to come up with my next words.

"If I do it, you do it," I demand daringly.

"You're on. On the count of three," he says with a devious grin. "1 . . . 2 . . . 3!" he blurts after he pulls off his pants. I loop my thumbs inside mine and wait until he has his shirt covering his face before I take off my shorts. When his face is covered, I pull them off quickly and yank up my pajama pants. Luckily for me, his shirt gets caught on his ears. By the time his shirt is off and on the floor, I'm already wearing my pants.

"That shouldn't count!" he says, pissed by my cleverness.

"What? I did it." I smirk as I walk over to my dresser to grab one of my many bonnets. *A black one will do tonight.* I see the earrings resting on the dresser. I'd completely forgot about them.

"But—"

"I guess I'm the sharp-witted one in our friendship," I say as I put the earrings in and my bonnet on. I tighten it with the strings, tying a bow in the front. "If I were you, I would have waited until my pants were off," I suggest as I wink and laugh.

"But . . ." he starts, then he grins. "But you wore that tank top outside, too. You don't want all of those outside germs in your bed." *Crap.* I had forgotten about that part. *Thank the world that I am wearing a sports bra under this.*

"Fine . . . but no googly eyes," I say, looking at him and wagging my finger.

"Ruby, I'm ashamed that you think so low of me . . ." he jokes. I take off my tank top. His jaw goes slack, and he gapes at me. To be honest, there isn't much to look at in that department. I think I basically have glorified "man boobs." But I feel flushed anyway and walk over to my bed and jump on it. I flop down and roll back and forth, rustling the covers just how I like them. "Bed comfy enough for you yet?" Zach asks as he approaches me, trying not to smile. I laugh.

"Yeah, thanks for asking," I reply, lying flat on my back. He's standing at the end of my bed.

"Can I have a pillow?" he asks. He eyes the three pillows behind my head.

"Actually, no. I need all three pillows to sleep sweetly and soundly, but I can get you an extra blanket to lie on," I say earnestly.

"But those pillows look comfy," he pouts. I position myself so I'm holding all the pillows over my head but against the headboard. I spot him eyeing me mischievously and can almost see the wheels turning in his head.

"You wouldn't dare," I warn.

"Then you don't know me that well," Zach responds, before lunging on top of me. I let out a soft squeal.

"No! Don't take my pillow babies!" I squeak, holding them with my nails. Zach pins me to my bed. His bare chest is above my bare stomach. His feet pin mine down, and his hands grip my wrists. I struggle underneath him, but he doesn't budge.

"I want a pillow," he demands. I shake my head.

"You aren't getting one," I say softly, hyperaware of the position we are in.

"Yes, I am." He removes one of his hands from my wrists and starts tickling my armpits.

"Hey!" I laugh. "S-stop th-that." I laugh so hard I bring my arms down and let go of the pillows. Zach grabs one. He sits up on my pinned legs and holds up the pillow above his head.

"I am the king of the world!" he proclaims dramatically in a soft voice, shaking the pillow in the air.

"Shh!" I hush him. "Lisa will hear you!" Although, it shouldn't be too much to worry about. The room is pretty insulated besides the stairwell. I look up at his adorable face, and he looks down at me. And it's normal. Normal and safe. Just two friends sitting on a bed. The guy on top of the girl, both shirtless. Just friends. I sit up, staring at him. Then I shove him onto the pullout bed.

"Fine! You win. Now go to sleep," I concede, getting under my covers. He does the same.

"Night, Ruby, and thanks for the pillow," he adds as he lies on top of the covers. I lean over and flick the light switch next to my bed and stare at my ceiling. After a few moments, I break the peaceful silence.

"Zach?" I ask, but he doesn't respond. I look over the edge of my bed and see him snoring lightly. My eyes go from his cute boyish face to his sexy, manly abs. He has a six-pack that makes me tempted to touch it. I reach my finger down and draw a smiley face, dotting its nose right on his belly button. He smiles gently in his sleep, which sends a flurry of something in my stomach. I pull away from his body and lie back on my bed. A small grin rests comfortably on my lips as I lay there, eyelids growing heavy, and fall into a deep sleep.

CHAPTER 5

*T*he hot sand burns my toes and my pajama pants stick to my legs. The desert sun is pounding down on my face, leaving droplets of sweat on my sun-absorbed skin. I keep walking until I finally see a town. I let out a sigh of relief as I run to it.

"Help!" I scream. "Anyone, please, where am I?" I walk toward a small building that looks like a jewelry and accessories store. I enter and scan the store for anyone. It's stocked with satchels, shoes, jewelry, and clothes. "Hello?" I yell, but again, no response.

As I walk through the store, I come upon an ear-piercing machine and a chair with a headrest. The headrest is a u shape, and when someone puts their head in it, it pierces both ears at once. I sit on the velvet cushion on the machine and lean my head on the headrest. I need water, *I think as I slide my hand along the armrest of the chair. I hit a switch that turns the machine on and scream as it pierces both of my ears and inserts studs into them. Thankfully, they miss the spot where the ruby studs are in place, going slightly above them.*

I stumble away from the machine and to a mirror. Looking at my throbbing ear-pierced ears, I notice silver studs in them. It's cute. I can't lie, but still, I think the pain was uncalled for. I move away from the nightmare chair and browse the store, savoring the relief from the desert heat.

"Hello?" I call out again, scanning the room one last time. Deciding that no one is near, and, hopefully, no one will be coming, I help myself to the store's merchandise. I hunt the shoe aisle for something I can put on my naked feet and spot some adorable red sandals. After putting them on, I walk through the rest of the store, filling my arms with earrings, necklaces, and other pieces of jewelry, before dumping it all on the checkout counter.

I search the accessories area of the store again and find some super cute bags. I grab a white backpack and stuff my loot from the counter into it. Walking behind the counter, I pop open the cash register. "Damnnnn," I say breathily, following with a long whistle. The register is filled with hundreds of dollars. The people in this town must have been in a hurry to leave if they left all this money, I think, and my stomach fills with worry. I push the concerning thought to the back of my mind and grab wallets to put all the money in. I keep the bills separate, placing all the ones, fives, tens, and twenties in their own wallets. It takes ten wallets to get all the money out of the register, and I stuff them in the white backpack.

Next, I change my clothes. I find a cute safari vest with matching shorts, strip down, and put on the clothes. A sigh of relief escapes me as my sweaty legs are free.

My last stop on this fantasy-like shopping spree is the toy section to find something for Maria. I spot an adorable puppy backpack with shiny pink straps, and I pull it off the shelf before stuffing it full of toys. When it's full, I grab another one and fill it with kids' makeup and costumes. All the money I earn and save is going toward my college fund, so I haven't had a chance to show her how much I appreciate her. I'm well aware this is a dream, but hey, it's the thought that matters.

I whip Maria's bags over my shoulder, grab some makeup for myself, and grab the rest of my dream swag. Then, with cracked, thirsty lips, I walk out of the raided store, my loot on my back, and into the abandoned town. I find a grocery store and run inside. I exit with a water bottle in my hand and three in my now excruciatingly heavy bag. Across the sandy road, I see a motel with windows along the front first floor. From inside, I spy movement.

"Hello?" I call out, making my way toward the entrance of the motel. I walk into the lobby and see a woman on the floor, gagged and with her wrists bound tightly *to her feet behind her back. "Oh, my gosh," I whisper, rushing over to help the poor woman dressed in tattered clothes. I kneel in front of her and take off her gag first. I untie her feet and wrists. All the while, she stares at me. "You must need water." I stand and walk to where I dropped my bags and pull out a bottle. I give it to her, and she drinks it all the way down, gulping and splashing water all over herself. I help her stand up and lead her to the sitting area of the lobby, making her sit on a couch. She looks up, staring at me. Her deep brown eyes hold dashes of red, and they bore into mine. Her brownish reddish curls are in two nappy braids that extend to her navel. She reeks of bile and sweat and urine, and it takes everything I have to make sure my expression doesn't fill with disgust. Her face is stained with tears, mud, and dirt. But through the dirt, grime, and stench, she has a beauty to her.*

"Ruby?" she whispers, her voice raspy. "Is that . . . really you?" This catches me off guard.

"Yes . . . How do you know who I am?" I ask while backing away from the woman.

"Well," she starts, looking down and clearing her throat, "I would hope that I know your name," she adds, slowly looking up to meet my eyes. "Since I did name you." Once again, the foul-smelling woman has caught me off guard. I'm frozen for a moment, letting her words process in my brain. Everything seems to move in slow motion. I feel myself gasp, and then my hand clamps over my mouth. I don't know how long I stand like that before I speak.

"No," I say, my voice slick with doubt. But the more I stare at her, the more the doubt slips away. She only nods, tears streaming down her face.

"My name's Ruby too, y'know," the woman claiming to be my mom says, smiling. The more I look at her, the more of a resemblance I see between us. I let hope course through me, and I fall to my knees, crawling to her. "But I go by Rubes."

"But . . . but . . . they said you were dead." I pause as realization strikes me and let out a short, hysterical laugh. "Right. You died in a plane crash. This is all a dream." A pang of sadness surges from my heart.

"No, Ruby. Your father and I are alive . . . We were on that plane so we could get you somewhere safe . . ." she says, tears still creating a waterfall on her face. "We had to hide, we had to hide, but—"

"My father? Where is he? Is he here? Can I—?" I interrupt. Choosing to forget this is a dream, I once again allow for hope, and perhaps some denial. I have a dad and a mom. *A family.* A real family.

"No, Ruby. I don't know where he is. Bloodstone . . ."

"What's Bloodstone! Did it do this to you?" I ask, concerned. What is going on?

"Please, Ruby, let me explain." I nod and sit back, dragging my hands down my face. This is a lot. This is too much. This is—

"Bloodstone isn't a what, he is a who. My little brother, your uncle, wants to dispose of us. Our family history dates back to ancient times. Our ancestors discovered that we have an amazing gift: the ability to wield unique and miraculous abilities." I nod, trying to follow what she's saying, believing half of it.

"How?" I question skeptically. Mom lets out a reluctant sigh of defeat.

"I don't know. We don't know. Each of our bodies is linked to jewels or gems that are all considered birthstones. When in contact with your linked stone, a dormant gene is turned on, giving you access to your ability." Now something is making sense. Last night is making sense. A weird, unrealistic type of sense, but hey, an explanation is an explanation. It's enough for my last remaining pieces of doubt to fizzle. Although a dream, maybe some of the things she is saying are true.

"Our ancestry is full of bondage and discrimination. Enslaved people didn't have diamonds or rubies lying around, so their genes would stay dormant." My mouth forms an O in understanding. *"We had thought it was some Black urban legend, giving our people hope and pride. Things changed when my mother, Adelaide, was gifted a pearl necklace from my father. She discovered that she was able to travel wherever she wanted with merely a thought."* I lean in closer, grasping the knowledge of my ancestry, something I wasn't sure I would ever know.

"After awakening her gene, she sought more information. She relied on literature and old newspaper clippings, piecing together the urban legend to what we know today. Eventually, she legally changed her last name to Gem and as technology grew and the reality of the legend was passed down through the family, a tradition was created: name the child after the stone of their birth month." Mom takes a big gulp of water before continuing.

"There is still so much we don't know, so much we probably will never know." Generational trauma surges through my body, roaring through my head. Mom's lips are moving, but I can't hear what she's saying. She's talking with her hands as she looks between me and somewhere in space. Hundreds of years of my culture and people being trailed through the mud, hanged from trees, burned with an audience, and beaten to a pulp. I'm filled with pain, sorrow, and anger. I will never know the truth about our abilities or why we are like this. Years of racism and White supremacy made sure of that. Seeing my mom's lips still moving, I force the thought away, fixing my attention back to her.

"Your necklace, Ruby. Once you are able to control your powers, you won't need it anymore. Using your ability while wearing your stone, though, will enhance the gene, making you stronger." This is a lot to process. She's been talking for not even ten minutes and my brain is already hurting. I look down at my necklace, stroking the stones gently. I clutch it and look back at my mom.

"You mentioned this earlier, but I'm confused. Naming us after our stones, I understand. But what about the months that have multiple?" I ask, leaning on my birthstone knowledge. "What then? What separates a citrine from a topaz?" Mom pauses, racking her brain for an answer, before she shrugs.

"I don't know, but the legend speaks of magic," she affirms, a small spark in her eye. "Maybe that part of the legend is also reality." A new feeling sits in the air, something filled with curiosity and mischief. I'm about to ask her to tell me more about the legend, but I don't have to.

"Sometime in the late sixteenth century, one of the many boats that hauled our people to the Americas was undergoing some trouble. The crew grew sick and started to hallucinate. They were yelling about witches on the boat and started to throw people overboard in a rampant rush of panic. But when they would count how many slaves were left the next day, it would be the same number: none were gone. At one point, the ship began to turn around, taking our people back to Africa. The crew blamed the slaves, and they wanted answers. So they went through all means to get them, seeming to forget that the slaves did not know their language." A chill runs through my spine at my mother's words. The transatlantic slave trade

isn't anything new to me. I was taught about it briefly in school and watched a couple of documentaries. Nevertheless, I listen intently.

"The torturing lasted for twelve days before the crew was able to gain control of the ship again. Further, the treatment toward the slaves only worsened. But with hushed whispers and the squeezing of hands, they would rise. The pain became bearable. They had more nutrients, they were getting stronger.

"They heard whispers of comfort before fingers brought food to their mouths. Whispers of diligence to a person in pain from a whipping, only for the pain to be eased soon after. Hands of warmth for those who had chills, and hands of cold for those with fevers." My mother's eyes are sparkling, filled with pride at the power of our ancestors. I can't help but feel a sense of pride too.

"They counted twelve. Twelve pairs of magical hands. Twelve strong whispers. And when the ship would finally dock somewhere in the Carolinas, twelve bodies were unaccounted for. They say that good spirits chose twelve people on that ship, gifting them abilities to provide aid for their folk on the ship and future hardships to come.

"For the enslaved people, The Legend of the Twelve was a sign of hope and freedom to come. It was something they told their children, engraving it in their head so they would tell their children, and so on." She takes another drink of water, wiping the excess liquid with the back of her hand.

"My mother called them the First Twelve, magical spirits of slaves who have passed, giving their kin aid from the dead. Whispers of another birthing of a total of twelve every hundred years soon became added to the legend: the power of the First Twelve reborn. And sometimes, it would be more than twelve, those women being able to birth children at a surprising rate, in which their slave masters would take advantage of." Another chill erupts through me. This is my ancestry. My family.

"When Adelaide wore her pearls for the first time, she felt whole. Within a matter of days, she realized she could teleport. After getting over her initial fear, she reasoned it with the Legend of the Twelve.

"Now, I'm not sure if the First Twelve are indeed 'the first twelve.' I think it dates back even further than we thought. I think that those twelve weren't

approached by spirits, but already had their genes activated. They most likely were forced on the boat and tried to use their abilities to save their people. But beyond that, with magic and how it began . . . I don't know. I was going to do the research into our lineage. I swear it. But life happened. Then this happened. I wish I had more answers for you, Ruby," mom says, smiling at me sadly. *I'm about to ask more questions about my grandmother, but mom's face turns serious.*

"I don't know what my brother's plan is completely, Ruby. I wish I did. All I know is that it can't be good." The quick switch of topic from my history to my present nearly gives me whiplash, and I'm struggling to keep up. *She shifts her body, readjusting her position. I hold back a gag at the aroma that comes with her movements.* *"Every 100 years, a full line of Gem children begins. On the 100th year, to the day, I gave birth to your sister, Garnet."* The gag pauses in my throat as I freeze. *A sister? A full line of children?* Siblings. I have siblings. *She sees the expression on my face and smiles softly.*

"I have brothers? Sisters?" I ask, my shock replaced by eager joy. My mom nods in response.

"I gave birth to twins nine years ago," she remembers dreamily. This makes me freeze.

"Nine years ago," I whisper. Anger boils in my bones, but it's different from before. For my whole seventeen years of living, my mom has been alive. And not once had she tried to see me. I think she feels the tension form in the air.

"Please, Ruby, listen." My lips stretch into a thin line. *"When I discovered the manner of Bloodstone's plan, I knew we had to hide. The plane was going to take us someplace safe. So we could be together."* Her eyes fill with tears. *"But something went wrong."* I blink. This is where my story starts. *"Your father and I went into hiding. We . . ."* she says, trailing off. *"We knew that the crash was no accident, so we thought it would be best—"*

"To abandon me," I interrupt. *"You abandoned me."* My heart drops and agony slices through my chest. This is worse than them being dead. Not only did she never come to look for me, but she abandoned me first.

"No, Ruby. I knew my brother was looking for us. If he found us, I don't even want to imagine . . . The best option then was to separate. Make it harder for him

to find us. It was the only thing we could think of. So we split everyone up. Two of you were left in Ohio, and the others we took to other states. We just wanted you safe and hidden.

"But five years ago, he found us, and he separated me from your father, and I don't know where your dad is." She's crying again. *"My brother is searching for all of us, Ruby. And he has been doing whatever it takes…"* Mom trails off, silent tears streaming down her face. It takes me a second to realize what she means, but when it clicks, my jaw falls. My uncle has been torturing my parents for years so that he can find me. Me and my siblings. *I let out a small, slow sigh. I understand now.*

"You've been protecting us." Mom touches my cheek and nods.

"If I don't know where any of you are, then he won't know either. Do you have more water?" she asks. Even though she finished her first bottle, a film of ash lines her cracked lips.

"Oh, yes," I say, running back to my bag and grabbing her another bottle. I give it to her, and she takes a couple of deep gulps.

"Ruby, you have to stay hidden, so lie low. The further apart you are from your siblings, the safer we are." She takes another sip of water, her eyes scanning my face. Her pupils dilate, and her look shifts, a soft smile appearing on her lips. *"You are so beautiful, Ruby."* Tears prick my eyes, and against my will, they drip off my eyelashes. She reaches up to wipe them away. The foul odor is still prevalent, but I ignore it. *"You have your whole life to live. It's not fair for you to drop it all for some cause you didn't sign up for."* My tears are falling fast now. *"Let me keep protecting you."*

"And I appreciate that, Mom," I start, reaching up to hold her hand that rests on my cheek, *"but I've wanted to be part of a family more than anything in the world,"* I explain, squeezing her hands into mine. *"And now that I know I have one, I can't just let that go! Especially when I'm so close…"* I trail off as I see concern fill her face.

"So close? Ruby, what—" I interrupt her. Rising joy takes over me and a smile fills my face.

"I think I already know one of my sisters." I'm sure of it. Dread fills mom's face as she senses my confidence.

"How can that be? We were so careful," she exclaims, covering her mouth with her hand. *"It has to be a coincidence, just some other kid."* But I smile. Moon and I are sisters; we have to be. There's no way we aren't. Because to be honest, what normal parent would name their daughter Moonstone? Not to mention, being Black does help to narrow down what may be a coincidence or not. Of course, I may just be jumping to conclusions, but this is a pretty big presumption I don't mind having. The concern that marks her features melts away as she sees my happiness, and she grasps my hands. My hands. I'm holding my mom's hands. She looks past me, and the smile disappears from her face. Her grip tightens, and my knuckles slide against each other.

"Ru-Ruby, you have to get out of here, now!*"* she says quietly but urgently.

"Why?" I ask, worried. I look to see what she is looking at, and a chill runs down my spine. A black and red shadow forms in the distance, creating a small tornado of sand in its place. I feel the blood drain from my face.

"Look at me and listen." My head snaps back to face her. The urgency and fear in her tone are new. *"This is a dream. Sometimes, this can happen, but I don't have the time to go into details. Even though this is a dream, everything I said to you is true. Where you see me now, it's like where I am in real life. Except, this is a limbo dream world, a mixture of reality and fantasy."* She tightens her hold on me, and I gasp in pain. I look down at my hands. My fingertips are turning purple. *"But . . . Bloodstone can't find you. Don't let him. He has abilities too! He can . . ."* She looks past me again, her eyes filled with fear. *"You have to get the hell out of here,"* she says urgently. *"Find Adelaide."*

"But—"

"Ruby, WAKE UP!"

"Wait, Mom, I . . ."

"Wake up!" she screams as she closes her eyes tightly. I shake my hands away from hers and cover my ears. Her screams make my ears throb with pain, and I press down hard. My hands feel wet, so I pull one away: blood. She backs away from me, eyes still closed. When she opens them, her eyes are pitch-black, and her

beautiful dirty skin melts away until there are just her bones and eyeballs. Her finger bones reach to touch my face, but I don't move. I'm frozen in place. The tip just barely brushes across my nose before I snap back to reality. I jump up, screaming and running, grabbing my bags of loot, and racing toward the door. I push on it, but it doesn't open. I turn back and see the skeleton that used to be my mother walking toward me. I'm panting as I'm ramming my shoulder into the door, willing it open. After three more hard hits, the door busts open and . . .

I jerk awake, gasping and thrashing in my bed, tears streaming down my face. Zach springs from the pull-out and hops on the bed next to me. He says something, but I don't hear him. My eyes are closed tightly, and my hands cover my ears. Something touches my arm, and I claw at it, screaming again. I hear a hiss of pain. More words. Someone is talking. Something is happening. I don't know, I don't know. I just . . .

"Ruby!" My eyes shoot open, and I see Zach kneeling on the bed in front of me, pulling my bloodied hands away from my ears. "What happened? Are you okay?" he asks, scanning my body with his eyes.

"Yes," I reply, gulping in air and sniffing. "Just a nightmare." He lets me go, and I notice the scratch I left on his arm. "Oh my God! I'm so sorry," I say, gesturing toward his forearm.

"Don't sweat it. C'mere." I get from under my covers and crawl toward him. I lay my head in his lap and let my tears of fear fall silently. *That was terrifying.* Zach leans away, grabbing something, then rubs my back. I let out a sigh of pleasure. He's holding me close, one hand rubbing my back and the other hand wiping the spots of blood on my hands.

"Maybe I shouldn't have taken the pillow from you, huh?" Zach adds, and I giggle tiredly. He continues stroking my back, which lulls me into a sleepy state. I snuggle closer to him and use my right hand to grasp onto my left thumb for comfort, holding it as if it were a small doll. He pulls me in closer, leans back against the headboard, and continues stroking my back.

"Feel better now?" he asks. I nod against his thigh. After a few minutes like this, I am nearly asleep when I hear his voice.

"Hey, Ruby, where did you get that stuff?" whispers Zach curiously.

"What stuff?" I ask sleepily. He stops stroking my back and points to the end of my bed. I follow his finger, my eyes widening when I see what he is talking about. Lying there in a small pile of sand is the white backpack and cute puppy bag from my dream.

CHAPTER 6

The next few days go by quickly. Ani, Camy, Jordyn, Moon, and I spent the week laughing, studying, and goofing off. Yesterday, Moon and I hung out after the football game, watching Disney movies and gossiping to the sound of chirping crickets.

"Not gonna lie, Ruby. Ani is going to be screwed for this quiz on Monday," Moon said, plopping a chip in her mouth.

"Yeah . . ." I trailed off. Moon readjusted her position on the couch and leaned toward me.

"Ruby, she has got every question wrong this week."

"I'm sure it wasn't . . ."

"Ruby. Every. Question," Moon emphasized. "Like it would be impressive if it wasn't so concerning." She placed another chip in her mouth. "And an aerospace engineer? We've gotta help her."

"We will! Tomorrow, remember?" I said, referring to the scheduled study session.

"Yes . . . but how?"

"Right." I chuckle. "Do we even know what we're doing?" So the rest of our movie night had become a "save Ani's grade" planning session. Moon and I both know the material well, so after practicing teaching each other for an hour or so, our confidence in tutoring Ani rose significantly.

I still haven't told any of my friends, especially Moon, about my crazy dream. I feel bad about not saying anything. Since my mom—if it was even *really* her—told me I could travel in my dreams, I have been praying before I went to sleep each night, asking God not to send me any. I need to focus on what I know and what I can control. And if that means pushing aside crazy dreams and weird abilities, then I intend to do so.

I open the fridge and pull out all the ingredients needed for pancakes, Maria's favorite breakfast food. As I mix the batter, she waddles down the steps drowsily and rubs her eyes.

"Good morning, Maria," I say as I mix the batter.

"Hi, Ruby," my six-year-old stepsister says groggily as she sits on a stool.

"I have a surprise for you," I announce, thinking of the puppy backpack.

"Really?" she asks. I pour the batter into the pan.

"Yes," I say as I turn to face her. "If you eat breakfast with me, I'll give it to you as soon as it is ready." Maria frowns.

"But what about mommy? She doesn't like me eating with you unless I'm sick." She pouts, upset she won't get her surprise during breakfast. I roll my eyes, pushing back my irritation, and look at Maria.

"Then be sick." I turn back to flip the pancake. One thing Maria is good at is acting. Her face brightens, and she runs upstairs to her room. By the time she comes back, there's a stack of golden-brown pancakes on the island. When I see her, I almost don't recognize her as the girl who was here a minute ago. Her usual rosy cheeks are now pale, her wet, black hair sticks to her face, and her silk nightgown appears to have barf all over it. However, I know she is faking because there's a grin on her face.

"You really have perfected 'being sick,' haven't you?"

"Well, y'know, there's a lot of times I didn't want to go to school…" She trails off and runs up the stairs. I tiptoe behind her, and she knocks on her mother's bedroom door.

"Mommy," she says as if her tongue is swollen. "Mommy, I don't feel so good." I hear footsteps coming toward the door. I wink at Maria, then hide behind the corner just as Lisa steps from her room.

"Oh, you poor child," she says, worried about her daughter. "Ruby! Get up here and please help Maria. She's covered in *bile*," she says, disgusted. I step from the corner and scurry to Maria.

"Yes, Lisa," I respond as I steer Maria away from the door. When we round the corner, she jumps with joy. "Shh," I say, trying not to giggle with her. "You're sick, remember? And what about your nightgown? That better not stain it," I admonish, referring to the "bile" all over her gown. To answer my question, she peels it right off her dress. "Oh, you're a smart cookie!" She grins, proud of herself. "Get rid of the makeup, and I'll meet you in my room."

"Okilly dokilly," Maria says, saluting me, then running off. I walk down the stairs and fix two plates of pancakes and two glasses of milk. I grab a serving tray from the top of the fridge, place the food on it, and head up to my room, where Maria is impatiently waiting for me.

"So? What is it?" she asks eagerly, looking around the room.

"Eat while I get it for you," I say as I walk to my bed. I bend down and reach underneath it. I feel the fluffy bags and tug it from under my bed. "Close your eyes." I hold the bag behind my back. She silently obeys, but not before shoving some pancake into her mouth. I lay the bag in front of her on the floor. "Okay, you can open them now."

"I love it," she gasps, grabbing them and squeezing them to her chest. She puts the bags down and gives me a huge hug. "Thank you, Ruby!" she says. When we break the hug, she stands up and models with one of the backpacks.

"Oh, magnificent! Bravo! That is so your style," I say, happy that she is happy. "Make sure you hide it from your mom, though," I warn. Maria nods. Lisa hasn't let her play with toys ever since she was two when she threw her doll at a wall. She said, "If little girls could mature faster, I want that to happen to you, Maria. Toys are just a distraction." I let her play with my old toys all the time though because, after all, she's just a kid.

"Did you think that I only got you the bag? There is stuff inside," I reveal, interrupting Maria's fashion show.

"I was wondering why it was super-duper heavy," she says, plopping herself back on the floor and dumping the contents from the bags. She empties out makeup and costumes for her acting, along with finger and hand puppets.

"Wow!" she exclaims, stunned at all the items. She reaches inside the only pocket on the backpack and pulls out a tiny multicolored square. "What is this?" she asks, holding it up to the light and examining it.

"Oh, let me show you," I say, taking the square from her hand and bringing it over to the corner of my room where all of my old toys are. I rip the plastic from around the square, and it immediately unfolds itself into a tent-like puppet stage.

"Amazing!" Maria squeals, running to it. "I love it!" She runs back to the pile of things on the floor, stuffs them in her puppy backpacks, then dumps it all back out inside the puppet stage tent. "Lemme put a show on for you, Ruby."

"Okay," I reply, bringing beanbag cushions from my closet and over to the front of the stage. I place stuffed animals in all but one of them.

"But let me prep first," she says from inside the tent.

"Go for it," I respond, settling into the empty beanbag cushion just as my phone vibrates with a text from Ani.

Ani: When can I come over?

Me: Why r u coming over?

Ani: To study, remember?

Me: Oh, yah, ok, ummm 10 min. That's when Moon will be here. Come in thru my window tho, on right side of the house, top floor by the big tree.

Ani: Perfect

I am about to put my phone away when it vibrates with a text from Moon. When I hear light tapping, I turn and see her at my window. I smile and head to unlock the window.

"What's up, my guy?" she asks me, poking her head in before stepping inside.

"Not gonna lie. I totally forgot about studying. Maria's about to put on a puppet show, and Ani will be here soon."

"How could you forget? It was all she talked about yesterday," exclaims Moon as we make our way to the front of the tent. She picks up one of the stuffed animals in the beanbag chair next to mine and sits down. Five minutes later, there is a puppet on the stage.

"Thank you for coming, Ruby," Maria announces in a deep voice.

"And Moonstone," I add.

"She here too?" Maria asks, going back to her regular voice and poking her head out.

"Yeah."

"Okay then," she replies. "Thank you for coming, Ruby *and* Moonstone."

"And Ani," adds a voice. Moon and I turn to see Ani climbing in through the window. She sits on the other side of Moon but has no math books or bag. She's wearing an oversized sweatshirt that goes down to her knees and large golden hoops nearly hanging to her shoulders.

"Okay, guys. Please stop interrupting my introduction. I am trying to put on a *show* here."

"Sorry," we respond in unison.

When the show starts, Moon whispers to Ani.

"So where are your math books?"

"What math books?" she responds, paying most of her attention to the show.

"You needed help with that problem, remember?"

"Oh yeah, right. I, uh, forgot them."

"That's okay, I brought mine," Moon whispers as I elbow her in the rib. "Ow."

I point to the show she completely forgot about. When Maria finishes, we all stand up and give her applause and congratulations. When the cheers die down, I let her know the three of us will be studying.

"Don't mind me! I can keep myself busy," she says and runs to the bathroom with her makeup kit.

"Hey, guys," starts Ani, "is it okay if we go get my books? I left the sheet of paper that has the problem on it and all my notes. I know that we can just use yours, Moon, but I really would like to have mine." Moon gives me a look that screams *obviously*.

"Sounds good to me. Where do you live?" Moon asks.

"A couple roads down. Not too far," Ani directs.

"Hey, Maria, we're going out. We should be back soon, at the latest noon . . . Don't tell Lisa," I say, as I am the last girl to go out of the window.

"You live here?" I ask in awe. Ani lives in the *legendary* house of the neighborhood. From where we are, all we see are trees, a driveway that curves into the woods, and a medium-sized shed. Ani points to it.

"Put your bikes in there." We all put our bikes inside, then we start the long trek up the cement driveway. That's when I spot it, the house. The house I've only heard rumors about—the house that has been here forever. *No one told me this house was for sale,* I think. *Ani is the new girl, so how was this not the talk of the town?* The siding of the house is a cherry wood color with brick stones. It has three garage doors, and there's a bus in the driveway.

Instead of going into the legend house, Ani leads Moon and me to the backyard. The land is surrounded by forest, and there's a pool with a diving board. *I hope she invites us over to swim sometime,* I think as we continue walking. She walks past the pool and stops in front of a huge oak tree. The width of the tree is about twelve feet wide, and it is taller than the house. I glance at Moonstone and find that her mouth is ajar. To my left, I see Ani on the ground, searching for something.

"Uh, Ani, did you bury your books?" jokes Moonstone, chuckling curiously.

"Huh? Oh no, I didn't bury them. You'll see," she adds, looking back and grinning. She drags her hand across the ground until she finally lays her hand on a root. "Aha!" she exclaims and pulls up on the root. A section of the grass in front of the tree lifts, almost like a trapdoor, revealing a slide. "Go inside," states Ani. My jaw drops. *What in the world?* I look back at Moon and see an expression mixed with amazement, awe, and bewilderment. I'm sure my expression reflects the same emotions. I'm about to go inside a fricking tree. A *fricking tree.* I'm silently grateful I decided not to rock an updo or 'fro today. My hair is in two low pigtails with two twists in the front to shape my face. Moon is already taking down her high bun of braids, not wanting it to get caught on any roots.

Nervously, I walk toward the slide and sit down. I turn to look back at Ani, and she ushers me to go. So I do. The slide stops after a few seconds, and there are coil stairs that go up the tree. *We must be inside the trunk.* Moonstone is right behind me, then comes Ani. She pushes past us and heads up the stairs, but I don't move. A tap on my shoulder tells me I should keep going, so I grasp onto the railing. I place my red sneaker on the first step, then the next, wondering what awaits me at the top of this not-so-normal tree.

CHAPTER 7

When I reach the top, I can't believe what I'm seeing. I step into the room, which is about the size of a large one-room basement, and walk around. There's a huge circular wooden table in the center of the room, surrounded by faux tree stumps as chairs. It's almost the size of a conference table, fit to sit . . . twenty maybe? When I look up, I notice a canvas of fake leaves and glass. Around the circumference of the room are cabinets, a microwave, a fridge, a stove, and an oven. Straight ahead is an archway that leads to a sitting room with beanbag chairs and a flat-screen TV, and five other doors leading to other places in this quite literal tree house.

"Wow, this is . . . wow," says Moonstone.

"What is this place?" I ask in awe.

"This is our safe bunker," Ani says, her arms outstretched. She pushes her round glasses up her nose and beckons for us to follow her. Ani makes her way to the sitting room and flops into a beanbag chair.

"Why?" Moonstone asks, confused. "What do you have to be safe from?" Ani stares off into space, clearly avoiding answering the question. The silence that emerges from her lack of a response quickly grows heavy.

"This . . . is . . . uh, well, are your books here?" I ask, dismissing the obscurity of the situation. Ani looks at me as if I am a kindergartener.

"Ruby, Moon, I never needed any help. I just needed to get you two alone so that we can talk." Moon and I exchange concerning glances.

"Um, okay, so what do you want to talk about?" asks Moon cautiously.

"Our past," she responds seriously.

"Our past? I think you mean your past," replies Moonstone. "Right, Ruby?" I look at Moon, confusion written all over her face. What do I say? I have no idea where this is going, and I'm filled with unease.

"Moonstone, Ruby, I suggest that you may want to sit down. This may take a while." Moonstone sits in a milky white beanbag, and I make my way toward a red one. "First, we should start off with something simple. My name isn't Ani, well, at least not my given name. My real name is . . . Tanzanite," I am almost at the chair when she says it: *Tanzanite.* I feel light-headed instantly. I need water. I feel the room begin to spin right before my knees buckle and I faint into the chair.

When I come to, I'm soaked with water. My black bra is clearly visible through my white top. I look up to see Ani, or "Tanzanite," with an empty bucket over my head.

"Ruby, you okay?" asks Tanzanite, concern written on her face.

"No, not at all! What is going on here? Why are you here? Mom said . . ." I trail off.

"So you knew?" Tanzanite asks, totally missing the "mom" part.

"I recently found out," I say quietly. "You're probably not even from Alaska, are you?" Tanzanite shakes her head, grinning.

"Nope. New York."

"What is going on? Knew what?" questions Moon, looking between us confusedly.

"How about *Tanzanite* tells you?" I reply, sitting in the chair and wringing out my hair. It couldn't have been too long that I was out for. I feel like the amount of water that was dumped on me was unnecessary.

"Okay, Moon, this may sound a little weird," Ani starts. Moon crosses her arms, impatiently, "but . . . um . . . how should I put this? You, Ruby, and I are all sisters." Moon stares at us blank-faced for a minute. Suddenly, she cracks up laughing.

"If this is all some ruse so that we don't study—" Moon starts, but Ani cuts her off. Irritation flashes in her features.

"Look, your parents died in a plane crash. Okay? Cry about it. Then you get adopted. Good for you. You're one of the lucky ones, avoiding the foster care system and getting a good family. But something doesn't feel right. You had to have felt it. You *know* something deeper is going on," Tanzanite explains, eyes beating into Moon's. I shoot Tanzanite a glare for being so harsh. Moon becomes nervous and looks to me for help, looks to me to deny what Tanzanite is saying to her. I don't know what to do or say, so I give her an apologetic, strained smile and shrug. Her nervous face fills with hurt.

"This is true, Ruby? You knew? You knew that we were sisters, and you didn't tell me!" Moon yells, pain abundant in her voice.

"In my defense," I respond, hands up in innocence, "I only found out a couple of days ago . . . and under the circumstances, I didn't think that the information was true," I defend, looking Moon straight into the eyes. Something is missing, though. Her face is emotionless and her eyes empty. She's shut down on me.

"Ruby, I'll tell Moon everything. It's hot today. You should go outside and dry off. You're all wet."

"Like I don't know that," I state, waving my hands all over my body. I get up and leave the room, thankful to not have to tell Moon everything, hoping I won't have to tell Tanzanite how I know. I pick the first door I see, and it leads outside to a balcony. There are many paths that trail on each branch of the tree. It's a maze. To the right of the door is a sun chair. I lay on it thankfully. No more stress, no more siblings, no more truth, just . . . now. I close my eyes and soak in the sun. Suddenly, a voice startles me.

"Hey, who are you? You aren't allowed up here," says a boy's voice. I shoot to sit up straight and see a guy a little older than I am with hazel eyes, staring at me. Serious and curious. He's wearing shorts and a dark green T-shirt. His eyes bore into my face, and after a while, he winces in pain and touches his temple. His loose curls bounce as he shakes his head. Seemingly upset about something, he covers his face with a mask of security. His eyes come back to look at my face, but they slowly drift down to my chest. He tugs at the collar of his shirt.

"You're wet . . ." He shakes his head again, putting on a flirtatious smile. "Here, I know where towels are." He goes inside the "tree" and comes back to find me sitting in the same position I was in before. "Here you go," he says, but instead of giving me the towel, he starts drying me off. He starts with my hair and moves down to my face. I do nothing. His attractiveness has stunned me into silence.

He's like your classic light-skinned boy, but with an extra dazzle of charm. His loose curls sit atop his head, with a clean taper fade on the sides. He dries my hair carefully, making sure to not cause any frizz. Moving the towel down my neck and on my chest, he starts drying my chest a little too much, gently squeezing the water out of my bra. I realize what he is doing a split-second too late and I shove him away.

"Get off of me, you perv!" I yell, bringing my knees to my chest. He takes a step back, putting his hands up in innocence.

"I was only drying you off," he says, throwing me the towel. I catch it. "And after you dry off, I can show you around. Maybe we can even have some fun," he adds, eyeing my body. I shrink under his gaze. "I have the perfect bra that would look excellent on your breasts. All the other girls were too big to fit in it, but you're just the right size." My jaw drops. "And don't worry, I won't tell anyone you're up here." I scoot farther away from him.

"You're disgusting. Leave me alone!" I say angrily.

"No, it's okay. All the girls say I'm fun," he coos, wiggling his eyebrows and coming closer. His eyes look hungry for me. I scoot back even more.

"And I *am* allowed up here. Tanzanite brought me," I add, bringing my legs closer to my body. Her name still feels awkward on my lips. His flirtatious grin disappears, and his face is serious once again. Faster than I can react, he grabs me by the throat and tilts my head up to face him.

"Who are you?" he asks, face as hard as stone. There's a spark of something else there too. *Fear? Hope?*

"I'm . . . I'm R-Ruby J-Jenk-ins," I stutter out. His face falls with relief, and he lets me go to scratch his head.

"Oh, Tani found another Gem. She's beating me now," he says, more to himself than me.

I look at him in horror. It. Can't. Be.

"And you are . . . ?"

"Peridot, your brother." He bows to me and grabs my hand and kisses it. I wipe the kiss away. "Sorry for earlier. On occasion, one of our sisters would bring non-Gems up here to gather intel or whatnot. I don't know what came over me. You just have a sexy—"

"Stop. Just stop," I interrupt him, disgusted. But then again, I thought he was hot too, before I knew . . . *At least I didn't say it out loud.* "What exactly is a Gem?" His mind seems to go somewhere else. My question snaps his attention back to me.

"A Gem is one of our siblings. Garnet came up with it. You're a Gem, I'm a Gem. Finding a Gem means you find one of our brothers or sisters. Y'know, Peri Gem, Ruby Gem, Tanzanite Gem. It's our last name, just makes things easier," he says, still eyeing me curiously. I start to relax though. Peri seems to be a nice guy. A whore too, maybe. But a nice guy. His sense of humor, though, not the most appealing. I flash back to my dream . . . *Gems.*

"Great. How many kids did our mom have?" I ask rhetorically, dropping my head onto my knees.

"More than ten, less than thirty. Somewhere around there." My head shoots up, and I gawk at him. "Yeah 'cause there's you and me, Garnet, Tani, Ziri, Citrine, Sapphire, and others. We have headway on their location, and we're getting ready to start a Gem hunt too. But . . ." Peri trails off as Tanzanite walks outside.

"I see you have met Peri."

"Pervy Peri sounds more accurate to me," I reply, looking directly at Tanzanite and rolling my eyes, avoiding eye contact with my brother.

"Moon wants to speak with you," she declares, looking at me. Then she turns her gaze toward Peri. "And I need to talk to *you*," she says, poking him in the chest. I leave them be as I head inside to Moon, who's sitting in the beanbag chair. I sit next to her, but she doesn't move. She just stares out into space.

"My *life*, my *whole* entire fucking life has been a lie," she says, not looking at me.

"Been there, done that!" I intone, trying to lighten the mood. She glances at me, not amused.

"Did she tell you that we have to live here? She didn't say why. She just said that I have to. I mean, she's part of my birth family. But . . . but she said that my adoptive parents are going to think I am dead. *Dead*, Ruby! They have done everything for me, and they are going to think I am *dead*! It will crush them. It's crushing me." A tear slips from her eyes, and she lets it fall from her cheek and onto her skin, where she doesn't even bother to wipe it away.

"I didn't know about that, Moon," I say, placing my hand on her back and rubbing it, then I stop suddenly. Maria will think I am dead. The only person for her to be herself around will be gone. Jordyn and Camy will never see me again. And Zach. Zach will think I am dead. *Zach*. I rub my forehead.

"Tanzanite said that Garnet, our oldest sister," she says, struggling with the word 'sister', "is going to pretend to be a high school student that we know. Two days from now, she's going to pretend to drop us off at school, and we're going to die in a car accident." *Two days*. Moon lets another tear fall, and another.

"So tomorrow will be our last day at our houses, ever?" I ask flabbergasted. She nods. *No*. "No. No. There has to be another way. We don't have to go. We can stay home. Pretend none of this ever happened."

"But . . . can we really?" she asks, looking into my eyes. She fiddles with her braids. "And I already asked Ani . . . Tanzan . . . whatever her name is. She's not really giving us much of a choice." She throws her hands up in the air. "And we have a family. *We're* a family. By blood, something I have always wanted and wondered about. I think that we have to do this, not just for them," she says, looking around the room, "for ourselves too." We both sit there, stuck. Just this morning, things were normal. Well, as normal as they could be for me at least. But everything is changing so fast that I can basically feel the pain of the whiplash on my neck. I'm about to reach for Moon's hand when Tanzanite walks in.

"Two days. You'll text somebody you know tomorrow night that *Alex*, not Garnet, is taking you to school so that they know. And you will both need to write a will and give them to me tomorrow evening. Please state your name in the will and that all of your belongings be loaded up and donated to the 'Gem Foundation.' Don't ask if it is real, it isn't. But the world thinks it is. We have a website and everything," she says, giving us a wink. She sees our confused faces and shrugs. "It's just some excuse for us to keep all of your stuff." She smiles sweetly, then her face goes back to business. "Are we understood?" We both nod solemnly. "I have stuff to do here, but you guys know the way out." She turns and leaves the room.

Tanzanite seems like an entirely different person than the "Ani" I met nearly a week ago. This girl is all business. Moon and I both stand and head toward the door that leads out of the tree quietly, preparing for the last few moments with our family.

"Maria," I say, knocking on her bedroom door. It's early in the morning, but she opens it.

"Ruby!" she squeals, smiling brightly. "You've just saved me from reading *The Odyssey*," she groans. "Reading is fun, but not *this*. I don't know why mom makes me read this stuff," she complains, waving the book in the air before tossing it aside. I give her a small smile. I saved her, and now her savior has to go.

"Maria, sit down. I need you to listen to me, very closely." She nods eagerly. She soon recognizes the distress in my voice and silently obeys.

"I gotta go away for a while." She starts to say something, but I hold up my hand. "Don't try to talk me out of it because . . . I have to." She stares at me, tears welling up into her eyes. *This is hard. How do you explain to someone your entire life is a lie and that you're some freak of a human?*

"Why can't you stay? Is it mommy?" I shake my head. She sniffs. "Well, if you are going away, I am too!" she declares, jumping up and yanking clothes out of drawers. Her pigtails bounce as she tosses the clothes over her shoulder.

"Maria . . ." I stand next to her, but she doesn't stop throwing clothes. "Maria, stop." She doesn't. "*Stop*!" I grab her arms and turn her to face me. Tears stream down her face.

"No, Ruby! Where you go, I go. You can't leave me! I thought we were friends." She sinks into her bed and wipes at her tears angrily. "I thought we were friends." I sit beside her and pull out a smart phone with a yellow case on it.

"Maria, we are friends." I lift her chin so she can meet my eye. "Look . . . you're going to hear some things on the news, okay? But it's not true." She sniffs, her dry tears being replaced with fresh ones. "I bought you this phone." I hand it to her, and she takes it. It was my first purchase with the dream money.

"Ruby, I already have a phone," she says, confused.

"Here is my new phone number," I say, giving her a slip of paper. "It is the only number that is allowed to go on this phone, do you understand me? You can talk to me and FaceTime me whenever you want. But, Maria, you can't tell anyone you're still talking to me, do you understand? If you do, I'll get in big trouble, and we don't want that." She nods, not fully understanding, but trying to.

"Why do you have to go?"

"I can't tell you. I'm sorry, Maria. I really am."

"You're leaving me with *her*," she says quietly. I cringe. I wish I could just take her with me too. "I hate her. I *hate* her," Maria whispers angrily, batting at her tears. She chokes on a sob "And . . . and now I kinda hate you too." We sit there in silence for what seems like forever until her small voice breaks it. "When . . . when do you go?" she asks. I bite the inside of my cheek and stare at the ceiling. *Be strong, Ruby.*

"Tomorrow." She winces but nods. "I love you, Maria, okay? I will always love you, from now until forever." I pull her into a tight hug, and we stay like that for a long time. I don't want to let go. I can't. Letting go means I'm leaving her. I squeeze her harder, silent tears racing down my face. I open my mouth to speak, but what I need to say next catches in my throat. I pause and take a deep breath. "Take care of Snowball for me," I say, letting her go and standing up. "I left you some money and instructions in her room." I sniff as I turn to go.

"Ruby?" she says when I'm almost out of the door. I turn to face her, soaking up what may be the last time I see her in person. "I love you too." I smile sadly and leave her sitting on her bed, clutching her new phone and treasuring the last time that we truly had together.

From there, I go straight to Zach's house. I climb up the big tree by his bedroom and watch him sleep. I have no idea what time he wakes up. I try to remember his goofy smile and dark hair. I won't see him again, and as the seconds tick away, the weight of that fact seems to grow heavier. He wakes up in what feels like hours later, but, really, it's only minutes. When he sees me, his eyes widen before he laughs. I can't hear it though, and that pains me. He opens the window and lets me in.

"Good morning, Ruby." I don't answer. I just flop onto his bed and scream into the pillows. A rush of cedar and nutmeg flow into my nostrils, and I am filled with woe. *What do I tell him?* He thinks I am being funny. "Sure, you can hop into my bed. You can hop in whenever you like." I take my head away from the pillows and look at him, eyebrows raised. Seconds later, he realizes what he said and he drags his hand along the back of his neck in embarrassment. "I-I mean, y-you know . . ." he trails off. I giggle.

"I get what you mean." I lay my head back on the pillows and breathe in his sweet, earthy scent. I don't want the last day I see him to be sad. It has to be happy. It has to be. "Let's play Egyptian Rat Screw," I say, going through his drawers to find a deck of cards.

"Uh, sure. But they're not in there." He reaches under his bed, pulls out the deck, and starts dealing out the cards on his carpet. I sit there, remembering the feeling and savoring today. We play until I win, so not long at all.

I texted his mom on the way over so she wouldn't walk in and freak out when she saw me. At some point, he goes downstairs to bring up some of the breakfast his mom made, and I turn on our comfort anime. But I'm hardly watching it. I am watching him. How his cheeks go up when he laughs and how his eyes twinkle in the light of the TV. Later, we go outside to play soccer and basketball. I don't even care when I lose. I just cherish the time I have with him because, after tonight, it will all be gone.

"What's up with you today, Ruby? I beat you in soccer and in basketball and you don't fuss about it? That never happens." He places the back of his hand on my forehead. "Are you sick?" I smile up at him.

"I am perfect." I lay my head on his shoulder. "And just so you know, I *let* you win," I lie. He chuckles and wraps an arm around my shoulder. We're sitting on the tree branch by his bedroom, facing toward the sunset. I have been with Zach all day, but it still doesn't feel like enough time. If only I had more time. Part of me feels guilty for not seeing Camy and Jordyn, but they both had plans today. So there wasn't really anything I could do. I gotta remember to call them later. "Zach?" I ask.

"Hmm?" he responds, pulling me in closer.

"You are the best. You really are," I admit, tugging his shirt. "I'm going to miss your smile and miss your laugh and miss—" He interrupts me.

"Miss what? Ruby, I'm not going anywhere. *You* aren't going anywhere." I sniff. *Dang, I can feel the tears coming already.*

"Look at me." I sit up so he can turn his head to face me. I lay my hands on his face, feeling every bone structure on him. My hands memorize every part of him, then they move down to his neck and both arms, to his chest, stomach, and legs, and end with me pulling off his shoes and touching his toes. I know it's excessive, but I don't care.

"Ruby." He laughs, confused. "What are you doing?"

"Remembering you," I say, tickling his toes. He attempts not to smile, but he can't help it. He reaches for my hands and holds them still.

"Why? Why do you need to remember me? You can't get rid of me, Ruby. Where you go, I go." I immediately think of Maria and pinch the inside of my wrist. *Don't cry, don't cry, don't . . .*

"You are one of my best friends, Zach," I say as I feel the tears welling up again. *I have to make this quick.* "And I know I'd tease you and stuff, but I hope you know I never meant anything by it. You have always been there for me, always, in my best and worst moments, and I love you for that," I say. *Okay, I have to leave now.* I'm about to, but I hesitate. If I'm never going to see him again, then I have to do this. If not, I'll regret it forever. I muster up my courage and kiss him on the cheek, right before making my way down the tree. He doesn't move until he notices me walking farther and farther away.

"Ruby!" he yells after me, confused. He climbs down the tree.

"Bye, Zach!" I yell to him, finally letting the tears fall. I'm too far away for him to notice. He yells my name again, running after me. "Goodbye Zach" I whisper, and when I turn the corner, I will myself to be invisible. I haven't taken the necklace off since we stole it back from Lisa. I clutch the ruby and walk away, leaving Zach spinning in circles, calling my name.

I find the root and let myself into the tree, tucking my necklace under my shirt as I walk up the stairs. Tanzanite is there, waiting for me.

"I have the will, Tanzanite," I say, knowing my face is probably stained with tears.

"Please, call me Tani. We're sisters, you know," she responds, smiling. It turns into a frown when she sees my face. She sighs and runs her hands up and down her arms. I can't get over how pretty she is. She's wearing an oversized brown sweatshirt with some geeky pun on it: *I may be nerdy, but only periodically.* The symbols for neon, erbium, and dysprosium spell out "nerdy." Her hair is in a cute messy bun of wavy curls on the top of her head, with several strands out to shape her face. Her usual large gold glasses are on her face, and the look is completed with some ankle socks and giant gold hoops. "Don't be mad at me, Ruby. This has to be done."

"Sure," I concede, dropping my will on the table and turning my back to her. I make my way back to the exit. "I'm sure there was no other way." And I leave Tani like that, feeling guilty, and I like it.

RUBY'S WILL

LAST WILL AND TESTAMENT

THIS IS MY WILL IN CASE I AM TO DIE UNDER THE AGE OF 18. I HOPE THAT THIS WILL BE CONSIDERED AS REAL AND VALID.

I WOULD LIKE MY BODY TO BE DONATED TO THE "GEM FOUNDATION" AS WELL AS THE REST OF MY BELONGINGS. THE NUMBER TO CALL CAN BE FOUND ON THE WEBSITE. THEY SHOULD TAKE CARE OF THE REST.

WITNESSES: MOONSTONE ADDAMS AND ANI JOEL

RUBY JENKINS

CHAPTER 8

I wait at the curb of my driveway for the car Garnet is supposed to be driving. When the blue 2021 Honda Civic finally pulls into the driveway, I walk to it and knock on the window. It rolls down to reveal a girl.

"Garnet?" I ask. She looks at me and smiles.

"At your service." She winks. I nod at Moon, letting her know it's okay, and we both climb into the car.

"You ready to die, Ruby?" jokes Moon in the back seat. She looks happier than the last time we saw each other, but I can spot the nerves in her voice.

"Yeah . . . Garnet, how are we going to die anyway?" I ask.

"Oh . . ." she replies as she stops at a stop sign. Looking at me through the rearview mirror, she winks again. "You'll see." I'm quiet after that. If I am going to drop off the face of the Earth, I would like to know how. I look at Garnet. The day that I am meeting her is the day I "die." I assume she was there at the tree bunker, just someplace else. *Why didn't she want to meet her two new sisters?* Her hair is dark red, styled in finger waves. It reminds me of my hair, but darker, almost black. Mine is a lighter, red velvet cake color. She's light-skinned with freckles running along her nose. Her lips and eyes are full of life and color. But, there's something else in her eyes too. She looks like the kind of girl who keeps secrets for pleasure's sake.

"Is that your natural hair color?" I ask, trying to make conversation. And I'm curious too. It looks like she dyed it.

"Yes," she replies, then changes the topic. "Peri's in that green car right over there," she says, pointing out of the window. She honks her horn, and through the rearview mirror, he waves back at us. "We're going to follow him onto Necknoe Road. That's where it's going to happen, okay?" Moon and I nod.

"Garnet, please tell us how this is going to work," pleads Moon as we approach Necknoe road. Garnet touches her ear and nods. She must have an earpiece in.

"Stop asking. It'll be explained once it's over," she says steadily. Moon sinks into her seat. We are currently on Entice Drive, which intersects with Necknoe Road. Garnet stops the car about fifteen hundred feet from the intersection. No one else is on the streets. I look to my right and see the green car that she said Peri is in. Garnet touches her earpiece again and smiles. She slams her foot on the gas and starts driving fast, and so does Peri.

"Garnet!" I screech. Moon cries next to me, gripping the seat, yelling at our sister to stop. *These people are maniacs!* Garnet turns her head and honks the horn, still smiling, still driving. I think I hear the other car's horn, but I'm not really paying attention. At this rate, fake death might turn into *real* death.

"Garnet, stop the fucking car!" screams Moon through her tears. But Garnet is still smiling. *Fuck this shit*, I think as I unbuckle my seatbelt and try to get a hold of the front wheel. But it's too late. I scream as the blue Honda Civic crashes into the other car. Glass shatters, and I hear metal tear apart. The last thing I see is Garnet's dark red hair and haunting smile, right before a searing pain flows through my body and everything turns black.

I wake up in a bus, freezing cold. My teeth chatter as I look down to find that I'm wearing a white dress that looks like a hospital gown but feels like silk. *So*

this must be Heaven. I turn to my right and see Peri sitting in the seat next to mine. *Nope, I must be in Hell.*

"She's awake, guys!" yells Peri to the front of the bus.

"I don't feel so good," I say as I try to move my arms. This bus is like a school bus, except it's painted blue on the inside and half of the seats in the back are gone. The cushions on the seats are comfy though, and there are seat belts.

"Well, you just died, so you shouldn't feel good at all," says Moon, clutching her stomach. The three of us are all a little beaten up. Bandages cover our arms and scratches sprinkle our faces. "I feel like I was just used as a punching bag for hours."

"What!"

"I woke up before you. Peri told me that we're immortal or some shit, so we died . . . but didn't," Moonstone says nonchalantly. She grins when she sees my reaction. I have a feeling she likes knowing something I don't. I gape at her. *Immortal? This is insane.*

"I didn't say all that," Peri explains. "Basically, we have a gene that—" he starts, but I interrupt him.

"I know about the gene," I reply. He and Moon both look at me, confused. I still hadn't told anyone about my dream or my necklace. *Crap.* "I mean, I heard you say it." They both nod, believing the lie, while Peri hands me warm soup in a mug.

"Yeah, so you just had an NDE (near-death experience). Medically, you were dead. Your heart stopped. But give it some time for our cells to do their regeneration thing, and boom! You're back!" Peri explains, talking with his hands. I purse my lips. *Interesting.* I think back to the moment right before the crash: Garnet's smile, the honking, metal scratching metal, then nothing. Nothing until now. I shake my head.

"Where are we going now? Back to the house?"

"We have to go shopping later," replies Garnet from the front of the bus. "You need to—Peri, is it on the news?" she asks, interrupting herself. Garnet must have just died, too, but she seems totally normal, except for a slight tiredness and scrapes on her skin. I look at Peri, and the same goes for him.

"Nah, not on Channel 3, 5, 9, 11, or wait . . . it's on 12. I'll turn up the volume." There's a working TV mounted on the wall of the bus, and I look up to watch.

"This is Jessica McAnderson, and I have breaking news. There was a severe car accident on the intersection of Necknoe Road and Entice Drive. No witnesses so far, but your name, dear?"

"Ani." Tani is on the screen.

"Did you see the accident?"

"No, but I know two of the people in the accident. She told me she was riding with Alex, her high school friend, and that's her car." She sniffs, tears pooling in her eyes, obvious—only to us—they are fake. "Just this weekend, we were all talking about life and death. About how we all want to continue to have an impact on the world even after our death." She chokes on her words. "That's why I ask that all their belongings and body be donated to the Gem Foundation. The Gem Foundation's mission is to research causes that can affect children and young adult's early deaths," Tani explains. A tear falls from her face, and she wipes it away angrily. "Why did this have to happen to them? Why . . .?" She throws her head into her hands and weeps. The news reporter reaches out to comfort her.

"Thank you, Ani. You're a good friend." The reporter turns back to the camera. "LHS has decided to close school today to honor the three young students. We reached out to their families but haven't heard a response." Peri shuts off the TV.

"Ruby, we're going to your house right now, so stay hidden," says Garnet from the front.

"Gotta pick up your shit," explains Peri.

"And Moon's stuff?" I ask.

"Got it already while you were still out," says Moon, steering clear of the windows.

"Ruby! Why can I still see your head?" yells Garnet from the driver's seat.

I duck my head and busy myself by chipping the nail polish off my fingernails, still trying to process that I just died. I *just* died. The bus pulls up to my driveway, and Garnet slams on the brakes. I fall off the seat and land on the floor with a thud. Squeezing my eyes shut, I wince. The pain is less than I expect it to be. My cells are regenerating quickly, and for a moment, I'm thankful for my weird abilities. Getting up, I peek out the window, curious about why we stopped suddenly. There, standing in the middle of the driveway, is none other than Zach.

CHAPTER 9

"Where is she?" he demands. "I have to see her." Garnet looks straight at Zach, then back at me. "Hide," she mouths to me, and I crawl to the back of the bus, hug my knees to my chest, and wait.

"She's not here," says Peri's voice as he steps out of the bus. They're talking, and I strain my ears to hear the conversation.

"You shouldn't be taking her stuff. Someone who knows her should," Zach replies, his voice as hard as stone.

"It's what her will says and what she wants. Now we're just—" Peri explains.

"Who are you?" interrupts Zach. "I don't trust you." *He's adorable, but he has to go. I have to help load stuff on the bus—my necklace is inside.* I took it off and the ruby studs for the car accident because I didn't know what was going to happen and didn't want to lose it.

"Listen, we're on a tight schedule here, so if you could please move—"

"No." I can't see what is happening, and I'm pissed. *I'm here, Zach,* I think. He is *right there,* but there is no way for me to comfort him. But also, things need to get done. There's so much I still don't know or understand. I lean my temple against the side of the bus. *Damn, I really don't know anything.* I almost burst into hysterical giggles. *I don't know these people, but just died for them! I don't even have any evidence of their intentions. This could all be some sort of ruse, and I'm just a gullible idiot.* But also, I feel like everything I've learned is too surreal to not be true. And last I heard, turning invisible is not the norm. And yet . . .

"You realize, *buddy*, this is what she wants. Do you not want to give her what she asked for?" There is a long pause. Then I hear Zach sigh in defeat.

"Okay," says Zach, giving in. "Okay but let me help."

"I don't think that is the best . . ."

"I will *not* move unless I help," demands Zach stubbornly. A few seconds later, Peri speaks.

"Garnet, turn the bus around. I guess you can help. I won't be able to carry all this stuff down on my own anyway." Garnet turns the bus around, backs up the driveway, parks, and hops out. "I'll meet you inside," Peri says as I hear the back door of the bus, in which I am leaning on, opening. I hold my breath and pray Zach won't be there.

"Ruby!" Garnets whisper yells. She's holding the back door open with one arm. Her other hand rests on her hip. "You have to get out of here!" I crawl a few seats toward the front.

"Wait," I whisper urgently. "There's something inside I need to get."

"What is it? I'll get it for you," she says back.

"No, it's too important," I plead. She stares at me, searching my eyes for the truth.

"Fine, but be quick, and stay hidden." I let out a sigh of relief.

"Thank you so much." I leave the bus and scurry up my tree. My priorities are the birthstone jewelry and my new cell phone so I can talk to Maria. I have to make sure Zach doesn't keep my necklace as a memento or something. When I reach the branch to the window, I see Zach and Peri inside.

"So, what are you taking?" Zach asks Peri.

"Everything but the furniture. That can stay," Peri says, voice hard. Then it softens, turning into something mischievous. "Were you dating Ruby?" At the sound of my name, I see pain written all over Zach's face.

"I wish . . . but no, we were just really good friends," he says. Heat engulfs my face. He wishes he had dated me before I died. *I wish I dated you too, I think.* I look at Peri and wait for him to respond. A playful grin grows on his face that makes my stomach curl.

"She had a really sexy body. Anybody would have dated her to get a hold of that." I roll my eyes. From what I know about Peri, he loves to get on people's nerves. And for Zach, he is pressing all the right buttons. Zach's hands turn into fists.

"Please don't talk about her like that," he responds, finding packing tape on my desk and heading over to the forest of boxes to tape them up. He pivots to see Peri at my drawers, holding up my pink lace bra. Zach's face turns foul. "The way you got me about to lose my shit!" growls Zach, ripping my bra from his grip and stuffing it into a bag. "You don't know shit about her. Go pack up those boxes over there or something. I'll handle everything else." Peri's face twists in anger. I guess no one gets in the way of him and a bra.

"Dude, I know her. You just go back to the boxes."

"Like hell you do!" swears Zach. My eyes widen at his words. I have never heard him this upset before. "This is the first time I've heard of you, *Peri*. The first I've seen you around here and—" Peri interrupts him.

"Well, did you know that her birth mom's alive, her dad too? But fine, if you think you know her then, you do the drawers." Peri shoves a startled Zach out of the way and walks to my bed, ripping the covers off and stuffing them in a bag.

CHAPTER 10

S o my dream is true. Everything is true. The doubt that still lived inside of me evaporates. My parents are *actually* alive. They want to find them. I want to find them. Suddenly, I want Zach to leave. He isn't part of this, and he shouldn't get involved. I wait until I see both Zach and Peri leave for the bus with boxes and bags. Once they're gone, I open my window and hop into my room. I have about five minutes before the guys will come back, so I work fast. I grab my white bag from my dream on top of my dresser and put the birthstone jewelry in it.

I run to my bed, reach under my pillow, and pull out my new cell phone and throw it into my backpack too. It's bulging with the items from my dream still in it and with the new added stuff. I'm about to head out when I realize I should put the necklace on, just in case. Digging through the bag, I find it and put it on just as I hear footsteps coming up the stairs. *I want to be invisible,* I think, still holding my bag. Not only do I turn invisible, the bag does too. *Amazing.* I can turn anything invisible. *That's wild,* I think as I go to my desk and pull out my field journal. I'm probably going to need this too. Better to take it now than search through boxes for hours later. I close the drawer just as Zach walks into the room. He looks distressed. He walks straight to my bed, picks up a pillow, and breathes it in. I know my "death" is killing him, and I wish I could comfort him. But I can't. I leave him like that as I crawl out through the window, with him breathing in my scent, remembering me.

I pull out my phone and text Tani, explaining to her the situation and telling her I'll pull up to the house on my own instead of on the bus. I then shoot a text to Garnet and start the trek to the house. The brisk September breeze provides me with a much-needed dose of tranquility. The once nauseating pain is now a barely noticeable throb, and it doesn't hinder my stride. When I get to the house, I send another text to Tani. She texts back, telling me to enter through the garage, and I watch as the doors open. I step into the house in what seems to be a mudroom.

"Over here!" she says from the left of me.

"Where do I put my stuff?" I ask her, readjusting the bag that's on my shoulders. She looks confused, looking around for something.

"Ruby, where are *you*?" *Right . . . crap,* I think, remembering that I'm invisible. *Welp, no time like the present.* I make myself visible and smile embarrassingly. It's clear when she can see me because her jaw drops. "You already know how to use your power?" she asks, dumbfounded. Her eyes fall to my neck where she sees my necklace. I just shrug.

"It was an accident." She continues staring at me curiously before nodding. She has her secrets. I can have my own too. I follow her into the huge open floor living room and kitchen. "Wow," I whisper. The floors are all an elegant hardwood, and the ceilings are at least twenty feet tall. We turn right and go up one staircase. Directly across from it, across the kitchen, is another one. When we make it to the top, she opens the door directly in front of us.

"This is your room." The room is pretty big, not as big as my room before, but it definitely has a better feel. In my old room, I felt so alone. I know that won't be the case here. I walk around the space. There are four windows that overlook the driveway and four doors that belong to a closet. Just then, I see the bus pull up. I'm surprised by how quickly they got here. Then again, the walk wa s a *walk.*

"They're back!" I call to Tani. "Where's Moon's room?"

"Through your bathroom—it connects with your room. I'mma go downstairs to help unload, and then we'll all talk. There are some things that need to be shared . . . on both parts." I ignore her jab at me and walk into my and Moon's bathroom. The walls are a grayish blue with marble-tiled floors and counters. We each get our own sink, and we share a toilet, tub, and glass shower. At the end of the room is a door I assume leads to Moon's room.

Her room is significantly smaller than mine but has a much cleaner feel. Her walls are the color of milky blue, and against the right wall is a brown birch ladder, leading to a loft. Under her loft is a white desk and a daybed. Unpacking everything will be hell, but it'll be nice to have a fresh start. I'm excited to learn about my siblings and myself too.

Hours later, when all my stuff is brought up and is in my bedroom just how I like it, I receive a text about a family meeting in the tree bunker. When I walk up, there are a couple of pizza boxes on the circular table, surrounded by both familiar and unfamiliar faces. My mouth waters at the sight of the food, and I make myself a plate quickly. I haven't eaten anything besides the soup from this morning, and I'm starving. When my plate contains four slices of cheese pizza drenched in ranch dressing, I take a seat next to Moon.

Everyone is talking and laughing except us two. It's clear they've known each other for a while. A pang of jealousy runs through my heart. The odds that I grew up in the same neighborhood as my blood siblings is crazy. Why didn't they come find me sooner?

"Okay, guys, settle down. I think we'll start with introductions," Garnet says as she walks in. She reaches for a plate and loads it with pizza. The room didn't get any quieter. "Y'all shut up!" she yells as she takes a seat.

"Damn, why you gotta be so mean about it?" Peri huffs as he sits down. Garnet flicks him off, and I try to hide a smile. The way they interact is amusing. It takes a couple more seconds for the room to quiet down before Garnet speaks again.

"I figured we'd all go around, talk a little bit about ourselves, share who you found, if you found someone, and share any other information that would be beneficial to the group." We all nod as Garnet speaks. "So I'll start. I'm Garnet.

I'm the oldest at twenty." She smirks. "I am the founder of the Gem hunts, and I have found Peri and Tani. I have the power of petrification, not by looking at people, though. I have to touch their heart with my bare hands," she explains casually. *I won't be giving her a hug anytime soon,* I think as she points to the girl sitting next to her, telling her it's her turn. Her gloves don't go unnoticed.

"Hi." She gives a little wave. "I am Sapphire, Saph, Appy, Phire." She winks at me. "You can call me any of those. I'm seventeen." Her voice enchants me. She's also gorgeous. Her hair is in ombre butterfly locs that go from black to a deep, dark blue, and golden charms sprinkle across her head. Her clothing gives me a bohemian vibe with her brown, long-sleeved, flared shirt. Something about her is eerie, but I can't place what it is. I lean toward her, squinting intently, and when she turns her head, I see it. Her eyes are blue, somewhere in between a deep navy and royal blue. I've never seen eyes like that before. "I'm fluent in ASL because of my power, siren song. Wearing these," she says, pulling out a pair of sapphire earrings, and flashing us a sapphire bracelet, "enhances my power, but it still works when I don't wear it. I found no Gems . . ." She trails off, her eyes s pacing out.

"Siren Song?" Moon asks, eyes full of interest. Sapphire smiles softly.

"Yeah. I can compel people to do things with my voice," she explains.

"And you fucked up with that, didn't you?" Peri chuckles. Sapphire shoots him a glare, her jaw set with irritation.

"For example . . ." She shifts her body to face Peri. "Peri, you've got a booger in the back of your nose. You should pick it," Sapphire says, her tone melodic. Her chin is dipped slightly, and her eyes sparkle. Without hesitation, Peri digs his finger in his nostril.

"Hey! I was only joking!" Peri says defensively.

"Well, I didn't think it was funny," Sapphire huffs. My eyes are wide as I watch Peri's finger disappear farther into his nose, almost to the point of being dangerous.

"Cut it out," Garnet says with irritation. Sapphire leans against the table, telling Peri he can stop. He tears his finger out of his nose in relief and opens his mouth to say something. Luckily, Garnet speaks before he does. "Your turn, City." The smallest girl sits up at the sound of her name.

"I'm Citrine. I'm nine." Her light-skinned face is framed by loose curls that fall just below her shoulder blades, her hair a mix of browns and oranges. "I don't know my power yet, but I will soon! And I will be great at it." She grins, showing off her shiny white teeth. "Anyway, because of me, we know that mom and dad are still alive. I—" Moon interrupts her.

"Because of you? I don't get it?"

Citrine glares at her.

"I was getting to that," she says, annoyed, her eyes boring into both Moon's and mine. I flinch away and avert my eyes. "I am nine. You're what? Seventeen? Mom and dad supposedly died right after y'all were born, so if that was so, then I wouldn't exist. But guess what? I do." She flips her hair and grins.

"I'd just like to say that I came down to that conclusion," says Tani, claiming her words.

"Whatever," replies City, rolling her eyes.

"City? But that isn't a birthstone, is it?" asks Moon, trying to follow along.

"Citrine. I already said that. *Citrine*. When I go on my first Gem hunt, my undercover name will be Katrina. I can't wait!" she says excitedly.

"Well, you will have to try," says Garnet. "Zircon found someone for you, but you're not ready yet. You need to know your power," she says and Citrine slumps into her seat, upset. "Go," says Garnet, looking at a girl with glasses that are too big for her face and Bantu knots. She reminds me of Tani slightly in her features.

"Yeah, I'm Zircon, but I go by Ziri. I am sixteen, and Tani's twin." They smile at each other. "Technopathy is my power," she says while twirling a zircon ring around her finger. "Computers, coding, electronics, it's what I'm good at. I can hack any database in the world. Once I hacked the Pentagon . . ." She trails off, then gets back on track, pushing her glasses up her nose again. "Technically, I am the one who finds all the Gems, but do I get credit? No. My first ever was Tani, though, before I knew anything that was going on." She shakes her head and taps the side of her nose. "I found you, Moonstone, and Ruby just happened to be here. You use Snapchat and Instagram, so it was easy to find you; but we weren't expecting Ruby. I had to change Tani's *entire* class schedule because of you." I blush. Social media isn't my thing. I once saw a sad picture of a man on a motorcycle, dragging his dog by a leash as he rode. The dog's entire right side was rubbed clean of its hair. After I saw that, I deleted all social media. Thinking back on it now, I can feel the tears well up. I'm thankful Tanzanite interrupts my thoughts.

"You know who I am. You know my age. My power is enhanced intelligence," she says. "Basically, I'm just really smart. I know statistics, linear algebra, calculus, number theory. I never needed help with math, well, any class for that matter," she adds, looking between Moon and me. "I found Sapphire, Moonstone, and Ruby." She shrugs. I gape at her.

"Eighteen, Peri. If you don't already know me, I've got rizz." He wiggles his eyebrows at me, and I roll my eyes and let out a chuckle. There is something wrong with that boy. "I have claircognizance. I can look at you and know a lot about you, except only when I wear this Peridot chain. I'm still working on the skill without it." He pulls it out from under his shirt. "That's how I got Citrine. Really, Tani should be one Gem ahead of me, but thanks to Ruby, she is two Gems ahead." He glares at me playfully, and I roll my eyes again. If we keep this up, my eyes might get stuck back there. "I wasn't wearing it when I first met you," he says, gesturing to me. "So I just thought you were some other chick." I nod, now understanding why he looked so focused at our first meeting. He had wanted to use his power.

"I'm Moonstone, but I go by Moon. I'm seventeen. I have no clue what my power is. I just learned about the gene or whatever." She waves her hands around everywhere. "I am excited, but I still don't understand why I had to 'die,'" says Moon using air quotations around the word *die*.

"And that will be answered soon," responds Garnet. A tight smile pulls on Moon's lips, but she relieves some of the tension with her next words.

"And also, the name Gem Hunt," Moon starts, smiling brightly, "totally gives Webkinz Curio Shop; and I'm *kinda* in love with it." At that, Ziri and

Sapphire break into a fit of laughter. I scrunch my eyebrows, confused at what's so funny.

"You're so right! I didn't even peep!" Ziri says, still laughing. The rest of us are looking at one another, puzzled. "No!" She gasps in disbelief. "You've never heard of Webkinz?"

"I've heard of it, but I just haven't played," I say. Peri, Tani, and Garnet nod along with me.

"Webkids?" Citrine asks, confused.

"Don't worry. I'll put you on," Ziri says, winking at Citrine. She takes out her phone, typing urgently on the screen. When she looks up and sees us all still looking at her, she apologizes. "Anyway, so sorry. Continue."

My lips twitch and I speak.

"I'm Ruby, also seventeen. My power is invisibility." It rolls off before I can stop myself. I see Moon's face drop, clearly upset that I didn't tell her. *Crap*. In my defense, how do you tell your best friend that you can turn invisible? It's not like I was prepared to have that conversation. "I . . . um . . . dream traveled to mom a few days ago." Everyone gapes at me. I guess it's not something common around here. I shrink in my seat.

"You did what?" asks Garnet, amazed.

"You can dream travel?" asks Tani, befuddled by what I'm saying.

I take a deep breath and attempt to speak with confidence. "Yes. Apparently, we all can. That's what mom said. She was telling me how it's like this limbo world, a place that mixes reality with fantasy. I don't know. I found her in this motel somewhere in this abandoned desert town. She said that it resembles where she is in real life."

"So we have to go to her!" says Citrine, standing up and pumping her fist in the air.

"No, we can't." I shake my head. "She said no, that it wasn't safe for us. But maybe . . ." Everyone leans in, eager to know what I have to say. It's cool to be new to something and know more than everyone else already here. It feels great, like I'm needed. "How much do you know?"

"That they are alive. That's about it," says Garnet. I can tell she is slightly irritated that I know more than her. I'm sure she had to take a real hard gulp to swallow her pride.

"Our uncle on our mom's side, his name is Bloodstone. That's the birthstone for March. He kidnapped our parents five years ago." I look at Citrine. "Mom said something about completing the line of children. I think it ends with Citrine . . ." I trail off. "Anyway, if the whole point of us dropping off the face of the Earth is to find them, I'm down. But I think that's the last thing mom wants. That's why she did all of this in the first place," I say, waving my hands around. "Separating all of us, I mean. She made it sound like he wanted to hurt us. She wants us to stay hidden and apart," I explain, looking at each of my siblings. "But honestly, screw that! When I saw her, she looked awful. Like she hadn't eaten in days and showered in years. We have to do something."

"Tell us everything," Garnet demands. I dive into the memory, recalling a surprising amount of detail. I explain to them about the Black urban legend and how we may exist the way we are due to a mix of genetics and magic. At the word *magic*, skepticism fills Tani's features, but I ignore it. Wetness is present under my arms, and I shift uncomfortably with the feeling.

"So like," Peri starts, looking between Moon, Sapphire and me, "how did this all work out anyway?" We all look at him, confused.

"What do you mean?" I ask.

"Like, how the fuck did mom give birth to Moon, you, and Sapphire all in the same year?" he asks, scratching the back of his neck. "Last I checked, that's not how pregnancy works." I look up in thought, but nothing comes to mind. He's right.

"I assume it has something to do with the gene . . . and *magic*," Tani replies. When she says *magic,* she nearly gags, and I have to hold back a chuckle. "Like nine months before Moon was born, the egg was fertilized. A month later, Ruby's was fertilized, and then later, Sapphire's," she says, gesturing over to me. "You probably were all in the womb together at some point but were just born in your respective months." She looks over at Peri.

"And on all our birth records, the signature of the attendant and local registrar are all the same, even though we were all born at different hospitals. Mom and dad must have trusted them with the truth." Ziri adds before looking back at Tani, who continues.

"So you're correct, Peri. It isn't how pregnancy works, but we all spent nine months being created . . . probably." We all nod and shrug at that. It doesn't make complete sense, but at least it makes more sense. "But also, there's not a lot of resources for us to fact-check . . ." Tani trails off, and the weight of the matter makes the air heavy. Frustration visibly roars through Peri, and he tightens his hands into fists.

"Bullshit," he grumbles, staring intently at the floor. "We never really fucking know anything, and that's just some bullshit. Not about the pregnancies. Not about why we are the way that we are. Or *what* we are . . ." None of us say anything. What is there to say? When your people have been enslaved for hundreds of years, it's not like they would advertise their supernatural behaviors. That'd be their one-way ticket to a rope, pistol, or whip. And that's *if* they knew. Like mom said, peridots and pearls aren't just lying around for slaves to unlock their special gene. But maybe . . .

"Imagine," I start, staring dreamily at the wall behind Peri, "that our ancestors actually *knew* what they could do. We could be related to Harriet Tubman who could have had super speed or invisibility! That could have been how she was so successful in bringing so many slaves to freedom. Or Ida B. Wells with enhanced intelligence . . . Booker T. Washington with siren song!"

"Hmm," Tani says, her sweatshirt sleeve pulled over her hand, bundled in a fist. She bites her nail through the sleeve in a stint of deep thought. "Maybe after all this is over, we can focus on that. Connecting the pieces of our history, comparing legend to reality—and maybe figure out who we are and why we're like this," Tani adds thoughtfully. The heaviness in the air seems to dissipate at this. Maybe our history isn't a complete loss. With Zircon and Tani's abilities, we could really find some sort of truth. I'm drifting away in thought, contemplating about our great-great-great grandparents, when I remember the last thing mom told me.

"Adelaide," I gasp out, looking between everyone. "At the end of my dream, mom told me to find Grandma Adelaide. Maybe we can get some answers now." Garnet sucks in a breath and stands up, gazing at the table. Everyone else stands up, too, so Moon and I follow suit. Garnet locks eyes with Tani, and Tani nods.

"Follow me," Tani says. We go through a door adjacent to the main room, and it leads to a room filled with chairs. The chairs are all facing one computer with about eight monitors reaching along the entire back wall. My jaw gapes.

"We need to find Adelaide," Tani says, but Ziri is way ahead of her, logging on to computers and doing her techy thing. I'm trying to follow what she's doing, but I can barely keep up. Windows are opening and closing, and the language she's typing in is something I don't understand. Maybe she's breaking through firewalls?

"I found her, Adelaide Gem. She's in a nursing home in Pittsburgh, less than three hours away. She's in the early stages of Alzheimer's disease." Ziri pushes her glasses up, then turns to face us, eyebrows raised.

"Road trip?" Citrine asks excitedly, hands clutched in front of her chest with hope.

"We would all fit on the bus . . ." Peri adds, attempting to persuade the eldest sister. I don't think he needs to, though. Garnet already looks like she's on board.

"We'll leave around eight tomorrow." Citrine is jumping up and down with excitement, and I catch a glow in everyone else's eyes too. "After that, we'll focus on finding our other siblings." *We're going to meet our grandmother.* My excitement bubbles quietly in my chest, and I'm excited for what tomorrow brings.

CHAPTER 11

This is my first road trip in years. Before Terry died, Lisa, Maria, Jack, Paris, and I took trips to nearby states to weird museums and science centers all across the Midwest. Back then, Lisa wasn't as mean to me, and never when Terry was around. With his death came her hatred, and I didn't know what to do but take it.

The drive to Pennsylvania was smooth. Everyone was asleep, except Citrine, Garnet, and I. Citrine was acting as if she drank two energy drinks this morning. She was bouncing off the walls and speaking at the speed of light. For the entire ride, she was staring out of the window, eyes full of happiness. Occasionally, Garnet checked the rearview mirror and smiled when she saw the nine-year-old. It was impossible not to.

I, on the other hand, was not looking out of the window. I spent the ride with my head down, eyes glued to my notebook in hand. With everything that was going on, I wanted to keep track of everyone and their powers, characteristics, and backstories. I didn't know how many other siblings existed, and if there were a lot, I wanted to be ready with a strategy to make things less overwhelming. So the majority of my time was spent making pages in my journal for each of us. I even gave myself my own page, writing what I knew of my abilities so far: invisibility and fast cell regeneration. I tried doodling sketches of my siblings to help me remember who is who. It took a ton of attempts and one hundred or

so eraser marks later, I gave up. When I have time, I'll replace the sketches with p
ictures.

I also took the time to write what mom said in the dream. I cursed at myself, wishing I had done so as soon as I had woken up. Recalling the details was a lot more difficult, but I got most of them. The Legend of the Twelve was the most important. After that was done, I slept until Garnet woke us up. We had arrived.

Now we're in the lobby of Sweet Water's Nursing Home, waiting to check in at the front desk. The lobby smells exactly how I expected it to, like disinfecting wipes and old people. I hope Adelaide's room has a sweeter smell. The lobby is a large room in the center of the building. Right off it is a cafeteria and a lounge. The color scheme of the building is beige and green, and the furniture is a mixture of light and dark floral patterns.

Finally, someone comes behind the front desk to assist us. The man looks at all of us curiously before opening his mouth to speak.

"Hello, who are you here to see?" he asks. I squint to catch the name on his nametag: Jason.

"Hi, we're here to see Adelaide Gem," Garnet says, a smile on her face. I haven't spoken to Garnet much, but I've quickly learned she's in charge, with Tani as her right-hand man.

"Can I have a name?"

"Garnet Gem. We're her grandkids." The man looks at us suspiciously before typing away on his computer.

"I'm sorry. Garnet is not listed as a registered visitor. Grandchildren of Adelaide you said?" At his words, something in the atmosphere shifts. He doesn't believe us. Looking into his eyes, I see skepticism and something else. Concern maybe. He's leaning to the left slowly, as if to not be suspicious. I look to see where his arm is leading, and it's to a phone. Sapphire sees it, too, and she steps from behind me quickly.

"We're here to see Adelaide Gem. We're her grandchildren. And you *will* let us visit." Her voice is harmonious again, like when Peri got on her nerves. I watch the man freeze and his pupils dilate. A few seconds later, he smiles happily.

"Enjoy your visit! Adelaide will be so happy to see you. She's in room 178, down that hall and to your right." Sapphire thanks Jason before leading us down the hall. Garnet, Tani, and Peri give her prideful pats on the back as we make our way to the room. With the eight of us walking together, we get many curious looks from residents and staff, but none of us really pay them any mind. We all have one thing on our mind, and that's Adelaide.

Things between Moon and I have only gotten worse after last night's meeting, and I haven't had a chance to talk to her yet. But it's also clear she doesn't want to speak to me. For the last hour of the drive, she was awake. I tried to talk to her, but she pretended not to hear me, with her earbuds in and staring out the window. I noticed that she's gravitating toward Sapphire, though. A couple of minutes after I tried to catch her attention, Sapphire also did and was successful. The two shared a seat for the rest of the ride, talking and giggling among each other. Even now, she walks a couple steps ahead of me, probably wanting to whisper to her blue-haired sister.

Adelaide's room door is open, and I watch Garnet peek in. She tells us the room is too small for all of us to fit in and that she'll be right back. She and Tani step into the room, out of sight. Peri, Sapphire, and Moon are by the doorway, blocking it from Citrine's, Ziri's, and my view. I don't completely mind though. My eyes are fixed on Citrine. I didn't really have a chance to see her outfit before. She's wearing a loose yellow-orange dress that goes down to her knees. Her cappuccino-toned face is done up with light makeup. She styled her golden-brown curls in a bun at the top of her head, with two strands out to frame her face.

I look at everyone else in the hall and curse myself under my breath. They all seem to have gotten the memo I had missed. Everyone looks neat and cleaned up: nice blouses, a polo, a long skirt. I, on the other hand, am wearing a sweatshirt and leggings. I pinch the inside of my wrist, shuffling my feet. *Damn it.*

"Ruby," Tani says, poking her head out of the room. My head whips up to face her, and she gestures for me to come inside. "We need you." She tells my other siblings that she'll FaceTime them so they're included, but to get out of the hallway and find a place to sit. When I step into the room, I see what they mean. The area is so small, there's only enough space for a bed, a small table, and one chair. By the window is a gray-haired woman in a wheelchair.

"Why do you need me?" I ask Garnet and Tani.

"She won't talk to us," Tani complains, dialing someone on her phone. "We figured, if you resemble our mom, maybe she'll talk to you." Tani waves to the phone at my other siblings as Garnet gestures for me to approach the woman. I haven't been around old people often. Both Terry and Lisa's parents are no longer living, so the only time I see people of this generation is in passing. I walk toward my grandmother slowly, until I can see her face. Her thin silver hair is in a small 'fro at the top of her head, and her mocha-pigmented face is filled with gentle wrinkles.

"Adelaide?" I ask quietly, but she doesn't respond. She's still looking out of the window silently, unmoving besides the blinking of her eyes. I clear my throat and give my sisters an awkward look before trying again. "Adelaide," I say, louder this time. Slowly, her head turns to face me, and when her eyes meet mine, her face lights up.

"Rubes! Rubes, you came to see me!" Before I can move, she grabs my arm and yanks me into a hug. My nostrils are overwhelmed with a fancy scent as I topple onto the woman, crushing in the hold of her hug. From where I am, I see Garnet and Tani, and I mouth, *Help me*. Then Adelaide is tossing me back to my feet, hands rubbing my arms.

"Let me get a good look at you. Aw, Rubes, you stay looking so young. My baby." She's about to pull me into another hug, but I step out of her grasp.

"Adelaide, I—"

"Now, I know you didn't just call your mother 'Adelaide.' See, this is why you need to visit more often! You're forgetting who your mama is!" Her eyebrows are furrowed, but there isn't a hint of anger in her eyes. She's happy to see me. No, to see her daughter. My eyes widen with acknowledgement. Adelaide hasn't seen my mom in five years; Bloodstone has her. The next words I say are awkward, making Garnet put her head in her hands.

"Sorry ma-mama. I just got caught up in . . . uh . . . work," I lie, attempting to fit into the role of my mother.

"You best not let work steal you away from me again, girl," she says, whacking me playfully. We spend the next thirty minutes talking about Rubes and Bloodstone's childhood. Adelaide asks me if I remember falling off the tree or coming in second at the spelling bee, and I just nod and add vague comments. But it is cool hearing about my mom when she was younger. It gives me a new image to think about rather than the dirty woman from my dream.

Adelaide talks about her husband and asks about my mom's law firm, sending a weight of recognition to my shoulders. Of course, my parents had a life before me, but they really gave everything up to keep us safe. She's about to go into some other story, but I interrupt. *Damn, can this woman talk.*

"Mama, can you tell me about the Legend of the Twelve?" At that, Adelaide's face softens, and she nods.

"You always cared so much about our ancestry." She goes into the same story that mom went into, almost retelling it exactly. Where the stories differ is at the reason we were given our powers. Adelaide says it was a gift from God to prepare us for the turmoil of slavery that he could not prevent. Mom said she believes it started in Africa, before the Atlantic Slave Trade, with a genetic mutation.

"And what again about the full line of children?"

"The children you'll have! Oh, I can't wait to meet my grandbabies," she says, clutching the quilt in her lap. I look over at Tani and Garnet. They both gesture to me to ask more.

"Me?"

"Yes, you. Rubes, I'd been told you this, girl!" She whacks my arm again. "I'm telling you, it gotta be you. You have that mark on your belly . . ." Adelaide reaches to pull up my sweatshirt, but I grab her hand, eyes wide.

"Now, mama, don't do that." I laugh nervously, clasping her hands out in front of me.

"Rubes, let go of my hands this instant. What has gotten into you?" I let go of her hands slowly and step out of reach. "The mark on your belly is God's mark of the full line. The ancestor who gave birth to a full line before had a diamond-shaped beauty mark on her belly too," Adelaide adds, gesturing toward my navel. "God is preparing your body to carry the line. You won't have a choice in the matter."

"I won't?"

"No. Whether you try to or not, God will be putting a baby in you. You can either help Him along, or He'll treat you like the Blessed Virgin Mary. It's the magic he put in our blood, Rubes. It will get you through it, however it may be. I just hope I'm here to help when it happens," Adelaide says, eyes misting. She dabs at them with her blanket again before speaking. "Where is Nurse Sophia at? She has to fill my water," Adelaide mentions, turning around and looking toward the door. Her eyes trace over Tani and Garnet before looking back at me. "Who are they?"

"Mama, can you tell me about your powers?" At that, Adelaide lets out a hearty laugh.

"What powers, dear? Mine have long been going away, like my hearing and eyesight," she says, smiling. "You know your mama is growing old. She can't do the things she used to." She must have gotten closer to me again, because she grabs my hand and tugs me close. "Power is fickle," Adelaide begins, "but Gems are forever." Her eyes stare deeply into mine. They're filled with love and faith and happiness.

"What else about us is different, mama?" I ask, letting her hold me close.

"Just our power. The full line of children, though, they're a special thing. Different from you and me. My grandbabies are going to help fix this broken world, I just know it," she says surely. "You know, your brother is going to make the world a better place with God's gift too." The soft smile on my face freezes, losing all joy that came with it.

"What?" I ask, my voice nearly caught in my throat. Adelaide lets go of my hands and rolls over to the calendar on the wall.

"You know, Nurse Sophia has a liking for Stoney," Adelaide says, leaning in close to the calendar. Garnet and Tani do so, too, their eyes filling with worry. "I keep telling her he will visit again soon . . ." I move close behind her, a pit of dread growing in my stomach. On today's date, written in big red letters: Stoney's visit, 2 p.m. I pull out my phone slowly to check the time: 1:45 p.m.

Tani is already telling the siblings on the phone to head to the bus while Garnet attempts to straighten up the room so it looks as though we were never here.

"Mama, I have to go," I say to Adelaide as I make my way to the door.

"No, Rubes, won't you stay?" Adelaide reaches for me again, but I take a step back. Garnet is flipping through the calendar, snapping pictures of all the months which causes Adelaide to look at her. "You're not Nurse Sophia. Who are you again?" More for her than me, I rush to Adelaide, enveloping her in a hug. She kisses my cheek and pats my back before letting me go. "Won't you stay?"

"I have . . . a client who needs me, Mama. I have to go," I concede, thinking up the lie on the spot.

"That's my girl." Her face is full of delight as she tells me she loves me, waving goodbye as I step out of her room.

The ride back is full of angst and concern. Since everyone heard the conversation between Adelaide and me, there isn't much to fill in. The unpleasant atmosphere only worsens as we arrive home. Garnet is barking orders all the way up the bunker tree.

"Guys, we have to move fast! Citrine, go inside and pack your things. You, too, Sapphire. We have Gems for you both. We were looking for a better time, but it's now or potentially too late," Garnet surmises. On the ride back, Tani was going through the pictures of Adelaide's calendar that Garnet took. A couple weeks from today is a day that was starred, reading *The Big Day*. The day after is a visit between our uncle and grandmother. Garnet thinks that "The Big Day" involves our family, so she started putting things into motion immediately.

"You could have told me that while I was on the bus," grumbles Citrine as she jogs out of the room, Sapphire right on her tail. Zircon is tapping away at a computer with lightning speed, and Garnet is standing over her, barking out orders.

"What is going on?" asks Moon, completely confused. I am too. Things are happening so fast, and my brain is spinning.

"We are sending people out to find all our brothers and sisters. I think this is a lot more serious than we initially thought. You'll need to go too," Zircon explains, typing wildly. "Jasper, he lives in New York. I know you just got here, but pack your bags 'cause that's where you're going." Moon looks like she is about to object but thinks better of it, nods, and leaves the room.

"What about me?" I ask, but Garnet ignores me.

"We leave this upcoming Monday! So move it, move it!" she calls after Moon. That's a week from yesterday. We still have time; I don't understand why everything is in such a rush. "Ruby, you're going to Tennessee. Zircon found a boy named Emerald there. Checked with birth records, and everything seems legit."

"What am I supposed to do, exactly?" I ask, confused.

"You have to tell him his true identity and get him to come to Ohio with you, understood? Just like what Tani did with you and Moon. Just be nice and cool and—Peri, *why are you sitting around*? Go!" He gets up fast and leaves the room. "Pack your stuff, Ruby. For the next few days, you and Moon are going to have some training," Garnet says, turning back to face me. "We figured that our parents wouldn't just pretend to die for no reason. So all of us here have training in self-defense and in our powers. And you and Moon need some of that," she says, not even looking at me. I nod and back up toward the door. She turns back to Zircon and Tani, talking quietly about who knows what.

"Okay," I say, not knowing what else to say, and leave the room, becoming mentally prepared for the few days I have left before Monday.

CHAPTER 12

"Spar against me, Ruby," Citrine's cute, adenoidal voice challenges me. We're in the basement in a large sparring room with cushioned floors and a mirrored wall.

"With what?" I ask.

"Your hands, silly!" she says, laughing a little. Then she puts her hands up into fists in a fighting position. I mirror her.

"Okay," I reply and go to punch her face, but she sidesteps it and punches me in the gut. I groan, but don't fall. For a nine-year-old, this girl is strong.

"This is too easy," she says, smiling. She probably thinks she will win this match. I lift my foot and trip her. Citrine falls to the ground with a thud, and I grab her fists and sit on her stomach. She struggles under me, and after a while, gives up.

"Did you say 'too easy?'" I tease, grinning like a dummy. Her eyes go from hazel to a darker orange, and she glares at me.

"You cheated! This is not fair. You are bigger and stronger than me. It doesn't count!"

"'All is fair in love and war,'" I quote. "Plus, being bigger and stronger isn't cheating," I acknowledge as I get off her. She sits with her legs crossed, letting out her anger. She takes deep breaths, moving her hands toward her nose, then down to her chest. When she relaxes, her eyes go back to a soft hazel, and she eyes me curiously. "Can I see you use your powers?"

"Sure." I take a deep breath and call on my invisibility. My body warms, and when a gasp erupts from Citrine, I know I've done it.

"That's amazing." She breathes, looking around the room to see if there is any flaw in my invisibility. "Once I find my powers, whatever they are, I will be able to use them like you," she declares, smiling into the open space where she thinks I am. I turn visible and kneel beside her.

"Maybe you can find your powers right now."

"I can't," she says, frowning. "Garnet has been trying to find a piece of citrine jewelry for months, and she hasn't found one affordable yet. At least, that's what *she* says. I can't turn on the gene without a citrine," she whispers, her eyes welling up with tears. Besides Moon, she's the only one who doesn't know their power, and I can tell her envy is getting to her. Suddenly, I remember something: I found a citrine tiara in my room. *Ugh,* I mentally groan. This should have been something I shared at the family meeting.

"Give me a second." I don't wait for her to respond before I run upstairs and find the dream bag I neglected by my desk. I run back downstairs with the bag, and as I walk into the room, I reach into it and find the tiara. "Will this work?" I pant out as I half jog, half fall back into the room. Getting places in this house is a workout. I lift the tiara, and her jaw drops.

"No way!" She takes it from my hands and puts it on her head. Her hair is pulled back into a high ponytail. "Where did you find this? Is it real?" she asks, awed at her reflection, dazzled by the stones on her head.

"Yes, I'm pretty sure it's real. It was in one of our mom's old jewelry boxes. I found it last week," I reply, happy to see her happy, the memory of her sparring defeat forgotten.

"I-I am going to try." Backing away to the wall, I try to give her some space. She does crazy dances and lists off names of powers that may be hers, but nothing happens. "Are you sure this is real, Ruby?" she asks, confused about why her powers are not coming.

"I'm sure." She tries for what seems like hours. Each time she fails, she becomes more and more aggressive. Then, suddenly, she turns on me, her eyes a darker orange, anger written all over her face.

"This isn't real!" she exclaims, approaching me slowly. Each step seems to be calculated. "You gave me hope, and now it's gone! Why did you do that, Ruby?" Her hands are in fists, and she takes another step. I gulp. The glow in her eye is of complete hatred and anger. When Citrine asked me to come downstairs with her, I thought this would be a nice sisterly bonding experience. And it was, for the first hour, when she wasn't about to lose her shit.

Her hair turns a dark auburn, and her eyes become hooded. Her glower sends shivers down my spine. What makes it even scarier is that it's like her features are turning to match her emotion: pure fury. Her face and hands turn red, and I back into the wall. She wants a fight, and I don't want to be the punching bag.

"Citrine, it's okay. You'll find your power. It just takes time," I add, trying to calm her down. I think that makes it worse because her eyes glare into mine and she screams at me.

"You *lied* to me! Sisters don't do that. I *hate* you!" And on the word "hate" fire shoots from her fists, and her hair lights into flames. *Oh. My. God.*

"C-calm d-down, Citrine," I stutter, backing into the wall more. She doesn't even notice she's on fire. She reaches for my throat, but I duck out of the way and turn invisible.

"Where are you, Ruby! I'll get you for this," she growls as she slowly paces the room. "You can't play me just because I'm a kid, the fuck? Who do you think you . . . ?" She stops as she meets her reflection in the mirror. "Woah!" she breathes. Her eyes relax, and the fire extinguishes from her hair and hands. She holds up her fingers and examines them. When she snaps her fingers, a small flame is born. I turn back visible, shaking in fear. "Look, Ruby," she says, referring to the fire on her fingertips. "*This* is my power." She grins at me, but I don't grin back. Citrine has no tolerance or patience. Anyone who pisses her off could end up in ashes.

"Citrine, m-maybe you should take the crown off," I stutter out, still keeping my distance from her. She frowns at me, her outburst totally forgotten.

"Are you kidding? I have my powers now. I'm never taking this off!" She smiles, making the flame larger in her hand.

"Well, while you do that . . ." I say, grabbing my bag and backing out of the door, right into Sapphire.

"You okay?" she asks, oblivious to what just happened. I grab her by the shoulders and stare her right in the eyes.

"Citrine has her powers now." Sapphire smiles.

"That's great! She always wanted hers. How did she get them? What are they?" I shake my head. She doesn't get it.

"It's fire manipulation," I say. At that, Sapphire's face twists into horror.

"Shit," she whispers. I nod and let go of her shoulders. She looks over me to see Citrine admiring her flaming hands and hair.

"If I were you . . . Don't get on her nerves," I warn Sapphire. "She has a temper." Sapphire nods in agreement.

"Don't I know . . ." She trails off. Her hand is on the doorknob, but she hesitates. I leave the room when she speaks.

"Maybe I'll just hang with you," she says, letting go of the doorknob and rushing over to me. As we walk upstairs, I tell Sapphire about the jewelry I found and pull out the moonstone necklace. I push open the white bookcase door that leads to Moon's room and find her in her loft. Sapphire and I climb up to join her. Moon is lying on the floor on her phone. I can tell she's still agitated with me because once she sees me, her head shoots back down to her phone. I sigh.

"Moon, I know you are still pissed at me, and I understand. But you have to see my side of this. Honestly, I thought I was going crazy, and I didn't want to freak you out or anything . . ."

"I get it, but don't get it," she says with a sigh, turning off her phone and tossing it aside. "I'm your best friend. We tell each other everything. It made me upset that you knew about this before I did," she admits. I can feel the tension in the room, and I know Sapphire can too. She is probably thinking about which choice is better, Citrine or this, because I'm thinking that too. I remember the reason I came and pull out the milk-stoned necklace.

"This is yours. I found it last week in a bunch of mom's old boxes." She takes the necklace and looks at it closely. "Do you want me to—?"

"I got it." She lifts the necklace, putting it around her neck, and takes in a breath.

"I know, right?" says Sapphire, watching her. "When you wear it, you feel . . . great. Free from all problems. You feel like you've found a part of you." Moon looks at her and nods.

"Wow," she breathily responds. "How . . . how do I figure out what I can do?" she asks Sapphire, not me.

"They just come to you when you call on them. Usually that happens without you knowing, though. So just wear it all the time. Your powers should come," she explains.

"Okay," she says, smiling for the first time that we've been in her room. "Thanks, Sapphire."

"No problem," she replies. I quickly grasp that I'm the third wheel in this conversation, and I take my leave.

"Well, I just came by to drop that off and apologize, so now I'mma head out," I say. Moon doesn't even acknowledge me. "I have to talk to Tanzanite and Garnet. Do you know where I can find them?"

"They're in the tree," Sapphire replies as I stand, and she doesn't get up with me.

"Thanks, see you guys," I say, about to make my way down the loft. But something rushes into my head, causing me to pause. "Hey, Sapphire, can I ask you something?" She and Moon had just begun talking again.

"Sure," she says, turning her body to face me. "What's up?"

"There was something that you said when you were introducing yourself that I've been meaning to ask you." She looks at Moon before meeting my eyes again.

"Okay. What was it?" Sapphire asks, eyebrows scrunched in confusion.

"What's it like? Siren singing people? And why are you fluent in ASL?" I ask, making my way back into the loft. When I finish my sentence, she sucks in a breath and slouches. I catch Moon give her a look of curiosity and concern. She's quiet for a while, and Moon cuts in.

"If you aren't comfortable, you don't have to answer," Moon says, giving me a look that conveys, *Why did you do that?* I toss her back a look of confusion and innocence before turning my attention back to Sapphire.

"I didn't mean to intrude. I was just curious," I explain, rubbing the sweat off my hands.

"No, I know," Sapphire insists, looking between the both of us. "I'm just trying to figure out where to start," she says before taking a deep breath. "The short story is that my adoptive parents were ... are ... ? They're still alive, I mean. It just doesn't really feel like they're my parents anymore." She plays with one of her blue locs, looking at the wall in front of her. "Anyway, I'm a CODA. Child of deaf adult is what it stands for," Sapphire clarifies. "My dad was Deaf, and my mom was hard of hearing. So I became fluent in ASL." She opens her mouth as if she wants to continue, but pauses, looking between Moon and me. She lets out a sigh before starting again. "But when I was ten, people were making fun of them, and the Deaf community as a whole, and I just got so *mad*," Sapphire says, clenching her hands into fists. "I had this on," she says, holding up the wrist with the blue bracelet, "and I told the boy who was saying mean things," she pauses, "'I hope you break your arm, bully!' And he did. Right in front of my eyes."

My eyes widen, and I look between Sapphire and Moon. Moon places her hand on Sapphire's clenched fist, and she looks up, giving us both a tight smile.

"I was nonverbal for a couple years after that, strictly using ASL. After a lot of therapy, I started to speak again. That's when it really hit me what I could do. What I *did*." I nod with understanding. That's why she was so upset when Peri made the comment about her "fucking up." He had to have known he was stepping into sensitive territory. Sapphire shakes her head and puts a beautiful smile on her face. "Anyway, that's why I'm fluent in ASL. And in terms of siren singing, it feels like pushing someone, but with my voice. So whatever I say, it kinda feels like I'm pushing them into doing it. If that makes sense." I nod, thinking back to her sing-song voice at the nursing home.

"Yeah, I get it. Thanks for explaining, and I'm so sorry that happened." At that, Sapphire shrugs.

"I am, too, but at the same time, I'm not. The kid deserved it. And imagine what else I might have accidentally done if I didn't realize what I could do." Her eyes go distant for a second before she blinks it away. I sense that there's more to the story than she's letting on, but, of course, I don't want to pry.

"Thanks for sharing, Sapphire," Moon says, looking at her carefully before looking down at what lies forgotten on her chest: the moonstone necklace. Sapphire notices and grasps both of Moon's hands, eyes full of hope.

"Don't worry, Moon. I don't know what your power is, but this is a safe environment to figure it out. I can help you." At that, Moon smiles. "And hey, if it does end up being a little more on the dangerous side, remember, everyone here has fast regenerating cells. You shouldn't be able to do much harm."

"Yeah, okay," Moon replies, hanging on to every word of encouragement Sapphire offers. With the sound of someone yelling downstairs, I'm reminded that I have to talk to Garnet.

"Thank you again, Sapphire, for sharing. And I'm sorry, but I have to go talk to Garnet before I forget." Sapphire looks at me and lets out a symphonic laugh.

"Don't sweat it, Ruby. And thanks for listening. As siblings, it's important for us to share things like that," Sapphire adds, and I nod. She's totally right. The more and more I think about this situation, the more surreal everything feels. I medically *died* and am living with people who are basically strangers to me. *God, I hope it will all be worth it.*

When I arrive at the tree, I head straight to the room with all the computers. I guessed that Garnet and Zircon would be here, and I was right.

"Sup, Ruby?" says Garnet, looking up as I enter the room.

"Do you have a map of this thing?" I ask, waving at the tree. "If this room wasn't right off the main room, I probably wouldn't have found it," I say, plopping myself into a chair next to them.

"I can print one off for you right now," says Zircon as her fingers fly over the keyboard. I was half joking, but I'll gladly take a map if one already exists.

"Thanks," I respond. We hear the printer start, and Garnet walks over to it and grabs the piece of paper that comes out. She hands it to me, and I put it in my bag. I'll memorize it later. "Good news. Citrine has her power! I stumbled upon a citrine tiara a couple days ago," I add. Garnet cheers.

"Yes, she'll be more prepared for anything that could happen." Garnet and Zircon high five, but I dissolve their happiness.

"Bad news, it's fire manipulation."

"Shit!" says Zircon, twirling her chair to look at me finally. I smile.

"That's the same thing Sapphire said." I laugh. I can't help it. They look so scared.

"That explains her short temper, though. How did I not see this coming?" asks Garnet rhetorically as she face-palms.

"Good news more!" I say, using horrible grammar. "We might have a sister named Opal. I found this," I add, pulling out the opal studs and laying them on the table, "in a bunch of mom's old jewelry boxes. I haven't gone through all of them yet, but I'm guessing that there may be more there." Garnet looks at them closely, then pockets them. She looks up at me, and a prideful smile fills her face.

"Good work, Ruby," she says. Then her face turns to business. "Is there anything else we should know about Bullshit?"

"What?" I ask, confused.

"Bullshit? BS? Bloodstone is . . . I don't know. It just sounds a little off," complains Zircon, and I laugh.

"Who came up with that?" I ask, still laughing.

"I did," announces Peri as he walks into the room with Tani.

"That makes sense," I agree, smiling. "Good, most of us are here. We should all know, except maybe Citrine, she—"

"Would get angry and burn the house down." I nod as Peri speaks. "Yeah, I just talked to her, pissed her off, and she fucked up my pants," he says, pointing at his burned jeans. "These cost me seventy-five bucks, and she isn't paying me back!" He rolls up a chair and sits next to me. Tani does the same.

"Okay, BS—" I start.

Peri interrupts me.

"Bullshit. Now go on." I roll my eyes.

"BS—" I repeat.

"Bullshit. You have to say 'Bullshit.' If I had Citrine's powers right now, I would burn his mouth off.

"I don't cuss like that," I say, turning to face him. I take a deep breath and begin to speak again, but Peri does first.

"Ruby, just say what you fucking need to say. We can't fucking wait all fucking day, so stop being a pussy!" Peri exclaims before cracking up. He's such a comedian.

"Peri, shut your mouth and let Ruby speak." Tani groans, nudging him in the ribs. He mumbles something under his breath before nodding his head toward me, a sparkle in his eye.

"Anyway . . . Bloodstone has powers too. Mom was about to tell me what he can do, but the dream went downhill before she could. For all we know, he could turn us against each other. Before we go to him, we should have our powers down pat and a concrete plan," I conclude. Everyone nods in agreement. "Also, mom said that Bloodstone thinks we're dead, but I don't think so anymore."

"Why do you say that?" asks Garnet, raising her eyebrows.

"He just thought we were dead until it said on the news that Moon and I died in a car accident. I'm betting he's smart, which means he's probably looking for us. *All* of us," I muse, frowning.

"This is really bad," remarks Tani, head in her hands.

"And you don't have to be super smart to know that." Peri slumps in his seat.

"I think that Garnet and Ziri should stay here. The rest of us can go on the hunt," Tani suggests. Zircon nods, agreeing, and faces her monitor again.

"Peri, you're going to California, San Diego. There's a girl who is seventeen named Diamond." Peri takes out his phone, opens a notes app, and jots down everything Zircon says. Tani has her phone out and ready too. "She's the captain of the cheer team at Westport High. You'll be going undercover as a junior. From there, you know what to do."

"Yes ma'am," he agrees, saluting Zircon. "My name will be . . . Todd. Ask me why." We're all silent for a bit, not wanting to satisfy him, but Tani caves.

"Why?" asks Tani tiredly.

"Because it is one of the sexiest names ever," he coos, grinning. Zircon turns to him.

"Yeah . . . that can't be true," she says, trying not to smile but failing. "Anyway, all of those websites are biased."

"But isn't Diamond a common name? How do you know she's a Gem?" I ask, getting us back to the point. Ziri turns to face me, a smug smile on her face.

"For every Gem I hunt, I cross-reference the name for all children born in the U.S. between 2002 and 2012. Then, I narrow down with race and middle name. All of our middle names are of our birth months." Ziri explains how mom left information for Garnet in a safe deposit box, one that she couldn't access until she turned eighteen. Inside were pictures, documents, money, and a key to this house. One document was her birth certificate. "With the full names of our parents, finding you all is a piece of cake. At least, relatively. The harder part is being smart about it. I can't leave a trail, and I can't get caught. So hacking hospital and school records can take some time."

I purse my lips, impressed at Ziri's techno-wizardry.

"Tani, are you ready for yours?" She nods, and Zircon fires away. "You're going to Arizona to find a girl named Turquoise. She-she's our triplet." Ziri and Tani exchange a warm glance before Ziri continues. "Anyway, she's sixteen and is a sophomore, like us. I have no idea who she is, what she likes, or anything like that, so you're on your own there. But you're you, so I'm not worried," Zircon says, hacking into the school database.

"I am indeed me," Tani purrs, brushing her hair off her shoulder.

"I'm enrolling you now. You know what you need to do." Before leaving any time for Tani to speak, Ziri moves on. "Peri, you're already enrolled at Westport." I take out my phone, knowing I'm next. When I do, I see I have twenty new messages from Maria, but I don't dare text her back right now. "Ruby, you know his name, Emerald, Tennessee. That's all I told you yesterday, but I have more. You two are free to go now," she says, speaking to Peri and Tani. They assume they are not wanted and quietly leave, but not before Peri says one more curse word that makes me roll my eyes. "He lives in Knoxville and goes to Allan-West High School. It looks like he does track and cross-country. It is cross-country season right now, so that's what you should do. Since this is your first hunt, I'll help you do it." I nod, wondering what I will need help with. "I am giving you a week. You should arrive at Deluxe Knox Hotel on Sunday, and I booked it for seven days. So you have seven days to bring Emerald home." I nod. This is going to be tough.

"Now we are short on budget. There is only so much money that mom and dad left us in the bank account, so the hotel is not the best, but it's walking distance to the school, which is good. It's only a five-minute walk. I'm looking at images of the hotel right now, and it is more like a motel . . . It's not the best, Ruby. Never take your necklace off. Also, bring your own sheets and check for bedbugs." I shiver.

"That bad?" She nods in response. "How short of money are we, exactly?" I ask.

"Actually, we're very financially stable. We just do this to keep y'all humble," Garnet says with a wink. "And for emergencies, of course." *Great.* Citrine walks into the room holding a flame on her fingertips.

"Can we order pizza and celebrate? I got my powers!" She's smiling like a dummy.

"Good thing you're here, Citrine. You ready for your first Gem hunt?" asks Zircon. The fire disappears from Citrine's fingers in surprise.

"Hell yeah!" she shouts, coming close and sitting in the chair that Peri sat on before.

"Citrine November Gem, don't you dare cuss again. If you do, I'll take the tiara off your pretty little head," chides Garnet.

"No, no, please don't! I promise, I'm sorry," she pleads. Ziri tells her to take out her phone to record her spiel.

"There's this girl named Topaz who lives in Illinois. Since her name is Topaz, I'm ninety-nine percent sure you have a twin," says Zircon, clicking away at the keys.

"I have a twin?" Citrine questions hopefully.

"It looks like it. She's on the swim team, so you will be too." Citrine's face falls.

"But I *hate* swimming," she complains.

"It's only for a week. You'll be fine." Ziri explains how she'll temporarily install a camera into her tiara so that she can monitor her. Garnet will drive her to Illinois and set up cameras in her room and leave her a bike for transportation to and from school.

"Look at me, Citrine," Garnet stares into her hazel eyes. "If anything bad happens, if someone comes after you, you burn them and run to the hotel room. We can see you there and know you're okay." Citrine nods, her look of excitement now replaced with worry. "It shouldn't come to that, though. The place is in a really good neighborhood, so I'm not too worried," Garnet reassures her, patting her on her head. "And don't lose your temper during school. Do you understand? If you feel yourself about to, breathe like how I taught you, or just take off your tiara . . . Actually, do both for good measure," Garnet warns.

"Breathe in through the nose and hold. Out through the mouth and relax," she recites, demonstrating her technique.

"Good, you will be fine," urges Garnet, reassuring everyone, including herself. "Now, go get Sapphire, okay? It's her turn." Citrine leaves the room.

"Why can't you just stay with her? Wouldn't that be best? She's only nine years old," I say, worried for Citrine's well-being.

"I have to stay here and help Zircon. We're keeping eyes on all of you, but she can't do it alone. So I have to stay," explains Garnet. "With all of you out at once, you'll be returning at different times. I have to make sure the house is ready and have some other things to attend to as well." I nod in understanding just as Sapphire and Moon walk in, giggling about who knows what. "Good, you two are both here we need to catch you up on your hunts."

Ziri tells Sapphire that she'll be hunting for Pearl, our seventeen-year-old sister from Chicago. She has a foster sister named Alex, and if their living situation is concerning enough, Garnet will allow Alex to stay with us. Moon will be in Lake Placid, New York, hunting thirteen-year-old basketball player, Jasper.

"Do you know your power yet?" Ziri asks, watching Moon fiddle with her necklace.

"No, but I am trying."

"Well, try harder. You have until Monday. That's when you head out, clear?" asks Garnet, making sure everyone knows the plan.

"Crystal," responds Moon as she gets up and walks toward the door. Sapphire follows her, but not before Garnet grabs her arm.

"Help her," she whispers. Sapphire nods before leaving to follow Moon. When she catches up with her, they giggle out of the room. I leave the tree as the sun is setting, thinking of how the heck I'm going to get Emerald to come to Ohio. As I walk around the pool and toward the sliding glass door, I see a face in the reflection, hiding in a bunch of bushes. I squint, thinking it's Citrine trying to scare me, but when the figure moves to reveal themself, I gasp. *Zach*.

CHAPTER 13

I whip my head around. "Zach?" I whisper harshly. He comes out from behind the bushes and runs to me. Embracing me in a breathtaking hug, he spins me in circles.

"I thought you were dead, Ruby. I thought you were *dead*." He lets go of me and stares into my eyes. Then he kisses me on the forehead. His hands hold me by my face. "I thought you were *dead*." It's clear he wants answers, but do I give them to him? I could just play it off like I am the wrong person, but that'd be idiotic.

"We can't talk here," I say, looking around him to see if anyone is watching us. We're holding hands.

"Ruby, I thought you were dead. I thought you were dead. I thought you . . ." He trails off, whispering to himself while stroking my twists. The night before the accident I spent four hours putting my hair in twists. I didn't want to have to worry about it with all that would be going on.

"Look at me, Zach." He hadn't even looked away. "I'll meet you at our spot in the park tonight at midnight. I know it's a school night, but if you want to talk, it's the only time I can. But you need to go," I say, pulling away from him. His grasp tightens.

"Ruby, I thought you were dead," he says to me. I look down.

"I know, Zach, I know . . ." He lifts my chin.

"No, I thought I would never see you again. I was broken, Ruby. I haven't eaten, slept, or gone to school. I thought . . ." A tear slips from my eye.

"Zach, I can't talk right now. Midnight, tonight, at our spot in the park, and I'll tell you as much as I can." I look at him deeply. "I'm okay."

"It doesn't matter that you're okay. I mean, it does. What matters is I thought you weren't." He looks as if he doesn't want to leave, but my eyes plead for him to go. If Peri finds us, let alone Garnet, things could get bad. He releases me and backs away toward the driveway until he's almost out of sight. "Midnight!" he yells, and his body disappears from view.

Pinching my wrist anxiously, I walk into the house to find Citrine, sitting on a couch wearing pajamas in front of the windows where Zach and I were just standing minutes before. *Damn, damn, damn, damn—*

"Who was that?" she asks calmly and curiously, flames dancing on her fingers.

"No one important," I lie, walking away, hoping the conversation is done, but she presses on.

"I thought you were supposed to be dead to the world, but I guess you're not. Maybe I should go tell Garnet that you need to die again." She gets up and makes her way to the door. *That little . . . Ugh.* I turn on her.

"Please, no, Citrine. He found me. I don't know how, but he did it, not me," I beg her.

"Come to my room. You tell me everything there, or I tell Garnet everything." She skips to her room, and all I can do is follow her. When I walk in, I'm surprised she didn't know about her power before. Her walls are a light orange, and she has red sheets on her white bed. The color blue is absent, except for the clothes in her closet. She doesn't seem to notice the irony. She just sits on her bed, twirling fire between her fingers. I sit in a papasan in the corner of the room, brainstorming what I'm going to tell her. Across from her bed is an electrical fireplace, and she watches it before turning her attention to me.

"He is my *friend,* okay?" I whisper. "I've known him ever since I was a little girl, younger than you. He saw that I died in the news, so he was at my house when Garnet and Peri were picking up my stuff. I don't know how he knows

I'm here. He was just hiding in the bushes. I-I don't know." Citrine shakes her head in disbelief.

"You must have told him something," she surmises. I shake my head.

"But I have to now, right? He saw me after I died. I have to explain it to him."

"What exactly are you going to explain? This is all a secret, and you can't just tell people," she says, crossing her arms.

"What else am I supposed to do?" She bites her lip, staring at the fireplace, but then her face brightens.

"Kill him."

"What? No!"

"Just think, it will get him out of the way. Just kill him." A devilish grin appears on her face and with a snap of her fingers, flames erupt in her hand. "Or I can."

"No one is killing him, Citrine! That's out of the question." At that, she giggles, extinguishing the flame.

"Or do you have a crush on him?" I feel my face twist into shock and embarrassment. She rolls back onto her bed, breaking into a fit of giggles. "Fine then. Don't kill him. I can clearly see that you *love* him." My hands grip the chair.

"I don't!"

"Do to!" She sits up and looks at me, serious again. "When are you going to talk to him?"

"Tonight, at midnight," I look at the clock above her bed. It's only 8:40 p.m.

"I'm coming too!" she announces, getting up and walking to her closet. She throws open the doors and shuffles through the clothes to find something to wear.

"Uh, no, you are not," I say, pushing myself out of the chair. At that, she turns to stare at me.

"Ruby, the first time I left this house was to visit Adelaide, and I have been here for nearly a year. I'm coming with you," she adds, turning back to her clothes before she sees the look of pity across my face. What else can I do but concede?

"Fine! But if you come, you have to promise not to tell anyone." She turns back to me, smiling and holding up her pinkie.

"Pinkie promise," she says, I bring my pinkie to hers and they lock.

"Meet me in the laundry room at 11:30 p.m." She nods, and I leave her room for my own. I take my phone and respond to the now thirty-five messages I have from Maria. They're all sad, saying she misses me and that she wants to FaceTime soon. I respond that we can and tell her to have a great day, knowing she won't see the message until tomorrow. I put my phone in my pocket and flop onto my bed. It isn't like the bed I had before at all. It has a circular bed frame with a rectangular mattress in the middle. On the headboard are color-changing LED lights. I turn them on and change the color to red, then I set an alarm for 11:00 p.m. Grabbing my nearest bonnet, I cover my twists and lie there, thinking of what to tell Zach, before falling asleep.

When I make it to the laundry room, Citrine is already there. We are both dressed in all black, but her hair looks nice and cute in two pigtails. It looks like she even put some makeup on too.

"Please don't tell me you're going out looking like that," she says, pointing at my face.

"What's wrong with my face?" I ask, wiping away at it.

"It is so plain. I can't be caught dead with my acquaintance looking like that. Come here, let me fix it."

"But . . ." Citrine grabs my shoulders and pushes me down on the floor. She takes off her backpack and pulls out a hair tie, tying my twists in a high ponytail. Suddenly, I feel a wave of nostalgia. Maria used to do my hair all the time, and put makeup on me too. I hold in the tears that threaten to leave my eyes as Citrine's fingers move through my hair. I take off my glasses to make it easier for her.

"Don't you have contacts?" she asks, pulling a couple twists out in the front.

"No, just thinking about that gives me the chills." She fluffs my hair and comes around me to face me.

"Now your face." She sees my worried look and gives me a smile. "Don't worry, I'm quite talented. There's not much to do when you aren't allowed to leave the house." Citrine brushes my nose with highlighter and puts on eyeliner, eye shadow, and lipstick. It's so dark that I can't see the colors; she's working with the moonlight. I silently pray I don't end up looking like a clown. "I'm always here, and I get bored a lot. So I busy myself by doing makeup on dolls. Sapphire doesn't let me touch her face—she says it's her prized possession. I did Tani's one time though!" She applies gloss to my mouth. "You look perfect. Rub your lips." I obey and stand up, ready to go. Following Citrine, we enter the garage.

Toward the back, I see five scooters, all different colors. They're like adult motorcycle scooters, but for kids. Like the ones you would find at Walmart or see the rich kids riding in the neighborhood. She goes to an orange one and takes off her tiara. After placing it carefully in her backpack, she puts on a helmet. I walk to a red one. "You know how to ride?" she asks me, raising an eyebrow.

"Not a clue," I respond nonchalantly.

"It's pretty simple, like a bike with no pedals." She pushes out through a side door instead of opening the garage, and I copy her. She hops on and goes down the driveway. I get on mine steadily, turn it on, and squeeze the thing on the handle, causing it to jerk forward. *Breathe, Ruby, Breathe . . .* I press it again and keep it steady, going at a nice pace down the driveway, and gradually get the hang of it.

I lead the way as we do twists and turns down the many streets of the neighborhood until we finally make it out. After five more minutes on the road, we arrive at the park. By then, it's exactly midnight. I see Zach under the gazebo, our favorite spot. Citrine and I park the scooters, and she runs to the playground to play, but not before taking her helmet off and replacing it with her tiara. I take my own helmet off and walk to Zach.

"Hi," I say, walking to him and stopping only an arm's distance away. He gapes at me, his jaw slack. I bite my lip to hide my nerves and pick at my skin around my wrists. "Citrine did my hair and face," I explain, waving my hands around my head, all awkward. "Do I look like a clown?"

"No, you look beautiful." I feel my face flush, and I rock back on my heels, pushing up my glasses. "Ruby, what is going on? You *died*. I saw the accident on TV. No one could have survived that." I take in a deep breath.

"Zach, I didn't survive. I really did die . . . Well, kinda."

"But you're here, standing with me right now. I can see you. I can hold you." He pulls me in closer to him. "So you're not a ghost." I can't tell if he is being serious or joking around.

"Zach," I pause, considering my next words carefully. "You know how I can turn invisible." He nods. "That isn't all. I-I'm immortal too," I reveal. He sucks in a quick breath. "Well, not exactly immortal, but let's just call it that. Basically, my cells regenerate at a rapid rate, so if it's not . . . I don't know, getting burned or prolonged exposure, then I'll be fine." Silently cringing at my rambling, I lift my eyes to meet his slowly.

"Okay . . ." Unlike when he found out I could turn invisible, he doesn't pull away. Instead, he tightens his grip on my arms.

"I'm sorry, but I had to make everyone think I was dead. Zach, I found my birth family." And as if on cue, Citrine walks under the gazebo. She pushes Zach's arms away and moves to stand in front of me, and I wrap my arms around her. Zach takes a step back, giving her more space.

"Who is this?" he asks, smiling, leaving the immortal part behind. It's a little awkward, but I appreciate the effort.

"I'm Ruby's sister, Citrine," Citrine says, introducing herself.

"Well, it is a pleasure to meet you, Princess Citrine," Zach responds, bowing and kissing her hand. She giggles.

"I am not a princess, silly! I just wear a tiara for my powers." She smiles, but when she realizes what she said, she covers her mouth and looks up at me. I smile, showing her it's okay. This catches Zach off guard.

"What?" he questions, a look of confusion on his face.

"It's not just me, Zach." I nod toward my sister. "Go ahead, Citrine."

I see the excitement all over her face at these words. I move next to Zach and take a step back, my hand on his chest, telling him to take a step also, and he does. Citrine lets flames rise from her fingers in both hands. Zach inhales sharply and grabs my hand, taking another step back. She scrunches her face, concentrating, and she makes the flames form people. She must have been practicing this little display just for him to see. Zach gasps, and my grip on his hand tightens. Citrine creates a person in her left hand and another in her right. Each figure is clearly a girl and a boy, probably to represent Zach and me. Citrine bites her lip and furrows her brow in concentration as she makes the two people dance in her hands. Then their bodies dissolve to form a heart. She progressively makes the heart bigger and bigger until it explodes into flames and embers fall to the ground. She grins at us, curtsying deeply. Zach stares, dumbfounded.

"So . . . does it run in your genes?" he asks. He tries to make his voice sound casual, but I still hear it quiver.

"Yep. My uncle, Bloodstone, wants all of us. He has my parents, and we're going to stop him! Not just me and Ruby, but all my other siblings too," Citrine explains excitedly. Zach tries to follow along, but I see him struggling. I silently thank Citrine for not mentioning the legend and magic. Until we can find out more information, we should only explain with science. Well, as much science as we can.

"So there's more of you?" Zach asks and Citrine nods eagerly. "How many?"

"Not sure, but a lot," I respond. He nods stiffly. He's quiet for a couple of minutes, processing all the information before finally looking up at me, determination in his eyes.

"I want to help," he says. I frown. It's best to keep Zach out of something that doesn't concern him.

"I don't think that would be the best . . ." I manage, avoiding his eyes.

"Too bad. We are all in this—" Zach starts.

"If you want to, you die," says Citrine. Zach stares at her, confused.

She rolls her eyes and clarifies. "What is your excuse for suddenly disappearing? You have none. You join us, you never see your family again." Citrine puts her hands on her hips. "You seem too nice for that. You can't just ditch your family. I like you, and I don't like a lot of people. You seem like a cool guy, but you're already too involved. Any more, and you could really die. This isn't some game. You know Ruby is alive. Take her phone number, talk to her, whatever you gotta do. But then back off." For a nine-year-old, she said it better than I could've. A lot of Garnet's personality is reflected in her. Zach looks at me for help.

"She's right. I'm sorry, Zach." Knowing he would need it, I fished out a scrap of paper from my bag that I had scribbled my new number on. I slip my hand from his, replacing it with the paper. "I love you too much to make you risk your life. You have always been there for me . . . but you can't for this. It's too dangerous," I add, looking into his eyes.

I wrap my arms around him, pulling him close. My hands grip the fabric at the back of his shirt, and I squeeze my eyes shut. Although this wasn't supposed to happen, a selfish part of me is glad it did. His arms squeeze my body tightly, his chin resting on the top of my head. When I pull away, he isn't looking at me. He's staring at the ground, his hands curled into fists; he doesn't speak.

"Come on, Citrine, we gotta go back." She grabs my hand, and we turn from Zach and head to the scooters, Citrine lighting the way with her fingertips. I look back at him; he's staring at his hand where I left my number. "Bye, Zach," I whisper, and we disappear into the shadows, leaving him behind.

CHAPTER 14

"Moon, can we talk?" I ask her the next day. She's with Sapphire, dipping her feet in the pool and chatting it up.

"Sure . . ." Sapphire makes a duck face, eyes wide and looking at her feet. She whispers one more thing to Moon before she leaves. Taking her spot, I tilt my head toward the sun.

"I know you're still mad at me, I know, but how can I make it up to you? I thought I was going crazy," I say, defending my actions. I've told her I was sorry so many times.

"So, you should have told me."

"And what would you have thought?"

"I—" she starts, and stops, her eyes concentrating. She sighs with understanding. "I would have thought you were crazy too." She looks down at the water and kicks her feet. "Ruby, I'm sorry too. I know I've been shutting you out, and that isn't exactly fair," admits Moon, meeting my eyes. "I was just mad. Mad at you, at myself, at the world. It was easier directing all my anger toward you, and I'm sorry," she says. She pulls me into a hug, catching me off guard. "Just no more secrets, okay?" she says before letting me go.

"No more secrets." We shake hands on it. I lean back, close my eyes and let the sun shine on my face. I've missed her. When I open my eyes to look back at Moon, she's leaning forward, staring at something in the forest.

"Did you see that?" I follow her gaze but see nothing. She stands up and makes her way to the trees. "I thought I saw something fall." I get up and follow her as she leads the way into the woods. "There," she whispers, and I see a baby bird on the ground.

"How in the world did you see that?" I ask, amazed, as she picks it up and cradles it. I look back to where we just were. We can't be less than fifty feet away from the pool.

"It fell at the edge of the woods. I saw the tree. It wasn't too high," she explains casually. Cradling the bird, she walks back along the edge of the forest. "There." She points at a nest a couple of feet above her head. Moon puts the tweeting baby bird in her sports bra and makes her way, climbing up the tree. She reaches the branch swiftly and takes the bird from between her breasts, placing it in the nest. She whispers words to it I can't hear. "Mission accomplished!" she yells as she makes her way back to the trunk of the tree.

"Look at you, the hero!" I exclaim as I applaud her. She grins back at me and does a small bow, but as she does, her fingers slip from the grasp of the tree. Time seems to slow down. Her hands grab wildly for the branch again but it's too late; she's out of reach.

"Moon!" I yell as she falls. She screams. I shut my eyes and plug my ears, not wanting to hear her hit the ground, but the thud never comes. I open my eyelids a crack and see Moon screaming but not falling. She's floating in midair. "Moon." I breathe. Her body is curled tightly in a ball, as if she's ready to make impact with the ground. Moon opens her eyes too. They widen with fear.

"Ruby," she states, frozen in position. "What? What is going on?" she asks, still suspended in the air.

"Try to come down," I say as I stare at her, amazed. *Levitation.*

"I don't know how!" she screeches, shutting her eyes again.

"Just think it! Will it to happen," I explain shortly. She squeezes her eyes shut, and the next thing I know, she's floating to the ground. When her feet hit the grass, she looks to me for guidance. I smile. "You can levitate, Moon." Her hand shoots to the necklace, and she looks down at herself.

"So . . . what do I do now?" she asks, excited and confused.

"I guess just practice. Garnet was talking 'bout we should perfect them. I wouldn't out here though . . . You could just float off!" I joke. Moon nods in agreement, and we head back to the house. Once inside, we go our separate ways. It doesn't feel the same as it did when she was mad at me. It's a more casual departing rather than departing out of tension. I know Moon and I won't get the friendship back we once had right away, but I also know we will be okay. I just need to regain her trust. Peri is sitting on my bed when I go up to my room.

"Umm, hi, Peri," I say, confused. "What are you doing in here?"

"Garnet sent me to help you pack," Peri says, hopping off my bed and walking over to my closet. He throws open the doors and pulls out a dress. "Model this for me." He tosses the dress to me, and I stare at him.

"I am *not* wearing this!" It's a sleeveless red dress that ends at my thighs. Sequins surround the waist and trace the low neckline. "Where did this even come from?"

"At Emerald's school, there's a dance on Friday. Yes, I did research because I knew *you* weren't going to." I cringe. I didn't even think of that. "And you're going. It's the perfect time for you to tell him." I nod, slightly impressed.

"Okay, okay, I'll go, but I'm not wearing this. I don't even think this is mine," I say, dropping it on the ground and walking to stand next to him.

"All of these dresses are yours. Yesterday, I came into your room and found your size. Then Sapph and I did a little shopping. We got a lot of different types of outfits for when you're undercover. Red is clearly your color, so I bought quite a few red things . . ." Peri pulls out this fluffy high-low dress. It's tight at the top with detailed off-the-shoulder straps, turning into a bunch of fluffs and feathers when it reaches the hips. I gape at it.

"That is beautiful," I say, feeling the texture.

"Go put it on while I get a spare suitcase," Peri says, handing me the dress and leaving the room. I go into the bathroom and pull on the dress. It's gorgeous. It fits all my nonexistent curves, creating some cleavage and small grooves at my hips. When I step out of the bathroom, Peri is folding up clothes and putting them in the suitcase. He looks up as I step in and claps.

"Daamnn, Ruby! Show off that dress." I model, walking and striking a bunch of tiny poses.

"This is the dress," I say, grinning like an idiot. I feel like a princess.

"Good, throw it in the suitcase, not literally, and help me pack clothes." When we finish packing, Peri ushers me to his room. "I have a surprise for you." The walls are light orange, with three large windows on one wall. His bed is in the center of his room and is full of decorative pillows. If I didn't know better, I would think Peri's ability had something to do with art. His taste in fashion and style is exquisite. He pulls out his laptop and sits on the bed, beckoning me to join him.

"What are we doing?"

"One thing that one should always have on a Gem hunt is a Swiss Army knife, especially if you're a girl." I nod, understanding. "People be wildin'." He pulls up this website and helps me customize my own.

"Exactly how much money was in the bank for us?" I ask, as he buys a two-hundred-dollar knife and picks the next-day shipping option. He pauses at this question, hesitating to tell me. Then he just shrugs.

"Three million."

"Three million?"

"No, I'm just playing. We're broke as fuck," says Peri sarcastically.

"So, we're like, rich?" I ask, and he nods. "Good to know."

"We try to save money, though. You have no idea where our parents may be or what we may need to buy, like a boat or a jet, so we limit ourselves." He closes his laptop and turns to face me. "It used to be five million, but we bought the bus, and the tree, and you know, bills." Licking his lips, Peri continues. "If need be, Ziri can do some . . . rearrangement of government funds." My jaw drops, and I gape at him.

"Like steal from the government?" He grins crazily.

"Some *Olivia Pope B613* type shit," he says. I laugh at his reference to *Scandal* and nod. This family is wild. Stealing government funds? Superpowers? *What's next?* I'm about to ask Peri when the ringing of the doorbell interrupts my thoughts. His eyes widen and he runs to his window to try to catch a glimpse of the person, then runs to the door. I follow him out.

"No one answer the door!" Garnet's voice booms through the walls.

"Does this not usually happen?" I ask, confused. Peri looks at me, his eyes boring into mine.

"Not since I got here." Peri says as he rushes down the steps. *Not since he got here.* That could mean anything. He could have gotten here last week for all I know.

"When did you get here?" I whisper yell after him. He doesn't even turn.

"Two years ago." Garnet shoves past Peri and whispers something in his ear. He nods and leaves the area, going who knows where. The house gets eerily quiet. Everyone is in the foyer, staring at the distorted figure behind the wavy, textured glass.

"I know you're in there!" yells the person, pounding on the door. Garnet gives Zircon a glance. *Go,* she mouths, and we all hide. I go to my room. It overlooks the driveway, so maybe I will see the intruder. Everyone else seems to have the same idea, and we are all staring out of my window. I hear muffled voices from downstairs, then the door shuts.

"*Ruby*! Get your skinny Black ass down here, *now!*" Garnet yells. Everyone stares at me as I leave the room biting my lip and pinching my wrist. Standing by the front door is a red-faced Garnet and Zach. Zach sucks in a breath when he sees me, but he doesn't avert his eyes. "Let's have a little chat, okay?" demands Garnet, not even waiting for a response as she leads us to the library. I don't say a word to Zach—how could I? *I explicitly told him I didn't want him getting involved, and now he does this?* The library is surrounded by built-in shelves on three walls. Along it is a bar table, stools, and two monitors. There are several round tables in the middle of the room, but toward the back is a large desk and two chairs facing it. Garnet lets us inside, shutting and locking the door behind her. Sitting herself behind the desk, she gestures for Zach, and I sit across from her, eyes hard. "Ruby, do you mind explaining *this*?" she asks, waving her hand in Zach's direction.

"Not really . . ." This whole time I've been biting my lip. With the way this conversation started, I might just chew my way through.

"It wasn't optional," she replies, clearly irritated at me.

"Well, this is Zach," I start off. Zach reaches his hand across the table as if to shake Garnet's, but she pushes the hand away. He shrinks into his seat and looks at me. I sigh. "Zach is one of my friends. We've known each other for forever, and a few days ago, I found him in the backyard . . ."

"And you didn't think to tell me!" interrupts Garnet.

"Well—"

"Look, this is all my fault," interrupts Zach. "Let me explain."

"Please do because I'm not getting shit from her!" I flinch at her tone, which Zach notices. He goes on to tell Garnet about my odd behavior the day before the car accident. Explaining that he saw the accident on the news, he rushed over to my house to see me.

"So then, that dick, I mean *guy*, Paris or whatever, was acting all weird and said that Ruby's . . . or your . . . parents are still alive. I got suspicious, followed the bus here, and saw Moon get out. Then I needed some answers, so I watched for a couple days. Ruby found me, told me everything that I wanted and needed to know. She also told me not to get involved, but now this happened. I'm clearly involved now and know too much, so I want to help." Garnet looks from Zach to me. She picks up the phone on the desk and dials a number.

"Get your smart ass to the library now!" she says into it and hangs up. She crosses her arms and leans back in the chair. "Go unlock the door for him." I do so quietly. Seconds later, Peri comes rushing in. He goes straight to Garnet. When he sees Zach, he frowns.

"This guy?" he says with disgust, crouching next to Garnet.

"Yeah, somebody told him about our parents," Garnet says, looking at him. He rubs the back of his neck apologetically. "Now he knows too much. What do we do?" asks Garnet. They talk as if we're not right in front of them, irritating me.

"I can kill him," he says. I gasp. *What is up with these people and killing?*

"No!" I screech, alarmed.

"No, Peri, I don't want needless blood on our hands right now, and Ruby clearly cares for him," Garnet agrees.

"Well, he can't help. He is *normal* and no *Norms* get involved. Your rule, remember? Plus, how do we know we can trust him?"

"Of course, I fucking remember!" Garnet yells. She drags her hand down her face and sighs.

"We can trust him!" I interrupt. "And what about Pearl and her foster sister Alex? You said you would make an exception for them if need be!"

"To live with us, yes, I'd make that exception. Not to *help*," hisses Garnet, dismissing me.

"Well, we need to do something," says Peri, looking Zach up and down.

"I swear I will touch your heart right now," Garnet says, lifting her hand as a threat. Peri flinches away.

"May I just say something?" I ask.

"Well, clearly, Ruby, you have said too much," Garnet admonishes, not moving from her position. I slump into my seat and wait until I am no longer treated as though I've turned *invisible*.

"He can go undercover?" asks Peri.

"Only Gems."

"But hear me out."

"What Peri? Just what?"

"What if he went with Citrine? I know you don't like the idea of her going alone, and this dick is kind of buff. And—"

"Peri, shut up. That is actually a good idea, so shut up. Let me think." Garnet removes her head from her gloved hands and leans back in the chair. Her eyes don't move from Zach's face. "What is your story?" she asks him.

"Story?"

"Yeah, you're helping us now, not forever though, so if you want to, right now, you have to go to Michigan. So what are you going to tell your family?" Garnet explains. He clears his throat before explaining how he has family in Michigan.

"Well, I am staying out of school for the time being, and I do have my driver's license. My uncle is pretty cool, so wherever I need to be, he should be fine that I'm there, as long as I check in. That should be pretty good, right?" he asks Garnet. She nods, but Peri is still skeptical.

"Your mom will let you go to Michigan?" asks Peri.

"Yah, she's cool like that." Zach rubs his hand up and down his arm as Garnet's eyes bore into him. "Even more so now, with the grieving and whatnot." I cringe at that. Mrs. Klight treated me as though I was her second daughter. I can't imagine the pain she must be going through thinking I'm dead. After minutes of silence, Garnet sighs.

"Fine, okay? *Fine.*" She flops down into the chair. "You should meet Citrine. We need you at the hotel on Monday. I'll worry about food so you don't. Peri, get Citrine in here." Peri nods to Garnet as he gets up to leave the room. I pray that Zach won't say anything about Citrine, and I sigh with relief when he doesn't. I intend to break the awkward silence when Citrine walks in, Peri on her tail. Her eyes brighten when she sees Zach. I give her a glance that clearly says, *Don't say anything or else*, but she doesn't even look at me.

"Hi, Zach! What are you doing here?" Citrine asks, oblivious to my look. "We told you not to get involved! But it's nice to see a different face once in a while." Citrine giggles as she walks over to him. To all of our surprises, she daps him up. Garnet's face is fuming as she looks at them.

"Well, I see you've already met," she says through her teeth, her voice rock hard. Citrine clamps her mouth shut and looks at me apologetically. Garnet fills her in about the updated plan, slides Zach a piece of paper with all the information, then leaves the room with Peri.

"Ruby, can I—?" starts Zach. But I don't want to hear it. I told him to stay away, and he did the exact opposite.

"No, no you can't." And I get up and leave the room, leaving Zach sitting there with Citrine jumping in excitement.

CHAPTER 15

"**M**ove it, move it, *move it!* Why is Citrine the only one ready? Gur-rrls, we have an agenda here." I open my eyes and close them again. Garnet is yelling, clapping her hands loudly in the hallway. I open my eyes again to check my clock. It's 3:00 a.m. Let me *sleep.* I tug a pillow over my head.

There's no one else but me. No one is here trying to wake me up; it's just me and my bed and my covers, hugging me forever. Suddenly, they stop hugging me, and I'm left shivering without their grasp.

"Get up, Ruby," says Peri. I roll over so I can face him. He's grinning like a mad man. "And jeez, Ruby, you should start sleeping with clothes on, just a suggestion. I can tell you one thing. This happens *a lot*," he says, winking. I look down at myself and see my pink floral bra with matching underwear. Too tired to be embarrassed, I reach over, grab my pillow, and throw it at him.

"Let me *sleep*," I say, rolling over to hide my breasts from Peri's sight.

"I can't, Ruby. You're going to miss your plane."

"What plane? I don't have a plane I'm going to miss because no plane is leaving, and I'm not leaving the plane," I say groggily. I was just having one of the best sleeps of my life. The one where it feels like days have gone by.

"Ruby, it's Monday."

"So?" I question, reaching for the covers. *Monday. There was something important about it.* Then it all comes back to me in a rush. *Monday, the day*

I go to Tennessee. Monday, the day I go to some random school. Monday, the day I get my brother. "Okay, okay, I'm up. Get me clothes to wear." I roll out of bed and stretch. I don't have to turn around to know Peri is on his phone, paying little attention to me. "Clothes, Peri, get clothes." I say, snapping as I walk to my bathroom and splash water on my face. I tie up my hair and brush my teeth. When I go back into my room, my clothes are on my bed, folded neatly. I pull on a crop top that reads *NERD* and jean shorts. My suitcase is no longer in my room, so I assume Peri took it down. I grab a hoodie from my closet and walk down the stairs to find Tani and Citrine with their luggage.

"Finally! I've been ready since last night. I even slept down here," Citrine says, looking more awake than ever. I don't say anything. Everything is hazy. I don't even register when Moon and Sapph come to the meeting spot. Before I know it, everyone is here. Garnet is talking, and I know I should be paying attention, but I am just too tired. Next thing I know, we're all on the bus. After a given time, we get off. We are walking to this big building, the airport maybe. I don't really care. I just *want to sleep*. Peri is talking to me. I tell him to stop—I'm not listening. I'm walking with my eyes half closed, barely aware of my surroundings. A firm squeeze on my shoulders snaps me back to reality, and I punch the person who did it.

"What do you think you're doing?" I ask the person who is covering their face in pain.

"Waking you up, Ruby," says Peri, rubbing his eye. "We're saying goodbye to Garnet, Zircon, and Citrine now. I thought that you might actually want to *be here* when we do." Oh. Yes. This would be a moment I'd like to be cognizant for. I hug Garnet first.

"You've got this, Ruby. We really need you to pull this through for us, so don't mess up," Garnet says, pulling me into an awkward side hug. I know she meant for that to be encouraging, but her words leave me feeling anxious. Ziri is next.

"Don't worry. You'll do great! And we'll be with you every step of the way," Ziri says reassuringly. I pull her into a hug.

"Thank you," I say quietly. I take my time to talk with Citrine. I bend down so I can meet her eyes with mine.

"Ruby, I'm going to miss you so much," she says, tears forming in her eyes.

"It's only a week. You have to be a big girl in Michigan. Are you ready for that?"

"As I'll ever be," she says, hugging me.

"You're lucky, though. You have Zach. I'm sure he will tell you a bunch of stories about me that it will feel like I never left." I release her from the hug and stand up straight.

"Don't screw this up, Ruby," she says with a smirk, mirroring Garnet's warning playfully. I smile at her words.

"I won't if you won't." At that, she rolls her eyes. I wave goodbye to the three of them one last time as Sapph, Moon, Peri, Tani, and I head into the airport. Everything goes smoothly. We print out our tickets at the kiosks, put on our bag tags, then load our checked bags. Thankfully, all the lines are short, even the TSA line. Since I don't know how to drive and have no ID, Ziri made sure to print everything I'd need. Of all my siblings using flight as transportation, I was the only one sans license. When we are all through and have our carry-ons, we pull each other into a big group hug. We exchange "good lucks" and "goodbyes" before heading off to our gates; Tani, Sapph, and Moon head in one direction, and Peri and I head to another. After a couple minutes of walking, he stops at gate B9.

"Well, this is me," Peri says, throwing up a peace sign. I smile softly, then surprise him by pulling him into a hug.

"I won't have to see you for a week! Who'll tease me then?" I ask him playfully, my arms wrapped around him. He's stiff, but then relaxes in my arms.

"Don't worry, Ruby. I'm sure you'll find someone." I head to gate lucky number B13 and wait for my plane. I pull out my phone, seeing it's 4:00 a.m. An hour and fifteen minutes until my plane is supposed to depart. I take out a book and touch my ruby necklace for comfort. Zircon put a tiny camera into it so she can see everything I do. I won't apply the earpiece until later.

"Flight to Knoxville is approaching. All military passengers, passengers with a child under two, senior citizens, and first class please form a line so we can start boarding." I get in line. Peri and Ziri told me they don't like to spend a lot, but I secretly upgraded my seat to first class because if I am going to fly to Knoxville, I am going to fly in style. And in my defense, I didn't use any of the family money. I used the money from the dream.

We board the plane, and I plop into my comfy seat and slide my backpack underneath. The seats recline, and everything is high-tech. I look out of the window, and for the first time, I realize that I am *on* a plane.

My heart is racing. I put on my seat belt and shut my eyes.

Breathe.

My parents *died* in a plane crash, and that could *actually* happen to me. This is the first time I'm going to be on a plane that I can remember, and I'm scared. I listen intently as the flight attendants begin their safety rant, and I prepare for the inevitable takeoff. I grip the seat and shut my eyes as the plane starts moving.

Breathe.

It's taxiing down the road, and gains speed suddenly.

Breathe.

My stomach dips as the plane leaves the ground. My hands cramp as my knuckles clench the seat. I make myself reach over and shut the window blinds. *Breathe, breathe, breathe.* I lie back in my seat and close my eyes. *You're okay, Ruby. It's okay.* But I'm not okay. I'm borderline panicking. I squeeze my eyes tighter and push my back into my seat. After about ten minutes, I let slumber and lightheadedness overcome me and I doze off in my seat.

"Miss?" I hear a woman say as I feel a tap on my shoulder. "Miss, it is time to deplane." I rub my eyes as the flight attendant helps me to my feet. Everyone who was on the plane has disappeared.

"Are we in Knoxville?" I ask drowsily.

"Yes miss. We let you sleep until everyone was off the plane, but now it's time for you to leave." I pull out my backpack and get off the plane quickly. I find the baggage carousel and see that my bag is one of the only ones left. I yank it off the conveyor belt and make my way to the door. After I locate a bus stop, I sit on the bench and wait. I make sure my necklace is still on my neck and pull out my phone to text Ziri that I'm in Knoxville. As I do, I pull out the earpiece she gave me.

"Testing, testing." All I get is static. "Come in, Zircon. Do you copy?" More static. Then, suddenly, it clears away, and I hear her voice.

"You sound crazy. Just talk normally." I feel heat rush up to my face. "Okay, anyway, you have to check into your hotel. Take the bus that comes to the fourth stop. It stops right by the hotel. Then hustle your way to school. It starts at 8:15 a.m. You have thirty minutes, and the bus is coming . . . .now." As Ziri says the w ord *now*, a bus arrives and pulls up right in front of me.

"Wow, nice timing," I say as I pay the bus fare and hop onto the bus.

"Obviously," she says playfully while I take a seat on the bus. I play a couple of games on my phone until I hear the name of my stop and signal the bus driver. When the bus arrives at my hotel, my face twists in horror. The exterior is absolutely disastrous. I walk in, and the place reeks of sweat, smoke, and aerosol spray. I breathe through my mouth to avoid the smell.

"Hi. I'm Ruby Jenkins. I have a room here checked out for a week," I tell the teenager sitting behind the desk while handing her my ID. I didn't bother choosing a fake name like Tani did. I should be fine. She looks me up and down. Her hair is jet-black, and she has a skull nose ring. She pops a piece of gum in her mouth.

"You here to fuck?" she asks casually, snapping her gum in her mouth and typing away on the computer. Her words take me by surprise, and my jaw drops.

"Excuse me? No. I'm just here to stay for a week." She briefly looks up at me before she continues to type.

"I didn't mean anything by it. This is the hotel for fucking as they say. You're pretty hot. You seemed like you would be into that shit," she says, her eyes unwavering. I squirm under her gaze.

"Well . . . you're wrong. Now may I please have my room key?" Her black fingernails drop my ID and room key into my palm. It isn't like a modern hotel key, but it's an actual key. The number 167 is on it, so I assume that's my room number. "Thank you," I say as I turn right and head to the hallway that is room numbers 146 to 170.

"Hey, red head," she yells after me. I turn and look back at her, "don't complain about any noises, I'm not gonna do anything about it." I nod, not really understanding what she means, but thank her anyway and continue to my room.

When I open the door, I'm aghast. The carpet is stained everywhere, the beds are poorly made, and there's a "present" for me in the bathroom. *This can't be legal,* I think as I dump my stuff on the bed closest to the door. Checking the clock by the bed, I let out a sigh. I have thirteen minutes to get to school before class starts. I grab my backpack and zip out of the door. Let the hunt begin.

Chapter 16

The office receptionist has me sit in a comfy leather chair to wait for Emerald, but I can barely sit still. I can't wait to see his face. *Will he be objectively attractive like Peri, or will he have more of a boyish face?* A guy walks into the room, and I know immediately he isn't Emerald. I slump into my seat and wait.

There are three minutes before school starts, and I don't want to be late on my first day, even if I'll only be here a week. A thought pops into my head, and I shoot out of my seat. *What if he has an accent?* That would be so adorable! A Gem with a Southern twang. *OMG it sounds like I am crushing on him. I need to stop.*

Another guy walks into the main office, and a tug at my heart tells me he's my brother. His hair is a mix of brown and dark auburn and is styled in braids. If I blur my eyes and tilt my head just right, I can catch a glimpse of emerald. He talks to the receptionist, then glances at me. After they exchange a few more words, Emerald strides over to me and holds out his hand.

"Hi, my name is Emerald Koolard, but my friends call me Emmy." I shake his hand and open my mouth to say something, but he speaks first. "Now, I know what you're thinking, and yes. I do have an amazing name," he continues, still shaking my hand.

"I wasn't thinking that. But, anyway, I'm Ruby, and I moved from Ohio. I should be moving back there soon, just here for business stuff, you know?" He nods and puts his hand in the middle of my back, guiding me out of the office.

"Trust me, I know. My parents are gone all the time, well, not all the time, but at least one week a month. But I get the whole house to myself then," he says, grinning like an idiot. I smile back. We walk in a comfortable silence until he stops in front of a classroom. "Well, Ruby, turns out I'll be learning a lot about you, one, because I am your guide for the day and, two, because we have the exact same schedule, kinda wild. You're welcome to sit at my table at lunch—should be smooth," he says as we walk into class and I take a seat. He doesn't hesitate to sit next to me.

"I might just take you up on that offer," I respond, smiling.

"You better," he agrees, grinning just as the bell rings. Everyone settles into their seats, and class begins. I don't pay attention though. I'm just thinking of when I ask him to the dance and how I will tell him we're related. I think I'll be able to go with him if he doesn't have a girlfriend, but if he does, and I wouldn't be surprised, I'm screwed. I'd have to find some other way. Emerald nudges me and points at the teacher whose name I've forgotten.

"I'm sorry, can you repeat what you said?" I ask apologetically.

"I had asked what you think is the most important lesson from history," reiterates Mr. I-Still-Don't-Know.

"Oh, very simple, learning from your mistakes. Learning from the past so that it isn't repeated."

"And I assume, Miss Jenkins, that you have learned to pay attention during class." There are a few snickers that bubble through the other students, and I shrink in my seat.

"Yes, sir, that's all history now," I offer, trying to hide my embarrassment. The teacher smiles sweetly and goes back to his lecture of who knows what. I behave this way through all my classes, trying to develop the perfect way to tell Emerald. And the first phase of my plan starts at lunch. I'm at my locker when Emerald comes behind me and taps my shoulder. "Hey," I say, turning to face him.

"So, you sitting with me?" he asks casually.

"Of course," I say, nudging him away and turning down the hall. "You're the only person I know here. Where else would I sit?" There's something about him that just draws me in. I'm not talking about his face, but his personality. He's so carefree about everything; it's refreshing.

"Ruby," he says. I turn to face him. "The lunchroom is that way," he says, pointing in the opposite direction. I puff out my cheeks, turning around.

"I knew that," I assert as we walk down the hall. "I was just making sure *you* knew that, you know?"

"Whatever you say," he crones as we walk into the cafeteria. I follow him through the lunch line and to his lunch table, taking a seat next to him. The table is round and has eight seats. We're the first people to sit, and minutes later, the whole table is full.

"I think that this calls for an introduction," says Emerald. "Chad, drop a beat." The guy sitting on Emerald's left begins beatboxing, and I am afraid of what I got myself into. Emmy stands up, holding a cardboard juice box and tapping it with his straw. "Ladies and Gentlemen," Emerald raps. He brings the straw to his mouth as if it were a microphone.

"La-La-Ladies and Gentlemen, I, Emmy, am proud to say, that I met someone really nice today. Her name is Ruby. She is a beauty, and she is truly, the coolest thing that's ever happened to me, today. And I am happy to say, that we are in the same class every single day, science, English, calculus, you name it, we have it. That's all you gotta do, so on the count of three, repeat after me. One, two, one, two, three, Ruby!" he raps.

"Ruby!" the table echoes.

"Ruby!" he repeats.

"Ruby!" they yell. The way I am frozen in my seat. What's happening in front of me is straight out of some low-budget Disney movie. I swear I'm the main character because there is no way in *hell* this is actually happening. *Whoever is writing my story better pay for my funeral 'cause I am dying of embarrassment.*

"Emmy, out." When he sits back down, my face is as hot as Citrine's hands. I sense the hum of power under my skin, wanting me to disappear, but I will myself not to let that happen.

"The *hell* was that?" I ask through gritted teeth.

"If it makes you feel better, he did that to me too," says the girl sitting next to me, patting my back.

"You're a lunatic," I say to him as I put my head in my hands. He sits back down next to me, grinning like a dummy.

"Gotta love 'em," replies a boy who is sitting next to the girl.

"He has done that to every one of us, I swareh ta gawd," says a girl with red hair. "Him and Chad have been doing this shit for years. We all know how you feel." She rubs my back in comfort "It's like a so-called 'initiation.'"

"Hazing more like it," I mumble, my face flushed with heat.

"Okay, name time," Emerald announces, rubbing his hands eagerly. "Around the table going to the left, starting with me, Emerald." He nods his head toward Chad and takes a bite of his sandwich.

"Chad, the best beatboxer in town," he says, smiling kindly.

"I'm Lincoln, but people call me Link," replies a boy sitting next to him. I nod.

"I'm Logan," says the boy on the other side of Link. *Damn, he's fine.* He has these cute square black glasses and dark brown hair, which he runs his hand through about every second as he whips it around. He's one of those guys who doesn't know how hot he is, which somehow makes him more attractive.

"I'm Arianna," says a small Asian girl with jet-black hair. It goes all the way down to the small of her back in a braid. Two strands are pulled out in the front to frame her face. The one on the left is a pastel pink and the one on the right is a soft orange.

"I'm Scarlett-Courtney. Scar is fine too." I nod. Her hair is red like mine, but more of a natural red. Ginger.

"And I'm Avery," says the girl sitting next to me. "So you're in every single one of Emmy's classes?" she asks politely. I nod. While we eat, we chat about everything and nothing. It turns out, everyone is in band. My eyebrows shoot up my forehead when Arianna, the smallest of the group, mentions she plays the tuba. When the conversation lulls, I put my plan to action.

"Is there anything exciting that I should know about this week?" I ask everyone.

"No school tomorrow," Chad mumbles with food in his mouth. "Teacher workday." I nod, looking calm, but feeling worried. I have less time now to get Emerald on my side.

"*If* you have nothing to do tomorrow," starts Emmy, "you can come to work with me." I scrunch my face up in confusion, and Avery giggles.

"Emmy is a magician at kids parties, and he has a job tomorrow." I blink. I'm still confused why this involves me. "*LOL*, Ruby, he's asking you to be his assistant," explains Avery, still laughing about the face I made.

"You should go," replies Arianna. "It's fun, except the kids can be annoying at times. Everyone was yelling that it isn't fair that I was an assistant and they weren't," says Arianna, shaking her head. "They thought I was some kid at the party."

"So you've all been?" I ask, a sigh of relief almost bursting from my lips as everyone nods.

"So?" asks Emmy. I smile.

"Why not? What do I have to wear?" I ask, keeping the conversation going.

"Don't worry about that. I'll take care of it. What's your address so my mom can pick you up?"

I tense. "Ummm, how about you just pick me up at school? I will ride my bike here," I insist, hoping he will agree. I mentally groan. I'm an idiot. *On what bike?*

"No, it's okay. Just what's your address? It just makes more sense," he simplifies cluelessly. *He isn't getting what I'm hinting at.*

"I'll skate here," I state, showing I won't change my mind, but Emmy is persistent.

"Are you—?"

"If I am going, you'll pick me up here," I say, a little bit louder than necessary. Everyone turns to look at me, but I look down, letting my twists fall in front of my face. This time, he gets the hint, and he holds up his hands.

"Okay, okay, I'll pick you up here then," he says, and immediately afterward, the table is filled with awkward silence. I had made a scene. *Great, just what I need.* I attempt to break it.

"Here's my number," I say writing it on a piece of paper and giving it to Avery. I smile. "At my school, us band geeks had a group chat, so I am guessing you have one too."

Avery grins. "I'll add you right now." she says, pulling out her phone and adding me as a contact. "But let me warn you, the chat can get a little . . . wild," she adds grinning evilly.

"I'd be concerned if it didn't," I say, and we both break into giggles. These are my kind of people, just like my old friends. God, I love band geeks.

"Ruby, how'd it go?" Ziri calls me while I'm at my locker.

"Good, actually, great. We're friends, so that's good," I say, pressing the earpiece into my ear. "You made it really easy for me, y'know? Thanks for that," I say, leaning my back up against the locker next to mine

"Good, don't forget what you need to do." I roll my eyes. How could I forget? It's literally all I can think about.

"I know. I know what . . ." I start but I realize that Arianna and Emmy are standing next to me.

"Ruby . . . who are you talking to?" asks Arianna, eyeing me curiously. I push myself off my locker quickly.

"Myself?" I question.

"Did you know," says Emerald, "that talking to yourself shows a sign of intelligence?"

"Yes, I did," I reply, swinging my backpack on my shoulder. "And I talk to myself a lot." Shutting my locker, I walk with them down the hall and out of the school. I head straight to the first bench I see, putting on my Rollerblades.

"Bye, you guys," I say, pushing myself up off the ground and starting to skate away.

"Wait!" Emerald calls from behind me. I skate in a circle and turn to face him. With my skates on I am the same height as him. I wave at Arianna as she walks to her car.

"Do you have to go home right now?" he asks, walking toward me as I skate backward.

"Umm . . . not necessarily," I respond.

"Well, can you wait with me until my mom comes to pick me up?" I hesitate. The answer is clearly yes, yes, I should.

"Okay," I say, braking with my Rollerblades. Emerald isn't ready for the stop and walks right into me, knocking me off-balance.

"Sorry!" he apologizes, stepping around me quickly and catching me before I hit the ground. "Sorry," he repeats. He's literally holding me, and a smile tickles his lips.

"What?" I ask, grabbing onto his forearm and trying to stand up, but my Rollerblades keep me off-balance. He helps me stand, and we head over to a bench.

"Nothin'," he says as we sit down. I literally have no idea what to say to him, so I just swing my legs under the bench, letting the blades roll along the concrete. "So, Ruby, where are you from again?" he asks, breaking the peaceful silence.

"Ohio, it's pretty alright." I say, being as vague as possible for the time being. He nods, staring out into the crowd of people, waiting for their rides. I see him squint his eyes, as if he sees something.

"No way!" he yells, jumping from the bench and running into the crowd.

"Wait!" I yell, skating to catch up to him. When I find him, he's talking to this brunette. Her hair has loose curls that go down to her hips, and the tips are pink. She looks cute in a school skirt and random jersey. Looking at them talking, I know she's someone special, either to him or just to everyone. Her eyebrows are perfect, and she has a smile so warm it could melt ice. I squint to get a better look at her; she's mixed, Black and something else. They're speaking in hushed voices, and I strain to hear. I don't think Emmy knows I followed him so I stay hidden in the crowd.

"Do you remember what I told you about last time I was here?" she says in as smooth a tone as honey. I don't hear Emmy's response. He glances back in the direction of the bench, but it's invisible in the crowd of students. I come out of my hiding spot to stand next to him. There's a slight hint of surprise on his face, but it disappears.

"Oh, Ruby, this is Corallina. Corallina, this is Ruby." She flashes me a smile and extends her hand for me to shake. Her grip is firm with confidence.

"Corallina, Ruby is new here. She's from Ohio." Her eyes brighten at the word 'Ohio.'

"Ohio, really? That's cool," she says, looking me up and down with curiosity. "I'm not from Tennessee. I'm just here for a funeral." Her smile disappears.

"I'm sorry. You have my condolences," I say, tugging at a twist. She said that so casually it was kind of unnerving. She drags her hands down her face and leans on Emmy's shoulder. He puts his arm around her, which makes her smile again. They don't seem to be just friends.

"So," she says, her smile appearing on her face once more, "what part of Ohio are you from? And what brings you to Tennessee?

"The Cleveland area," I say, being vague but not. They both nod in acknowledgement. "And you know, business and family." I internally grin at my wit.

We stand in awkward silence for a few seconds, but then I can't help it anymore. I have to know.

"So are you two . . . like a thing?" I ask, cracking my knuckles to keep myself from impatiently tugging a twist or pinching my wrist. Slowly, Corallina removes Emmy's arm from around her and pats his chest.

"Ew, no. We've known each other since . . . forever really," she says, smiling up at Emmy. I push my glasses up my nose. "We're cousins." *Phew.*

"Oh, cool," I say. She nods, and the three of us stand in silence. Silence that could become awkward soon. Corallina sends me a look that screams, *Leave now*, and I quickly decide not to question it. "Well, I have some things I need to do. I'll let you guys catch up!" I say, skating away slowly. It looks as if Emerald is about to stop me, but Corallina speaks first.

"Thanks, Ruby. Hope to see you again," she responds sweetly, lightly tugging Emerald to a bench. He waves goodbye and follows her, like a puppy on a leash.

"Hi, Ziri. I have an update," I say, staring at my laptop screen and looking at her face through Zoom. When she gives me the go ahead, I recap today's progress.

"I'm going over to Emmy's house for some birthday party stuff. I think that things will go smoothly when I tell him." It may be a bold assumption, but I'm hoping to manifest it. "I'm planning for this Friday. There's a school dance that night. So either he'll ask me, or I'll ask him. Well, that is . . . unless he asks Corallina . . ."

"Who's Corallina? Is she a threat to the mission?" I see worry written all over Ziri's face, but I can't tell if she's serious.

"No, she's not a *threat*. Corallina's his cousin. She's in town for a funeral. It's all good. I was just overthinking out loud. He might ask her, just to spend more time with her," I explain.

"Good, Ruby. You know how important this is—don't forget," says Ziri, staring into the screen. I swear she and Garnet are like broken records. It's always "This is important, Ruby" and "Don't screw up, Ruby." Or "Our parents' lives depend on us, Ruby." *Like Jeez. I get it.*

"Understood," I say, saluting her. "Ruby over and out," I add, ending the Zoom call and flopping on my bed. Thankfully, there are no bed bugs or lice, and even though the covers look ugly, they smell freshly cleaned. As soon as I got home, I deep cleaned the room as much as I could. I can still smell the lingering effects of the bleach wavering out from the bathroom. Still on my phone, I call a different number, and when I hear her voice, I can't help but smile.

"Ruby!" Maria says, waving at me through FaceTime. Tears tempt my eyes as I tell her hi. We talk for nearly thirty minutes, and I soak up every second of it. Maria tells me how Lisa started to step up around the house, cleaning and cooking ever since my "death."

"I think it was a good thing," Maria explains, holding her phone as she lies on her bed. "Like, what is the saying? Something about a master of disguise?"

"Blessing in disguise?" I offer.

"Yes, that one!" She explains how Lisa has let up on Maria's reading and how she is feeling more and more like a kid. When she tells me that Lisa is even applying for jobs, that really makes my jaw drop. She's been living off Terry's life insurance and savings, not having to work for a dime. "Don't worry about me, Ruby. I'm okay," she says, answering the question I had spinning through the back of my head. *Maria's okay.*

After a couple more minutes of talking, we say our goodbyes, and I cuddle deep under the covers, happy. Seconds later, a thump reverberates through the room, jolting me upright. *Thump. Thump. THUMP.* I hear a moan from the room next door. *Someone's in trouble.* Sprinting out of my room, I knock on my neighbor's door. Silence. The thumping stops.

"Hello? Is everyone okay?" I ask, knocking again. The door unlocks and is opened. A boy is standing there. He doesn't seem much older than I am. His hair is dark and wavy, and he smiles when he sees me. He isn't wearing anything but boxers, and his six-pack screams *hunk.* My face heats up, and I look down. "Hi," I say, my voice barely above a whisper.

"Hi," he replies, looking me up and down. His eyes linger on my chest but soon creep up to my face. I shiver under his gaze.

"Ummm, I just heard some thumping, and I was just wondering if everything is okay," I say, shuffling my feet and gazing at his handsome face. He smiles.

"Oh, sorry, that was just . . . nothing. I'll try to keep it down," he apologizes.

"Oh, okay! Glad everything is okay!" I say brightly, backing away from the door and heading back to my room. I feel his gaze on me, but I don't turn around. I walk straight into my room and lie on my bed. I begin to drift off when my phone dings. I pick it up.

Unknown number: Hi Ruby, This is Emerald.

I smile and text him back.

Me: Sup Emmy, what's up?

Emerald: Are you sure you want to be picked up at the school?

Me: Positive. Time?

Emerald: 9:30, the party starts at 10:30 but I have to set up some shit.

Me: Okie Dokie.

Emerald: A'ight, C u then!

I turn off my phone and close my eyes, ready for what tomorrow will bring me.

CHAPTER 17

E mmy and I both arrive at the school at 9:30 a.m. I wave at him as I skate to his car, open the van door, and take a seat.

"Hello, Mrs. Koolard," I say, taking off my backpack and buckling up my seatbelt. She smiles in the rearview mirror.

"Hello, you must be Ruby. Emerald has been talking nonstop about you," she says, winking at me, and I smile. Emerald's mom is a lean brunette with dimples. Her hair is parted into two braids, and she's wearing jeans and a T-shirt.

"I hope they were all good things," I add.

"They were wonderful things," she replies. She drives us, playing some smooth jazz before we reach the house. "Well, you youngins have fun, y'hear?"

"Yes, Mama," Emerald gets out of the car, and I exit as well. "Ruby, can you help me unload the trailer?"

"Sure." Inside the trailer, I see boxes and boxes of magic supplies. I help him empty everything out in multiple trips and take it to the backyard. I watch as he says goodbye to his mom and comes up to me.

"Ruby, I can set up everything. I'm kinda particular about it, so, for right now, you can change."

"Change into what exactly?" I question, recalling our conversation from yesterday. Emerald grins as he pulls out a revealing purple leotard covered in golden stars and a large lilac tulle peacock skirt. I feel my face get hot.

"No way am I wearing that." I push the outfit back toward him.

"Ruby, you have to. It's part of the show."

"Yeah, some show. Emmy, it's not my style, okay?" I say, standing my ground.

He sighs. "I guess you shouldn't have come then. You can leave if you want." He turns and throws the leotard in a bin and gets back to work. As much as I don't want to wear the outfit, I know I have to. That manipulative son of a—

"Ugh, fine, just give it to me." He turns to me with the brightest eyes.

"Great," he grins, handing over the leotard. "Mrs. Taylor is inside." I head to the patio and knock on the French door. I find Mrs. Taylor, and she directs me to the bathroom.

I undress quickly and squirm into the suit. When I look in the mirror, I have to admit, it looks great on me. The costume shapes my rectangular-shaped body into an hourglass figure, pushing up my breasts and pronouncing my hips. I grab the hair tie from my wrist, tying my hair into a bun of twists, and pull a couple of strands out to shape my face. I grab my unused makeup kit from the dream and apply dark purple liquid lipstick, basic purple eyeshadow, black eyeliner, and black mascara. I reapply the eyeliner several times before I give up. Almost symmetrical will have to do.

"There, this will be fine," I say to myself, smacking my lips one last time. I step out of the bathroom and make my way to the backyard. When I open the screen door, I see a total transformation. There is a stage with sparkly purple curtains and a banner that reads *The Magnificent Emerald*. I don't think I was in the bathroom for that long, but I guess I was. *Must have been that damn eyeliner*.

"Wow, this is some setup you have here," I say, walking toward Emerald. His eyes widen when he sees me, and he looks me up and down. I squirm. "Is this satisfactory?" Emerald chuckles.

"*Satisfactory?*" He looks around the yard and lowers his voice. "You look fine as fuck, Ruby."

"I think it's the skirt," I admit nonchalantly, running my hands through the fluffy lilac fabric. "When are the kids supposed to be coming?" I change the conversation quickly, not wanting to stay on the route it is going. Not with my *brother*. Emmy glances at his watch.

"In a few minutes, actually. We should get ready. Follow me." He leads me to the back of the stage "So your job is simple—you're just my assistant."

"Yes, I understand that, *Magnificent Emerald*, but what am I assisting with exactly?"

"Oh!" he grins mischievously, "you'll see." I notice him fidgeting with something on his finger and take a closer look. It's a ring, an emerald ring. I reach for his hand and pull his fingers to my face.

"Wow, Emmy! This is beautiful. Is it real?" I ask, inspecting the ring closely. He pulls his hand away and shoves it in his pocket.

"Nah, just part of the costume. Found it at a thrift store," he interjects, walking away to peek behind the curtain. "Here comes the crowd."

"Cool." I turn away. After all the time Zach and I spent examining my mom's jewelry, I know a real gem when I see one. That is definitely an authentic emerald. Either he is ignorant of the fact, or he knows what he can do. Either way, I make note to pay close attention to his behaviors.

"Are you ready?" he asks, tapping me on the shoulder. "All ya gots to do is introduce me."

"Okay, I can do that." I walk toward the curtain.

"Oh, and Ruby," I look back at him. "Your name is The Ravishing Ruby." At that, my jaw drops.

"Awww, hell no!"

"Ruby."

"I said 'no.'"

"I'll owe you," he pleads, grasping his hands in front of him and giving me puppy dog eyes. I hesitate.

"Fine!" I open the curtain and step onto the stage. In the crowd, I see the faces of many children and adults, some bored and others happy. There are more people here than I expected. I clear my throat. "Ladies and gentlemen, boys and girls. I," I smile at all the kids' faces, "The Ravishing Ruby, am pleased to introduce the most spectacular magician in all of Knoxville, The Magnificent Emerald!" I clap, and the audience soon follows suit. A puff of smoke arises from the stage floor, and from it, Emerald appears. The crowd goes wild.

"Thank you, thank you, everyone! Who's ready to see a show?" announces Emerald. Cheers erupt from the crowd of kids. I reach up and tap my glasses. Ziri had installed an undetectable camera in the lenses right before I left. She said it was to *collect data,* and *report back evidence.* And since I'm nearly positive that is a real emerald on his finger, he'll probably be using his powers, whether he knows so or not.

Emerald starts by doing a few simple card tricks that even toddlers can do. But as time continues, his tricks become more elaborate, only a few involving me. The crowd eats up his show, and even I have to admit he has talent.

"And for my last trick, I shall do something never accomplished before at this household." There are a few chuckles from the audience. "First, I will need a few volunteers." Hands shoot up from the crowd. "Ravishing Ruby, may you please pick four volunteers?" Emerald asks, turning his gaze to me.

I nod and step into the crowd. For the first volunteer, I pick the birthday boy. He practically jumps to the stage, full of glee. I chose a petite girl as my second choice, and she thanks me and runs to the stage. I go toward the back of the yard and choose a woman with frizzy hair third. The crowd erupts as she makes her way to the stage.

"Go, Mrs. Hoffman!" shouts a boy in the audience. "You're the best teacher ever!" Nods of agreement ripple throughout the crowd. For the last volunteer, I pick a lanky boy with an adorable smile. He stands shyly and makes his way toward the stage, with me right behind him. Emerald has rolled out a huge plastic tank I hadn't noticed before. Also, new on the stage, are metal chains, a large chest, and a straitjacket. All of this must have been in the boxes we unloaded. Chills creep up my spine. He's taken off his costume and is now in a simple T-shirt and shorts.

"You, little girl, will you help me put this on?" The girl nods and helps him with the straitjacket. "Make sure it's tight." He turns to the lanky boy. "Can you and Mrs. Hoffman open the chest? I need you to show the audience that there are no secret doors, loopholes, or anything of that sort." Mrs. Hoffman and the boy open the chest and show the audience that it's empty.

"As tight as I could get it," says the girl, stepping from behind Emmy.

"Perfect," he assures. He meets my eyes and winks, but I don't smile back. "Ravishing Ruby, can you please help me into the chest?" Gasps flare up from around me, including my own. I form a grim smile and nod, walking over to Emmy and guiding him toward the chest.

"What are you doing?" I whisper aggressively.

"Putting on a show," he responds. I help him into the chest, and he gives me a reassuring smile. In no way do I feel reassured. "Audience!" he says, standing in the chest. "The Ravishing Ruby will be locking me in this chest, and with the help of a few dads in the crowd," four men raise their hand. A shock of betrayal goes through my body. Emerald told them beforehand, but not me, "they will raise me into that huge tank in which our birthday boy has been filling with water." I jerk around to see what I was too distracted to notice before, a boy filling the tank with water from a hose, and it's already three-fourths of the way full.

"You can stop there, Tanner. That's perfect. *Ladies and gentlemen*, the chest I will be locked in will soon be submerged in that tank of water." Murmurs flow from the audience. "I shall attempt an escape. The Ravishing Ruby will set a timer for three minutes. If I'm not out by then, please get me out—and call an ambulance." The audience goes dead silent at this. "Please feel free to take any pictures and record this attempt of escape, 'cause if I do make it," he forms a broad grin, "you have proof of the impossible." I help him sit down in the chest, then step to the side so I can close it. "Oh, and kids?" The crowd leans in. "Don't try this at home," he says earnestly. "The timer will start once I'm in the water. Goodbye for now!" He glances at me and whispers, "No matter what happens, get me out only after the three minutes are up. Promise me."

"Emmy . . ." I start.

"Promise me!" he grits out. I gulp and nod. He curls into a ball, and I shut and lock the chest. The dads make their way toward the stage and hold the chest up. The volunteers and I wrap the metal chains around the chest and lock them. After the volunteers make their way back to their seats, the dads lift the chest and put it in the water.

"Time starts now." I say, pressing the timer on my phone. Then we wait. From the tank, we can see the chest jerking and moving. Almost everyone in the crowd has their phones out, recording.

He has two minutes and forty seconds left.

The chest stops moving, and I can tell everyone is holding their breath. I look into the crowd and see Mrs. Taylor, her eyes full of fear. She's holding her phone in her hands, ready to dial 911. My guess is Emerald didn't tell her about his little trick.

We're down to two minutes and thirteen seconds.

I am pretty sure that this will be the longest three minutes of my life. I fidget on stage, my hands alternating between tugging a twist of hair and tugging at the skin around my wrist. My eyes never leave the tank.

One minute and forty-two seconds.

"Wait!" yells someone from the crowd. Everyone turns to look at Tanner as he steps over people, rushing to the stage. "Wait!" When he's finally on the stage, he bends over panting. "He-he told me to put the key in the chest," Tanner rambles, his eyes full of panic. "I-I thought I did, but it's in my pocket. We have to get him out!" Everyone is motionless.

Fifty-nine seconds left.

"I'm calling 911," Mrs. Taylor says, fingers ready. I think back to what Emmy said.

"No, don't call yet," I interject, regret filling my stomach. Everyone turns to face me. "We have to give him three minutes. He still has time left."

"How much?" yells someone from the audience. I glance at my watch.

"Twenty seconds." Everyone shifts uncomfortably, and I see a few glancing at Mrs. Taylor.

"It doesn't matter. He's been in there for too long. Call 911!" yells Mrs. Hoffman. Time seems to slow. Emmy could be dead. I could have failed my whole mission just for some stupid birthday trick. My *brother* could be dying right now, and it would be my fault. The fear inside me increases.

"No!" I yell, my voice sounding more confident than I feel. I have to keep everyone calm, even if I'm not calm myself. "We give him the benefit of the doubt. No one calls until we open the chest! He could be alive and unharmed, and we would have called for no reason. No. One. Call." I glance down at my watch. It's fifteen seconds past time and still no sign of him. "Times up! *Get him out!*" I yell, terror filtering into my voice.

"Forget it, I'm calling," says someone else.

"No one's calling!" I screech. The crowd goes silent again, and I take a deep breath and smile. "This *is* The Magnificent Emerald," I reassure them. "I've seen this trick many times. He can practically do it in his sleep," I lie. Everyone seems to relax. He should be fine. He has the magical gene. And yet, panic still rises in me.

Five men go up to the tank and lift out the chest. They set it down on the stage carefully. Tanner passes me the key, his small hands shaking.

"We'll both do it," I tell him. He nods. I put my hand over his and, together, we unlock the chest. Tanner and I open the chest, and we both gasp. Everyone in the audience cranes their neck attempting to view the chest. I go behind it, and, with all my strength, tip it over. Only the straitjacket falls out. Now everyone is in awe. One of the dads steps forward and looks down at it, shaking his head in disbelief. He's wearing all black with a hat and sunglasses, hiding his face.

"Now *that* is one hell of a trick," he says, taking off his hat and glasses. Everyone gasps. Then whoops and screams and clapping explode from the audience. I shift my position so I can see the man's full face, except it's not a man at all. *It's Emerald.* The whole tank was clear plastic except the back wall. There's no way he could have escaped from that where no one could see him.

"The Magnificent Emerald everyone!" I shout, gesturing toward Emerald. He grins and bows to the audience. He looks over and shoots me a dazzling smile. I smile back, but not out of happiness, mostly out of relief. The thought of kicking his butt for not telling me of any of this ahead of time runs through my brain. He's gonna get it.

CHAPTER 18

"Why?" I ask for the tenth time. "Why did you not tell me about *that* before? It woulda been nice to know." I put the last of the props into the trailer of his mom's car. "I was panicking!"

"It's better when all reactions are real and you don't have to act," he responds casually. "I'm surprised you haven't asked how yet," he adds, getting into the front seat. I hop into the back.

"Asking *how* would ruin the magic part of it," I mock him, buckling my seatbelt. "Hi, Mrs. Koolard."

"Hello, Ruby. Still in costume I see." I look down and blush.

"Yeah, I was too mad at Emmy for keeping his grand finale a secret to notice I was still wearing it."

"Ahhh," she acknowledges. "The escaping part of his tricks. My least favorite." She whacks him on his head. "Stupid of you not to tell her. What is wrong with you?"

"Many things, Mama," he admits, lurching away before she could whack him again.

"He started doing magic tricks when he was really little. He went viral on YouTube, actually."

"You really haven't heard of 'The Magnificent Emerald' before now?" he asks, reaching his arm back toward me to hand me his phone. On it is a video of a little boy with a top hat. He's standing on a makeshift stage in a living room. As the video continues, he does some impressive magic tricks for a kid his age. His finale was him pulling a duck out of his hat, which then proceeds to chase him around the room as he's screaming and crying.

"Oh my God! I remember this! This is you?" I ask, handing him back his phone in awe. He takes it, nodding.

"Yeah. I don't do much of YouTube anymore. I stopped a couple years after that. Now, I just do live performances for events and birthday parties." His pride is evident in his voice, and I can't help but smile.

"Well, Ruby, it's pretty late. Should we just take you home?" asks Mrs. Koolard, turning on the car. I tell her to just drop me off at the school, but she refuses. We go back and forth for a couple of minutes before I give up, tell her the address of the hotel, and slouch in my seat.

"Ruby, are you sure you got the address right?" ask Mrs. Koolard as she pulls into the parking lot. I don't answer. I unbuckle the seatbelt and open the door. I feel my face hot with embarrassment.

"Thanks for the ride," I say, averting the pitying gaze I know is on their faces. I grab my stuff, shut the door, and run into the motel. The teenager that was there the first morning lifts her head as I open the door. When she sees me, she raises an eyebrow. I look down and remember I'm still wearing the costume. *I'll give it to him at school tomorrow*, I think. I avoid eye contact and rush toward my room. With my eyes down, facing the floor, I ram into something. I start to fall headfirst, but someone catches me inches before my forehead would slam on the tiles. "Oh, jeez. I'm sorry, I've been having a rough . . ." I trail off. I look up and see I'm in the hands of the hunk from next door.

"Hello, you," he remarks, staring down into my eyes. He helps me stand up, then looks me up and down. "What are you wearing?" he asks, a gleam of laughter in his eyes.

"Errr, nothing," I say, blowing a twist from out of my eyes. I feel my face burning.

"No, you are wearing something. If you were wearing nothing . . ."

I step back. "Um, just a long story. Actually, it's been a long day. I am really tired. Sorry again for . . . crashing into you." I inch my body around him to get to my room, but he steps in front of me.

"Where do you think you're going?" he asks, his arms crossed and a smirk on his face.

"To sleep," I say, stepping to the right. He follows suit, once again blocking my path.

"I don't think so," he insists. I can tell he's having a wonderful time. "You bumped into me and caused severe pain to my chest," he continues, clutching the area. I snort. "*And* I saved you from cracking your head on the floor. I'll say you owe me." I open my mouth to say something, but he's too fast. "You owe me twice," he emphasizes, poking the area between my breast and neck on the word *you*.

"But it was an accident." I put my hands on my hips. He smiles.

"I know, and you can make it up to me," he says. I sigh, giving up for the second time today.

"I don't even know your name," I declare, a smile tugging on my lips against my will. He is . . . interesting.

"Seth Huckson, seventeen," he says frankly. I loosen up a bit and think, *He seems fun. And, honestly, if I go back to my room, I'll probably just stress about the mission and cry myself to sleep. I need a break.*

"Okay, *fine*. What do I gotta do?"

"Photoshoot."

"What—?" I start, but he grabs my hand and pulls me into his room. It's a lot nicer than mine. Stainless bed covers and unbroken furniture. In fact, it seems like he has done it himself. "Wow," I admire, twirling around the room. "This place is heaven compared to my room," I admit, flopping onto his bed. "What were you saying about a photoshoot?"

"Wait, hold that position right there." He closes the door and walks over to his desk, picks up a professional-looking camera, and kneels to my eye level. I laugh, and he snaps a picture.

"LOL, okay. You *actually* meant a photoshoot." I flip onto my stomach and scoot closer to him. Seth slides onto the floor, leaning his back against the bed to show me the picture. I look so happy, like I'm a little kid who just saw a unicorn. "Wow. That was a great shot," I say, nudging his shoulders. "Looks like pretty boy's got some talent." He grins.

"This can be good," Seth says, his eyes gleaming. "We can make this fun. Do you wanna have some fun?" I smile. *Yes, I want some fun. I want a break from my mission. I want to chill and relax and at least pretend to be normal, just for tonight. My call with Ziri can wait.*

"Give me a moment." I grin, getting up and skipping out of the room and unlocking mine. *Ziri doesn't need to see this,* I think as I take off my glasses and my ruby necklace. I rush back to Seth's room and lean in his doorframe. "Hi, I'm the *Ravishing Ruby*, and I would love to be your model for this evening." With every step I channel my inner sexy, swaying my hips hypnotically as I approach him.

"Ooo, very professional," he croons, standing up and walking to stand across from me. "Jump up and down like you're having fun. Don't worry about me and the camera. Flop down on the bed too. Just be yourself." I stand on the bed and jump up and down. The tulle skirt is like an extension of my body, flowing with my every movement. This is *fun*. I'm smiling and laughing as I goof around. After a bit, I flop on the bed, rolling on the covers. I end lying on my back, head hanging off the end of the bed staring right into the camera.

"What next?" I ask, breathless.

"So I see you can do fun," Seth says, leaning against the wall. "But can you do sexy?" he asks, wiggling his eyebrows.

"Legit, every girl can do sexy. You just gotta ask . . ." I pause, rolling onto my stomach and pushing myself up with a sexy look on my face. I pull at my hair tie, and my twists fall loose, bouncing at my shoulders. " . . . if I do sexy *well*." I part my lips and sit on the bed, spreading my legs so Seth can have a perfect view of my leotard bottoms. He brings the camera back up to his face and snaps a picture.

"Yes, you do." I do many more sexy poses until an idea pops into my head. I do a sexy crawl from the front of the bed to where he sits in a chair taking pictures. I've never done something like this before. It's cool and new and intriguing and fun and *liberating*. I'm not insecure about how I look or feeling the stress of my new life. I *am* confident and beautiful. I feel like I have the power to do anything. He continues taking pictures as I reach the end of the bed. I climb off it and sit on his lap facing him, too close for him to take a clear shot. To his surprise, I pluck the camera from his hands.

"Your turn," I say, getting off him and sitting back on the bed, attempting to figure out how the camera works.

"What?" he asks, laughing.

"You're the model now. Go get in something nice, then come back," I say, glancing at his sweatshirt and gym shorts.

"Wait," he says, standing up. He points at me accusingly. "I never asked you to do that." He crosses his arms.

"You didn't have to 'cause I already did. Now shoo. Go change into something else."

"But . . ." he begins to object.

I give an obnoxious yawn.

"I'm getting tired. Maybe I'll just . . ."

"I'll do it, Ruby. I'll be right back," he interrupts, hands up in defeat.

"That's what I thought." I sit in his chair and skim through the pictures, barely recognizing myself. I see a sexy woman, not me. But maybe that sexy woman is me, or at least a part of me. A little voice in my head tells me this is a bad idea and that I should leave, but I ignore it. I'm having fun. I'm feeling *empowered*. With everything that's been going on, I've felt powerless. I was thrust into this new life without much of a choice and barely any time to adjust. But now? Here? I have control. Here, I'm The *Ravishing Ruby*, someone who isn't part of some science fiction family or who's dead to the world. And, yeah, maybe this wasn't a well-thought-out decision of mine, but at least I feel great. Plus, no one will know. And if anything bad happens, I have my pocketknife in my bag.

"How's this?" he asks, coming out from the bathroom buck naked.

"Oh my God," I say, closing my eyes. "I said 'sexy'! Not naked!"

"Are you saying I don't look sexy naked?" he asks, opening his mouth in mock surprise. "That's a first." I hear the bed squeak as he sits on it and take a peek through my hands. He's sitting in front of me, legs slightly too far apart. I put my hand back over my face fast, squeezing my eyes shut.

"Nope, can't do it. You're gonna have to put it away or cover it, else I'm leaving." I hear more squeaking, then silence. I take another peek and see him with a pillow over his crotch. I fully open my eyes and relax. "Alright, you just be your *sexy* self while I snap some pics," I say, putting my feet up on the chair. I rest my wrists on my knees to hold the camera steady. Seth makes sexy dances and poses, sometimes with the pillow covering his ding dong and other times the blanket or his hands.

My favorite is of him lying back against the headboard with his legs apart, with only his penis covered by the blanket. When he first got into that pose, I was laughing so hard I was on the verge of tears. He begins to crawl down the bed sexily like I did, and then he's in front of me, everything exposed. I squeeze my eyes shut, and he laughs. He grabs my knees gently and pushes them down so my feet are no longer on the chair but the floor. Then he copies me, and sits on my lap, grabbing the camera from my fingers. I giggle. "Copying my tricks, eh?" He smiles. Seth leans over past my shoulder and puts the camera on his desk, then faces me.

"We should do this again sometime, but with both of us modeling at once."

I laugh. "Maybe," I smile shyly, wanting to look away from his eyes burning into my gaze, "but not tonight. It's getting late, and—" I begin, but I am interrupted by his lips against mine, soft and delicate. He tastes of chocolate and mint—mint chocolate. Although I don't like chocolate so much, his lips and tongue are sweet in my mouth. I have only seconds to make a choice. Kiss him back or push him away. The me from a few months ago would have pushed him away. Heck, the me from this morning would push him away. But what about the me I just discovered? The sexy, model, *daring* me. Am I ready to go back to the nerdy, invisible freak? Am I ready to go back to the responsible one? *It's just a kiss*, I think, but my heart feels as if it might erupt from my chest. *Just this once*, and I kiss him back.

The kiss starts off gently but he deepens it with pure need. *Lust.* His hands are on my back, and they make their way to my stomach. They continue up onto each of my breasts, and he squeezes. At first, I think it was an accident, but he continues to knead them. My eyes pop open. *Hell no*, I think, and I shove him off me lightly. "I gotta go. It's getting late, and I'm tired," I say. He leans back and plants kisses down my arm.

"You can sleep with me," he says between kisses. He keeps kissing me up my shoulder and down between my breasts.

"I have stuff to do tomorrow," I counter, pushing his naked body off me lightly. I totally forgot about his nakedness. I avoid looking down as he stands off me.

"But you still owe me," he says.

I sigh. "I really don't." I wave my hands around the room. "My debt has been paid." *I had fun while it lasted, but it's time for me to focus back on what I came here to do: get my brother.*

"I thought you were having fun." He frowns slightly.

"I was actually, a lot, but I have priorities. And you're not one of them."

He nods in understanding. "Well, I hope I can be," he says hopefully.

I smile. "Not gonna happen pretty boy."

He smirks. I think he's liking this too much.

"Fuck me," he declares. My jaw drops. He leans in so that his mouth is right up against my ear and he whispers, "I will give you so much pleasure you're gonna want to eat me for breakfast, lunch, and dinner." I gape at him as he backs away. *Is he dumb?* "And I know I'm gonna want to eat you that much too," he adds, licking his lips.

"No," I say, moving from around him and making my way toward the door. *This has gone too far, extremely too far.* He blocks the way.

"But I saved you. You could have gotten a concussion if it weren't for me, and what would have happened if you did?" I don't say anything. For one, I would have failed my mission. Pathetically. Ziri would kill me, and then Garnet would kill me again. He may be stretching the truth, but I was gonna land on the floor headfirst, no doubt. I do owe him . . . a lot actually. I move around him to get to my stuff.

"Anything but sex," I concede, bending down to grab my bag. He shifts his body and stands in front of me, resting his hands on my head. When I look up, I come face-to-face with his erect penis. I try to squirm away, but he holds me there. I break into a cold sweat.

"Fine. Head," he says, looking down at me.

"I am not putting that in my mouth!" I state, attempting to move again. Nothing.

"Can you at least make out with my dick? Twenty seconds. That's it,"

I sigh. I can kiss it, as long as it's not halfway down my throat. *I'll just get it over with and be done. I can do this. Just a kiss, and I'll be done with this.*

"Fine!" I say, giving up and kissing his dick.

"Wait! I didn't set the timer!" he says, but it's too late. I'm giving him what he wants so he can give me what I want. A way out. I start at the top of his shaft and kiss my way down to the tip. It's not as bad as I imagined. Plus, it tastes kinda minty. Seth moans with pleasure, hands never leaving my head. I form my mouth around the tip and kiss, letting my tongue dance. His hands tighten on my head as he sighs.

Ten more seconds, I think as I do a few tiny pecks. Then I let my tongue lay on the tip and wiggle it around as I inch my mouth up more.

Five more seconds. Suddenly, Seth pushes my head up and thrusts his dick far into my throat. I choke. I struggle to get out from his trap, but he shifts his body so I am sandwiched between the wall and him. I try to scream, but it comes out as a gurgle.

"Ruby, don't resist," he says, shoving his dick farther down my throat and moaning with delight. This was a mistake, a *huge* mistake. I claw at his legs as tears stream down my face, but he won't budge. I smack his legs with all my might, but he just laughs. "If you wanna slap something, slap my ass." I feel around my bag for anything that I can use to defend myself.

My hands slide across something smooth and small. *My pocketknife.* I flick it open and think of where to strike. His penis is off-limits because it's all down my throat. My best bet would be his butt. I grip the pocketknife, and, with all my strength, stab upward into the bottom part of his right cheek. He screams and pulls away from me just as I yank out the knife. I cough, trying to catch my breath as he pulls his hand away from his wound, revealing blood.

"What the fuck was that for?" he yells, eyes glaring at me. I close the knife quickly and slip it under my costume by my hip. Grabbing my bag, I leap to the door. I can almost reach the knob when I'm yanked back by my hair. I yelp. "Now you owe me again, bitch!" he yells, pulling me back toward him. I scream, but his hand covers my mouth. He pulls me into his chest, one hand on my mouth and the other hand searching my hands before wrapping around my waist. I can taste the blood that stains his hand, and I cough again. Struggling in his grasp, I tug and wriggle, tears stinging my eyes.

His left hand slides from my waist down between my legs. I scream into his hand. His fingers move the leotard bottom exposing my crotch. *I'm an idiot. I should have walked away.* He presses his fingers up against me, and I whimper and struggle in his constraint. "And to think, this all could have been avoided," he says. My limp right hand comes to life and I tug the knife from where I hid it, stabbing him in his thigh. He screeches and wretches away, letting me go.

I start for my bag but change my mind, marching over to the bleeding boy lying on the floor. I kneel and hold the knife to his throat. Tears stream down my face, but my voice is steady with anger.

"If I see your face again, I swear to God," I spit, pressing the knife slightly harder into his neck, "that I will not *hesitate* to cut off your dick and feed it to you." With my free hand, I choke him, bringing the knife to his chest and slicing a cut, not deep enough to be lethal but enough to scar. "Here's a little reminder." I push myself up off him and walk to the desk slowly. After I pick up the camera, I pop out the SD card. I want to smash the camera to pieces, but instead, I put it back down, pick up my bag, and walk out the door, leaving Seth bleeding and groaning in pain on the floor.

When I get into my room, I deadbolt the door and lean against it. I can't hold it back anymore. I fall to the floor sobbing and gasping for air. Snot runs down my chin, and tears slide into my mouth. My nose is so congested I can barely breathe. I was caught up in the adventure. I thought I could do anything and that everything would be okay. I was mistaken. It was a stupid lapse of judgment. This never would've happened if I were back in Ohio. I was hooked on freedom like a drug, and now I'm facing the consequences.

It's not your fault, Ruby, I tell myself, trying to calm down. *You said no. He was manipulative.* I squeeze the palms of my hands into my eyes, and another sob escapes me. *I'm here. I survived. I'm okay.* Shivers overwhelm me, and I tug on my twists, hoping it will ground me. The shaking only gets worse. *No, I'm not okay. But I will be because I have to be.* I lean my head back against the door and breathe. I think of Citrine's mantra: *Breathe in through the nose and hold. Out through the mouth and relax.*

I get up slowly, grab a pair of clean clothes, and step in the bathroom. When I pass the mirror, I halt. *Who am I?* All I see is a girl, a stupid and less naive girl. I strip off the costume and turn the shower on. I don't even wait for the water to warm before I step in. I let the cold water blast against my skin.

I wish I could do more. File a report. Make him pay for what he did. Who knows how many girls this could have happened to before . . . or how many will be after. I gargle and spit and gag on the water, the minty flavor burning my mouth. But I can't do more. To file a report, I'd have to exist, and to the world right now, I don't. Maybe Ziri can do something. Put him in the system somehow. But that would require me to tell her, and I'm not ready to tell *anyone.* *I said no,* I tell myself again. I can still feel where his hands were on me. I grab a cloth and rub hard on my skin, tears streaming down my face, but his touch won't go away.

Chapter 19

I don't go to school, and Ziri is pissed at me. I can feel myself dissociating. Hours pass by as if they were minutes, and my eyes don't seem to focus on anything. School is the last place I want to be after what happened. Faking smiles, feigning interest. I'm like a zombie in my own body. It's too hard.

"You only have three more days until Friday, Ruby! Missing a day will bring that down to two!" she yells through the screen.

I take a deep breath.

"I don't feel good, okay?" I say, rubbing my shoulders and turning away from the screen. *Focus, Ruby. Don't think.*

"Come on, Ruby. This is serious. This isn't a game." Garnet appears on the screen, leaning over Ziri's shoulder.

"I know, okay? I understand that." I take off my glasses and tap the side of them, causing a memory card to slip out. I hold it so they can see. "I got some footage of Emerald yesterday. You can see if you saw him using his powers." The irritation in my voice grows. I take a breath and continue, attempting to ignore the thoughts of Seth that creep into my mind. I shiver. "I saw him wearing an emerald ring, so it's likely . . ." I don't need to finish my sentence.

"Send it over," orders Garnet. I upload the video and send it over to them all in silence. I know I have to talk to them, but all I want to do is lay in bed. I can feel myself building a mental wall, blocking out the memory of Seth and the emotions that come with it. Like the third little piggy, I could build my wall of brick. But even that seems too fragile to hold back the feelings. Instead, I choose b rick *and* thick steel plates. I watch their expressions as they watch the video. Both of their jaws drop when it reaches the end.

"I've never seen anything like that." Ziri turns to her right and types on another keyboard. "It could simply be magic, but a lot of those tricks are rudimentary." Her fingers fly over the keyboard. She scrolls down the screen, furrowing her eyebrows in concentration. "Like, the chest and stage could have had a trapdoor underneath it or something . . ." Her eyes brighten. She slams her fists on the table and pushes her chair back, spinning in circles.

"You found it?" I ask curiously. Several more layers of steel plating and my wall will be set. I'll deal with what happened, but later. I just have to make sure that *later* doesn't turn to *never*.

"The only one I could find. *Escape Artistry*. That's the only way he could have escaped that undetected. I mean, it's just straight up impossible," Ziri explains. "Wild. Absolutely wild."

The wall is complete. With a deep breath, I focus on the task at hand.

"What exactly is that though? Something I should be worried about?" I ask. She shakes her head.

"Nah, not really. Blah, blah, blah. The user can escape all manner of bonds, blah, analyzes knots, situations, fetters . . . nothing that should put you in any harm, at least according to this. His abilities could be a little different. But if he's wearing that ring, or if he already mastered his powers, you won't be able to tie him up or anything of that sort."

"Why would I have to tie him up?" I ask. Ziri and Garnet exchange a glance.

"Some people resist." Garnet shrugs. "Okay, we have to go check on the others. Don't screw up." She ends the call. *Too late,* I think.

I spend the day surfing the internet and sleeping. I just need a break from everything, even myself. Someone knocking at my door wakes me with a jolt. *Seth.* With that, my mental wall attempts to tumble, leaving all my hard work in vain.

"Ruby?" I hear a muffled male voice, and I tense. "Ruby, open up." I don't dare, but the knocking doesn't stop. I creep out of my bed and grab the pocketknife on my desk. It still has blood on it. I'd forgotten to clean it last night. I tiptoe to the door and thrust it open, holding the knife in front of me.

"Seth, I swear I'll call the cops if you don't . . ." I say, my eyes focusing on the face. It's not Seth. "Emerald, what are you doing here?" I ask, startled. I close the knife quickly and hide it behind my back. Hopefully, the blood blends in with the knife's red color. I'm not ready to answer any questions yet. He runs his hands through his braids awkwardly.

"Can I come in?" he asks nervously. I open the door wider, and he steps in. "You weren't at school today," he states, taking in the scene of the room. I shrug, crossing my arms over my chest. I point to the chair for him to sit, and I settle across from him, cross-legged on the bed.

"I wasn't feeling very well," I say.

He sighs. "Ruby, when you said . . . I didn't realize . . ."

"I know," We enter an awkward silence, and I'm desperate to break it. "How did you know where to find me anyway? I mean, the room?" I ask, shifting uncomfortably.

"The girl at the front desk," he responds. I'm not surprised. More silence.

"Sooo, why are you here anyway?" I ask, trying to make eye contact with him. He resists.

"Just wanted to make sure you were alright."

I think about last night. I am definitely not alright.

"Why wouldn't I be alright? I'm *fine*." My voice goes an octave higher.

He stares at me oddly. "I have your costume." I change the subject, getting up from the bed and walking over to the closet. I grab the costume and drop it on his lap. "Sorry, there's no washer here, so I couldn't—" I start, but he interrupts me.

"Don't trip. Are you sure you're okay?" he asks. I obviously can't tell him the truth, so I nod, staring at the dress attentively. When I'm satisfied, I relax in relief. *Good. I got all the blood off it. Baking soda can go a long way.* "Well, there's this thing this Friday," he continues. *The dance.* I perk up and lean in, pushing my embarrassment and self-loathing aside. I have work to do.

"This Friday?" I ask.

"Yeah, it's this stupid school dance. And, of all themes, it's Hollywood." He tugs at one of his braids and shifts in his seat. My heart leaps. *Stupid?* If he thinks it's stupid, is he even planning on going?

"Stupid?" I squeak. He bites the inside of his cheek and looks down.

"I was thinking, maybe, it would be less stupid if you came with me." Emmy brings his eyes to meet mine slowly, and I smile.

"Are you asking me to the dance?"

"I am," he says, smiling shyly. I don't hesitate.

"I'd love to go with you," I reply, grinning. His smile grows, and he laughs a little.

"Great! That's-that's great. This'll be fun," he says, coming over to sit next to me. He looks up at me and smiles. *Oh my goodness, he looks so cute right now. Not like in an attractive cute type of way, but a brotherly way. His eyes are so hopeful. Telling him that we're related may be more awkward than I thought.* "Do you know what you might want to wear? I know that it's last minute, but at least the color?" I smile.

"Red, it's my favorite color," I say.

"That makes sense. Your name *is* Ruby. You already are as beautiful as rubies, so it would make sense for you to like that color too," he adds, staring intently at my eyes. I look down at my hands, feeling my face heat up.

"Thanks."

"You shouldn't have to thank someone for telling the truth," he responds. I look away, hiding my smile. *Why does this kid have to be so gosh darn cute! Any girl would be lucky to have him.*

"Not to be rude or anything, Emmy, but I have a lot of stuff that I need to get done," I say, tugging at the curls in front of my face, "and I really should get started on that." He nods in understanding, and we both stand and walk toward the door.

"I'll see you tomorrow at school then?" I nod and open the door.

"Yep." He steps out into the hall.

"Good, see you tomorrow."

"See you," I say, closing the door as he walks away. I sprint over to my phone and start to text.

Me: He asked me to the dance.

Garnet replies immediately.

Garnet: I'm impressed, Ruby. Now don't screw this up.

I let out a huff. That seems to be Garnet's favorite phrase. I turn off my phone and flop onto my bed. *Screw up? It seems that has been my favorite activity as of late.* It can't be that hard to tell someone I'm related to them. I should plan it out, the exact words I'm going to say. I clear my throat.

"Surprise! I'm your long-lost sister, and we have other siblings in Ohio! You have to come back with me so we can find our parents; they're alive." I cringe and slam my head into a pillow. That was terrible. I lie in bed for a while, tossing out ideas, but none of them are smooth.

I think back to how Tani told me and shrug. Hers wasn't that smooth either, so it'll be *fine.* The moment I decide to give up practicing revealing our secret, my wall begins to tumble. *No. Not yet.* I rush to my knockoff AirPods and shove them into my ears, playing some random Spotify playlist. The wall doesn't rebuild itself, but it stops breaking. I take a deep breath and turn to my side. *Things are fine.* But there's still a pit in my stomach as I drift off to sleep.

CHAPTER 20

F riday comes in a breeze. Everyone at school is giddy about the dance later. As I roam the halls after the last bell, I see the student council hanging up decorations. This is going to be a huge night. A night in which I not only have to tell Emmy who he really is, but I also need to convince him to come back to Ohio with me and leave his old life behind. When I turn the corner and see Corallina and Emerald talking, I walk up to them, a smile on my face.

"Oh, hi, Ruby. How are you?" she asks sweetly as I approach. I tell her that I'm fine and the adjustment to Tennessee is going smoothly. When I ask her how she is, she explains that she's here to pick Emerald up from school, then she'll be leaving for home later.

"Oh right! How was the funeral?" I ask, recalling the reason she's here.

"It was early afternoon yesterday, and it was really beautiful," she says, bringing her hand to rest on her heart. "We're having a family get-together soon," says Corallina. I glance back at Emmy and see that any compassion I saw in his eyes before has disappeared. Now they are clouded, and distant, and something else slightly. The corner of his mouth twitches up. "Emmy has a surprise for everyone, and I just can't wait!" She shoots him a glance, snapping him back to the present, and he scratches his head.

"Family get-together? So like, a family reunion?" I ask. Corallina looks back at me smiling broadly.

"Yes. Exactly," she replies, a glimmer in her eyes. "I just can't wait!" she continues, elbowing Emerald. He laughs, causing a pain to course through me. Emerald won't make it to that reunion. He'll be with me.

"Well, I should go . . . Pick me up at seven?" I ask, directing my question at Emerald. Guilt is rising in me, fast. When he confirms, I wave goodbye to him and Corallina and jog down the hall.

As soon as I make it out of the school, I call Ziri.

"Ziri," I say as I shove on my roller blades.

"Hey, Ruby, I heard you were asked to the dance. Good job!"

"Yeah. I knew what I was doing." I feign confidence, chuckling as I stand to my feet. "How is Citrine doing? Did she get Topaz?" I ask, checking up on my competition.

"Yeah. Topaz agreed to come. Garnet is on her way over there right now to get the disappearing part done with. It shouldn't be too hard because Topaz is in foster care. It didn't take a lot of convincing, I'm sure," Ziri adds, the pride in her voice fully audible.

"That's great, and what about Moon with Jasper?"

"Oh, that's going really well actually! They seem to have bonded right away, even though it took what seemed like *forever* for Moon to talk to him. He's as shy as a turtle! They'll be coming home soon," says Ziri. I can hear the smile in her voice.

"I'm glad to hear it. Thanks for the update. I gotta go get ready for this dance now. Talk to you in a bit."

"Alright, bye." Ziri hangs up just as I enter the motel. The teenager is there again, smacking gum and filing her nails, with her feet propped on the desk. Her makeup skills are flawless, but the color choice is so dark it just makes her look a little scary. I smile at her as I walk down the hall and enter my room. I open my suitcase and pull out my red feathered and tulle dress.

My heart leaps as I hold the dress against my body. Tonight is going to be amazing. I look back down into the suitcase and notice a plastic bag under the dress. Inside is a ton of makeup and a note. *Gotta hide all of those blemishes, P.* I scour at the note and crumple it. *What a jerk,* I think as I feel a small smile forming on my lips. I look back into the bag and see foundation, highlighter, primer, and concealer, and I realize I don't know how to use any of it. I can do a simple brush of mascara and swipe of lip gloss, but the rest is all new to me. After I fall back onto the bed, I stare at the stained ceiling. I have three hours to get ready. The shoes and the dress I have, but not the face. And I want to go to this dance feeling like a million bucks. For all I know, it could be my last one.

After the . . . event with Seth, I've been feeling anything but pretty. I feel like an imposter in my own skin, and I hate it. When I look in the mirror again, I don't want to see "that girl," the weak, naive girl who barely managed to get free. I want to see the strong woman I know I am, that I know I can be. Suddenly, I have an idea. I lunge for my wallet and pull out ten bucks, fling open the room door, and sprint down the hall.

"I have ten dollars," I say to the teen girl as I slam it on the table. She looks up from her nails and at me.

"And?" she asks, smacking her gum again.

"There's this dance tonight, and I want you to do my makeup. I have all the stuff already," I say, sliding the ten dollars closer to her. She takes her feet off the desk and sits up straight.

"Me?" she asks, confused.

"Your makeup skills are flawless, and, as for me, I can only do the basics. I really need your help," I say, beginning to sound desperate. She looks me up and down, and I notice her features softening. She smiles at me.

"My shift ends in fifteen minutes. Order some Japanese hibachi steak for me, and get a movie from Redbox. Do you know how you want your hair styled?" she asks, eyeing my mess of twists, some having already untwisted themselves.

"Uh, maybe a twist-out?" I say, my hands flying to my head. She chuckles.

"I have some ideas. When do you have to be ready by?"

"I'm being picked up at seven," I reply. She looks at her watch.

"Fuck, three hours? Girl, you better be on your way and order that food if you want to be ready in time." A grin spreads across my face.

"Thank you, thank you so much!" I say, sprinting to my room.

I am just putting in the movie *Spiderman* when I hear a knock on the door. I open it to see the girl, but she looks totally different. Her dark hair is in a simple braid that rests on her shoulder. The edgy clothes that she was wearing before are gone, replaced with a peach cami and jeans. I must have been staring because she clears her throat, snapping me back to reality. I step aside, letting her in.

"My name is Stephanie, by the way," she says, walking straight to the food, dropping her stuff, and sitting cross-legged on my bed. I follow her footsteps and sit on the bed across from her. "You have to eat first," she says between bites, "so that you don't mess up the makeup." I nod in response as I open my box. My stomach grumbles as I look at the steaming teriyaki chicken, rice, and vegetables. I didn't realize I was this hungry, and I shovel down my food eagerly.

"My name is Ruby," I say after a while. I was so hungry that I forgot to introduce myself. "You look different . . . the nice kind of different," I say, pointing out the obvious. "Not that you didn't look nice before!" I ramble. She sighs and sets her food beside her, leaning back on her elbows.

"The whole bitch facade is something I just keep up when I work. That way people won't bother me. I told you, people come here to do crazy shit, and I have no interest in that." She shrugs, grabbing her food again. "That person, h er *personality*, that's not me. But she does keep me safe. Her armor does too." She picks at her food and sighs again, looking up to meet my eyes. "The pay is good, like really good, eighteen dollars an hour. So I stay." I nod, understanding her situation. We eat in more silence until she gets up and throws her stuff away, taking a sip of her Pepsi. "Gulp it down, Ruby. I've got work to do."

"Right," I say, shoveling down the rest of my food and chugging my own drink. I run to the bathroom and wash my hands.

"Wash your face while you're at it." I do as she says and shake my hands dry while I jog out of the bathroom. She cleared one of the beds, and my red dress is on it with my heels right beside it. "Damn girl," she says as she sees me come out of the bathroom. "You're gonna be a fine ass bitch tonight." I grin in response and run over to turn on the movie.

The first thing Stephanie does is throw a sheet on a mirror, banning me from seeing my reflection until my transformation is complete. As she does my face, she explains what each product is and how to use it. We talk about life, and it turns out, she goes to the same school Emerald does. She tells me all the school gossip and all her dreams and wishes. She wants to be a hair stylist after high school, and she's waiting for a response from one of the beauty schools she applied to. She pulls out her phone and shows me her Instagram page. It's full of herself and random people with different styles of nails, hair, and makeup. She's even more talented than I thought. She complains to me how everyone at her school is fake, and that I am the first real person who she's met in a while. *How ironic.*

A couple of hours after laughing, nail filing, make-up brushing, and hair styling, I'm done. As I admire my long ruby red nails, Stephanie takes pictures on her phone, zooming in on my hands. My pointer and ring fingers on both my hands are glittery with red sparkles. The middle fingers are in a French tip style with a white flower off-center in the middle of the nail, and the top of the nails are red. My pinkies look exactly like my middle finger but without the white flower. Instead, small red rhinestones snake from my cuticle to the tip of my nail. My thumbs are nude on my nail bed and extend to clear acrylic, sprinkled with small red sparkly butterflies. The nails are the perfect length, where I can still manage my surroundings easily.

"These are beautiful! Thank you so much, Stephanie!" I say, reaching to pull her into a hug, but she stops me.

"Let's get you in your dress and shoes first. Then I'll snap some pictures of you. And *then* a hug."

"But—" I start.

"No buts. Your date will be here in fifteen minutes," she reminds me, ushering me up. Stephanie helps me put the dress on, making sure to not mess up my face and hair. "Done," she says, grabbing her phone. With a quick look around the room, she sighs. "This room is a mess. I can't take pictures here." She taps her finger on her phone case, thinking. Suddenly, she brightens. "Come with me." I follow her out of the room and up flights of stairs as fast as I can. She opens the door to the roof and ushers me outside. Soft floodlights stream onto the roof, giving us the perfect lighting.

"Wow," I say, turning around in circles. The sky is a beautiful shade of orange, pink, and purple, and in the distance, we see downtown. The streetlights are on, too, giving us the perfect background. "I think this is the prettiest part about this motel." I smile.

"I know. I come up here to clear my mind sometimes." She looks at her watch. "Come on. We don't have much time." She points where she wants me to stand and snaps nearly fifty pictures, all from different angles. I do a variety of poses, spinning and laughing. When she turns on the flash, my heart plummets as I flash back to Seth's room. *Another photoshoot, but not another mistake.* Shaking off my nerves, I strain a smile, reinforcing my mental wall. It seems like it is taking forever when she finally puts her phone away. "Alright, let's go."

We run down the stairs, me being careful not to ruin my curls. When we make it back to my room, I give her my number so she can send me the pictures. "Don't post them until tomorrow please," I say, my legs bouncing with anxiety. "I don't want people from school seeing it until after they see me, and don't at m e."

"No problem. You're looking like pure fire tonight," she says, reminding me that I still have no idea what I look like. I walk up to the mirror Stephanie had covered with a sheet and rip it off. I can barely recognize the person staring back at me. Her lips are a full, deep red. Her eyes are big and bright, and her cheeks are slightly rosy. The weirdest part is that her lips are mine. Her eyes are mine. Her *face* is mine.

My hair is in six parts going around my head and one in the middle. In each, there's a feed-in style braid that ends about one-third of the way to the back of my head. The entire back is loose, my curls bouncing at my shoulders.

I reach down and grab my glasses, putting them on. For the past few days, I've felt like a shell of my former self. But now, I'm starting to feel like myself again. I'm reminded that I am capable. That I am *that bitch.* I thought what happened with Seth would take that away forever, but it didn't. I feel confident, powerful, amazing, like I can do anything in the world. I feel beautiful. What happened to me, happened to me, but it doesn't have to define me.

"Wow." I breathe. I turn around and find Stephanie recorded the whole reveal. I run over to her and wrap her in a hug. "Thank you so much," I say, squeezing her tightly, trying not to let my grateful tears slip from my eyes.

"Anytime, Ruby," she says, returning the hug. I realize this girl who I thought was a complete bitch is one of the nicest people I have ever known. A rush of shame runs through me.

"Sadly, this will be a one and done thing." I pull away and head to my wallet. For everything she's done for me, ten dollars is dirt cheap. I pull out three one-hundred-dollar bills from my dream and fold them in my hands.

"Why? You're just going to a dance," she asks, confused. I walk back to her and hand her the money.

"Oh," I say, stepping back and sitting on the bed. "I'm leaving this weekend. I have to go back to Ohio," I explain. "Here, giving you ten dollars for your work would be a shame." Her jaw drops as she stares at my hands.

"Ruby, I can't accept—" she starts, but I interrupt her.

"Take it. I appreciate you." I place the bills in her hand and fold her hand closed. She accepts it gratefully.

"Dang, why do all the good ones have to leave," she says, sitting down on the bed across from me. "Thank you." She holds up the money. "It was really nice meeting you, and if you ever need makeup tips or a place to stay in Tennessee, you know who to call." I laugh and start to say something when someone knocks at the door. "Looks like your Prince Charming is here, princess!" she exclaims, walking up to open the door. "Go to the bathroom. His reaction when you reveal your new look will be priceless, and I have to get that on camera." I nod and scurry into the bathroom just as she opens the door. When I hear his voice, my stomach becomes a bundle of nerves.

"Oh, hey," Emerald says.

"Hi, Ruby's in the bathroom," Stephanie replies. "She should be out soon." I take that as my cue to step out. Taking a couple of deep breaths, I open the door. When Emerald sees me, his jaw goes slack. I glance at Stephanie, and she has her phone out, recording the whole encounter.

"How do I look?" I ask, doing a little twirl. His jaw is still dropped as he takes in the whole sight of me.

"Like a gem," he says, standing up. "Ruby, you look amazing." I smile at him. Thoughts of Zach flood my brain, taking me by surprise. I wish that he got to see me like this. If he looked at me the way Emerald is looking at me right now, in complete awe, I think I'd melt. Emerald's look makes me do something else though: fill with pride.

"Let me get a picture of the two of you," Stephanie says. "Not in here though. How about outside?" I grab my purse, peeking inside to make sure my wallet, room key, phone, and knife are in there, then follow Emerald and Stephanie out of the door. We stand facing the motel so the light from it can illuminate our faces. Emerald wraps his arm around my waist, and I wrap mine around his. He's a good half a foot taller than me, so I have to stretch a little. Stephanie snaps a few photos, then puts her hands on her hips. "Well, if you two aren't the hottest couple of the night, I don't know who is." I grin and run over to give her another hug.

"Thank you, for everything," I say.

"I'll text you the pictures tonight," she whispers in my ear. I step back and walk toward Emerald. "You two have fun. Just not too much fun, if you know what I mean." My face heats up, and words start tumbling out of my mouth.

"Don't worry, we won't. Ever. I mean, we will have fun. We just won't do what you are insinuating . . . Let's go Emerald or we'll be late. Bye, Stephanie." I wave. Stephanie is bent over in a fit of laughter as she tries to wave back. I bite back my own grin and link elbows with Emerald. "How are we getting to school?" I ask.

"My car," he says, stopping in front of a black car.

"Your car?" I say, gaping at it. "I didn't know that you could drive." I open the door on the passenger side and step in.

"My mom likes being in control of my performing business and insists on driving me to my gigs." He starts the car.

"You're lucky to have such a good mom."

"I know," he admits, driving toward the school.

"I never really had a mom. I thought she died in a plane crash. And I was raised by my stepmom who pretty much fit the fairy tale role," I grumble, staring out of the window.

"Thought?" I turn to Emerald. His knuckles are white on the wheel.

"What?"

"You said you thought your mom died in a plane crash. Does that mean that she's still alive?" *Shoot!* Emerald is looking at me now. I don't know how I'm gonna explain that trip up.

"Ummm," I say, looking away and back to the street. "*Emerald, stop!*" I yell. He slams on the brakes, nearly hitting a family crossing the street.

"Shit!" He runs his hands through his braids.

"What the fuck kid!" says the man I assume to be the father.

"I-I'm s-s-so sorry," Emerald stutters out.

The man reaches for his kids and wife, turns back to Emerald, lifts his middle finger, and says, "Go to fucking Hell, you son of a bitch." I'm frozen in my seat. The family makes it across the street and walks into a restaurant. Emerald is as pale as a ghost. He doesn't even notice when the light turns green.

"The light, Emerald," I whisper. He looks up and tightens his grip on the wheel. We drive in silence until we make it to the school. He parks and leans forward, resting his forehead on the wheel. "Are you okay?" I ask him.

"I fucking almost killed a family. Why the hell would I be okay?" he says, harder than I anticipated. I shrink away.

"Sorry," I mumble, scooching as far away from him as possible, trying not to make it too obvious that his yelling got to me. He sighs and lifts his head, dragging his hand across his cheek.

"Fuck, Ruby. I'm sorry. I screwed up. I didn't mean to yell at you. I just, I j-just can't believe that almost h-happened. I'm a good person. I'm a good person," he whispers repeatedly under his breath. A wave of concern rushes over me, and I place my hand on top of his. He looks up to meet my eyes.

"You *are* a good person. They're okay. We're okay. Don't dwell on what could have happened. It's all over now. Nobody got hurt." I smile at him. "Let's just go inside and have a fun time, okay?" I have no idea how I am supposed to drop the bomb that we are family, but now doesn't seem like a good time.

"You're right. Thanks, Ruby." I squeeze his hand and smile at him.

"Let's go," I say, stepping out of the car.

CHAPTER 21

School dances in Ohio are nothing like the school dances in Tennessee, I think. The school is transformed into everything I would imagine Hollywood to be like. The concrete leading up to the school is covered in stars, each with names on them. Everyone is dressed in their best. The school even hired photographers to act as paparazzi, ambushing innocent friend groups with their yells and flashing lights.

This is going to be fun.

We walk through the entry hall which looks normal. Emerald slips his hand in mine and looks down at me smiling. I smile up at him.

"Pretty cool, huh?" he says, staring into my eyes. Against my better judgment, I blush.

"Yeah. Even if you didn't ask me, I doubt you would have said this was stupid." I laugh and tug at my dress gently with my free hand.

"Let's agree to disagree," he affirms, giving my hand a slight squeeze. As we near the end of the hall, the music gets louder, and I notice color-changing lights. When we step into what once was the cafeteria, there's a DJ on a stage at the front of the room, blasting some sort of remix. Hundreds of sweaty teens jump and dance to the music, forming a large, and continuously growing, mosh pit.

"Wow!" I spin around in a circle, taking in the sight. "This is wild." I turn to face Emmy. His face is full of admiration. "What?" He shakes his head and smiles at me.

"Let's dance!" He grabs my hand and pulls me toward the crowd.

"Wait!" I say, trying to plant my feet into the ground. "We can just dance out here."

"It'll be more fun in there, trust me." He gives my arm one final tug, and I stop resisting. Pushing his way through the crowd, he reaches the dead center, grabs both of my hands, and jumps up and down. I follow his lead, laughing and smiling as I jump to the beat. He keeps his eyes on me the whole time. Such innocence and blissful happiness. How am I going to tell him that everything in his whole life started from a lie? We dance for what seems like hours. Fast songs, slow songs, and boring songs. I go on my tip toes and yell into his ear.

"Can we go sit down? My feet are killing me!" He grins and nods, pulling my hand as he weaves me out of the crowd, which is no easy feat.

"Where do you want to go?" he asks, eyeing the edge of the cafeteria for open seats. I do the same, finding none.

"We can go over there." I point to an empty hall at the edge of the lunchroom and lead the way. Compared to the other room, the hall is nice and cool. I can actually feel the air conditioner. I lean my head against the lockers and breathe in. The air is fresh and clean in my lungs, not a hint of sweaty teen in its scent.

"Emmy," I say, turning to face him. But before I can say anything, his lips are against mine, and he's pressing me up against the lockers. All rationale leaves my brain, and I'm trapped. I can't think, or see, or hear as his lips dance over my frozen ones. *Who is this? Seth.* My mind is rushing, trying to comprehend what is happening. *Not Seth, Emerald.* This. Is. My. *Brother!*

"Stop!" I say, coughing and wiping my lips. Emerald chuckles uncomfortably, fidgeting with one of his dangly braids.

"Wow, was I that bad?" He looks sad and nervous.

"Yes! I mean no! It was fine, but that's besides the point!" I say, talking with my hands and wanting to gag. "I—we . . . this," I say, pointing between us, "can't happen." He takes a step closer, playing with the tulle of my skirt.

"But it seems so right," he says, leaning in again. I move my hand to cover his mouth.

"Stop talking. Just stop." He sighs and takes a step back.

"Ruby, I thought we were having a moment." He frowns, looking away from me.

"We were. I mean we did . . . but not the moment you think." I sigh and put my face in my hands.

I can do this.

Crap.

Fuck.

"Emmy, there's something I have to tell you, and it's not going to be easy to hear. But I just need you to listen and not interrupt, okay?" He turns back to look at me.

"Let me guess, you just want to be friends? Yeah, I've heard that before," he says, cracking his knuckles.

"Nah. We're already more than friends," I say, sliding down the lockers until I reach the floor. His eyes brighten, and I hurry to clarify. "But not in the relationship way," I explain. Emerald moves to sit next to me, chuckling.

"So, what's in between that, Ruby?" He puts his elbow on his knee and leans forward to look at me.

"Family?" I whisper.

"Yeah, okay, and how is that supposed to work?" I look at him, then down at my feet, then up at him again.

"Because . . . you're my brother," I breathe out. He freezes, looking at me, confused. Then he bursts out laughing.

"Ruby, are you high or something?"

"Okay, okay, just listen. Let me explain. You're adopted right? Yeah, well, me too. I can guess where you were adopted from, too, Ohio. Am I wrong?" He looks away from me. "You're seventeen, just like me! So you must have been on the plane that our parents died on."

"Ruby, that doesn't mean—"

"Shh, I'm not done." I grab his hand and pull off his ring.

"Ruby, what the fuck?" I pull out my ruby necklace and show him.

"See, Ruby has a ruby, and Emerald has an emerald." He just blinks at me. I look down. I really should have practiced this more. "I know you can't do your magic show without this," I say, holding the ring up between my fingertips. "You say it's your good luck charm, but you've almost died when you weren't wearing it. Am I wrong?" He looks away. He *knows.* "It's your power. Your gift. All of our siblings have one." His head whips back at me.

"Siblings? As if what you're saying is true, they're more people like me?" he asks, rubbing his ring finger on his right hand.

"Like us," I reply, holding my ruby and closing my eyes. Emerald's eyes widen.

"Fuck. Ruby, what the fuck did you just do?" He backs away from me, looking around the hallway wildly. "Ruby, shit, where are you? What—"

"Emerald," I say softly, channeling all my energy to make myself visible, but slowly, that way he can watch me appear. It takes a lot more concentration than I thought, and by the time I'm fully visible, I'm slightly light-headed. He jumps and presses himself against the lockers.

"What . . . what—"

"You aren't normal, Emerald. *We* aren't normal," I try to explain. I reach my hand out to rest on his shoulder, but he jerks away. "You have to come back to Ohio with me. You have a family who wants to meet you. Who wants to love you." He widens his eyes again before turning from me, making his way down the hall.

"Shit."

"Emerald—"

"Shit," he says, tugging at his hair. He breaks into a run.

"Emerald, you can't tell anyone this!" I say, running after him "Emerald!" I yell. He stops and turns to face me. He snatches the ring from my hand and turns away from me without another word.

I let him leave. There is no way I'll be able to get through to him if he's in denial. I thought I explained it well. I think back to our conversation; things went better toward the end, but the beginning was rocky. I press on the earpiece to call Ziri.

"Give me some good news, Ruby."

"I told him."

"Damn, Ruby, that's some great news! Where is he? Can I talk to him?"

"Umm, he didn't really take it well . . . He just ran away."

"Ruby, you gotta follow him!" Ziri responds urgently.

"But—"

"Ruby, go!" I sigh as Ziri hangs up on me. I make my way to the front of the school, smiling and waving at my new friends. I peek out the glass doors and see Emerald pacing back and forth in front of his car, talking urgently into his phone. As students leave, the paparazzi ambushes them. I can't draw attention to myself just yet. I turn invisible and go straight to Emerald. I find him pacing by his car anxiously.

"Emerald," I say, making myself visible as I walk into the light. He turns and faces me, hangs up the phone, and walks to me. "I told you not to tell anyone, Emmy."

"I know. I didn't tell details. I just needed to . . . I don't know. I'm sorry I ran out like that," he apologizes, tugging on his hair. I chuckle.

"You're gonna pull out all of your hair if you keep that up." We both stop walking when we're standing face-to-face. "There's so much more you need to know." I reach for his hand. He takes mine, hesitantly. "I know this is hard to hear," I say looking down. "It was hard for me too." I slowly look up to meet his eyes. "But we need you. Our parents need us." He squints his eyes in confusion and nods. I'm about to hug him when cameras start going off suddenly. I shield my eyes. The paparazzi.

"Let's get out of here," Emerald says, tugging me back toward his car. When we're safe inside, he starts the car. "Okay, where to?"

"My place," I say as I pull out my phone and call Ziri back.

"Give me some good news, Ruby," she repeats. I can hear her typing away on her keyboard.

"We'll be at the hotel in a couple of minutes, and then we can—" I say, interrupting myself to glance at Emerald, "work on phase two," I finish, turning away from him and looking out of the window. I feel Emerald's eyes on me, but I ignore it. Maybe I should have waited to call back home . . .

"Yeah . . ." Ziri says, her voice trailing off. "I'm searching up flights. Aha, Garnet will get on the first plane out. She'll be there by tomorrow morning. Tell Emerald to meet you at the motel tomorrow at 10."

"Okay, thanks, Ziri," I say, then hang up and lay my phone in my lap. Emerald shifts uncomfortably.

"Was that—?" he starts, unable to finish.

"Yeah, Ziri. She's our little sister," I say, not knowing exactly where to look.

"Oh, cool," he says, tightening his grip on the steering wheel. This atmosphere is completely different from the one on the car ride to the school. This one seems heavier, more tense. "So when do we start? Next month?" he asks, and I cringe, turning my face toward the window.

"Try tomorrow morning," I whisper. Emerald sucks in a quick breath.

"To-tomorrow?" he asks quietly.

"Time isn't a luxury we have, unfortunately." He pulls into the parking lot and parks the car. I decide to tell him everything and go into detail about the First Twelve and how our parents have been kidnapped and tortured for years. I explain how our uncle is behind everything and has a powerful unknown ability, something we'll probably only be able to defeat if we have the numbers for it. "You have to pack your things tonight . . . and say your goodbyes."

"My goodbyes? Ha, you make it sound like I'll never see my family and friends again," he says, chuckling. I turn away from him as a tear of guilt falls down my face.

"It's because you won't," I say softly. I feel him freeze and the car grow colder.

"What?" he asks, his voice cracking. I thought it was hard when I died. It's even harder telling someone they will. I think back to the days that led up to my death day. I was lucky and had more time. Time to plan, to pack, to make my last memories. I sigh.

"I'm going to call Ziri back. I can stall the inevitable until Monday maybe, but then we have to go," I say, turning back toward him. I watch his face turn emotionless. "It's not fair of me to ask you to do this. It wasn't fair of Ziri not to give you more time. She's just . . . stressed. I'm stressed. I don't—" I say, choking on incoming tears. "I don't know what's going on, I don't know if our situation has gotten better." I wipe my eyes and unbuckle my seatbelt. "I do know that seven hours for you to say goodbye is not right." He's silent for a long time. I stay and wait. I can't leave him like this.

"What's going to happen? Like, how is this going to work?" he asks. I am about to look away from him again, but I stop myself. I take a deep breath and build up my confidence as I turn my whole body to face him.

"You're going to die."

CHAPTER 22

Tomorrow morning, Emerald dies. I met up with him yesterday with all of his friends . . . our friends. I told them how I was heading back to Ohio, and we reminisced about my time here. Emerald was visibly sad. As we walked through town, I pulled him aside.

"I don't mean to sound like a jerk, Emerald. But this is your last time to make memories that will last a lifetime, and you need to take advantage of that. Don't throw it away." I reached for his hand and squeezed it. "I just went through this a couple of weeks ago. I know it's hard." He sniffed. "But—"

"This is evil, you know that?" he said, straightening his back. "Pure evil." He wiped his eyes and took a deep breath right before running up to his friends and throwing his arms around their laughing shoulders.

I go to the bathroom and brush my teeth. Dying was hard, and I'm just happy I won't have to do it again. Well, at least, I hope so. When I'm done, I grab my phone and head to bed. I snuggle deep underneath the covers and set my alarm for the morning. After sending Emerald a quick text reminding him of tomorrow's plan, I put my phone down, turn off the lamp, and close my eyes for some much-needed sleep.

I'm back at home sitting on the porch steps, waiting for the bus that will bring a reborn Emerald. A wave of guilt rushes through me, and I put my head in my hands. I took an earlier flight this morning, so I wasn't there with him when he died. But I should have been.

"Don't be too hard on yourself, Ruby," Moon says, coming up from behind me.

"I should have *been* there." I drag my hands down my face. "When I died, I had you with me, Moon. He . . ." I say, rubbing my eyes and pushing myself off the ground. "He had no one." Moon stays silent. I realize I haven't seen her in days, and the first thing I do is complain about my problems and mistakes. I shake off my self-disappointment and put on a small smile. "So how was New York?" Her eyes brighten up. It seems like things are finally on their way back to normal between us, and that comfort alone washes away my current self-loathing.

"Oh my God, Ruby, I wish you were there. So you remember how Jasper is a basketball player right?" she asks, moving closer to me. I don't remember, but I nod anyway. "Well, if it was, y'know, basketball *season*, my job would have been so much easier, but nope. It was straight out of a movie. It was crazy." She smiles wider.

"What was crazy?" says a voice behind us. We both flip our heads, and Moon squeals, running over to him.

"Jasper!" she says, resting her elbow on his head. "Ruby, this is Jasper." For someone who is supposed to play basketball, he is extremely small. Moon is even taller than him, and she is the shortest person I know . . . Well, she was.

"It's nice to meet you, Jasper," I say, coming over to shake his hand. He's obviously shy. He inches closer to Moon, but she gives him a little nudge. Warily, he reaches out to shake my hand.

"He's shy," Moon says, rustling his hair of twists. He whacks her hands away.

"Yeah, and what's so bad about that?" he asks, shaking his hair back to place.

"Nothing, except that you hide your fantastic and hilarious self! Don't worry, Ruby. Just wait until he breaks out of his shell." Moon goes to rustle his hair again, but he quickly dodges her, remaining in the shadows. When I meet his eyes, he gives me a small smile. I smile back as he studies me quietly. His eyes roam every feature, every bone structure of mine. It's not in a cynical way though, more . . . thoughtful, tactical. It still gives me creepy vibes, so when a car horn goes off that gathers all our attention, I silently thank Garnet for her impeccable timing.

The bus that once carried my lifeless body pulls up the driveway and parks. Emerald, Garnet, and Tani hop out, but my eyes are immediately drawn to Emmy. He's sluggish with his movement, clearly still weak from dying. I make a mental note to ask him how he is when we're alone.

"Need any help?" asks Moon, starting to head over to the bus. I follow close behind her, but Jasper doesn't move. He's now staring at Emerald, his eyes full of interest.

"Yeah, we have a bit to unload. Tani, Emerald was the last one, right?" Garnet asks as she pulls a duffel bag out from the storage compartment at the bottom of the bus. Tani nods, grabbing another duffel bag. Moon and I each grab one, while Emerald flexes and carries three. "Well then, I think it's about time for our first family reunion."

After dropping off Emerald's things in his room, we all head to the tree. I slow my pace to walk beside Emmy and hesitantly touch his hand.

"You okay?" I ask softly. He sighs.

"No, but I will be." When we get to the tree, I see confusion all over his face, and when Garnet pulls the root, opening the door, his jaw drops.

"You'll get used to it," I say, smiling and nudging him inside. When we make it to the "conference" room, there's a bunch of kids sitting around the table. Many of them are familiar faces, but I catch a lot of new ones too. The room goes silent as we take our seats. Garnet doesn't sit, though. She remains standing, all eyes on her. Her eyes are sparkling, and I can tell she's happy, really happy.

"Here are words I never thought I would be able to say so soon: Hi family." She smiles, her eyes meeting each and every one of her siblings. "I knew mom and dad the longest. Although I was little, I remember their love and mom's pregnant belly with one of you ready to come into the world. Looking at all of you now, I know that they would be proud, no, that they *are* proud.

"I know that we've all just met, and for many of you, this is literally flipping your world upside down. But I'm here for you—*we* are here for you. All of us have gone or are going through the exact same things you are feeling: confusion, fear, hope. We're all in this together, and it's about time you know exactly what *this* is.

"But first, we should all meet each other and trust each other because, right now, we're all we have." I look around and see nods and smiles spread across the room. "So I'll start. I'm Garnet. I'm twenty. It doesn't matter where I'm from. It just matters that I'm here now. My ability is petrification. So, basically, I'm Medusa." Tiny gasps erupt throughout the room. "But relax, it's only if I touch your heart with my hands. As long as I'm wearing these," she says, holding up her gloved hands and wiggling her fingers, "you guys are safe." She gives us all one last happy smile then sits down.

Tani and Ziri stand up, as well as this girl I've never seen before. Although her face is stained with tears and she has no meat on her bones, she's one of the most beautiful people I've ever laid my eyes upon. Her loose curls are styled in a half up, half down wash-and-go, and her face has perfect bone structure. But the most intriguing thing about her is her eyes. They're green. I've never seen green eyes on a Black person before, and it's a little eerie how natural it looks.

"Hi, I'm Tanzanite. This is Zircon, and this is Turquoise." Ziri gives everyone a huge smile, but Turquoise only gives a small wave. "You can just call us Tani, Ziri, and Turq. We're sixteen. My ability is enhanced intelligence. I basically know the answer to every question, I'm super great at strategy, and I have a photographic memory." She grins, giving everyone a wink. She nudges Ziri to go next, still smiling happily.

"I'm technopathic. Electronics are my life. I can control them as well as use them to my benefit. And with Tani's help, I can invent some really awesome things. I've lived in Connecticut my whole life . . ." Ziri pauses as her eyes go distant. She shakes her head quickly. "Then I found Tani and Garnet found me. It's a long story for another time." She looks toward Turq and reaches for her hand, giving it a slight squeeze. She's crying again. Everyone but Garnet and her triplets seem to be confused. When she speaks, her voice is quiet and weak.

"I had a mom and dad who loved me." The room goes dead silent. "We lived in Arizona until I was about eight. I loved Arizona." A faint smile crosses her face, and she stares off into the distance. Then she bites her lips and squeezes her eyes shut, tears pouring down her face. "My dad got transferred to a new work position in Georgia. It was so pretty there . . ." She sniffs, rubbing her eyes. "When we got there, I always felt pain, *so* much pain. It was like hitting your hip on the edge of a table, over and over, in the same spot, but all over my body. My parents took me to the emergency room the first night, but the doctors didn't know what was wrong with me. They asked my parents if anything recently happened in my life that was traumatic. They told them that we had just moved there, so I was diagnosed as being homesick. I tried to tell them I felt pain, but I could barely talk or move. And the screams . . ." Chills run through my spine. "I heard screaming all the time, cries of help." She lets go of Ziri's hand and rubs her right wrist. "When months went by and I never changed, my dad suggested taking me to a psych ward. He thought it might help me. When my mom finally agreed and we went to the ward, the moment I stepped inside, the horrible pain became tolerable. I could talk, move, laugh, and smile again, but as soon as I left, it started up again.

"Soon, my parents got me a room in the ward. The walls were white. The floors were white. But I got to keep my green bed sheets. My parents hired a tutor for me, and I stayed there. They would visit me every day," she's smiling again, "until my mom got pregnant. When the baby was born, the visits turned to every week, soon, once a month, and then, finally, they stopped coming all together." Her smile disappears, and she rubs her wrists faster. "The, um, nurses told me that my dad lost his job and couldn't pay for me to stay there anymore, so my parents gave up custody of me." Ziri reaches out to still Turquoise's hand. "I ran away, moved back to Arizona with some money they left me, and everything was so much better," she explains sadly. "My ability is ecological empathy. Basically, I feel everything that plants feel. I can control them, and even cast part of myself into one. But, living in a psych ward for six years, I can't control it. There's a way to stop it, but I can't. It's . . . it's just constant *pain*."

All the pieces click together. Turquoise is being tortured by her ability. I can't even fathom how hard her life must have been. The three sit down quietly.

"I found out what was really happening to me when I got here. Tani explained that it was because I always wore jewelry with real turquoise in it that my parents had bought me. But even when I take them off now, the pain is dulled, but I can still hear the screams." Turq leans her head against Ziri's shoulder, and Ziri combs a soothing hand through her curls. The other's stories are not as tragic as Turq's.

Aquamarine and Jade are eleven-year-old twins and polar opposites. Jade is loud, and Aqua is quiet. They both are telekinetic and telepathic.

Sapphire, Peri, Emerald, and Citrine share their powers to the group, siren song, claircognizance, escape artistry, and fire, respectively. They are followed by Citrine's twin, Topaz, who can control water.

"Hi. My name is Opal. I use they/them pronouns, and—" Opal starts, but Citrine interrupts.

"They/them pronouns? What does that mean?" she asks, cocking her head at Opal. Garnet sends her a glare, but it softens immediately with recognition. Genuine confusion and curiosity are on Citrine's face, and it makes sense. She doesn't really get to go out into the world and meet new people or stay up-to-date on how our society is evolving. Tani opens her mouth to explain, but Opal starts before she can.

"You know how there are boys and there are girls?" they explain. Citrine nods. "Well, I don't really identify with either."

"Identify?"

"Yeah. I don't always feel like a boy. I don't always feel like a girl. Sometimes, I feel like neither or both, and other times, I feel like something in between," Opal says, a soft smile on their face.

"But I thought we couldn't pick. We can pick?" Citrine asks, leaning in. Opal nods.

"Yep," they say, their features glowing. Atop their head are thick silver curls, the back and sides shaved.

"So if I feel like a girl, I can be a girl. But if I feel like a boy, then I can change?" With another nod, Citrine slightly leans back, slouching comfortably in her seat. "Well, I want to still be a girl. I like me like that." At that, we all chuckle a bit, continuing with our introductions.

Opal, Tourmaline, and Jasper are triplets, each having their own ability of mimicry. Opal can morph and communicate with animals, Tourmaline can mimic others' powers, and Jasper can shape-shift into both animate and inanimate objects.

The next pair of triplets catch me off guard. Moonstone is a triplet, with Alexandrite and Pearl. Pearl can teleport, Alex has super speed, and Moon can manipulate gravity: levitation.

Of all my siblings' powers, I think I envy Amethyst's or Diamond's the most. Amethyst has elasticity and Diamond has prehensile hair. Her black hair is in braided pigtails, and one of the strands is writing rapidly on a piece of paper. *Smart.* I should have been writing all this down. I don't know how I'm going to remember everyone's names, let alone their abilities. To be honest, I don't know how everyone even got here. More than half of the new names that were introduced I hadn't heard of until today. Ziri and Garnet must have put a rush on things while I was gone.

Listening to their stories, the majority of my siblings were in the foster care system or children's homes, not all of them in the best condition. People can disappear quickly and easily with the right motivation and tools. And, boy, do we have that.

What I'm most confused about is how everyone knows what they can do already. I make a mental note to ask Garnet later. Suddenly, it's my turn, and I nibble my lip, pushing myself out of my seat.

"Hi, everyone. I'm Ruby. I came here a couple of weeks ago and used to live just down the street all of my life. I can turn invisible." I do a quick display of my power, disappearing for only a few seconds before returning visible again. "Oh, and I'm seventeen," I say before I sit back down. I felt like my Cinderella story of a life wasn't something that needed to be shared. Everyone only shared information that was necessary for others to know. Unfortunately, that happened to be Turquoise's entire life. For good reason though. Now I know what topics of conversation to avoid while with her.

"There's a lot of us . . ." Opal says, looking between everyone. "A lot of things to keep track of."

"Which is why, hopefully, this will make things easier," Ziri says with a wink. Seconds later, the room erupts with the buzzing and dinging of phones. When I pick mine up, my heart warms, a smile broadening on my face. It's a family group chat.

"Which one of you is the uncivilized heathen with an Android?" Peri asks in disgust, referring to the green bubbles in the group chat. Friendly chuckles sprinkle the room as he and a couple others eye one another. After a few silent moments, Topaz quietly and slowly raises her hand, her face sheepish.

"Sorry," she says in a quiet voice, her cheeks seeming to darken. Peri's face immediately fills with regret, and a small snicker escapes me. He should have known better. Opening the message, I silently commend Ziri on her diligence. She's been doing what I have, just better. I'm still confused on the number of siblings that I didn't know about and am about to ask, but Garnet beats me to talking.

SIBLINGS	AGE	MONTH BORN IN	POWERS
Garnet	20	January	Petrification
Amethyst	18	February	Elasticity
Aquamarine	11	March	Telekinetic Telepaths
Jade	11	March	Telekinetic Telepaths
Diamond	16	April	Prehensile hair
Emerald	17	May	Escape Artistry
Pearl	17	June	Teleportation
Moonstone	17	June	Levitation/gliding
Alexandrite	17	June	Super Speed
Ruby	17	July	Invisibility
Peridot	18	August	Claircognizance
Sapphire	17	September	Siren Song
Opal	13	October	Animal Morphing
Tourmaline	13	October	Power replication
Jasper	13	October	Shape Shifting
Citrine	9	November	Fire manipulation
Topaz	9	November	Water manipulation
Turquoise	16	December	Ecological Empathy
Tanzanite	16	December	Enhanced Intelligence
Zircon	16	December	Technopathy

"Good work, Ziri. Now that the pleasantries are done and over, it's time to get serious," she says. "As you know, we're different. We have a genetic mutation in our DNA that gives us these capabilities. Just like a kid who's allergic to peanuts will have a reaction when they eat or touch one, we have a reaction when we are near or touching our gemstone." She brushes her fingers along her garnet studs. "But we don't need them. Because we thought ourselves to be normal, we never thought to try finding our ability. The stones simply unlocked them for us, starting our 'allergic reaction,'" she says, using air quotes.

She goes on to explain the legend and my dream travel to mom, as well as our short visit with Grandma Adelaide. At the word *grandma*, a handful of my siblings' eyes widen with surprise and curiosity. She defines what's known of the limits of our abilities and the terms of our rapid cell regeneration.

"And this reaction-unlocking of our gene can never be removed, only nurtured and wielded to our benefit. So now, our goal is to have the stones enhance our abilities; we just have to train how to use our powers without them."

"Train for what exactly?" asks Diamond, her hair taking notes rapidly. Garnet's face turns sour, but she continues.

"Our uncle, Bloodstone."

"Bullshit, but continue," Peri chips in from across the table. A few chuckles erupt, and I can't help but smile. This is my *family*. Sisters and brothers who I will learn more about and love more than I already do now. Garnet erases these thoughts away when I catch her glaring at Peri.

"Bloodstone's ability is muscle and blood manipulation, and he wants to use that to take over the world." Everyone goes silent, even Peri. I look around the room and see a mixture of emotions from my siblings: confusion, fear, and disbelief. I'm glad I'm not the only one. *How does she know?*

"What? Gar, I thought we were just saving our parents. What the hell are you talking about?" asks Ziri, a mix of confusion and fear written on her face.

"Yeah, I thought so, too, until I found this." Garnet pulls out a worn book and tosses it on the table. Tani reaches for it, flips to a random page, and reads aloud.

"September 15 1997.

Dear Diary,

I've met someone today! Well, I meet people every day of course, but I met a man. A handsome, smart man. I was taking the bus to work and saw him reading Wuthering Heights, *and I just had to talk to him about it. I said something along the lines of 'I absolutely hated that book. I have no idea what happened.' His head shot up and he looked at me, baffled. 'You hated this book? Why? It is so beautifully written.' His voice was so rich and smooth! 'I prefer* Jane Eyre.' *We started a debate on which book was better and continued the conversation all the way to my building! Diary, we work in the same building! We got on the elevator, talking about our favorite classic novels when he had to get off at floor three. Right as the doors were closing, I yelled, 'Wait, what's your name?' 'Alfonso,' he said. Alfonso. Diary, I have more to tell you but I will write it in the morning, it's late.*

Love Rubes."

Tani's jaw drops, and she looks up. "This is mom's old diary?"

Garnet nods. "I found it a couple of days ago at the bottom of some of her old boxes."

"And you didn't think to tell us?" Peri responds, offended.

"I'm telling you now! I thought to wait until we were all here," Garnet defends.

"What does this have to do with Bloodstone?" Ziri asks, still confused.

"Flip to the last page." Tani does as Garnet says and continues reading aloud.

"January 6 2005.

Dear Diary,

I went to go check on my brother today. I haven't heard from him in a while. So, I hopped in the car and drove to Pennsylvania. When I got to his apartment, the door was slightly ajar, and I was terrified. I didn't know what to do, but I knew I had to go in. So I turned invisible and stepped inside. Diary, the place was trashed. There were books everywhere . . . all over the floor. There were plates of leftover food on every table and boxes upon boxes of jewelry. I had a pit of dread in my stomach. Then I heard mumbling in one of the rooms. I tiptoed to it and pressed my hand against the door. I willed the door to become transparent to me. Like a one-way window or mirror or something. I saw B inside. He looked like he hadn't bathed in weeks! He was furiously writing something down in a book. I couldn't see it though. There was this map of the world on his wall with red marker all over it. Major cities like London, New York, Sydney, and Tokyo were circled in red. Then I heard his voice. I think he was talking to a recorder.

'Day 156 of World Domination. My power has been strengthening. I have priceless bloodstone artifacts I've added to my collection that have only helped me grow stronger. My skills have greatly improved. I am now able to control not only the body, but the mind. I've made a child murder his mother and laugh about it. I've robbed a bank by controlling a bank teller. I've convinced people to do things they never would have otherwise. It is awful, but this is my duty. Soon, I'll be able to make the world as it should be. For everyone. Well, except Brian Henry, Jr. I will make your life a living hell for everything you put me through.'

I don't remember when I started crying, I don't remember when I started moving, but I left his apartment so fast. I don't know what to do. I don't know what to do. I don't know what to do. I don't know what to do. I don't know what to do . . ."

"It says that hundreds of times," she mumbles. The room is dead silent. Everyone's eyes are filled with fear. My mind is overloaded with information.

"January 2005. That was right before the supposed plane crash." I look at all the siblings born the same year as me: Emerald, Moon, Pearl, Alex, and Sapphire.

"Okay, so what are you supposed to do?" We turn our heads to see Zach standing by the balcony. In the chaos of things lately, I forgot he was involved. I didn't even know he was here.

"I thought I told you to go home." Peri shoots daggers at Zach.

"Listen. Yes, you have insane abilities, but you're also just kids. If this man can control bodies, people, he can easily control you." Garnet's annoyance at his interruption disappears, and she leans toward him. "Think about it. You find the guy. What are you going to do, kill him? Not before he takes over your minds. If he gets to you, he can use you to take over the world with the bat of an eye. And if he has your parents, maybe that's been his plan all along." My eyes meet Zach's quickly before he looks at Garnet. "Without a well-developed plan, intense training, and a way around his manipulation, you guys are signing your own death sentences." His eyes find mine again. "And I am *not* going to stand by and watch that happen." The room goes silent again.

"He makes an excellent point, Garnet," Tani admits, looking over at her older sister.

"I knew we kept him around for a good reason," Citrine chimes in, attempting to break the tension in the room.

"I'm sorry. I am twenty-four carat confused right now. Who is this guy?" asks Pearl, eyeing Zach as if he's a threat. Pearl is relaxed in her seat. But she still has a way of making herself seem large, intimidating. Her style is a mix of goth and dark academia. She's wearing a light-weight black cropped sweater with ripped black jeans. Her ears are lined with piercings from the lobe to the helix, her nose with a small septum piercing as well. She has a piercing on her left eyebrow, too, an intricate silver-gold piece snaking up and under her brow. Her generously melanated face is expertly coated in dark makeup. Not so much that it is overwhelming, but enough so that it casts a shadowy edge over her mocha skin. Her hair is in dark brown locks, ending where her breasts begin. She sticks her tongue out slightly, revealing a pearl piercing. The amount of jewelry on her face isn't overpowering. It seems to balance well with her features and probably her personality.

"Ruby's friend who accidentally got involved and—" Citrine begins, but Garnet interrupts her. I shrink in my seat.

"Shh, just *shh*! Let me think." Garnet drags her hands through her short hair. Emerald is stiff beside me. I can imagine the wheels turning in his brain, trying to form a means of escape.

"I'm sorry." I interrupt her thoughts. She sighs annoyingly and looks at me. "I'm just a little bit confused. How did everyone else get here?" I gesture toward the unfamiliar names. "I only knew about Jasper, Turquoise, Pearl, Topaz, Diamond, and Emerald."

"I found Pearl in Arizona," explains Tani, a small smile of pride on her face, looking at everyone. "She was doing exactly what we're doing; getting the family together." Pearl readjusts her position and leans against the table lazily.

"Yeah, so when I got to Illinois, she wasn't there . . ." mumbles Sapphire, feigning irritation.

"I grew up with Alex in a foster home in Chicago," Pearl explains, glancing at one triplet. "In school, we had to do this ancestry assignment or whatever. That's when we found out that y'all exist." She gestures to us.

"So we started looking," Alex chimes in quietly. "Pearl and I both have been saving up money to buy a mobile home. Something we can live and travel in. We made plans to buy one soon after learning about you guys." Conversely to Pearl's boldness, Alex is the exact opposite. Her lace wig is a golden dirty blonde, flowing down to the center of her back; A pink fabric headband holds her hair out of her golden bronze face. She has only one piercing in her ears, in which pearly heart earrings dangle. Her makeup is soft. Shades of rouge and neutral tones, simple eyeliner, and plump glossed lips make her seem significantly more approachable than her dark demeanor triplet.

"As for knowing our powers, we found out about them a while ago," explains Pearl. "We didn't have much, but we did have real stones." She winks at us, stretching slightly. When she does, her navel is revealed, unsurprisingly, pierced as well.

"We focused on siblings who wouldn't necessarily be missed. Kids in foster homes like us or living on their own."

"And getting there was easy," she continues as she teleports out of the room. A few seconds later, she returns, an ice cream sandwich in hand. She takes a bite and casually waves her hand in the air. "We had everyone else: Opal, Tourmaline, Aquamarine, Jade, and Amethyst. On my way to getting Turquoise is when I ran into Tanzanite."

"Damn, what are the odds . . . ?" Peri breathes audibly. I'm glad I wasn't the only one confused.

"Yeah, we were really lucky," Tani says.

"And, hopefully, we're done!" Ziri puts her head in her hands.

"For real. Mom and dad were busy as hell." Peri chuckles. Everyone starts mumbling among themselves, and I'm pleasantly surprised Garnet lets them. With my confusion clarified, I think back to everyone and their powers, zooming in on the chart Ziri sent in the family group chat. Suddenly, I have an idea.

"Tory!" I shout, jumping to my feet. The room goes silent. She looks at me, her eyes wide and full of confusion. Her dark skin glows in the sunlight as she looks around intently, the charms in her silver Fulani braids jingling softly. "Tory is how we can win!" I step away from my seat and start pacing, the plan clicking together in my brain. *This can work!*

"Okay, Ruby, use your words," says Peri, and a rush of heat runs through my body.

"Right, yes." I tug at my hair as I pace excitedly. It's in the same style as from the dance since I haven't had a chance to wash it yet. "Tory can mimic others' abilities." I look her directly in the eye. "So we have to train you on Bloodstone's." Her face pales as Tani and Garnet nod slowly in agreement. "If you focus your training on muscle and blood manipulation, you can control Bloodstone! If you can mimic others' abilities, maybe you can suppress them too!" I smile, this really could work. "If he can't control us, we can . . ." I trail off. "What would we do with him?"

"Kill him," says Peri with no remorse. My chest tightens.

"Do we have to kill him? There has got to be some other way," Opal suggests, scratching their head. "Every life has a purpose." Looking toward them, I nod in agreement.

"Yeah, and his life's purpose is death," says Peri. *No, I will not have someone's life be taken because of me.* I go silent. Someone starts to talk, but I hold up a hand and shush them. I feel an idea coming, right on the tip of my brain. I squeeze my eyes shut, and when the idea pops in my head, I open my eyes.

"If our birthstones amplify our powers, there has got to be some sort of stone that does the opposite. That . . . that defuses our abilities." Tani's eyes pop open. "I know that you said that once our gene is activated, that activation can't be removed," I direct at Garnet. "But what if it can? Like something that wants to suppress the gene."

"I think I have an idea of what you mean." She whips out her phone and taps rapidly.

"This would be a great plan," Tory speaks for the first time since she introduced herself, "but I can only mimic powers if I've been exposed to them. I just need to be exposed to them once. The strength that I can manipulate the power is always about 25 percent less than the full power. If this plan was even slightly plausible, I would have to study Bloodstone for at least a week in order to understand the extent of his ability." My face falls. The room goes silent again. Everyone is thinking, planning.

"Maybe we can make that work," says Pearl. Everyone's heads snap in her direction. She snaps a piece of gum in her mouth. "If we know where our uncle is, I can teleport you there, and you can study him."

"Okay, yeah, but he'll see you guys," Garnet counters, but Pearl is ready. She pops her gum again before smiling wickedly.

"Not if Ruby comes with us." She grins. All eyes turn to me, and I shrink in my seat for the second time today. "Can you cast, Ruby?"

"Cast?" I ask.

"It's when you spread your ability to others. Like making us all invisible," Tani explains, clearly liking Pearl's idea.

"I-I've never tried it before."

"Well, just think about it. If we know Bloodstone's location, me, Tory, and Ruby can go back and forth. We can train Tory and gather intel on his plans so that we can pick the perfect time to ambush him." Pearl pounds a fist into her palm. A thoughtful look crosses Garnet's face. "A genius plan, that's what it is." She smirks, proud of herself.

"That—" Garnet starts, nodding her head. "That might just work." Even Tani is nodding.

"It seems like a pretty solid plan. It'll only work if all three of you are completely prepared," Tani says, agreeing with Garnet. She turns toward Ziri. "Do you think you can find his location, hack his emails, and find out as much about him as possible?"

"I'll do my best," Ziri says, getting up to head to the computer room.

"So what do we all do then? They get to have all the fun and we—" Citrine starts. Garnet snaps her head toward her.

"*Fun?* This is not a game, Citrine. This is now a matter of life and death. We not only have to save our parents, but the whole fucking world." Citrine goes quiet and sinks in her seat. Garnet turns her face from her to the rest of our siblings. "And what the rest of us are going to do is develop a concrete and foolproof plan, *and* we are not going to complain about it." She side eyes Citrine. "Every second counts."

CHAPTER 23

I spend the next week and a half training, my only moment of rest being Saturday afternoon to celebrate the October triplet's birthday. Since the weather was nice, they asked for a pizza night backyard party. I tried to relax and have fun, but my lack of progress in my training loomed over me. Casting is much more difficult than I thought. I not only have to focus on making every fiber in my body invisible, but others' too. Luckily, Zach did not hesitate to help me.

"Just breathe, Ruby. Focus."

"Zach, I've been trying for days, and nothing is working! How . . . how am I supposed to do this? I can't do this." I drop to the floor and pull my knees to my chest. "Everyone is counting on me. I can't fail them, Zach. I just can't." I struggle to hold in my tears of frustration, but a couple slip down my face. I quickly wipe them away and let out a sigh. Zach bends down to sit next to me.

"Just remember what Garnet said: '*Let your ability flow like water.*' Let's try again." I growl as he pulls me to my feet. The same pathetic apple that has been haunting me for the past week sits on a pedestal in the training room. "Let your ability flow into the apple."

"You make it sound easy," I huff as I glare at the apple.

"You have to relax, Ruby."

"I am relaxed, Zach! I am chilling. You know, just *chilling.*"

"You sound as if you're boiling," he mumbles, stepping to the back of the room to give me some space.

You can do this, Ruby. Just breathe, relax, breathe, relax, breathe . . . I take in a deep breath and focus on the apple. Making things invisible that I am not directly touching is significantly harder than I thought it would be. Sighing, I close my eyes and picture the red fruit. I erase the stem slowly, followed by the skin, meat, and seeds. I feel a slight pressure against my temple, but I push through. Sweat runs down my face, but I don't dare move. I twitch as it tickles my cheek and neck. *Please be gone, please be gone, please.* I cautiously open my eyes and gasp. The apple's gone. I snap my head toward Zach.

"Did I just . . . .?"

"Whatcha doin' in here?" asks Citrine, munching on the apple that was just on the pedestal. I let out a growl of frustration and stomp toward her and snatch the apple from her hand. "What the fuck was that for?" she yells.

"Language," Zach warns her.

"Fuck you too. I'm mad now," Citrine says, her face growing red. Flames tickle her fingertips. "I only came down to see if you needed any help!"

"Seriously, Citrine, fix your language," I say, letting out a frustrated sigh. I shove the apple back into her hands and walk over to the wall.

"God, you're such a hemorrhoid." Citrine sighs, frowning slightly, before taking a bite of the apple, full of cattiness. My head turns to her slowly, and I hear Zach choke down a chuckle. She meets my eyes with a raised eyebrow, challenging me to come up with my own insult. I hold her gaze for a few seconds.

"Since when?" I ask, cocking my head to the side. On top of my frustration of failure, I am *not* in the mood to be tossed around. I won't give her that satisfaction.

"Since you started to look like one," she deadpans. Zach coughs, clearing his throat to hide his laugh.

"No, since when did I ask for your input?" I say slyly, a small playful snarl on my face. Yes, I'm irritated. But the insult she gave me was so uncalled for and absurd that I can't help but be a little amused.

"Hemorrhoids don't get the option to ask. Go back to being a pain in the ass." My eyes widen at her, and she tilts her head, a small smile on her lips. *Damn, she got me.* I give her a slight nod of respect and she gives me a small smile in return, before she hides it by taking another bite of the apple. Our bickering was a nice but short stint of stress relief, and I'm silently thankful for her hotheadedness. But with it being over, the weight of my importance becomes heavy once again. I turn back toward the wall, leaning my head against the cool surface. *This sucks.*

"I've been trying to cast for days, and nothing is working. Nothing is working." I feel Zach come up behind me, and I lean into his chest. "I'm getting irritated and impatient with myself. Everyone is depending on me, and I'm scared. What if I mess up? What if I can't do it? What if we get caught because of me?" Zach brings his hand to my hair and massages my scalp. I feel him about to say something, but Citrine beats him to it.

"So what if you mess up? You beating yourself up over something you are struggling with is not gonna help you." She chews the apple loudly. "This is really good." She clearly cooled down fast.

"City, you are the last person to talk. You were literally me a couple weeks ago," I say, struggling to keep the tears from flowing. She takes another bite.

"Yeah, well, getting angry isn't going to help you because you're not *me*. That's something that becomes more clear everyday. But being angry doesn't always get you what you want. I *learned*, and now I am *sharing* that knowledge." I shove away from the wall and start pacing the room.

"Well, *thanks* for that," I say. The advice that Citrine gives me leaves me feeling irritated. Why is this nine-year-old girl talking to me as if she's the wisest? I hate feeling weak and useless and belittled. I hate myself. My whole body aches with annoyance, and I just want to sleep. I just want to sleep this all away. These powers. The potential apocalypse. Sleep all the danger away but keep my family. *My family.* I have to do this for them. I stop pacing and throw a determined look toward Citrine. "Get me another apple." She straightens her back, salutes, and scurries out of the room.

"Thatta girl," says Zach, looking at me admiringly and patting my head. A rush of butterflies erupts in my stomach. *Gosh darn it, why is this man so amazing?* Citrine returns and places a new apple on the pedestal before walking to the corner of the room.

"You got this, Ruby. Remember, you aren't a punching bag, no need to beat yourself up. I believe in you." Citrine gives me a thumbs-up and takes another bite of the apple. I chuckle, shaking my head. *Thanks, City.* Instead of imagining myself peeling the apple away, I take a different approach. Without a path, water will flow aimlessly with no direction and no destination. I close my eyes and take a deep breath. I imagine the room is black. The only thing there is me, the apple, and the pedestal. I build a small white groove with my mind, starting from my temple to the center of the apple. I summon my invisibility. I feel warmth rise from the bottoms of my feet and through my veins until it reaches the top of my head. I imagine it flowing through my temple and into the groove, straight into the apple's core.

My power.

My ability.

Me.

The apple is now a part of me. We are connected. I let out a sharp exhale and open my eyes. The apple is gone.

"I did it," I whisper.

"Yeah, Ruby, you did," Zach says, his face is full of pride. I turn to where the apple was and grin. I release my grip on the apple's visibility, and it comes back to sight. I repeat the same process I did before, and the apple disappears again.

"It's not like water," I say, turning the apple visible and invisible with greater ease. "I thought it was at first. But it's not like water at all." A smile tugs at the corner of my lips. "It's like electricity. All I need to do is connect the wires, and I'm the power source." I'm smiling freely now. I throw away the imagery of a groove and replace it with a dazzling copper wire. I run the wire through the apple and back to me before repeating the same process for the pedestal: a parallel circuit. "I am the power source and the controller of the switches." This time, I make the apple and the pedestal disappear. A couple of seconds later, I bring the apple back but leave the pedestal invisible so it looks as though the apple is levitating in the air.

"Wow," says Citrine in awe as she stands up slowly. A burst of applause erupts from her. "Yay, Ruby!" The clapping grows thicker and louder, and I turn to see Garnet, Pearl, and Tory in the doorway.

"She's getting the hang of it," Zach says proudly. Garnet's gaze lands on him, and she sighs.

"I would ask why you're here, but I think I'm just going to give up with that question." Zach chuckles but doesn't hide his grin.

"I think we're gonna move on to a more complex object next, like a bed or a couch or—"

"Or a person," Garnet interrupts. My head whips in her direction, and I stutter.

"A-a person?" The confidence I just gained diminishes immediately. "Garnet, it took me a week to make this apple disappear. I don't think I'm ready for that yet." I pinch the skin around my wrist anxiously.

"Well, Ziri has finally narrowed down our uncle's location, meaning that your training needs to speed up. You'll be heading there Monday."

"Monday?" Zach exclaims. "That's three days from now. I don't think that's such a great idea."

"Yeah, Garnet, I literally suck at this, and-and *lives* are at stake. I shouldn't be going on this mission yet. I'm not ready."

"I know that, Ruby," Garnet responds. "That's why I *need* you to be." She gives a curt nod and leaves the room. Pearl gives me a thumbs-up and follows her.

"You've got this, Ruby. I believe in you," Tory says before leaving the doorway, Citrine skipping behind her.

"Zach, how am I—?"

"Let's not think about that right now. Let's not think about the day, the time, or the situation. Let's just focus on you."

"Zach . . . ." He steps toward me and grabs my hands.

"It's just me and you now, Ruby. Just me and you." He leans his forehead against mine, and I'm immediately relaxed. "Now make me disappear." I let out a deep breath, give a slight nod, and close my eyes to focus. I imagine Zach.

Beautiful, smart, funny Zach. His dark hair, caring eyes, fit body, intelligent mind. And then I imagine a wire. A wire connecting my mind to his, and his heart to mine: a circuit to let my invisibility flow through.

Summoning the power is much harder. I created the same old circuit, just with a stronger resistor: Zach. What if I don't have enough strength? The apple and pedestal already made me break a sweat; can I really do this? I shake my head. No, I have to push these doubts away. I am strong enough. I *am* strong enough.

Garnet's voice rings through my mind. *"Your ability is like a muscle. The more you exercise it through practice and precision, the stronger you will get. Let your power grow, Ruby. Don't be afraid of it because it's who you are."*

And if I'm not strong enough now, I will be. I have to be.

"I can do this," I whisper under my breath. *I know I can.* Warmth surges through my body, and I push it through Zach. I hear him gasp, but I keep pushing. I channel my invisibility through his body and back into mine over and over again. I feel sweat drip down my forehead. Should I open my eyes? Did I do it? I squeeze his hands and take a peek, but it just looks like I'm squeezing a ir.

"Wow," Zach says, squeezing my hands back. I'm elated. Elated and amazed with myself. But I have to focus. I grit my teeth and let go of his hands, taking a step back. "What are you—?"

"Walk to the other side of the room," I interrupt, gritting my teeth as I continue stepping back. "I want to know how much distance I can keep this up for, and how long." I hear his steps.

"Ruby—"

"I know, I know. I just learned this today. I know this is my first time. I know not to push myself too hard and to go easy on myself. I just need to know what I can do, what I am capable of doing *now*. This way, I can see my improvement. I have three days, Zach. I don't have the luxury of time." He's silent. Maybe he nodded? That's something that he would do: a gesture while being invisible. I chuckle and let my back hit the wall. "Are you there?"

"Yeah," he says, his voice at the other end of the room. The room is about ten meters long, or the length of a school bus. It's harder to keep control at this distance but still manageable. We stand apart in silence. Me focusing on not losing my grip on him and him doing who knows what. When at least ten minutes have gone by and I've gotten a slight headache, I know I can aim to do more. If I remember correctly, the wall to my right leads to a large hallway where I can see the stairs. I press my hand to the wall and feed my imaginary wires through it. The whole imagery process is getting much easier, and I feel myself becoming more comfortable with my ability. *I've figured you out.* I push my power through the wall. My headache becomes more intense, and my ears begin to ring. I push through the pain.

"Ruby!" Zach gasps. The wall is gone when I open my eyes. In its place is the large hallway and a flabbergasted Garnet and Ziri. I smile. Garnet meets my eyes and smiles back, giving me a nod of approval. I wink back at her and remove my own visibility with ease. Two people and a wall. Now I just have to do three people and half a wall, and I should be good.

Mom could do it, the half a wall, one-way mirror thing. It said so in her diary. She didn't tell me she could turn invisible too! Maybe the fact that she and I have the same power means that I am stronger than she is. Stronger than my siblings are. Perhaps the strongest of them all? I feel my cockiness getting to me, but I don't care. I'm on a high of endorphins, and I'm not ready to fall.

I weave a web of wires through Garnet, Ziri, and a now gaping Moon who just came down the stairs. I then move my focus back to the wall. *Making the wall into a one-way mirror is going to be difficult.* I have to make one side of the wall look like it's still there while making the other side invisible. How would I do that? If one side of the wall remains, with the other side that's invisible, all you would see is the interior of the wall: plaster and wood. *No, I have to do something different.*

I imagine myself rewiring the wall. To be honest, I have no idea what I am doing. I'm letting my gut choose the path. Letting my instinct choose the direction. When I feel the satisfying feeling of completion, I flip the invisible switch. I open my eyes. Garnet, Ziri, and Moon are gone, and I still see the stairs. Did it work? I am so concentrated on my work I don't hear the door open.

"Ruby!" I jump and lose my grasp on Zach. Before I lose my grasp on anything else, I turn my focus back to my skill. I look toward the doorway but don't see anybody else.

"Ruby, you're amazing." It's Ziri's voice, but I don't see her. *I did it.* I close my eyes. I still feel the connection to the wall and the three other girls.

"She is, isn't she?" Zach says, pride written all over his face, along with his goofy smile. That smile. A smile I would live and die for. I hear pacing back and forth.

"This could really work, this could really work." It's Garnet. "You made the three of us invisible, and the wall, and then *not* the wall." There's a pause. "Or . . . the wall still." Another pause. "Damn, a one-way window." I smile, grinning ear to ear and nod, forgetting that I am still invisible.

"Congrats, Ruby." This time it's Moon. *Moon.* I miss her so much, and I can feel her coming back to me. A bolt of joy roars through me, recharging my nearly empty battery. This time, I let the cockiness get to me. I make the ceiling disappear and the left wall, while alternately bringing each person back to view. Garnet, Ziri, Moon, Zach, like flashing lights. I wonder if they can feel it, the warmth. When my invisibility surges through them, do they feel it enter and leave their body? I'm so delighted I don't notice the gathering of my siblings in the hallway, peering through the now completely transparent wall. I weave my wires through them now. *Poof!* Tani, City, and Turq are gone in an instant. Followed by Peri, Opal, and Diamond. Their startled gasps and oohs and aahs only make me feel more elated. I want to do more. I want to push myself until I break. Will I even break? *I'm my mother's daughter. Born the same day as she, with the same abilities.*

My hand is still against the wall as I make myself visible again. I want to try something new. We all know the wall is there, but if I can make it invisible, maybe I can make it disappear completely. I release my hold on everything except the wall. I think my siblings are talking, but I block them out.

I place both my hands against it, grit my teeth and push. My head is pounding mercilessly, but I couldn't care less. I have to know if I can do this. But rather, something even more useful pops into my head. I make the wall visible again but continue to push my power through it. What is my ability really? The manipulation of light? The removal of matter? Can I make matter invisible to the point that it barely exists? I keep the facade of the wall, but I can feel something changing. The wall . . . the wall no longer feels like a wall. It feels like foam, something that I can push myself through. So I do.

The gasps and claps that erupt through my siblings give me delight as I push my way through the wall to the other side. I'm smiling at them all, bowing and waving, as their hoots and hollers bounce around my brain. I turn to push myself back through the other side, but something doesn't feel right. All the applause becomes muffled in my brain, and everything is blurry. My headache is unbearable now. The ringing in my ears is echoey. I feel my face erupt through the wall, and I look around. All the voices and colors in the room blend. I think I see Zach right where I left him. And is that Garnet's dark red hair?

"Ruby, are you okay?" I hear someone ask. I don't know who it is or where in the room it came from. All I know is that I want this pounding to stop. I feel nauseous. I need to lie down. *Maybe I pushed myself too hard.* But now I have something greater: confidence. Before, my idea was just wild, but, now, it's become reality. A reality I will have to face in three days' time. I push my arms through the wall, and someone grabs my hand. The scent tells me it's Zach: cedar with a hint of nutmeg. I smile and lean into him as he helps pull me out of the wall.

"I did it," I whisper. Everything goes black as I collapse onto his body.

CHAPTER 24

I wake up still in the training room. My head is on a pillow and there's a blanket overtop me. But something's wrong. I am lying on my stomach, and there is a searing pain in my right foot.

"She's awake!" I hear someone exclaim. Moon, I think. I go to turn my head in the direction of the voice but it's too heavy. I moan and try to curl myself into a ball. Everything is too bright. I let out a yelp. My right foot won't budge.

"What the . . . ?" I trail off as I look down at my foot, or should I say, where my foot used to be. All I see is my ankle. The rest of my foot is in the wall. *I must have passed out before getting all the way out.* I let out a chuckle and cringe in pain. Of course, something like this would happen to me.

"Thank God," I hear Zach say. I peek up and see him rushing over to me. "Here, I'll help you sit up." He pushes my back up and wraps his legs and arms around my body so his chest is like the back of the chair for me. He brings water to my lips, and I drink eagerly.

"How dumb do you have to be," Zach sighs as Peri continues. He crouches down in front of me and taps my ankle, "to get your fucking ankle stuck inside the wall?" I frown. He whips out his phone, snapping a selfie of the two of us before I can react.

"Shut up, Peri, and don't touch her," Zach says possessively, holding me tighter. His whole presence gives me comfort, and I lean into him.

"Very dumb, I'm assuming." He chuckles and slides against the wall to sit beside my leg. "You, my dear sister, are quite the dumbass."

"I said—" Zach starts, but Peri interrupts.

"I heard what you said. I simply chose to ignore you." I feel Zach tense, so I move my hand to his and rub small circles on his inner wrist. He relaxes, but only slightly.

"How long have I been out for?" I ask, leaning deeper into Zach's chest. *It's cold in here.*

"Well, let me see," Peri starts. "You were putting on your little performance around lunchtime, and it's now . . ." He looks down at his watch. It's new. I spy glimmers of peridot studded around the circumference of it. *Okay, with the drip!* "three a.m., so you've been out like Sleeping Beauty, little miss Ruby."

"Damn, wow. I . . . um . . . sorry?" I say, trying to get more comfortable. But you can only get so comfortable with your foot stuck in a wall.

"How are you feeling, Ruby?" asks Zach, playing with my twists.

"Exhausted, in pain, but happy and fulfilled." I crane my neck to look into his eyes. "I feel accomplished." He smiles back down at me. I get lost in his eyes, but Peri snaps me out of it.

"*Awww*, look at the two lovebirds." He reaches toward me and pinches my cheek. He goes to pinch Zach's, but he swats his hand away.

"Dude," Zach says, clearly irritated by Peri's presence. I clear my throat uncomfortably.

"Um, can I get my foot out of the wall now? It hurts like hell," I say, cringing again with pain. Garnet's voice comes from behind me.

"I mean, if you're up for it. You need to be able to do . . . whatever the hell it is you did before, which was amazing by the way." I smile and push my glasses up the bridge of my nose.

"I know it hurts, Ruby, but maybe we should wait until you have—" Zach begins.

"We've got it!" Ziri exclaims, bursting into the room with Tani right on her tail. She's pacing excitedly, a tablet in her hand. "It only took forever, but we've got it!"

"Got what, Ziri?" asks Garnet, immediately forgetting about me and my current situation.

"Remember how we were talking the other day? About the possibility that there's a stone that can dampen our abilities since there are ones that strengthen them?" We all nod, and Ziri lets out an excited giggle. I've never seen her like this. "Well, there are many, actually, that have the damper effect. But they are very weak, so irrelevant."

"So why did you bring them up?" Peri mumbles under his breath. Luckily, Ziri didn't hear. I shoot him a glare, nonetheless.

"Musgravite is the strongest. Sadly, it is also very expensive. The larger the stone, the greater the power. Garnet, we are definitely going to want a team on this!"

"I've been doing some calculations, but we really need to do some research first. I need to know the radius in which the stone has an effect. I assume that it will be proportional to the size of the stone specifically," Tani adds giddily. "I haven't done experiments in so long. I am really, *really* excited, really, really—"

"How did you even find this out?" Peri interrupts. "It's not like people know about us and what we can do." Ziri and Tani look at each other and grin.

"That's why it took us so long," Ziri says. She reaches into her pocket and pulls out a small smooth stone, barely larger than my fingernail. "This is how we found out."

"We scavenged mom's old jewelry boxes. If there was a stone that existed that could diffuse our powers, mom, of course would have it somewhere!" Tani says delightfully.

"What! I went through mom's stuff so many times and never saw this rock." Garnet reaches for it, but Ziri pulls her hand back. I notice she is wearing thick gloves, and Tani too.

"Don't touch it. It irritates our skin. That's why you couldn't find it because mom didn't want it to be found. It was in a secret compartment under one of the boxes. Even though it's small, we immediately knew when we found it. Not only because it made my skin red and itchy, but mainly because it felt harder to breathe when I was holding it. Usually, I can always feel the hum of electricity around me, but in that moment, I just felt nothing. And then Tani tried, and she said she felt the weight of the stone too. She also couldn't find a complex derivative with ease, so we knew for sure this had to be it."

"I forgot what being dumb feels like," Tani chimes in happily. "I absolutely hate it. I don't know how you guys . . ." she trails off as we all stare back at her. "Sorry," she says, covering her mouth. "Anyway, we took the rock back to the computer room. I did some simple tests with what we had around the house, and with the help of the internet and about five rock and mineral identification books, we were able to find the name of the stone: musgravite." Her gloved hand reaches into Ziri's, and she holds the stone up to the light. I notice some of Tani's energy diminishes, and a bit of spark returns in Ziri's eyes. "I don't know the specific radius of effect that this rock has. All we know is that it only affects the person if it is in direct contact with their skin. Holding it through the glove, I simply feel tired, and my head feels slightly heavy. I still have the basics of my intelligence and wit." She gives us all a wink.

"We just have to put a small team together. The plan is to make the perfect stone," Ziri says, grinning.

"The perfect stone?" I hear Moon ask. I forgot she was in the room. Then again, I can't really turn and see her. I'm sitting like an awkward pretzel, and my mobility is highly restricted.

"Yes," Tani says. "We need to make a formula of other minerals to make the perfect weapon. One that won't irritate the skin and will do the most damage with the smallest amount of radius of affect. If we get this on Bloodstone, we want to be able to still have our full abilities, even if we come near him."

"Even *this* small piece is strong enough to affect both Tani and I if we are touching skin to skin," Ziri says as she takes the stone back from Tani and places it in her pocket carefully. I used to think I was smart. *Compared to the two of them, I'm as dumb as a rock.*

"Okay, this is great news. Thanks for the update you two." Garnet goes behind the two girls and squeezes their shoulders. "You guys can pick and choose your team tomorrow, but, for now, get some sleep."

"Yes! Okay, good night, guys!" Tani says, waving and heading out of the room.

"Night!" says Ziri right on her tail.

"And now the attention goes back to you, dumbass. Would you like to get your foot outta the wall now?" Peri asks, getting my attention. I nod eagerly.

"Yes, please. It hurts so badly."

"Okay, Ruby, whenever you're ready, do what you did before," Garnet encourages. I give a curt nod and close my eyes. I feel more refreshed than I did when I first woke up, which I'm thrilled for. I call upon my invisibility, and I feel the familiar warmth I've come to love. I focus on the wall, doing the same process as before, but this time, it comes with so much more ease. I barely break a sweat. When the wall becomes the weird consistency it was before, I pull my foot out and relax more comfortably in Zach's arms, releasing my grip on the wall. I let out a sigh of relief.

"Now time to check this bad boy out," Peri says, wiggling his fingers as they get closer and closer to my foot.

"Maybe I should do this one, Peri. Not to say that you aren't a good nurse but . . . you aren't," Garnet says, lightly pushing Peri out of the way. He scoffs and stands up.

"Fine then, if my hands won't be of use here, I'll go somewhere in which they will be." Peri turns to march out of the door.

"And where exactly is that?" Zach asks. When Peri whips his head around, there's an evil grin on his face. He holds up his left hand and twiddles his fingers.

"My bedroom, obviously," he says as he backs out of the door with a wink. Zach lets out a grunt of annoyance, and I choke on air. Garnet doesn't even seem phased by his innuendo. All of her attention is directed at my foot, as it should be. It's been in the wall for way too long. I can't feel any of my toes. Zach cringes, and I'm sure it's because he's looking at my foot. I'm too scared to do so myself.

"So this is disgusting and really bad," Garnet says. "Basically, your foot is dead."

"Dead?" I exclaim, and my eyes jolt to my blackened foot.

"My guess is, in the . . . fifteen-ish hours that your foot has been in the wall, it hasn't been getting any blood flow. This might be bad."

"Wait, but I can still feel it," I say. "I feel pain at the heel of my foot. It can't be dead then, right?" Garnet's eyes widen, and she looks at my foot again. Then she claps happily and stands up.

"Awesome, then it isn't dead yet! That is actually some fantastic news. That means your body can heal itself and amputation is not necessary! Fabulous." She brushes off her hands and heads toward the door. "Zach can take you to your room and help you get into bed. Your foot will still hurt by the time you wake up, but you should be able to walk on it." Garnet looks toward me. Her eyes darken as she looks at Zach. "Help her then *go home.*"

"I will, I will," Zach says as he helps me to my feet.

"He wouldn't leave until he knew you were okay," Garnet says, her eyes soft as she looks into mine. I blush. *Gosh darn it, why do I blush so much?*

❖ ❖ ❖

When we get to my room, I stumble over to my bed and flop down onto it.

"Ahh, I am so ready to just sleep," I say, grabbing my pillows and snuggling into them. Zach chuckles.

"And that is fantastic, but let's get you out of those dirty clothes, shall we?" he suggests. I nod eagerly and use his arm to help me stand.

"There we go." I stand in front of him, chest to chest. Leaning my weight on my good foot, I look up into his pretty eyes and give him a small smile. They're filled with awe, joy, and something else . . . passion maybe?

"Ruby . . ." he trails off in a whisper. I love when he says my name. Butterflies fly from my stomach to my chest.

"Yes, Zach?" I ask as I feel my face flushing again.

"You're amazing, you know that?" He tucks a twist of my red hair behind my ear. I feel myself getting giddy and try to hide my smile.

"*Staahhhpp*," I say, hiding my head in his chest. He chuckles and backs away slowly, lifting my chin so my eyes meet his.

"I want to hear you say it." He stares intently into my eyes.

"Say what?" I ask, trying to keep my voice steady.

"That you're amazing." He brings his hand to rest against my cheek and slowly leans in closer.

"Okay," I say, grinning a little and trying to smother my uprising giggles. "*You're* amazing," I reply.

"Ruby," he growls, getting closer. I think my heart skips a beat. I've never seen him like this, but I don't think I mind. He's even closer now, our lips barely an inch apart.

"I'm amazing," I whisper. I can barely breathe. He's so close, and I don't want him to go away.

"Say it again," he demands. It's like he's moving in slow motion.

"I'm amazing." It's like the whole world freezes. We don't move, our lungs breathing in unison. At this moment, nothing else matters. Only us. His arm tightens around my waist, and he pulls me into him, our lips finally colliding. It's like putting the last piece in the puzzle. Our lips latch onto each other's, moving in an intricate dance. My hands wander up his back and spread over his waves delicately.

I let out a whimper. I've wanted to kiss Zach like this for so long, and it's better than I thought it would be. I want more. I pull his head down into mine urgently, coaxing our kiss. His arms tighten around me as he pulls away to leave a trail of kisses down my neck.

"Zach," I gasp out. I want him. I *need* him. I grab his head and bring his mouth back to mine, clutching on to him as if he were my lifeline. And maybe he is. The kiss seems to go on for an unsatisfactorily length of time when he pulls away, leaving me breathless. I try to pull him back, but he holds his ground. "Zach?"

"You have to get some sleep, Ruby," he says as his hands trail from my back to my shoulders, then down my arms to hold my hands.

"Stay with me," I say, pouting and squeezing his hands. "Please stay."

"Trust me, I wish I could. All I want to do is hold you . . ." He stares deep into my eyes. "But I made a promise to your sister, and my parents." He starts to turn and go. I pull him back, and our lips crash together again. I kiss him passionately, hoping my gratitude and love for him is translated through our lips.

"Okay," I say, pulling away. "Goodnight," I whisper, as he slowly lets go of my hands and heads toward the door.

"Goodnight." I watch him leave and close the door behind him. I stand there for a few seconds and try to process what just happened. Then I let out a squeal of happiness. I giggle and do a goofy dance.

"Ouch!" I yelp, forgetting about my injured foot. I limp back to my bed and fall onto it, a smile written all over my face.

CHAPTER 25

When I wake up, I take a quick shower, put on a T-shirt and some joggers, whip my hair into a high ponytail, and limp my way back to the training room. My foot is healed except for some minor bruising. When I get there, I focus on the wall. From the last time we went over the plan, I remember my job is to keep us all invisible and to make a wall into a one-way mirror so we can see everything that Bloodstone is doing from a distance. Out of the three of us, my job is the most important. I can't mess up.

"What are you up to?" asks a voice. I jump, turning to see Emerald leaning against the doorframe. I haven't talked to him since we got here, and I low-key missed him.

"Nothing much, just practicing, y'know?" I grin, returning the wall to its normal state. I take a step toward him, the pain in my foot barely noticeable now.

"Well, you wanna take a break? I kinda wanna take a walk. Get some fresh air y'know?" he asks, but I frown.

"Yeah, but I can't really do that. I used to live out there. Someone will recognize me." I wrap my arms around my waist. Emerald laughs and walks over to me. He throws his arm around my shoulder and walks me to the door.

"You can make us invisible, remember?" he says, still laughing heartily. I smile sheepishly.

"Oh, right." I readjust my glasses.

When we get outside, I look up and notice there isn't a single cloud in the sky, and it's the perfect temperature: not too hot, not too cold. I take in a breath of fresh October air. *This feels nice.*

"So what exactly were you doing down there?" Emerald asks curiously as we walk down the driveway.

"Just prepping for the mission on Monday." I spy a dandelion and bend to pick it up.

"Which is?" he asks. I look at him, my eyes roaming his. I thought everybody knew.

"We're going to spy on our uncle," I say. He sucks in a breath.

"Really? You're still doing that? Couldn't it be dangerous?"

"Well, yeah. That's why I've been training so hard. It really all comes down to me. I can't mess up, Emmy. I just can't," I groan, pinching my wrists. I look down. I've been doing this a lot as of late, tugging and rubbing the skin around my wrists. I think it's because of the stress, or anxiety . . . or both. He sighs and runs his hands down his face.

"I . . . I just hate bad people. Why are people bad?" He looks left, then right before we cross the street.

"I don't know, but I wish they weren't," I reply. I realize that we are too far from home now, so I make us invisible, but not entirely. This morning, I realized that if I made Tory, Pearl, and myself invisible, people wouldn't be able to see us, but we also wouldn't be able to see each other. So I created a bubble. A bubble in which we are invisible to those outside of it. I put a bubble around Emerald and myself, hiding us from the world. "Sometimes, I wish all the bad people would just disappear," I grumble. Emerald's head snaps toward mine, and I notice a spark of fire in his eyes.

"Me too! Imagine if there was a way, Ruby. The world would be so much better if we could eliminate all bad. Think of what the world would be—happy." He sighs, smiling. "The world would be happy."

"Yeah," I agree as we turn a corner. I stare up at the cloudless sky, deep in thought. "But would it? Just like light cannot exist without dark, can good exist without bad?"

"Yes," Emerald says confidently. "It can."

"And how do you know?" I ask curiously.

"I just do." He stops walking suddenly and grabs me by the shoulders. "Think about it, Ruby. If everyone had a heart like yours, wouldn't the world be a kind and safe place? No kidnappings, no sex trafficking, no rape." My mind shoots back to the motel, but I push those thoughts aside, reinforcing my wall quickly. "Hell, those words wouldn't even exist anymore! We could leave all the bad in the past!" His eyes are blazing. I shake him off and take a step back.

"Yeah, in theory. But even good people do bad things." I tug at my twists, staring at a couple of kids playing catch in front of a house.

"So, then, they aren't inherently good, are they?" Emmy asks, cocking his head and tapping his temple.

"Good and bad are a social construct. What may be good to you could be bad to someone else. It's all about perspective," I say matter-of-factly. "Like Robin Hood. He'd steal from the rich and give to the poor. Is he a good guy or a bad guy?" Emerald pauses and tilts his head up toward the sky, the sun illuminating all his features.

"He's good," he says, starting to walk again.

"But he's stealing. Isn't that bad? A sin?" I ask, skipping up to be in step with him again.

"Yes, but the good he is doing outweighs the bad." He throws his arm around my shoulder and pulls me into the grass as a couple passes us, walking their dog. When they are out of earshot, I speak.

"Okay, but why do *you* get to determine the weight of giving and stealing? What gives you that power?" I ask, compelled by his thinking. He tilts his head, looking up to the sky.

"Hmm. I never thought about it that way."

"Mm-hmm."

"But I know I'm a good person. I know I have a kind heart and soul and that I care about others. I want to make the world a better place. I *will* make the world a better place.," he says confidently as we cross the street again. "I'm willing to do whatever it takes." I touch his hand.

"I know that, Emerald. That's what we are doing, stopping our uncle to make the world a better place."

I move out from under Emmy's arm to balance along the curb.

"But be careful with that last thing you said. I'm sure that's what some villains think. Take Syndrome from *The Incredibles* for instance." I stumble, regaining my footing. "What did he say? '. . . when everyone's super, no one will be.' Which is true. He started his whole ideal because he was rejected by Mr. Incredible for not being special. For not being super. Because if everyone is special, then no one is *really* special. He was willing to do whatever it took so that people wouldn't feel the pain of rejection he felt. So is he doing good or bad?" I ask, pleased with myself for my analogy.

"He's bad. He clearly did bad things—" Emmy starts.

"Aht, aht, aht, but remember what I said? Even good people do bad things. Hell, I've done bad things." I look toward my brother. "He's bad because he was going to do whatever he had to do to get what he wanted. And he wasn't going to repent about it either. He held no burden." I jump off the curb and give him a hip bump. "Gotcha there, didn't I?" I say smiling. He smiles back and throws his arm over my shoulder again.

"A burden is the key. Paying for your evil actions in full, that's what's the difference between a horrible person and a good person who has done horrible things," Emerald says. I nod.

"That's what I've always thought." I say, pushing up my glasses. I reach into my pocket to grab my phone. "Shoot!"

"What is it?"

"Well, looks like break time is over. Garnet wants to talk to me, Tory, and Pearl about the plan. We should head back." Emmy nods his head in agreement, and we turn around. We walk back in a peaceful silence until he sighs. I shiver as a cool breeze ruffles my hair, and he pulls me closer to him. I gladly accept his body heat.

"Hey, Ruby?" he asks as we walk up the driveway toward the house.

"Hmm?"

"If you had the power to make all the bad people disappear, would you?" he asks. I stop walking. He does, too, looking at me thoughtfully. *Would I?* I think about what lies behind my wall, and it makes my stomach twist. *What if I could have taken away Seth's malicious intentions? If I could just* poof *all the people who aren't good, wouldn't the world be as Emerald described?*

"I . . . I don't know," I say, letting the invisible bubble dissolve around us as I begin to walk again. "But I know I have the power to make one bad person disappear. Our uncle." I look back at him and smile. Although the world may never know we saved it, I'm glad that I will know that we did. And we will save the world because the alternative is unthinkable. Emmy catches up to me but doesn't say anything. When we get to the house, I tell him I'll see him around and make my way to the tree. Garnet, Pearl, Tory, Tani, Ziri, and Peri are all sitting at the conference table when I walk in.

"How is your foot, Ruby?" Garnet asks as I take a seat.

"Really good! I can barely feel the pain anymore!"

"That's good! So you're set for Monday?" Garnet asks. I nod. She raises her eyebrows at Pearl and Tory, and they nod too. "Fantastic. Tani and Ziri have been working nonstop. Not just on the diffusing stone, but also on drafting a plan for you three." Garnet nods at Tani and Ziri, and they both stand up.

"Our uncle is in Hawaii. It seems like he's been there for a fat couple of years," Ziri explains. Pearl lets out a low whistle.

"Well, shit," she says, moving to sit up straight. She leans forward, putting her elbows on the table. "I'm good at teleporting, but not that good. You've got to be fucking crazy if y'all think I can teleport three people across an ocean," Pearl adds, looking around the room.

"Luckily, we aren't," Tani says. "We booked a flight for you three. It leaves at noon on Monday." Pearl nods, satisfied.

"Bloodstone lives in a mansion at the bottom of the volcano Mauna Kea, which is on the island of Hawaii," Ziri explains, her tablet in hand. "We booked you a nice hotel about sixty-five miles from there. I know it's pretty far, but it's decently close to the airport, which is convenient." I smile at the words "nice hotel."

"Does that work for you, Pearl?" Pearl cracks her knuckles.

"Holy shit," she swears under her breath. "I'm flattered that you believe I can do that. The farthest I've ever ported was twenty-five miles, and I was exhausted. Ten-mile porting is even pushing our luck," Pearl admits. "I can do five easily, though. I'm gonna need stopping points." Ziri goes to stand beside her and shows her the map. "It's easier and safer if I know exactly where I'm porting to. I have to see the area," she explains. We all nod in understanding. Pearl smacks her gum and points to the tablet. "The halfway point can be here. We can have small stopping points along the way." I strain to see from across the table, but it's no use.

"Hold on," Tani says. The room has lots of glass and is always illuminated by natural light. When Tani goes to the wall and pushes a button, shades roll down over the windows and a screen comes down from the ceiling. A projector I'd never noticed turns on and displays a zoomed in map of Hawaii: our hotel, some roads, hella vegetation, and an X on what I assume to be BS's house. "That better?"

"Much, thank you," I reply. "How did—?"

"Screen mirroring," Ziri says, grinning. She zooms in on a forest.

"It takes me about a minute or so to gain back my energy for jumps this far," Pearl states, pointing at the screen. "Ruby, can you keep us invisible during that time?" I nod. Pearl smirks and relaxes back in her seat. "Well, then, we're good to go."

"How long do we have?" Tory questions, speaking for the first time.

"I booked the hotel for two weeks, but if you need more time, that's okay. Our next plan revolves around you, so you have to be ready," Ziri responds.

"How exactly does your mimicking ability work?" Tani asks curiously. Tory shifts uncomfortably in her seat.

"Well, I only found out a couple days ago when I got here, so I'm not really sure. All I know is that if I've seen you do your ability, I can copy it." To demonstrate, she turns herself invisible and then visible again. Then, with a flash of blue light, she teleports from her seat next to Pearl, to behind Garnet, and back. I purse my lips, eyes widening in awe. "It only works if they're in the room, though," Tory adds. "It's like I'm leeching off your power." She sits back down and looks around the room. Tani looks down at the table, tapping her chin in deep thought. Her head shoots up, and she stares intently at Tory.

"Leech you say?" Tani asks. Tory nods.

"It feels like I latch a part of myself to them, and then I have their ability," Tory clarifies. Tani grins.

"So what if instead of you leeching off of them, you leech off of their stone," Tani suggests. Garnet's eyebrows shoot up. She looks impressed. I am too. Tani never ceases to impress me. Tory gives a small shrug.

"I don't know, but I can give it a try. It'd still have to be someone's ability I've actually seen, though," Tory points out. "I subconsciously gather info on how to wield it just by watching."

"And who have you seen?" asks Ziri. Tory's foot begins to bounce under the table.

"Well . . . everybody's except Garnet's to be honest. At least, everybody's that can be seen. I can't mimic Tani's, Peri's, or yours. You three have a connection to specific intelligence I can't replicate." Tory gives a small smile. "I've been studying everyone while they've been training." Now, Garnet looks dazzled.

"Peri," she demands, "go borrow someone's stone."

"Anyone specific you'd like to mimic, Tory?" Peri directs at her as he stands and walks toward the exit of the tree.

"Opal's," she replies.

"Make sure Opal doesn't come in here either," Garnet says. Peri nods and leaves the room. When he returns, he has an opal choker between his fingertips. He tosses it to Tani, and she catches it, handing it to Tory. She places it around her neck, sucking in a quick breath.

"I think you're right, Tani," Tory purrs as she begins to transform.

"What's Opal's ability again?" I whisper to Peri.

"Oh, you'll see," Peri whispers eagerly. I watch as Tory's nose grows longer and her skin turns orange as she grows smaller and stouter. Soon, she disappears under the table. Seconds later, a fox jumps onto the table and trots around the circumference. *Animal morphing.* None of us expect what happens next. The fox gets engulfed by blue light and teleports across the room. We all gasp. Tory can use multiple powers *at once.* I'm in awe. The fox then morphs into a black panther, and it prowls the room, circling all of us. The panther disappears, but we can still hear its footsteps: invisible.

"Amazing," Ziri breathes out. The panther goes to where Tory was sitting and licks its paw. It morphs again, but back into a human. There in its place, is a naked Tory. Her arms are covering her chest, and her legs are crossed. Everyone is staring at her, and she shrinks in her seat.

"Ta-daa," she says timidly. She reaches down, grabbing the clothes that fell off her when she morphed.

"Holy shit, that was awesome!" Peri says, giving her a round of applause. She smiles softly and ducks under the table.

"Thanks," she says sweetly. When she comes back into view, her clothes are back on. She unclips the necklace and reaches over the table, handing it back to Peri. Garnet's staring at her, thoughtfully.

"So, if we manage to get our hands on a bloodstone . . ." she begins.

"Then she can practice here," Tani finishes.

"It would be safer," Ziri adds.

"I'd still have to go and see him use his powers," Tory counters. "The more of his ability I see him use, the more I'll be able to replicate."

"That brings up another thing," Pearl adds. "How do we know he's going to use his powers? What if he doesn't the whole time we're there?"

"Then we're back to square one." Peri sighs.

"Either way, the trip won't be in vain," I chime in. "If we're going to ambush him, it'd be nice to know the layout and gather any other intel that we can." Everyone nods in agreement.

"Well, then, it's settled," Garnet says. "You three are still going. We hope that he uses his abilities. Even once is good enough?" Tory nods. "And if not, we can still plan our means of attack."

"If you guys can pull this off, we'd have such an advantage, perhaps even on his weaknesses," Tani says excitedly.

"You guys better not—" Garnet starts.

"Screw up? I know. We won't," I say, finishing her sentence. "I haven't let you down yet, have I?"

CHAPTER 26

I wait by the pool for Zach. He texted me earlier, asking me if I was free. Today is the only day he can see me before I go to Hawaii. I'm in a light blue, checkered, one-piece bathing suit. For mid-October, it's *hot* outside. So I thought I'd go swimming at the legendary house before the pool closes for the winter. I'm kicking my feet in the water when I see Zach emerge from around the corner. He's in swim trunks and a T-shirt.

"Hey." He comes to sit next to me.

"Hey," I say back. He pushes his tote bag toward the lounge chairs and slips his feet in the water next to mine.

"Are you nervous?" he asks, watching our feet move under the water.

"Very much so." I sigh and lean back, angling my body at the pink sky. "I don't want to think about it though. Tomorrow, and for the next two weeks, I'll have no downtime. All I want to do is relax." I give him a light nudge. "And enjoy my time with you."

"Well, in that case . . ." Before I realize what he's doing, he pushes me into the water. I let out a yelp right before I'm completely submerged. I come back up and wipe my eyes. He's laughing at me.

"Jerk!" I call out and splash him with water.

"Stop that! It's cold!"

"Yeah, no *kidding*," I say, keeping my head above the water and swimming closer to him. "Come in. You get used to it."

"Okay, okay, I'm coming." He stands up and walks over to the diving board. "Three . . . two . . . one . . . *Geronimo*!" He does a cannonball into the water. I laugh and swim over to the shallow end so I don't have to tread water. He swims over to me and emerges from the water mere inches from my body. I feel my cheeks heat up. He shakes his head, splashing water all over my face. His waves are now a small afro. I laugh and wipe my eyes.

"Why, hello there," I reply, smiling.

"Hello to you too," he says quietly, looking deeply into my eyes. He wraps one arm around my waist and the other to rest against the nape of my neck. His hand entangles in my hair, and he pulls lightly, tilting my head slightly to the right. He leans in slowly, his breath tickling my ear.

"Can I kiss you?" he whispers in question. My heart leaps to my throat, blocking my airway. Butterflies flutter in my stomach and tickle my pelvis.

"Yes," I whisper back. He turns my head toward him, lifting my chin so my lips graze his.

"Say my name," he purrs. The butterflies get stronger, and I bite my lip, my face on fire.

"Please, Zach. Kiss me." I manage to look into his eyes before I'm entangled with his lips. Wrapping my arms around his neck, I run my hands through his wet hair, playing in it. The other day, he told me he's going to grow it out, and I'm looking forward to playing with his future curls. He runs his arms down my back as he pulls me in, resting his hands on my ass. Zach squeezes, and I moan into his mouth. He freezes and pulls away, holding me at arm's length and piercing my gaze with his. His eyes are wild with need as he looks me up and down. Goosebumps creep up my spine. He reaches for me again, tugging me into his arms.

"I want you, Ruby," he growls into my neck. He tilts my head to the side again, exposing my neck and biting down on my skin. I gasp, wrapping my arms around him and clutching his wet skin. His teeth gnaw on me while his lips and tongue graze on my skin.

"Zach . . ." I moan, pushing up onto my tippy toes to give him more access to my neck. I've only seen this side of him once before, when he kissed me in my room. He makes me melt, and I lust for him. I push his head deeper, and his tongue dances in spirals around my skin pleasantly. He pulls away, tilting my head and exposing the other side of my neck, eager to give it some attention too. I lean into his chest, pressing myself against him. He snarls and grips onto me, turning primal. After he moves away from my neck, he rests his forehead on mine.

"I'm done swimming now," he announces, his voice a smooth liquid pleasure. "Let's go upstairs." My tongue is dry in my mouth, so all I can do is nod. He bends down and slides his arms under my knees, scooping me up into his arms. He carries me out of the pool and into the house. I lean into his chest and close my eyes, listening to his heartbeat. *Bum ba dump, bum ba dump.* We make it to the stairs in a peaceful silence, listening to one another's breaths.

"Well, lookie what we have here." I whip my head around to see Peri lounging on the living room couch, a glass of wine by his side. I didn't know Peri drank, but, honestly, I'm not surprised. Zach pulls me in tighter.

"Pay no attention to him," Zach says in a deep voice, turning my head to meet his eyes as he makes his way up the stairs, dripping water all along the floor. "The only thing I want on your mind is us." His eyes are filled with passion.

"Okay," I whisper, never looking away.

"Just remember to use protec-" The closing of my bedroom door cuts off the rest of Peri's sentence. Zach carries me to the bathroom that Moon and I share, locking the door to her room. He sets me down beside the bath, plugs the drain, and runs the water. "Zach what—?"

"You have a big day ahead of you tomorrow." He lifts my chin up. "I want you to have a relaxing night. You're going to need as much strength as possible." I nibble on my lip and nod. He moves his arms to rest on my shoulders, hesitantly and we sit in a peaceful silence, staring into each other's eyes and getting lost in them. A bit of time later, he leans in, reaching past me to turn off the water and check the temperature.

"Perfect," he whispers into my ear as he backs away, pushing himself to his feet and turning toward the door. "Enjoy your bath, Ruby," he says, his hand on the knob. My heart drops. *He's leaving?* I kinda assumed that he'd stay, or . . . I don't know . . . bathe with me. I feel myself blush harder.

"Zach!" I whisper, staring down at the floor. I hear him stop. He makes me feel something I've never felt before. When I'm with him, I feel as though I'm perfect. My flaws and blemishes nonexistent. I feel comfortable, safe. "You-you can stay." I don't have to look to know that he's frozen in place. After a few moments he sighs.

"Ruby, I don't think that's a good idea. You . . ." He trails off as I walk toward him. I stop when I'm mere inches away and put my head onto his chest.

"I want you to stay," I mumble under my breath, my voice full of need.

"Hmm?" he asks, wrapping his arms around me. I muster my courage and look up at him.

"Please stay, Zach," I repeat, reaching up to clutch his nonexistent shirt. "I want you to stay." I pull away from him and turn toward the bath, taking a deep breath before grabbing my swimsuit and pulling off the strap. I hear him suck in a breath.

"Fuck, Ruby. Wait," he says, but I ignore him. This may very well be the last time I ever see him. *What if the mission goes wrong? What if Bloodstone finds me and kills me, or worse, forces me to work on his side?* This night that I have with him, I have to make the best of it. I push the suit down over my hips and let it drop to the floor. Zach lets out a gasp, but I don't dare turn. If I do, my confidence might shrivel into nothing. I walk to the sink and bend down to pull out the bottom drawer. Before stepping in the tub, I reach inside and grab two blue bath bombs. I may have some confidence, but not enough to sit in clear water with him. I finally turn to look at him, giving him a small smile and tilting my head toward the tub.

"You coming?" *OMG the* balls *that I have right now. I can't!* I'm so proud of myself, I'm giddy. I want to dance and giggle and . . . I step into the tub, letting the water engulf my naked body. Surprised by its warmth, I shiver, letting the water settle just below my chin. Zach's silence makes my brain buzz with insecurities and doubt. I'm too afraid to look at him, so I fix my eyes on the dissolving bombs. This couldn't be more awkward. I sink deeper, trying to cover my inflamed cheeks. But then I hear rustling and clothes dropping to the ground. Part of me wants to peek and see, but the other part is too embarrassed.

He dips one foot into the water, then another. He sits down across from me, his legs outstretched, toes touching my hip. I summon the courage to look up at him. I've never seen his face so shy. His eyes are looking everywhere but at me. The fact that his confidence level fluctuates as much as mine blows my mind. I don't know what to say. I don't know what to do. *Maybe this was a bad idea. How do I act? I don't—.*

"C'mere," Zach says finally, his eyes full of assurance. I blink once. Twice. He gestures for me to sit next to him, so I crawl over there. He wraps his arm around me and smooths my hair with his hand. It's still in twists, and I know I'll regret it later. But for now, this is fine. I lean my head against his shoulder and sigh, scooting closer to him. He radiates a soothing peace and I relax completely.

I hesitantly place a hand on his chest. His heartbeat makes me smile, and I watch the subtle movement my hand makes with each beat. I feel as though I'm doing something reckless, but at the same time, I don't. My mind flashes with the memory of Seth, and I freeze. I shut my eyes but the thoughts take over. The photoshoot. The knife. My stupid decisions. I cringe, feeling as though I am sinking. I've done so well, burying the memory, convincing myself that it didn't actually happen. But, now, I'm filled with shame.

"Hey, hey. What's wrong?" I hear him say. But it's too late. The memory has consumed me. I need to go. I need to run. I need to do *something*. Because, if I sit still, it will be all I can think about. But I want to stay with Zach. I close my eyes, trying to push the thoughts away, but that only makes it worse. My mind confuses me, flashing images of Seth and Zach. For a second, I forget who I am with now. Startled, I open my eyes, scanning the man with me rapidly. *Zach*. I fidget with my hands, sighing. Everything was so nice before my brain ruined it for me.

"I'm . . . I'm fine." I say, moving to sit across from him. Concern is written in his eyes. *No, no. Let's go back to the way things were.* "Talk to me, Zach," I say, twirling my finger around the blue water. *Don't think. Don't think. Just forget, Ruby. Forget. This is Zach. Zach is safe. Zach is home. Zach is—*

"Okay, hmm. Terra's birthday is this Thursday," Zach says, a smile tugging at his lips with the thought of his sister. My face brightens, and the memory slips back to the place my subconscious hides it.

"Really?" I ask, unconsciously leaning closer to him. "How old is she turning? Are you guys going to do anything cool?" Zach chuckles.

"She's turning fourteen. And yeah. A couple of her friends are coming over after school Thursday since there isn't school Friday because of the instructional day. They're spending all of Friday together. They finna do something goofy." He smiles at me, his eyes twinkling. "They're gonna buy fancy dresses at a thrift store then go to a spa. And then after that, she wants to go to the movies in the clothes they bought at the thrift store, after washing them of course. I got stuck with being the chauffeur."

"Well, isn't that very brotherly of you," I say, poking him in the chest and smiling like an idiot. When his eyes sparkle the way they are now, I turn to mush. "That sounds so much fun though! I want to do that too!" I say, enthusiastic. "Like, go to the supermarket all dazzled up!" He tilts his head back and laughs.

"Yes, of course you would want to, Ruby." I stick my tongue out and wink at him, throwing up a peace sign. He laughs again, grabbing my hand and pulling me toward him lightly. "Is this okay?" he asks. We're so close that my nipples are touching his chest, sending a shiver down my spine. *Here we go again.*

"Yes." I giggle, snuggling closer to him. I lay my head on his shoulder, resting my hand on his stomach. I put one of my legs over his and sigh in his grasp. "Yes, this is very much okay," I say, unable to contain my smile. I never thought this was something I would ever do with anyone. Especially someone as important as Zach. "Is this okay with you?" I ask him.

"Mm-hmm." He holds me tighter. We lie like this until our heartbeats sync, and I feel myself dozing off in his arms. "Ruby, don't fall asleep on me."

"Why not?" I mumble, snuggling deeper. "I'm comfy." He chuckles.

"Because you haven't even soaped up yet."

"It's okay. The bath bomb is soap enough. I sleep now," I say, half conscious. He shifts from under me and I let out a whine. He moves me so that I'm sitting between his legs. I'm so tired I can barely keep my eyes open. I fall back onto him and curl into his chest. He pushes me off him again, and I groan. "Zach," I whine. A cold substance touches my scalp and I shiver, arching my back. "What the . . . ?" I gasp, my eyes shooting open. Zach places something in my hand and I look down. My red loofa.

"You soap up, and I'll wash your hair." His hands begin to massage my scalp, and I arch my back with a moan. I clamp a hand over my mouth as his hands freeze near my ear.

"Mmm, don't do that, Ruby," Zach growls into my ear. He starts to untwist my hair and his fingers feel great. I tilt back my head and sigh. "Soap up," he demands, and I do as he says. But every time his fingers move through my hair, I pause. My breath catches in my throat. Then I hear his voice in my ear, cooing me to continue. With Zach here, I feel both safe and dangerous. My headspace is different too. When he talks and touches me, it's as if everything around me darkens and melts away except for the both of us. And with each breath, touch, and sound one of us makes, I'm overcome with a wave of pleasure. Something overtakes me. *Love? Need? Lust?* I turn around and push Zach's legs together, wrapping mine around him so that we are face-to-face.

"You can wash my hair this way," I hear myself say in a tone I don't recognize. Zach stares into my eyes intently. He pulls me close so that our chests collide. When his hands entangle with my hair once more, I push myself onto him and kiss him. He kisses me back just as intensely, our lips entwining, gliding to the rhythm of our heartbeats. I moan into his mouth, and he lets out a growl, his hands leaving my hair to cup the bottom of my ass. I feel his dick harden between my legs and I deepen the kiss. This . . . this feels really *good*. I want more. I *need* more.

"Zach," I whisper between kisses, "please stay with me tonight."

"Of course, Ruby." His fingers move back in my hair and I sigh, leaning back slightly so his hands apply more pressure. I reach behind his head and grab the shampoo bottle, squirting some onto his hair. We take turns washing each other's hair and soaping ourselves up. When we're both clean, I pull the drain plug and grab the detachable faucet head to wash any remaining soap off the both of us. I rise to climb out of the tub when he stops me. I look at him, confused.

"Stay." I do as he says and watch him get out of the tub, my eyes locked on his hips. When he comes back, his waist is wrapped in a towel, and he has another one in his arms. He motions for me to stand up, and as soon as I do, he wraps me in the towel and lifts me into his arms. I giggle and snuggle closer to him. He carries me into my bedroom and lays me on the bed. "Where are your pajamas?" Zach asks.

"I can grab them," I say, starting to sit up, but I stop when my forehead hits his finger.

"No," he replies, smiling down at me. "I don't want your pretty little feet to touch the floor." I blush and tell him where he can find my underwear and pj's. He comes back with an oversized T-shirt and a plain black pair of underwear. "Put these on, and I'll be right back," he says before heading back into the bathroom. I throw on the shirt and slip on the underwear.

Walking over to my desk, I grab my brush, parting comb, and leave-in conditioner. In the back corner of my room is a floor-length mirror. I shuffle toward it before sitting cross-legged. Parting my hair in half, I brush each side, tying them into two detangled ponytails of curls. I braid both, tying them off with a tiny elastic rubber band. My braids rests about half way down my shoulder, and I smile, satisfied.

My hair growth over the past couple of years has been amazing. My thick red velvet curls are extremely healthy, bouncing back with elasticity despite the abundant split ends I have. *I have to get a trim soon.* I push myself off the ground, put the products and brush back on my desk, and tie on my bonnet. Then I dive into my bed, waiting for him under the covers. I hear rustling and water from the bathroom. *What is he doing?* Ten minutes later, I hear the bathroom door open as I'm half asleep. The bed dips where Zach applies his weight, and he gets under the covers with me, wrapping his arms around my waist. I snuggle closer to him and am a little disappointed to feel the clothes on his body.

"What were you doing in there?" I mumble. I move my hand so it rests on his and use my fingers to tug at his thumb. I wrap my whole hand around it and sigh, pulling his hand closer to my heart.

"I was just cleaning up the bathroom for you," he says into my hair. I tilt my head up at him, pouting my lips in appreciation.

"Awww, thank you." I bend my neck to press a kiss on his thumb. He pulls me closer and lays a kiss on my cheek.

"Anything for you, princess," he mumbles, his voice filled with sleep. My heart leaps, and I freeze. *He just called me 'princess.'* I let out a happy whine and curl into a ball.

"I like that," I say shyly, my entire body filled with joy. "I like being your princess." He kisses me again, and I close my eyes, savoring the caress of his lips.

CHAPTER 27

Just as the plane is landing, I wake up. When I look out of the window, I gasp. I've never seen so much water. And it's so blue! I'm sitting in between Pearl and Tory. Tory is asleep in the window seat, and Pearl is sitting by the aisle, listening to music and reading *The Grapes of Wrath*.

The twelve hour flight happened faster than I thought. I slept through most of it though. This morning, I woke up to a kiss from Zach, asking me how I slept and if I was hungry. We stayed entangled in each other's arms until I had to get ready for my flight an hour later. After trudging my suitcase out to the bus, Zach had to leave.

"Be safe, Ruby. Promise me," he said, holding my hands in his.

"I always am," I said reassuringly.

"Promise me, Ruby, please."

"Okay, I promise." I held up my pinky, and he mirrored me. When they interlocked, we kissed our clutched hands, sealing the pinky promise.

"And if anything goes wrong?" he asked. I leaned in to give him a deep, passionate kiss.

"We'll pull out of the mission immediately. But nothing will go wrong, Zach." After that, I went to see Garnet so she could debrief us on the mission one last time. I know the plan better than I know the back of my hand. Get the info, and don't get caught. Probably easier said than done.

I turn toward Tory and shake her gently until she rustles. "We're getting ready to get off soon."

"Oh, okay." She rubs her eyes and sits up.

The trip from the airport to the hotel went smoothly. We swiftly grabbed our luggage and found a tram that would take us to our hotel.

"Hi, we're here to check into our room," Pearl says as we make it to the front desk.

"Of course. What's the name?" asks the man at the reception desk.

"Pearl Matinee," she replies. The man nods and types away on his computer. While they're busy, I take in the scene. I've never been on vacation before, and even though this isn't a time to relax, I plan on seeing as much of Hawaii as I can. The hotel lobby is quite grand. The room is in a giant semi-circle, with long windows stretching to the fifteen foot ceiling. Hanging in the center is a beautiful chandelier. The sun reflects off it, sprinkling rainbows in our presence.

There's a beautiful water fountain in the center of the room, pouring into another water feature. It's like an intricate river system that spiderwebs across the entire floor. Some of it is covered with glass while other parts are left uncovered, providing the room with a refreshing scent. I bend to get a closer look and gasp. There are fish in there! An entire ecosystem. I look outside into the courtyard and see a grand Salicaceae tree that towers above a pound. That's where the water must come from, or, maybe, empty out. *Or, maybe, it isn't a river after all, just a weirdly shaped pond.* "Ruby!" Pearl barks, knocking me back into the present.

"Yes?" I squeak, standing up straight. Pearl is waving at me from across the room. I hadn't even realized she and Tory had moved. I scurry across the room just as the elevator opens.

"Pearl called your name like five times," Tory says, laughing softly. I feel my cheeks heat up.

"Sorry, I was just . . . admiring the design?" Pearl rolls her eyes. When we make it to our floor, our room is a couple doors down on the right. Pearl swipes the key and pushes the door open. The room is fantastic. It has its own living room, kitchen, two bedrooms, and two bathrooms. *Wow, Ziri, you didn't need to do all of this!* But I'm not complaining. One of the bedrooms is clearly a room for kids. There's a built-in bunk bed that covers one of the walls, and on the wall across from it is a flat-screen TV. Sunlight flows in through the large windows. I head to check out the master bedroom where I find Pearl chilling on the bed, her luggage all over the floor.

"I call this room by the way," she states, not even looking up from her book. She's on top of a queen size bed with silk sheets. Blue and green drapes hang around the headboard, adding a splash of color to the room.

"Fine by me," I say, stepping out. I grab my luggage and pull it into my room. Tory is there already, sitting on the bottom bunk. *I guess the top is mine then.* After hanging up a week's worth of outfits, I decide to walk around and check out Hawaii. I ask Tory if she wants to tag along, and she nods eagerly. Pearl declines though.

"I didn't sleep at all on the plane, and I'm exhausted. I was thinking about checking out the hotel spa before our mission. Y'know, get in a little TLC and R & R before hell might break loose," Pearl says.

"Ooo! That sounds like fun too. What if we all did both?" Tory suggests, smiling brightly. "It's 4 p.m. now. Pearl, you can call the spa place and see if they can squeeze us in today. Then we can plan around that. But after today, we won't have much time to see the land. We should soak up as much of it as possible!" Tory says excitedly. I can't help but smile. Ever since Tory came *home,* she has mainly kept to herself. The only time I've really seen her talk is when she was talking about the mission. Once she comes out of her shell though, she's cheerful. She and Pearl hang out quite a bit and complement each other. Pearl is formidable, but when she's with Tory, she seems to soften a bit. She's less cocky and more lighthearted.

"I guess you're right," Pearl says, rolling across the bed to grab the phone and dial the front desk. After talking for no longer than a minute or so, she hangs up, turning back to us, grinning. "Spa at eight, bois!" she hoots. Tory squeals with excitement and reaches over the bed to tug on Pearl's arm.

"That means we have about three-and-a-half hours to sightsee! Let's go."

"Okay, okay. Jeez, stop that already," Pearl groans, but I see a twinkle in her eye. "I'm tired as fuck, but it will make the spa trip feel all the better, I guess."

When we're ready to go, the three of us leave together. I'm so excited I can barely walk at a steady pace. As soon as we step outside, we're hit with a refreshing breeze, and I sigh. Everything looks so pretty, it's almost surreal. On our way out of the lobby, Tory grabbed a map. She's standing dangerously close to the street, staring at the paper. Pearl walks up to her and puts her hand on Tory's shoulder gently, pulling her back.

"Let's see . . ." Tory trails off. "Wow, there's so much to do! We could go snorkeling or surfing or hiking or—"

"But sadly, this isn't a vacation," Pearl interrupts.

"Right," Tory confirms quietly. "Hmmm, there's a shopping district not far from here. The Kona Inn Shopping Village. That place looks nice."

"Lead the way," I say, and she nods, holding up the map.

As we walk, giant palm trees tower over us, and I'm grateful for the shade they provide. From time to time, we pass people sleeping under trees or on the side of the road, and I make sure to leave them a couple of dollars. When we get to the village, it's beautiful. Everyone is smiling, and pleasant music plays in the background. There are stores that sell authentic street food, clothes, bags, local artwork, and a variety of trinkets.

We go into every single store. Pearl spends most of her time and money in the stores that sell jewelry and accessories, while Tory loves admiring the art. I, on the other hand, am not really shopping for myself. I want to get something for all my siblings, Zach, and Maria. I go from store to store, spending more of the money I got from my dream. I buy trinkets and shirts and a ukulele for Moon. When my arms are covered with bags, my stomach grumbles. A sweet fragrance of teriyaki tickles my senses, and I begin to salivate. I follow my nose until I reach a food cart.

"Excuse me? What is that smell? It smells delicious."

"Huli Huli chicken," says the woman. "Would you like some?"

"Yes, please!" I watch as she makes me a Styrofoam bowl of rice and cabbage topped with the chicken. She puts in an extra scoop of the sauce, and it drenches the rice and cabbage in its flavor. I can barely stand still. *This food looks amazing.* I pay her quickly and look around for a place to sit. I find Tory and Pearl a few feet away sitting on a bench. I half run, half trip over to where they are and plop myself in a seat.

"OMG, I am so excited to eat this," I say right, before dipping my fork into the tender chicken and placing it on my tongue. "Oh my God," I moan, tilting my head back as my taste buds dazzle in the glory of the meat. "This is amazing." I'm giggling now. I'm so happy I could bounce off walls. I put another bite in my mouth, and I feel my eyes water. I look over at Pearl and see her staring at me, amused. Tory's laughing, her own plate of street food resting in her lap.

"Don't be giving yourself a foodgasm out in public, Ruby, jeez." Pearl puts a forkful of food in her mouth to hide her grin. I'm too happy to be embarrassed.

"What did you guys get?" I ask with my mouth full.

"I just got some fish tacos," Tory says, smiling.

"And I got Poke." Pearl flashes us an evil grin. "The vendor says there's octopus and sea snails and raw fish. It's really good." Tory grimaces.

"Raw fish isn't my thing. But, like, go crazy," Tory adds, taking another bite of her taco. "If you *do* end up getting seventeen tapeworms in you, let it be known that I *did* warn you."

"Mm-hmm," Pearl says calmly as she slurps up an octopus tentacle.

After we finish eating, we go shopping for a little bit longer. I have yet to find myself a souvenir, and, well, I want one. I drag Tory and Pearl with me through store after store, but nothing pulls on my heartstrings. Just as I'm about to give up, I spy something through the display window. On the mannequin's right wrist is a bracelet. I walk into the store and straight toward the jewelry. I slip it off the mannequin and admire it. It's a turtle.

"Ah, I see you like that bracelet," says a woman as she walks up to me. I nod. "The Honu is a symbol of good luck from our aumakua, our family guardian spirit." She takes the bracelet from my hand delicately and holds it up to the light. "This specific bracelet was made from part of a green sea turtle's shell that was found at the bottom of a coral reef," she says as she tightens her grasp on the bracelet. "I'm sorry, this isn't for sale." She tucks it away in her pocket and shows me to this wall of beautifully made quilts. "Might I interest you in one of these fine quilts though?" The quilts are, in fact, exquisite. A particular one catches my eye, and I know I have to get it.

The background is white, and sewn into each square is a different animal native to Hawaii. However, I cannot get the bracelet off my mind. It isn't like this is a chain store. It's family-owned. Maybe for just the right price, I can buy it off her. Plus, I think my family needs all the luck we can get.

"I really love this white quilt right here," I say, touching the soft fabric. "I'll buy this. But I also adore that bracelet. I can't get it off my mind. I'm willing to pay whatever it takes," I say, smiling. I've never really negotiated like this before. *Am I supposed to look stubborn? Do I channel my inner Karen?* The woman shakes her head.

"Please, miss, I'm sorry. It's not for sale." She smiles at me softly and places the bracelet over her heart. "This bracelet means a lot to me and is a family heirloom." My eyes soften with understanding. A wave of internal cringe rolls through me at the thoughts I had, and I push them away. "My great-grandmother made this for my grandmother, and it has brought good luck to this family. I cannot sell it." I nod my head.

"Well, then, I will just take this quilt. Unless, do you have any other bracelets like that one by chance?" She shakes her head. *Well, I guess we'll have to make do with the luck that we have.* When I'm done checking out, I find Tory and Pearl waiting for me by the door.

"Finally. That took forever. We're gonna be late for our spa appointment!" says Tory. She pauses for a second then breaks into a fit of laughter.

"And what's so funny about that?" Pearl asks, raising an eyebrow.

"Well, it's such a miniscule problem that I'm worried about, when I should be worried about how we have to save the world." With those words, the air fills with unease. I feel a weight fall onto my shoulders, which only makes carrying my bags even harder. The day was fun, and although the fun isn't over, I feel myself dreading the walk back to the hotel and the entire spa treatment. Because that means we are getting closer and closer to seeing the uncle who probably wants us dead.

CHAPTER 28

I should feel relaxed, but I'm anything but. The spa last night was excellent. I felt all my immediate stress and tension melt away. However, it seems it has returned overnight in full force. It's an hour before our mission begins and I should eat something, but my stomach is full of fear. I've already showered and dressed in all black, my pocketknife clipped onto my belt loop. I touch my ruby hoping it will give me some type of comfort, but I feel nothing.

I can tell Tory is nervous too. After all, this mission is all because of her. If she can't master at least some of his ability . . . well, we're screwed. She's sitting on her bed, her head in her hands. Her legs are bouncing rapidly. I should talk to her. Tell her everything will be fine and that we'll kick butt. Instead, I leave the room to pour myself a glass of ice-cold water. I gulp the water down, loving how it cools my hot throat, but I still feel parched. *An entire two weeks of this? I don't think I can handle it.* Pacing around the kitchen, I'm remembering everything that I've learned, recounting everything I can do. I cannot fail. Tory and Pearl can. We'll be fine if they mess up. But if I do? If I do, we will all get caught. I have to be perfect.

"You ready, *bitches*?" Pearl asks as she steps out of her room. I eye her with amazement. She looks stunning. She's wearing a black beanie with a tight halter neck crop top. Her high-waisted shorts fit her curves perfectly, and the fishnet tights and combat boots just bring the whole look together. Her makeup is impeccable too. She's wearing black lipstick, but her eyes are shadowed in a pretty shade of gold. Even her nails are black. In her ears are unique gages, custom-made I presume. There's a small pearl hanging from each gage. I spy pearls sprinkled in her other piercings as well.

"As I'll ever be," Tory says, stepping out of the room. She's dressed in all black, too, but she sprinkled color into her outfit here and there. She braided her silver Fulani braids into one braid so it rests on her back. Her makeup is faint but still there. She has heightened her natural beauty, which only makes her glow even more. She's wearing an off-the-shoulder black dress that fits her perfectly. It doesn't look as though it will constrict any of her movements. The bottom flows out, stopping at the lower end of her thigh. Underneath, she is wearing black tights and black flats.

"Yeah, what she said." I take turns looking at the girls. Pearl's and Tory's style are completely opposite. Pearl takes on an edgier look while Tory's look screams a mix of soft girl and cottage core, but in black. I don't have the words to describe my style. I'm wearing a plain black T-shirt and dark gray leggings with mesh creeping along my calves and thighs.

"Awesome," she says, walking over to the coffee table and spreading out a large piece of paper. She gestures for us to come. I cock my head to the side in confusion as I walk over. Lying on the table is a blueprint of a huge building. "So I came to a realization last night," Pearl starts as she smooths the creases out of the paper. "You know how it's better for me if I can picture where I'm porting to? Well, I didn't know the layout of Bloodstone's lair or whatever. So last night, I made a quick call to Ziri, and she faxed this over to the hotel." I notice the tape keeping the blueprint together. "Ziri and I were talking for a bit, but I wanted to discuss with you both too. This house is huge. Picking a standard port spot would be ideal. Ziri and I were thinking of the hallway between the kitchen, living room, and this room." She drags her finger across the map. "We think it may be an office or something." Tory and I nod in agreement. That plan makes sense.

"We should bring this with us," Tory mentions, eyeing the map carefully. I shake my head.

"I can make us invisible and make walls disappear, but I can't eliminate sound." I pick up the paper and give it a small shake. "The crinkles are way too loud. We can bring it on a phone, though." Tory furrows her brow.

"Yeah, no. A phone is not good enough . . ." She trails off, thinking. Pearl and I share a glance, but she shrugs. A few more seconds of confused silence goes by before Tory's eyes light up and she runs out of the room. When she reenters, she has an iPad in her hand with an Apple Pencil. "Email me the blueprints, Pearl. Tory grins. "I think it's important to note which rooms are irrelevant and which rooms aren't. If we're planning to bring the fight to him, it's important to know where. The blueprint gives us the layout, but without the furniture and stuff. We can make notes here while we're over there." I smile back at her. *Damn, it's nice to have some smart siblings.*

"Look at you, Ms. Smarty Pants," Pearl says, leaning over the table to punch Tory in the shoulder. Tory winces. "I also took the liberty of going on a morning run," she stands up to walk to the kitchen, "and by *morning run,* I mean I ported all the way to BS's place."

"*What?*" Tory gasps, shooting to her feet. I'm up too.

"Pearl . . . that wasn't safe. Anything could—" I begin, but she cuts me off.

"Yeah, yeah, whatever. I know it wasn't smart. But I'm back safe and sound, and, on my way up, I brought food from the buffet." She takes out paper plates from the fridge and places them in front of us, still smiling. When she sees our concerned looks, she leans against the counter and sighs. "Look, I was feeling really anxious this morning, okay? I hadn't done the route before, and not knowing about the landscape was freaking me out. We're taking a straight shot to Mauna Kea, and . . . I dunno. I was second-guessing the strength of my ability, okay?" I'm silent, not really knowing what to say. Tory pinches her lips.

"Okay, just let us know next time, okay?" she asks. Pearl grins and reaches to grab our plates to warm them.

"Sure thing, babe." She starts the microwave and turns to face us. "Turns out, I had nothing to be worried about. I kicked ass. Did better than I thought I would too. I was a little winded when I got back, but after some juice and food,

I was fine. I also took the liberty of packing us lunches—" This time, I cut her off
.

"Lunch over there is a terrible idea. One, I can't mask the smell. Two, crumbs. We have to assume that our uncle is 'smarter than the average bear.'"

"Fine then. Do we just not eat?" Pearl asks. Tory looks at me, concerned by this thought too. I pause. There has to be some type of compromise. My eyes light up with an idea.

"Okay, I've got it. We eat lunch in shifts. First, you two port out of the house and eat lunch in the woods or whatever. Like a picnic type thing, I guess. And then y'all port back and Pearl and I will port away to have lunch."

"Okay, but what about me?" Tory asks, concern written all over her face.

"I'll leave my necklace with you. You most definitely won't be able to keep the wall as a one-way window, but you can make yourself invisible."

"Sounds good to me," Pearl says and Tory nods in agreement. As we eat breakfast, we go over the plan again, all the way down to the nitty-gritty details. We decide that twenty minutes to eat is good enough, and at noon, Tory and Pearl will port away. If anything goes wrong on either side, we will text in the group chat. Calling would be useless since we can't talk. My stomach fills with nerves as we clean the counter. I slip my phone into my pocket and kneel to lace up my shoes. I'm trying not to look as nervous as I feel. When I stand, Tory and Pearl are ready by the door. Pearl gives me a curt nod. I throw up our invisible bubble and give her a thumbs-up. She grins.

"Hello, and welcome to the Pearl Express. Please keep your arms, legs, and feet inside the ride at all times." Tory lets out a giggle as I roll my eyes. But I'm grateful for the lightheartedness. "Here we go."

Suddenly, I'm taken over by a wave of nausea and a weird pressure on my temple. It feels as though I'm submerged deep underwater, and my ears are ringing. Just as quickly as the feeling came, it vanishes. I open my eyes to find us all standing outside on the edge of a plateau and the woods. Before I can readjust, I'm consumed by the feeling again. I squeeze my eyes shut. This feels so *weird*. I feel bile rise in my throat just as the feeling disappears again and we're in the woods. I'm so focused on not vomiting and keeping the invisible bubble around us I barely notice I haven't been feeling the pressure. Tory and Pearl are standing around me, concern written on their faces.

"I'll be fine in a sec." I gasp as I focus on my breathing. *That* is going to have to take some getting used to.

"You have a weak stomach," says Pearl, smirking down at me, but I ignore her. When I can finally see and think clearly, I look around the area, confused.

"Where are we?" I ask her. She leans against a tree and snaps the gum she's chewing.

"One more port, and we'll be in his house. I had to make sure that you were okay before throwing us in there," Pearl says as she crosses her arms over her chest. "You good now?" I groan as I rise to my feet.

"Yeah, I'm good now. Let's go," I reply. My stomach twists as we teleport into a hallway. The walls are light beige, and the floor is covered in dark hardwood. I double-check to see if I can feel my power flowing out of me. The familiar warmth resonates through my skin, and I give a confirmation nod toward Pearl. We walk through the hall until we reach the kitchen, and my jaw drops. This house is beautiful . . . no, *elegant.* The furniture and appliances are all shades of white, silver, gray, brown, and black, with the only splashes of color coming from beautiful paintings hanging throughout the room.

We walk around the open space but hear no one. Tory opens nearly every drawer and looks underneath each cushion. I eye her suspiciously, but choose to ask her about it later. The sound of a toilet flushing makes us freeze. Someone is in the hallway bathroom. We quickly tiptoe back to the hallway and wait. The sound of the sink flowing makes my heart beat faster. Any minute now, whoever's in there will walk out. What if we aren't invisible? What if I'm failing? *No, I can't think like that. Focus, Ruby, focus.*

The bathroom door creeps open, but all I can hear is the loud pounding of my heart. A man wearing a dark red robe walks out of the bathroom and turns toward us, coffee mug in hand. For a moment, he pauses, tilting his head up toward the ceiling. Then he smirks, shakes his head, and walks right past us, heading into the room at the end of the hall. I look toward Pearl for her instruction. She points to the room he just entered and mouths, *Main bedroom.*

She turns to point at the other end of the hall and mouths, *Office.* Pearl can't want us to split up yet, can she? She gestures for us to follow her, and I let out a shaky breath of relief.

We head down the hallway toward the office. When we make it to the door, Pearl pushes it open quietly and ushers us inside. I'm the last one, so I close the door behind me. I gasp when I take in the room. The office is nothing like the kitchen and the living room. In fact, it's the exact opposite. The kitchen was clean and pristine and elegant. This room is cluttered with books and papers and looks to be in severe disarray. On the back wall is a map of the world, covered in red string and sticky notes. I make a step to get a closer look, but Tory sticks out her arm to stop me.

"Be careful," she whispers. "If anything is moved or different than before, he could notice." I nod in understanding. I look down and give a silent thanks to Tory. If she hadn't stopped me, I would have knocked over a small stack of books. I pay careful attention to where I am stepping now. When I finally make it to the map, I gasp. All major cities are marked with red marker, and names, both familiar and not, are on the sticky notes. *This must be the map mom was talking about.* Why does our uncle want anything to do with these people?

Pearl is standing next to me, snapping pictures of the map. That's smart. I'm sure she'll be sending them to Ziri and Tani before the day is over. I spot Tory looking carefully through his desk drawers. Before I can make my way over to her, I hear footsteps in the hall. *He's coming.* I tap Pearl on the shoulder and point to the door. She gives a curt nod and hightails over to Tory, dodging spilt thumbtacks and trash on the ground. But before she can make it to her, the door opens. We all freeze, not daring to move.

He walks in casually, shutting the door behind him. My jaw drops as I take in the sight of him. He's still wearing the robe, except it isn't tied in the front, and it exposes his naked body underneath. I nearly choke on air. I stare at Pearl, wide-eyed, but she isn't looking at me. All her attention is on Tory. Tory's trying to shut the drawer that she opened before he notices it. My heart sinks to my stomach. This is not good.

Thankfully, he doesn't look in her direction. He lifts the coffee mug to his lips and takes a couple of more sips before setting it down on a coaster. My eyes widen as the coaster sinks down into the desk by the weight of the mug. The foundation underneath me sinks, and I struggle to keep myself calm. Pearl whips her head in my direction, fear written all over her face. It tilts into a sort of ramp, revealing a dimly lit passage that leads farther into the ground. I struggle to keep my balance as the floor continues to rumble beneath me. Bloodstone makes his way toward me, walking down the ramp as if this is something he does on the daily. It probably is.

I make my way to the side quickly and press myself against the wall. The ramp isn't exactly wide, so I can't risk him accidentally brushing against me. When he walks past me, I'm as stiff as stone. But he looks like a man on a mission. His mind is clearly set on something, and all of his focus is on that. I let out a breath when he disappears into the passage and make my way back to the office. Pearl and Tory are standing there, mouths gaping. *Fuck, fuck, fuck, fuck,* Pearl mouths as she stares at the floor. Clearly, she didn't know about this either. It wasn't anywhere on the blueprints.

Suddenly, the floor rumbles from beneath me and rises. My head shoots toward my sisters. We have to make a split-second decision. Dive into the unknown or wait until we have more information. Maybe Ziri can hack her way into giving us some type of directions. I see the same look in Tory's and Pearl's eyes that I imagine reflects mine. We slide into the tunnel, barely making it before it shuts us away from the world above.

The corridor is pitch-black. I blink my eyes, waiting for them to adjust to the darkness. A few seconds later, I make out the silhouettes of my sisters. My heart drops. I haven't been thinking of my invisibility this whole time! Did I falter? I let out a sigh of relief once I feel the familiar warmth coursing through my veins, smiling at the fact I can subconsciously maintain my power. I no longer have to focus on it completely. As I follow Pearl, or maybe it's Tory, one of them makes their way down the hall.

The air down here is stuffy and reeks of mildew. Our movements are in synchronized silence, truly making our presence nonexistent. I'm getting anxious as we continue walking. *It must have been five minutes already. How far down does this tunnel go? And why haven't we run into our uncle yet?* He wasn't that much in front of us, and it's not as if we've been walking slowly. Ten minutes pass and we're still in this hall. We need to stop and regroup. I whip out my phone and shoot a text in the group chat.

Me: We have been walking forever, we need a new plan.

Pearl: I agree. Now that I've been here, we can teleport here later. We gotta talk out next steps.

Me: K.

Tory: Sounds good.

Pearl teleports us out of the hallway and back to the woods. I clutch my stomach, waiting for the nausea and discomfort to fade.

"That was wild," Pearl says, plopping down on a rock. Tory nods in agreement. We started our mission nearly an hour ago, and we barely made it anywhere.

"We need to go back," I urge gently as I pace the small clearing.

"Yes, but what do we do?" asks Pearl, leaning her arm back on the rock and looking up at the sky.

"I don't know. Gather intel? Try to follow him? Something!" I yell, anxiously tugging at my twists. "We have to do something." Tory comes over to stand in front of me, placing a hand on my shoulder.

"Don't worry, Ruby, we will," she reassures me. "We just needed to talk it out, that's all." She smiles at me softly, and some of my nerves dissipate. I take a seat in the soft grass and look at my sisters.

"Okay. Okay. Let's go over what we know," I say. Tory whips out her iPad, ready to take notes.

"Well, we know that Bloodstone has a secret passage in his office that can only be opened via a coaster and a mug," Pearl recaps, staring at her fingers.

"And he has a map of the world, specific names marked down," Tory chimes in eagerly, then she frowns. "Aaand that's about it, unfortunately." I sigh, laying back in the grass. There has to be more, something we missed. I close my eyes and recall the room.

"What were the names again?" I ask my sisters. "The one's on the map?" Pearl whips out her phone, looking down at it.

"Some names of famous people. Dictators, celebrities . . . I see a couple murderers on here too." She examines her phone closely. "The rest, I don't know." I let out another sigh. *Why would Bloodstone have these names down? Inspiration maybe? Jealousy?* I make a mental note to think about it later and sit up.

"I want to go back to the passage," I say, looking between Pearl and Tory. "I know we didn't know where we were going, but let me try to look through the walls," I explain thoughtfully. "Maybe I can manage to see where we need to go." Tory and Pearl look at each other skeptically, trading unspoken words. Pearl looks back at me, concern written all over her face.

"Ruby . . . you remember the last time you pushed your powers," she recalls, referring to the day I got my foot stuck in the wall. I cringe. "We can't afford for that to happen here."

"But it won't! I promise," I protest. "Tory can keep the invisible bubble on us so I only have to focus on the walls." Tory's eyes widen, and her head whips between Pearl and I.

"I've never done an invisible bubble before. What if—"

"We can do a trial run now, Tory." I stand and walk in front of her. "Let's see how long you can keep it up. I'll time you." She looks at me skeptically, but eventually, gives in.

"Okay . . . how will I know when the bubble pops? Will I feel it?" she wonders, looking around nervously. I nod in response.

"You should feel it, but just in case, only entrap you and Pearl in the bubble. I'll time you from outside of it," I remark positively. "For a bubble, it doesn't matter how many people are inside of it, all that matters is the shape," I explain, eyes on Tory. I glance at Pearl. "If you stay close to Tory, she'll be able to keep it up longer. The smaller and less complex the bubble is, the easier it is for Tory to handle." Pearl gives a curt nod and goes to stand next to her younger sister, resting a reassuring hand on her shoulder.

"You've got this, babe," she says with a soft smile. Tory smiles back at her, then slowly looks at me.

"Okay, let's do this," she says, with more confidence. I reach for the back of my neck and take off my necklace. Carefully, I pass it to Pearl who puts it around Tory's neck. I walk to the edge of the clearing and take a seat, leaning my back against the tree.

"It's like wrapping yourself in a blanket," I explain to Tory. "Pretend like the invisibility is something you can just throw over yourself." She nods and when I say "go," her face twists in concentration. After a couple of stalled seconds, she and Pearl disappear. I start the timer.

"Did I do it?" she yells. I give her a round of applause.

"You did it, Tory! Now you just gotta keep it up!" For the next forty-five minutes, I examine empty air. There hasn't been any sign of them. Not a hint of an arm or glimmer of hair. As the time reaches an hour, I call out to them. "Alright! Let's call it." Pearl and Tory immediately reappear, Tory staring back at me excitedly.

"You're right, Ruby! It's not that hard. I barely broke a sweat." This is good. It shouldn't take me too long to tamper with the walls, but knowing that Tory can cover us if things go wrong is extremely comforting.

"Alright, let's go," I say, coming to stand next to Pearl and Tory.

"This is fucking crazy. We're fucking wild." Pearl looks between Tory and me. She smiles devilishly. "I love this shit."

The next thing I know, we're in the passage. The nausea and dizziness aren't as noticeable, and I'm extremely thankful for that. It takes a lot longer for my eyes to adjust. Blindly, I reach my hands out until I can feel two bodies. I squeeze the one to my left gently. When I feel a familiar hum of invisibility wrap around me, I know that Tory cast the bubble. Now, my turn.

I focus my attention on the wall to my right, laying my hand on it. As great as my technique of linking my powers through invisible wires is, a direct connection will have a better effect. Even though I gave Tory my necklace, I still have the ruby studs in my ears.

I push my power through the wall, and within seconds, we can see through it. But there's nothing. I can barely make out rocks and stones on the other side; this wall doesn't border anything. I push my power more, concentrating it to flow down the wall's entirety: nothing.

I move to the wall on my left, about to repeat the same process, but I stop. I know I can't push myself, but this is frustrating. This passage has to lead somewhere, and, theoretically, with my power, we should be able to tell where that somewhere is. So instead of focusing on flowing my power through one wall, I focus on flowing it through two: the left wall and the floor. There's nothing to the right of us, and above us is the house. Wherever Bloodstone is has to be below us or to the left.

I close my eyes and grit my teeth as I channel my ability. I feel it flowing down my body and out of my arm that is touching the wall, as well as down to my toes and through my feet. Furrowing my brow, I push myself more, maintaining my breath as the warmth flows through me. I'm so focused on my ability that I jump when a finger taps my shoulder. I follow the silhouette of the finger with my eyes as it points to a now visible room.

Linking my elbows with my sisters, we start the walk to the end of the hall. When we reach a door, I reach for the handle, but someone grabs my wrists. By the amount of rings I feel on her fingers, I assume it's Pearl. She squeezes gently, and the next thing I know, we're on the other side of the door. Bright lights illuminate the narrow stairwell we are in and I squint. I release my grip on the wall and wrap a bubble around us. Tapping Tory's shoulder, I tell her to let go. She nods and relaxes visibly.

I move to take a step, but Pearl stops me. She grabs ahold of my hand, then Tory's, before porting us down the stairs strategically, careful not to make any noise. When we reach the bottom, a short, narrow hallway leads us into a huge room made of concrete and metal. On the far wall is an enormous window, revealing the innards of the dormant volcano Mauna Kea.

I gape at the giant room, taking in the unique and odd structure. A balcony wraps around the left side, leading to other areas on the second floor. The ceiling is high and isn't even a ceiling at all. It's straight up rock and dirt, supported by metal beams throughout the space. I look over at my sisters, and they're in awe too. Tory has her iPad out, recording a video of the layout to refer to later.

Here, I think as I spin around, getting a better understanding of the foundation. When I meet Pearl's eyes, I know we're thinking the same thing. The battle has to be here. It's far enough away from civilization that no innocent bystander could get hurt. Even though we're underground, I'm not too worried. If anything goes wrong and we need a quick escape, Pearl can port us out.

"Get up!" Our heads whip to the left when we hear the man's voice. I check to make sure I feel the warmth of my invisibility, then nod toward Pearl. In a few seconds, we're on the balcony, right outside of a glass room. We peek inside the room and gasp in unison. *Mom.*

CHAPTER 29

Our mom is toward the front corner of the room, her wrists in chains, and she's sobbing on the floor. Her hair is chopped at uneven lengths and she's barely wearing clothes. The room she's in isn't extremely large. Against the wall opposite her is a maroon leather couch. An elegant wooden desk is centered in the back of the room, framed by blood red curtains against the rouge walls. It's like another office, but neater.

"Please," she pleads, curled up into a ball. "I don't know! I don't know!" Bloodstone steps into view. He's still only wearing the robe, not even bothering to tie it closed. Walking toward the couch, he drags his fingers against the wall. He sits gracefully, spreading his legs in comfort. In his right hand, he holds a flute of red liquid bubbling in his glass. He sighs, lazily taking a sip.

"I said get up," he says calmly. Mom lets out a gasp of pain as she struggles to her feet. "And come here." She grits her teeth as she stumbles over to him slowly, tears streaming down her face. The way she is walking is off. Her weight isn't centered above her body, but behind it, as if she wants to go back. As if she isn't moving with her own will. I exchange a nervous glance with Tory, and she nods uneasily, tears stinging her eyes. She focuses her attention on Bloodstone and our mom, biting her nails anxiously. When mom is directly in front of him, he barely acknowledges her. She furrows her brows and bites her lip, swallowing her sobs. "Kneel." His voice is rock hard.

Mom's knees shake violently as she tries to fight his hold on her. Now she has his attention. He leans forward, looking at her bitterly. "I said, *kneel.*" His eyebrows furrow, and mom winces in pain as her knees crash to the floor. With his free hand, he reaches out to pat her head, then wipes her tears with his thumb. "Good girl," he purrs condescendingly. He leans back against the back of the couch, amused.

"You know, Rubes," he sighs, interrupting himself with a sip of wine, "I don't know why you put yourself through this day-to-day." He looks at his fingernails in boredom. "You know what I want." Mom looks up at him, hatred in her eyes.

"I already told you. I. Don't. Know," she spits out. Before anyone can react, he grabs her by the throat. Her eyes stare in horror as she struggles to breathe.

"You forget," he hisses, leaning forward so his mouth is against my mother's ear. "Speak to me with respect or not at all." He releases her, chucking her to the ground. She lays there, gasping, her arms holding her up as she coughs. Our uncle pushes himself off the couch and walks along the wall out of view again. I tap Pearl on the shoulder and point to the corner of the room closest to us. She nods and ports us inside.

I nearly gag at the aroma wafting off our mother. Pearl's face scrunchies, and Tory has to cover her nose. We step back into the corner quietly. Bloodstone's fingers are pressing a button, activating an intercom on the wall.

"You can come in," he says. The door beside him opens, and a woman and young boy walk in.

"Mommy, what's going on?" asks the boy nervously. Mom's head whips in their direction, aghast.

"No! Brother, please," she begs, jumping to her feet. In response, Bloodstone lets out a sigh.

"You know what I want." He points to a spot on the floor, and, wordlessly, the mother walks to it, standing quietly. Her face is emotionless, as if she's in a trance. Bloodstone points again, this time to a spot directly across from the mother. The boy's face is wiped clean of feeling, like his mom's, and he goes to stand in the spot. Mom lets out a cry of outrage and rushes over to our uncle. Before she can reach him, the tension of the chain yanks her back.

"I already told you!" she screams, glaring at him. She's crying angrily. "I don't know where they are!" Bloodstone sighs and walks over to his desk, reaching down to pull open a drawer.

"I need your children, Rubes." He opens the drawer and pulls out a silver gun, staring at his sister intently. "I need your kids." He walks over to the boy and holds out the gun. The kid takes it wordlessly before his arms fall at his side limply. Bloodstone walks away casually, heading to a wardrobe along the wall. With a barely audibly exhale from Bloodstone, the mom and son awake from their trance.

"Benji!" she exclaims, looking at her son with fear.

"Mommy!" he yells. His legs move aggressively before his eyes fill with fear. "I can't move, Mommy!"

"Benji, put the gun down," his mom says, her voice shaking. Benji tries, but he can't. He shakes his hand violently, but the gun stays strong in his grasp. The mom looks anxiously around the room. When she sees my mom, she gasps, covering her mouth with her hand. Her eyes search the room rapidly before spying my uncle. "Please, you have to help us! My son and I can't move!" Bloodstone grabs a satin button-down shirt with tranquility, holding it for the woman to see.

"Do you like this shirt?" he asks her, his voice steady. The mom shakes her head in confusion.

"Sir, please, we need—" Bloodstone tosses the shirt on his desk before bending to open another drawer.

"I asked," he repeats, his voice still gentle. He pulls out a pair of folded leather pants and places it next to the shirt, "do you like the shirt?" The confusion on the mother's face melts and is replaced with horror.

"Let us out of here, you son of a bitch." Silent tears stream down her face. Bloodstone shoulders off his robe lazily and opens another drawer. Right as he does so, Benji lifts the gun to point at his mom. My jaw drops, and I cover my mouth. Pearl's face is hard, hatred in her eyes. Tory is barely managing to stay quiet. Both of her hands are covering her mouth, and streams of tears rush violently down her face.

"*Mommy*!" Benji screeches as he cocks the gun. The mom rips her eyes away from Bloodstone to stare at her son. A sob escapes her throat, and she holds out her hands calmly.

"It's okay, Benji," she says reassuringly through tears. Benji is crying, too, unable to control his emotions or his actions. Bloodstone looks at them amusingly, then over the boy's head at his sister. She's on the floor, knees pulled into her chest. Her hands are covering her ears and her eyes are squeezed shut. Bloodstone stretches before he sucks his teeth.

"Aht, aht, aht, Rubes. This show's for you!" Against her will, mom opens her eyes and removes her hands from her ears. The boy cries as his mom tries to reassure him, telling him it will be okay and that it will all be over soon. As she does so, Bloodstone sprays on cologne before pulling on his boxers.

"Look at me, Benji," the mom says, staring at her son adoringly through tears. "I love—" A gunshot rips through the air, and the mom falls to the ground. I clamp a hand over my mouth, smothering a sob, my hands shaking violently against my face. Tory bites down on her arm, trying to stop the devastation overcoming her. She moves her arm, about to let out a wail of distress, but Pearl grabs her, covering her mouth with one hand and holding her tightly. Disbelief and disgust fill my eyes as I examine the scene. The mom adds to the bloodstains on the wall that went unnoticed until now. *How many people did my uncle murder in this room?*

Benji is sobbing uncontrollably now. He rushes over to his mom, holding her dying body. Bloodstone watches him curiously as he puts on his dress shirt and buttons it down.

"Mommy, I'm so sorry." He gasps, holding onto her. She tries to say words but her mouth fills with blood. "No!" Benji screams as he stands up again. "Please, no! I'm sorry." He shoots his mom in the face, blood splattering on him and the wall. He shoots her again, and again, and again. "I'm sorry, Mommy. I'm sorry." He wails uncontrollably. Suddenly, he goes quiet. He turns to face my mom slowly before rushing over to her. He grabs her hand softly, looking into her swollen eyes.

"Will you be my mommy now?" Benji pleads gently. "My mommy's dead," he explains to her, as if she didn't just see him kill her. He turns to face his mother and shoots her again. She jumps. "See?" he asks, waving the gun at his mother's limp body.

Abruptly, he rushes over to his mom, staring down at her corpse. He examines it carefully, before shooting her for the last time. He skips to the desk and sets the gun down. Bloodstone nods at him gently, and the boy grabs his mom's foot and drags her lifeless body out of the door they came in.

"All you had to do was tell me, Rubes," Bloodstone says as he pulls up his pants and buttons them. He slips on pink pig slippers, then turns to face the mirror adjacent to the wardrobe. He carefully admires his reflection, stroking his beard thoughtfully.

"I told you I didn't know! And I still *don't know,*" mom grits out. Bloodstone closes the doors of the wardrobe swiftly and walks over to our mom, bending down to hold her chin.

"And tell me, dear sister. *Why* don't you know?" She doesn't respond, but holds her gaze on her brother. He taps her on the cheek lightly, just as his phone chimes. He sighs and straightens his back, pulling it out and smiling thoughtfully as he reads what it says. "Looks like I don't need you anymore," he says as he walks back to his discarded robe, picks it up, and leaves out of the same door as the mother and son.

CHAPTER 30

As soon as Pearl ports us into the clearing, Tory lets out a bloodcurdling wail and falls to her knees. I'm also on my knees, vomiting. The effect of Pearl's teleportation added to what I just witnessed pushed me over the edge. When my stomach is empty, I take a glance at Pearl. She's sitting on a rock, back straight as a toothpick, face completely emotionless.

"I . . . I can't." Tory weeps, gripping her hands in the grass. "I can't." Pearl reaches an arm out, but Tory jerks away violently. "Don't touch me!" she screeches as she struggles to scoot away. "Don't touch me . . ."

As I crawl away from my puddle of bile, I don't know what to think. I don't think I *want* to think. That would require me to relive that moment, and I can't do that yet. When I make it to the same tree I leaned against before finding the lair, I lay my back against it again, pulling my knees to my chest. I lay my forehead against my knees and sit there, my mind blank.

I don't know how long I stay like that before I feel a light touch on my shoulder. Judging by where the sun is in the sky, it must have been a while. I slowly look up to a standing Pearl.

"Let's go," she whispers. All I can do is nod. I push myself to my feet slowly, and we walk over to Tory. Her back is to us, and she's quiet. It's not the kind, lighthearted quiet she usually is. This one is heavier, filled with grief and

hopelessness. Pearl reaches out to touch her shoulder carefully, and she doesn't re
act.

A couple of pit stops later, and we are back in bunkbed room. Wordlessly, Pearl leaves and shuts the door behind her. Pearl is by far the strongest out of all of us. The only reason my invisibility held up in that room was because I was terrified. *If he saw us, what would he have done?* I quickly push the question aside, not wanting to even consider it.

Neither Tory nor I have moved from our spots. I want to talk to her, but what would I even say? That everything will be okay? We don't know that. *Actually, by the looks of it, everything will* not *be okay.* I'm walking as if I'm in a trance, time completely irrelevant to me. I grab a pair of pj's and walk to the bathroom. The shower I take is not comforting in the slightest. I'm a shell of myself, completely numb. Without thoughts.

I robotically climb up to the top bunk and lie there, staring at the ceiling. Tory hasn't moved from her spot on the floor. I think I'm concerned, but, honestly, I can't tell. Everything is so fuzzy that I can't sort out my thoughts. I only managed to shower because I didn't want to wear those clothes anymore.

"I can't." I jump as Tory speaks, not expecting her to talk. Leaning over the bed, I notice she's staring at the floor, pinching her arm. "I—" She chokes back a sob, bringing her legs to her chest. "I can't do that to someone!" she yells out. She pulls at her braids, and the sobs start up again. "I can't. I can't. I can't . . ."

I've lost track of time. It's been four, five days maybe. Tory and I haven't left the safety of our room. On day two, food started appearing on our desk in the morning magically, enough to last the whole day. I spend most of my time sleeping or staring at the wall. I haven't touched my phone since we went shopping that day. *Damn, that seems like forever ago.*

Tory and I haven't spoken again since. It's not that we're mad at each other, it's just there's nothing to say. Nothing that will erase the nightmares that come to us or the images we see every time we close our eyes. I don't know what she sees, and, frankly, I don't want to know.

Whenever I close my eyes, I imagine my mother kneeling in front of her brother. And my nightmares are the same every night: The pleads of Benji and his mother before the gunshots rattle my brain. *Will you be my mommy now?* I shiver as I turn over in my bed.

Why am I here? Why did I give up my life for this? Yes, I've always wanted to meet my real family, but was it worth it? *I had Maria and Moon. Camy and Jordyn and Zach. I never should have wished for more. Why couldn't that have been enough for me?* I push my palms into my eyes, tears threatening to spill.

A soft knock on the door stops the tears entirely, and I turn to face it slowly. Pearl walks in quietly, closes the door, and takes a seat on the floor. I assume that Tory must be in her bed because Pearl starts talking.

"We're going home," she says quietly. "Our plane leaves tomorrow morning." No one reacts. Pearl puffs out her cheeks before nodding sadly, taking a stand to leave.

"How am I supposed to do that to someone?" Tory whispers. Pearl whips her head to look at her younger sister. From where I am, I can't see Tory, but it's obvious she's been crying. Pearl starts to take a step toward her but thinks better of it. She thinks carefully, planning out her next words.

"Because you have to," Pearl states blankly. "We have to stop him. From whatever his goal is, and from doing *that* to anyone else again." It's quiet for a while after she says that. She twists the doorknob to leave, but Tory speaks.

"And if we fail, what then?" Pearl looks between Tory and me, and I finally spot it: Emotion. Fear, pain, determination, and something else. The next words Pearl says are full of purpose and truth, nearly snapping me out of whatever daze I've been in these past days. She's one hundred percent correct.

"Not an option."

The next eighteen hours move in a blur. I've become comfortable in my hypnotic state, my consciousness on low battery. It's nice to be dependent for once, the one who is being taken care of. But a part of me feels guilty. Pearl acted as Tory and my caretaker all week, with us both being smothered by the traumatic memories and heavy guilt. Because of that, I do what I always do when something terrible happens: I shut it out. This time is different, though. There's so much pain to lock away, it's easier to lock myself away, too, than to sort through it all. So I'm a zombie, brainless for as long as I can be.

We had packed our things right after Pearl left the room. I know Tory was itching to get as far away from Mauna Kea as she could, and a part of me was too. That was yesterday. Today, there were no issues with our flights; we had a layover in Las Vegas. Six hours later, I'm in the back of our family bus, silent as we ride to the house.

An immediate family meeting is called upon our return. We don't even have a chance to unload our things from the bus before we are ushered to the tree politely. I was surprised Garnet hadn't made any snarky comments. This was definitely a screw-up, both for Tory and me. Two weeks. We were supposed to be spying on our uncle for *two weeks*. We couldn't even make it to twenty-four hours.

When we make it up the tree, Tory and I take a seat next to each other silently. In the center of the conference table is a small pile of authentic jewelry; while we've been gone, they've been stocking up. Avoiding the looks of confusion and pity coming from our siblings, I look down. *Do they know? Do they know what we saw?* A surge of jealousy takes me by surprise. I wish one of them went instead of me. I wish I could be the one donating a look of pity and empty apologies. A hand reaches across me and grips my own. It's Tory. She doesn't look up from where her eyes are glued to her lap. I wonder if she's reaching out to comfort me or herself. Maybe both.

"Why are they back so early?" asks Citrine, clearly not reading the room.

"Citrine—" Tani starts, but she interrupts her.

"I thought you were supposed to come back next week." She raises her eyebrows as she looks around the room, pushing herself out of her seat. "Did you find something? Oh my gosh! We're going to save mom and dad, aren't we?" Before anyone else can speak, Topaz reaches up, tugging gently on Citrine's arm.

"Something's wrong," she says quietly, looking around the room. Citrine's eyes lock with mine, and she sits down slowly, concern sprinkled in her gaze.

"All right, everyone. I know most of you are confused about what's going on, but there's no reason to worry. Everything will be—" Garnet starts, but a strong voice interrupts her.

"No," Pearl says, standing up, staring into each of our siblings' eyes. "We have every reason to be worried," she speaks truthfully. "And we don't know if everything will be okay."

"Pearl—" Garnet begins, but Pearl holds up a hand, silencing her.

"No, Garnet. They need to understand the gravity of the situation. Sugar-coating will get one of us killed." The room is completely silent now. Garnet is silent as Pearl recounts our brief time in Hawaii. She doesn't skip a detail. Beginning with us arriving at the hotel and our adventure through the town, she describes the weather, adding notes of what attire should be worn when we go back. *When,* not *if.*

Pearl describes the layout of the house we were in, spending much detail on the office. She projects the picture of the map, explaining that we don't know what the names mean or why he has them. When she gets to the part about us entering the lair, she plays the video that Tory took, pausing to note key features: the glass that shows the insides of Mauna Kea and the office.

This is the part where I turn off my ears, gazing at my hands intently: one bouncing on my knee aggressively and the other tightening in Tory's grasp. When a hand rests on my shoulder again, my head jolts up. Everyone is looking at the three of us. Some have their jaws dropped, others their hands covering their mouths. My eyes lock with Emerald's, his face filled with confusion and pain.

"Excuse my language, but we all need to be scared as fuck right now," Pearl admits, removing her hand from my shoulder. "But we shouldn't hide from our fear," she continues as she paces slowly. "We just need to . . ." Pearl stops and I turn so I can see her. She looks as if she's about to talk again, but she doesn't. Instead, her eyes widen. I scrunch my face up in confusion as she walks over to Garnet awkwardly, pulling her to stand by her collar.

"Pearl, what are you—?" Garnet tries, but a hard slap to the face silences her. Tension immediately fills the air.

"Fuck you!" Pearl spits in her face before slapping her again. I'm rooted in my seat, jaw on the floor. I look between my siblings, but they're all as confused as me. Garnet is stunned into silence, looking intently at her sister. Pearl moves to hit her again, but a hand stops her. Peri.

"Pearl, you need to chill the *fuck* out," he says, gripping her wrist tightly. Tory's hand tightens in mine, and I'm nervous too. Before anyone realizes what's happening, water erupts from the sink, puddling around Peri's feet. His grip on Pearl loosens, and she rips her hand from his. He stumbles back, surprised. Peri moves to grab her again but he trips, nearly falling to the ground. The water turns to ice, freezing Peri's feet in place. "The fuck . . . What the fuck, Topaz?" Nearly everyone looks at the nine-year-old water manipulator, but she's shaking her head intensely, fear in her eyes.

"It's not me!" she defends, holding up her hands in innocence. Garnet uses this distraction to her advantage and tries to pull away from Pearl, but she's ready. Pearl shoves her against the wall, using her other hand to grab Garnet by the throat. "Fuck. You," Pearl growls, hatred filling her tone.

Now it's Zircon who tries to stop Pearl. "Stop this!" She moves to pull Pearl back by her shoulders. Pearl whips around, grabbing Ziri by her neck, too, unfazed by the nails digging into her skin. We're all frozen, Peri literally, unsure of what's unfolding in front of us. Full of concern, my eyes shoot toward Tani, but she isn't looking at me. She's looking past me.

"Tory," she says calmly. I turn to see Tory staring at Pearl intently, tears freely flowing down her face, her eyes hard. Her free hand is in a fist as she squeezes my already throbbing hand harder. "Tory, stop," Tani says relaxingly. Tory's eyes dart to Tani's, and she holds her stare. After a few seconds, Tory stands up , huffing out a sigh.

Garnet and Ziri gasp for air as Pearl lets them go immediately, and Peri shakes out his ankles as the water unfreezes from around him. Tory chucks something on the table before turning around to leave, slamming the door behind her. I lean closer to see what it is and my stomach curls uncomfortably. It's a bloodstone.

CHAPTER 31

The family meeting is immediately adjourned, and my siblings scatter around the property. Some go to their rooms and others to the training room. I linger at the table, processing what exactly just occurred. Tory was so furious, but at the wrong person. Yes, Garnet is in charge of this, but it's not like she sent us there knowing what we would see.

After what may have been ten minutes, I push myself up and head to the balcony. The sun is just setting, coloring the sky in pinks, purples, and reds. I take in a breath of fresh air and sigh as I sit on one of the lounge chairs, readying myself for what I need to do next.

What I witnessed my uncle, my own *blood* do, is something I wouldn't wish upon my worst enemy. The grief and trauma consumed Tory, causing her to react impulsively with anger and grief. I can't let that happen to me.

Closing my eyes, I start to break down my wall. Part of me wants to ram it with a sledgehammer, letting all the trauma and emotions storm out of their cage. But instead, I peel back my steel paneled wall slowly, revealing the other wall behind it. I choose to take that wall down, brick by brick.

The first brick I pull off is made of the high school friends I had to leave behind: Camy and Jordyn. I didn't get a chance to see them before I had to leave, and the guilt was painful. They had been by my side since middle school, and I made no time for them. The shame swarms around me, and I squeeze my eyes tighter. I can't let it.

"I'm sorry," I say, speaking for the first time in hours. *I'm sorry.* I'm sorry for taking our time together and our friendship for granted. A tear slips out of my clamped eyelids and I let it fall. "*I forgive you,*" I whisper softly, hugging my chest tightly. I'm not forgiving Camy, nor Jordyn; they did nothing wrong. I'm forgiving myself.

The brick dissolves into sparkles in my figurative hand, trickling off my fingers like a shimmering waterfall. Several other bricks along the wall dissolve with it, leaving rectangular-shaped holes in their place. The me inside my head peeks through a hole, seeing black ghostly shadows flying angrily inside.

Suddenly, a shadow rushes out, squeezing through a hole. As it does, the shadow changes from its ominous color to a glittery rouge, rushing past me briskly. Others do so as well, leaving the real me feeling lighter . . . more like myself.

I open my eyes, sitting up straight. I'm coming back. Everyone battles their demons differently, and I've never battled mine. Now I need to. I don't have any room left to hide the dark thoughts and feelings. Plus, compartmentalizing for this long can't be healthy. I need to feel like *me* again. I close my eyes again, figurative me taking off another brick. This one is of Mrs. Klight and Terra.

"I'm sorry . . . I forgive you," I breathe out, and another weight lifts off my shoulder. More bricks fall, allowing sparkling, coded thoughts to pass through. I take off brick after brick, repeating the same process. First the apology, then the forgiveness. Smiling, I feel pride flowing through my veins. *I'm doing this!* I pull off a brick and freeze. This one is about Lisa.

Of course, I know my stepmother was absolutely cruel to me, but I never called it what it was. I grit my teeth, watering again. *Neglect,* I think as I squeeze my hands into fists. *Emotional abuse.* After I take a deep breath, holding in the air. *I don't understand why you couldn't love me as your own, and I don't forgive you,* I reflect, *but I accept what has happened to me.* The thought that she is changing makes this acceptance easier, and I let out a relieved sigh.

Tethered to the thoughts of Lisa is my leaving Maria. She texts me a couple times a week, informing me she's okay and that she wants me to focus on my "mysterious mission." When she told me she didn't need me anymore, I wasn't hurt. I was reassured.

Twenty or so bricks dissolve, and mystical clouds of sparkles fly through. *Yes.* I grab another brick, a stupid grin of content on my face. My facial expression vanishes immediately when I see what the brick is: Seth.

I'm definitely not ready to sort through that situation, but I am ready to tell someone. I open my eyes and jump, obnoxious hazel eyes looking right back at me.

"Damn! How long have you been there!" I gasp, gripping the ends of my seat. Peri shrugs in response.

"A couple of minutes, I suppose," he says amusingly, eyeing me curiously. "That was pretty epic in there," he adds, referring to what Tory did. I'm silently thankful he didn't ask what I was doing or about my trip.

"Wild . . . but valid in a way, I guess." I lay back in the chair. "I get why she did it, but she should be directing that to the person actually responsible."

"And she will," Peri says confidently. "We didn't get to it in the meeting yet, but Tani and Ziri found how to make the diffusing stone." My eyebrows shoot up

"Really?" I lean back in the lounge chair, pulling a twist thoughtfully. "That's great news!" Peri leans back, too, taking in the darkening dusk.

"Some mixture of the musgravite and other stones blah, blah, blah. I don't know the smart stuff about it," Peri says, throwing his hands up. "I can tell you that it has to be mixed with your stone to only affect you." Sitting up straight, I rub my fingernails together in thought.

"So we mix it with bloodstone . . ."

"And he's weak as fuck."

"Brilliant." I breathe. "Damn, they really did that." With Tory being able to wield Bloodstone's ability and this dampening effect, our chances of winning increase exponentially. "We could actually win this." Peri nods along with me, optimism radiating off him.

"All we need now is a plan and a date," he says happily. *A plan*. This plan has got to be perfect; we have no room for error. I tighten my hands into fists and stand up.

"Yeah . . . yeah we can do this," I say, turning to leave.

"Where're you going?" Peri asks, getting up to follow me.

"I have to talk to Ziri." I walk past the conference table and to the computer lab. When I enter, the lab is set up completely different from before. The monitors and PCs are still in the same place, but to the left are several tables, covered in microscopes, stones, and hotplates. This must be where they were experimenting.

"Oh, hey!" Tani says friendly, waving at us. Her lace front wig goes down to the center of the back, moving calmly as she waves. Ziri doesn't turn from where her eyes are glued to her computer. All she does is throw up a quick peace sign before typing again.

"Hey, Ziri, can I talk to you?" I say as I walk toward her. I don't want to make a super big deal out of this, so I decide not to ask everyone else to leave. The concern and confusion would be all over Peri and Tani's faces.

"Sure, what's up?" she asks, rubbing her neck while looking at her computer. Her iconic hair is redone, each bantu knot without a hair displaced. Wrapping my arms around myself, I rock on my heels, bringing the courage to ask this of her.

"Can you find out everyone who occupied a room at the hotel adjacent to me when I was in Tennessee?" Ziri looks at me oddly, Peri and Tani mirroring her gaze. Maybe I *should* have asked them to leave.

"Yeah," she says, opening a new window and typing away. "But why?" I ignore the question as she continues to type. Within a few minutes, three names pop up on the screen, all unfamiliar except for one. I lean forward and point at Seth's name.

"I need you to put him on the sex offender's list." Ziri's head whips to look at me, worry written all over her face. I give Tani and Peri a quick glance, confusion and anger on their own faces. I look back at Ziri, pleading for her to do it with my eyes. After a few more seconds, she nods, turning to face her monitors. "It's good as done."

I wake up to the sound of the mourning doves cooing. I roll over and check my phone. It's 6:21 a.m. I push myself out of bed, grab clothes, and head into the bathroom. My bladder releases a tsunami of pee, so much so that I don't know if I should be concerned or impressed. Grabbing my phone, I find a hype playlist and turn it on, dancing to the beat. After I take off my pajamas, I turn on the shower, throwing on a shower cap over my hair. The warm water pounds into my back as I dance in it, soaping up every now and then.

I feel great. Refreshed and full of hope, I step out of my shower. I brush my teeth and wash my face before pulling on my clothes. Mid-October in Ohio is always unpredictable, so I dress in layers. I make sure to unlock both doors before exiting the bathroom and heading downstairs. I open the pantry door and grab flour, sugar, and vanilla flavoring.

With all the chaos of finding family, I've never had the time to actually spend time with them. So before I went to bed last night, I decided to do something nice for everyone. When I open the fridge, I sigh. There's no fruit.

"What are you doing up early?" I jump as Pearl speaks, startling me.

"Good morning," I say, closing the fridge with eggs and milk in my hands. I set them down and pull out an ear bud, still shaking my hips to the rhythm. "I'm making breakfast," I state, bending down to grab a large mixing bowl from the cabinet.

"I see that. But like, why?" she asks. I don't think she's being rude. She's just genuinely curious. I look up at her, smiling.

"I've never had breakfast with all my siblings before." Pearl freezes, taking in my response. Then she smiles kindly, leaning forward on the counter.

"How can I help?" The smile on my face turns to a grin. I've always made breakfast alone, and I'm happy to break the trend.

"Do you think you can go to the store and grab me a few things?" I ask, opening a drawer and pulling out a sticky note and pen, scribbling quickly.

"Yeah." She takes the note from me. "I'll be back in ten minutes," she says before porting away. I head back to the pantry to grab the crepe maker. When I come out, a couple of siblings are entering the kitchen, some yawning and others perky.

"Pearl came in and got us," says Citrine, walking in wearing her orange matching bonnet and pj set. Topaz is by her side, nearly dressed the same except in royal blue. "I've never had 'crates' before. How can we help?"

"*Crepes*, Citrine." I laugh, putting the crepe maker down by the island. Nearly all my siblings are surrounding the counter, and my heart warms. *Thank you, Pearl.* I tell them all to wash their hands and then put them to work. I have Citrine, Topaz, Jade, and Aquamarine set the table while Diamond, Jasper, Opal, and Emerald work on milkshakes and smoothies. Everyone else is on mixing duty with me.

Garnet turns on some music, and we laugh and dance as we make the crepes. A few minutes later, Pearl ports back with the fruit and other items I asked her to get. Now that the fruit is here, we can start cooking. I put Tani in charge of cooking the crepes, and Peri, Moon, Sapph, and I work on the filling. I decided on strawberry, blueberry, caramel apple, and Nutella.

Making the filling is easy; all the fruit is sliced and put in their respective pots, along with honey and a spoonful of sugar. We put the pots on medium heat and let them cook.

"Oh my gosh, I love this song!" Diamond says, running to the open part of the kitchen and rocking side to side to the beat. "Who knows it?" she asks, looking at us eagerly. Peri, Amethyst, and Alex make their way to Diamond, nearly toppling over. A couple of seconds later, the lyrics start; the four of them dance in unison.

I watch them, yearning and admiration swimming through me. Of course, I know how to line dance; I know the one that tells you to hop and the other one that tells you to kick. I've never learned one like this before, where it's just a straight up dance that, one day, everyone decided to agree upon. When they make it around one loop, Diamond looks at us standing at the side.

"C'mon! We can teach you!" Citrine practically carries Topaz over to the dance floor, and others follow. I turn the heat to simmer before heading over myself.

"I'll talk y'all through it," Peri says, not missing a beat. When the dance starts its loop again, he directs us with ease, saying each word on beat. "Right two step, left two step. Cross, undo, step cross, step cross. Right out, back. Left out, back. Back, step, cross, undo, prep for spin and . . ." He repeats his directions, and we all do our best to follow them. I burst out laughing when Citrine trips over her feet, falling on Zircon.

When the song ends, another line dance I don't know plays, but a lot more of my siblings do. Diamond, Peri, Pearl, Garnet, Amethyst, and Tory are leading the dance. Warmth flows through my body, and I'm unable to hide a grin. Tory is acting like her normal self again. She must have apologized to Garnet and Peri already because I sense no bad blood or tension. There's only fun and love. We dance to a bunch of other songs, enjoying each other's company before Tani's voice rings throughout the kitchen.

"Food's ready!"

"And the drinks!" Emerald adds. I grab a plate, laughing as I pick up a crepe. I explain to everyone that they pick the filling they want, add it to the bread, then fold it, showing them as I make my caramel apple crepe. After folding it, I add more filling to the outside, topping it off with a spiral of whipped cream.

My siblings follow suit, repeating the steps I displayed. Moments later, we're all at the giant rectangular table. Only two seats are empty, one for mom and one for dad.

"Before we dig in . . ." Garnet says, her face lit with happiness. I look around the table, everyone is happy. *Genuinely* happy. Not a glimmer of concern or fear in their eyes. "I am just so happy. Happy and thankful to all of you. I think . . ." She seems to be about to say something but thinks better of it. "Let's eat!"

We all eat and talk and laugh. We share funny moments about our old lives and things we want for our future. Tani wants to work for the CIA or NASA, whichever one gives her more fulfillment. Peri wants to go to law school, after he goes to undergrad first. He talks about how Garnet found him before he could apply to college, kinda like with me.

College. Just two months ago, I was writing essays, applying to schools with big scholarships: Ohio State, Michigan State, and Emory. Now the stress seems so miniscule. *After this is all over, will I want to go to college? If so, aren't I dead to the world?*

Ziri explains that, officially, I'm not dead, only to my town. She says, after all of this is over, if I want to go to college, I can. She can fake my last year of high school, even enroll me into any school I want. Although appealing, I think I want to get in on my own accord. However, I will gladly accept the fraudulent actions on my high school transcript. It'll be the world's "thank you" gift to me for saving its ass.

When we finish eating, we rinse our dishes before putting them in the dishwasher. We're all getting ready to pursue our usual activities of the day: training, researching, and planning. But before we can leave the room, Garnet stops us, holding up something.

"No fucking way!" Peri says, grabbing it out of Garnet's hands and heading over to the TV.

"What is it?" Turq asks, smiling brightly. She looks significantly better than when she arrived. She must have learned how to control her ecological empathy, making it so she can't feel or hear every little thing coming from nature.

"It's a Switch," Peri says, plugging it into the TV. He turns it on and looks at the games. "No way! There's Smash. We gotta do Smash." Peri sets up the game. My eyes light up, and I jog to the couch, grabbing one of the remotes under the T V.

"How long have we had one?" Ziri asks Tani, but she shrugs. A stupid grin is written over Garnet's face.

"After seeing everyone's joy while making breakfast, I had Pearl pick one up. I set it up as much as I could between dances." Peri looks at her, an emotion I can't place written on his face. He puts down his controller, walks over to Garnet, and pulls her into a tight hug.

"Thank you," he whispers sincerely, tightening his grip around her. Garnet hugs him back. It's such an intimate, sincere hug that I almost feel embarrassed for looking. He pulls away, nodding at her, before running back to his remote. "I call Dark Pit!" he yells, grabbing the controller. We all find seats by the couch, some of us on the floor, others on stools or on the couch itself. Tani is sitting between Garnet and I, and she reaches out, grabbing both of our hands and squeezing them tight.

"Thank you." She looks between us, happiness glimmering in her eyes. "We really needed this."

"Damn, we gotta unlock characters," Peri complains, looking at the small selection on the screen. So that's what we do. "Ugh, not you choosing Kirby!" Peri groans judgmentally. "That's so basic. I'm actually disappointed." I've always played as Kirby. He's been my go-to ever since I played at Zach's house.

"He's literally the baddest bitch in the building, and anyone who says otherwise is an opp," I defend, and it's the truth. Although small in size, Kirby has incredible skill and amazing abilities. He's basically Tory; he can replicate other players' powers.

We spend the rest of the morning and well into the afternoon battling against one another, unlocking character after character. We had plenty of crepes left over, which turned into our gaming snack. All twenty of us had the chance to play. I tried to avoid playing at the same time as Citrine, though. After the first round she played, Tani got up and returned with a fire extinguisher *just in case*.

I felt like a kid again. We all did. The pressure of saving our parents and the world was irrelevant for a couple of hours, and it was refreshing. It gave insight into what life could be like after. *After*. That is, assuming our nonexistent plan is a success.

As the sky darkens, some of my siblings leave, but not to go to their rooms. Ziri is on her laptop playing some online shooting game. Tani, Pearl, and Garnet are talking, drawing things out on an iPad. The two sets of twins—Topaz, Citrine, Jade, and Aquamarine—are playing a card game called Kemps. I look over and laugh as I see the tips of Citrine's hair on fire. I don't think she and

Topaz have won a round yet. Topaz keeps trying to comfort her, but it's not working.

Jade and Aquamarine are telepathic. They can talk to each other just by thinking. If you play any sort of game when you aren't on their team, you're basically setting yourself up for failure.

There are so many siblings I have yet to converse with: Alex, Turq, Aquamarine, Jade, Topaz, Amethyst, Diamond, and Opal. I want to talk to them, but it feels almost awkward if I were to do it by myself. I hand my controller to Jasper and get up, looking for them.

"Done already, Ruby?" Peri asks.

"Yes." I sigh, standing and stretching. "My eyeballs are tired." I round the couch and see all the siblings I just thought of—except the twins—plus Moon, sitting in a circle. I can't tell what they're doing, so I walk up to see.

"What are you guys playing?" I ask, taking a seat beside Moon.

"Spoons," Diamond replies. "Deal you in?" I nod, and she deals out the cards with her hair. Prehensile hair is an amazing ability; it's like she has two extra hands. Her hair is styled in two pigtails, braided down to her knees. They are thick and full, diamond-studded hair jewelry sprinkling them.

"We added a twist though!" Amethyst says, her arm stretching to reach for her cards. I've never seen her abilities in action before, and it's a little unsettling. Her arm lengthens at little to no effort besides the will of her mind. "Powers permitted." My eyebrows shoot up, and I look at my competition. Elasticity, prehensile hair, animal morphing, ecological empathy, super speed, and levitation. *Damn, this is not going to be easy.*

Opal winks at us before morphing into an octopus, one of their eight arms holding up their four cards. I'm incredibly impressed. Diamond passes the deck to Alex so she can start. Within seconds, she's gone through the entire deck, impatiently waiting for cards to make their way around the circle.

"This is why we told you not to do that," Diamond says, and Alex rolls her eyes, a card finally making it to her. Opal uses all seven of their free arms, picking up the cards Alex discards and passing them to Moon. Moon doesn't even touch the cards. She lets them float to her eye level, discarding the ones she doesn't need to me. I turned myself invisible, as well as each card I pick up, making them visible when I put them down again.

My technique is to make a spoon invisible and grab it when I have four of a kind. Unfortunately, that hasn't happened yet, so I keep passing cards to Amethyst, who passes to Turq.

I feel a little bad for Turq. Ecological empathy shouldn't be too helpful in this game. So I'm surprised she grabs a spoon seconds before Opal does. I lunge into the center of the circle, but I'm too late. All the spoons are gone. Opal flexes their four kings to us all, fanning themself with the cards.

"W-Wait," I stutter, flabbergasted. "Did you get four of a kind, too, Turq?" She shakes her head, grinning wickedly. "Then how did you know?" Wordlessly, she points to the thing behind her, not even bothering to turn to face it. It's a small plant on top of the fireplace. My mouth forms an *o* as I make my way back to my seat. She must have projected part of herself into the plant so she could see everyone's hands. *Damn, this is going to be tough.* Against my siblings' abilities, I'm going to lose. The best chance I have at staying in the game longer is to get the first four of a kind.

We play a bunch of additional rounds, laughing, lunging, and bonding. I end up being the first one out, so I step out of the circle so they can continue playing. I sit on the couch by them, watching them play while occasionally scrolling aimlessly through my social media apps. My phone dings and the notification fills my stomach with butterflies.

Zach: I miss you <3.

I smother down my giddiness and text Zach back.

Me: I miss you too <3<3<3.

He responds immediately.

Zach: Can I come over?

I look around the room. There's only about ten of us still down here. My family won't mind if I tap out.

Me: Yeah. It should be smooth.

Zach: OMW!

I turn off my phone and tell my siblings Zach is on his way over and I'm gonna call it a night. As soon as I say that, I'm ambushed with kissing noises, oohs, and winks. I roll my eyes and tell them good night before heading outside to wait for him in the driveway.

CHAPTER 32

Zach and I are in our pj's, under the covers in my bed. We put on a cartoon show for background noise as we talk and catch up. He tells me about his classes and how he's doing well. Apparently, he's already submitted applications for six out of the fifteen schools he's applying to. He explains how filling out his applications helped distract him from worrying about me.

As much as he would like to leave Ohio, tuition is cheaper for in-state students. He's finished all the Ohio schools he wants to apply to, and completed a couple in North Carolina, New Hampshire, and Washington D.C.

Zach's applying as a psychology major. He doesn't know whether med school or law school is in his future, so he chose a major that would work for either. *What would I apply to college as? Would I go STEM or the "businessy" route?* I don't know, but I have a couple of months to decide. There's no way I'd meet the November first deadline, but maybe I'll make the regular decision one.

I brush my thoughts aside. This is very much an after-I-save-the-world problem. When he's finished updating me, I go forth with mine. I start with how amazing the day was. How it was nice to hang with my siblings and not have to talk about things that carry so much pressure. Then, I move on to tell him about what happened in Hawaii. When I finish, he sighs, rolling on his side to look at me.

"Ruby—"

"I know, Zach. I know. I was there; it was bad." I copy his movements, facing h
im.

"I just . . . ugh. I just don't like the idea of you going down there." He cups
my face with his hand. "I understand that you have to, but I just don't like it."
I lean into his touch, savoring the feeling.

"I'll be safe. I promise. We're going to come up with a well-thought-out plan
and kick some BS ass. I promise," I say, laying my hand over his. "We're all gonna
make it out okay, *including* my parents." Zach nods slowly. I know he wishes he
could come when we go, but I would never let that happen. Neither would any
of my brothers and sisters. He would be completely vulnerable. A liability.

I can tell he's still anxious about it, so I lean my forehead against his, staring
directly into his eyes. "I'll make it back okay," I whisper, promising something
I can't guarantee. The discomfort of the unknown that weighed heavily in the
room disappears and is replaced by something more intense.

"Can I kiss you?" he murmurs, meeting my gaze. The way he asks makes my
stomach twist, and all I can do is nod. "I want to hear you say it." He leans
forward. Our lips are nearly touching, filling me with need. I lean in, the strong
urge nearly taking over me, but he pulls away.

"I need you to say it, Ruby," he says quietly, a spark of mischief in his eyes.
The cartoon is playing in the background, completely forgotten. Of course, if
I could manage words to come out, I would tell him. *Yes, Zach. Please kiss me.
When we kiss, everything seems right with the world, and I never want that feeling
to end.*

But instead, filled with stubbornness and nerves I say, "Fine," before turning
away, focusing my attention on the animated cat chasing a mouse. A growl
escapes Zach's beautiful mouth, but I don't dare turn to face him.

"Ruby," he snarls quietly. Another wave of butterflies rushes through me,
but I hold my ground, squeezing my legs together and ignoring him. I reach to
tug on one of my twists, watching as the mouse evades another of the cat's traps.
"Ruby, please," he whispers on my cheek, his lips just grazing me.

Here, I have two options: give in to what we both want or be a brat and see
what happens. I only have a few seconds to make the decision or else it will be

made for me. I think carefully. I haven't seen Zach in a week and a half-ish. I know it's a short amount of time, but I missed him. I didn't realize how much until I saw him biking up the driveway. For all I know, I could be leaving back to Hawaii at the end of the week. I should make the most out of my time. Throwing a leg over him, I pull us close, dragging my hands up his shirt.

"Kiss me, Zach." What originally was going to be a soft, delicate kiss turns terrifically devilish due to my shenanigans. Zach's tongue slides into my mouth as if trying to touch something it can't quite reach. When it finds my own, it expertly caresses it, inviting me to my own journey between his lips. I accept eagerly, pressing our mouths together harder, drunk on the taste of my childhood friend.

He rolls us over so he's on top of me, straddling my hips as his hand goes to my neck. He applies pressure to the side, causing a pleasurable ringing in my ear and a slight feeling of euphoria. A whine of need escapes me, and Zach moans, breaking the kiss to bite my neck. The ache of his marks is desirable, and I tilt my head, exposing more skin for him to tease. His tongue slithers across my skin, tempting me to pursue lustful acts.

"I need you," I moan, wrapping my legs around Zach's hips and pulling him close to me. "I need you now." With all my weight and newfound strength from training, I roll him over, with me on top of him. His head slams against the pillow, and he looks up at me, impressed. Leaning forward, he tries to kiss me again, but I shove him back down. I rip off my shirt and sports bra, revealing two small pear-like breasts.

Before he has a chance to admire them, I attack his neck, tilting his head by his chin. A sound I've never heard him make before slips through his lips, his arms wrapping around me. He pulls me in tightly, squeezing a satisfied sigh out of me. My teeth tug at his skin hungrily. After each bite, I comfort the mark with my lips, my tongue doing figure eights on his skin. His fingertips dance over my back, gifting me with a sensation that sends shivers to my other set of lips.

I'm no longer in control of my actions—my body is. As I tug at Zach's shirt, I whimper. I need to feel our chests pressed together. He moves my hips to his thighs and sits up to tug off his shirt. Crumbling it up into a ball, I chuck it across the room before shoving him on his back. I slide my hips down his legs, leaving a trail of kisses until I get to his waistband.

"Ruby . . ." he moans, his hands on either side of my face. Ignoring him, I tug on his pants, eager to taste what lies between his legs. Just as I'm seeing his shaft, he grabs me by the neck, pulling me toward him. Our lips crash together, and we inhale each other, our tongues and lips dancing in a coordinated tango that carries no pattern. His hands crawl up my stomach to my chest, massaging my breasts and perky nipples. I sigh in pleasure, rocking my hips against his pelvis, eager to return to what I was doing before I was rudely interrupted by his lips. I move to go back down, but he holds me still, kissing me hungrily with longing.

"Ruby, let's wait, okay?" I pull away from him, confused.

"Are you okay? Did I do bad?" I ask, becoming self-conscious. I crawl off him quickly, covering my chest with my knees. Zach sits up straight.

"No, Ruby, not at all. That was," he pauses, rubbing the back of his neck, "that was incredible." He breathes. I release a breath and cock my head, puzzled.

"Then why did you want to stop?" All lustful desire has evaporated, leaving only concern. Things were just great. I can't understand why he wanted to stop.

"Trust me, Ruby, I want to continue." He leans his head back on the headboard, staring up at the ceiling fan. "It's just that I don't want to have sex with you with the fear you won't come back," he explains, eyes glued to the spinning blades. "Because with that fear, Ruby, I won't be able to hold back."

Electricity erupts in my spine, and I nod in understanding, crawling back to him slowly. I lay next to him, my head on his chest as I wiggle my way under the covers. He wraps his arm around me, bringing me closer. Lips press against my forehead before his head relaxes against mine. We don't say anything for the rest of the night, simply enjoying the comfort of each other's presence before falling asleep in one another's arms.

"So Garnet, Ziri, Pearl, and I have been talking, and we think that it'd be best to split into two teams," Tani says, standing in front of a whiteboard. This morning was just as good as last night. We all had breakfast together, Zach included, before making our way to the tree to discuss the next steps. Against Peri's wishes, Zach is also joining the family meeting. He's sitting to the left of me, hand in mine, under the table. "For color marker purposes, we'll do Team Red," she says, drawing a large rectangle on the board, "and Team Blue." She draws another rectangle before handing the blue marker to Garnet.

"Team Red will be on rescue. We're assuming that BS has a room where he's holding all of the people he . . ." Tani looks around the room, cringing. ". . . uses, so Team Red will be getting them out of wherever they are."

"But how will you know?" Emerald asks, taking notes on a sheet of paper aggressively. I admire the focus, and I feel like I should be taking notes, too, but, honestly, I'm too lazy for that. He'll just have to share.

"We're gonna send a group in early to find their location." Tani explains. "Basically, day one, we scout out the area, and day two, we execute the plan." Tani grabs a green marker and draws another smaller rectangle. "Scouting will be me, Ruby, Garnet, Pearl, and Peri. Everyone else can enjoy Hawaii for the day." My siblings exchange hollers of excitement and a couple of high fives. Garnet picks up the discarded red marker and refers to the board.

"Anywho," she says, slightly irritated by our theatrics, "Team Red is Emerald, Alex, Moon, Amethyst, Citrine, Topaz, Tory, Jasper, Turq, and Jade." The marker squeaks as she scribbles everyone's names. "You all have powers suited for defense rather than offense, that's why you're on rescue." Citrine pushes herself out of her seat, huffing a breath of air.

"What?" she shouts, her fingertips and hair on fire. "You think my power is *defense?*" she spits out, disgusted at Garnet's words. Topaz is next to Citrine, ready to jump in if she gets too heated.

"No, Citrine." Tani remarks calmly. "We just think it'd be safer than the alternative." Slowly, Citrine relaxes.

"Oh." She takes her seat once more.

"But wouldn't it be more safe if they stayed home?" Turq asks, eyeing Garnet and Tani. "I just don't understand why we all have to go." I tilt my head with thought; she makes a valid point.

"Safety in numbers?" Peri questions.

"We've just been working toward this together," Garnet says, gazing around the room. "It'd be unfair to leave someone behind."

"Plus," Tani adds, "the power variety is something we can take advantage of if need be." The room is filled with nods of agreement from everyone except Turq, her face full of doubt.

"On Team Blue," Garnet continues, barely giving anyone time to gather their thoughts, "is me, Tani, Peri, Ruby, Ziri, Pearl, Opal, Diamond, Sapphire, and Aquamarine."

"Wait, why aren't Jade and I together?" Aquamarine asks, clutching onto her twin's shoulder.

"Because you guys are going to be our human walkie-talkies," Tani says, tucking a piece of hair behind her ear and grinning proudly. She must have come up with this. "Since you're telepathic, we can easily relay messages between the teams." Aquamarine's mouth turns into an *o,* and she tugs on her sister's arm, clearly excited. At this point, everyone is. They're all talking about the mission eagerly, thrilled to be able to put their powers to use outside of the training room. Their eagerness rubs me the wrong way. It seems like they all forgot what's at stake.

"Not to kill the vibe or anything," Diamond interrupts, "but like, we go in, kick ass, and then what? Like, what happens when we get Bloodstone?" Ziri smiles wickedly and looks at her intelligent triplet. As she does, Tani pulls something out of her back pocket: a syringe.

"This serum should shut off the gene in Bloodstone, hopefully permanently," Tani explains, holding the weapon carefully. "I just need to get close enough to him to inject it."

"What is it?" Citrine asks, leaning forward on the table. The sun glares off her tiara, causing rainbows to sprinkle the room.

"It's a mix of the properties of musgravite and bloodstone; and it's super concentrated." Tani holds it up in the light. "It's supposed to act as a form of gene knockout. We tested super small concentrations on each other," Tani points between her, Ziri, and Garnet, "and it seemed to have some sort of impact. So, hopefully, since this is a much higher concentration, it will have a lasting effect."

"And if it doesn't work?" Diamond asks worryingly. We're all silent now, looking at our smartest siblings for comfort. Garnet, Ziri, and Tani exchange a glance before Garnet speaks.

"We hope that it does." The room is filled with unease, but, as the three girls explain the plan, the tension seems to lift. Everything is well thought-out and planned to a T. It appears they went through every possible thing that could happen and accounted for it.

Everyone has a purpose. I'm in charge of keeping my team invisible, and Pearl is the transportation. For Team Red, Tory is both. She'll be wearing our stones on top of her's and Bloodstone's. If people are captured and locked up, Emerald is responsible for setting them free.

Garnet explains that Bloodstone will most likely have people working with him. Whether against their will or not, they aren't to be harmed.

"Avoid it, and if you can't, then minimal harm. These people probably didn't sign up for this." As more of the plan is discussed, Zach squeezes my hand, and I look over at him. Worry is written all over his face; I wish that this meeting would put him at ease. This morning, he seemed clingy and anxious. He followed me everywhere, even waiting outside of the bathroom door.

When Tani announces that we're leaving in a couple of days, I slouch in my seat. All of this running around all over the country has me exhausted. *Why can't the world just save itself?*

CHAPTER 33

Instead of staying in a hotel, we opt for a large Airbnb. Garnet and Tani are itching to get things on the move, and their determination and confidence is addictive. And yet, a sense of dread bubbles in my stomach. As the shuttle bus pulls up to the house, I smile as my siblings hoot and holler. Topaz has to hold her twin from running out of her seat, while everyone stares in awe at the house. I wish I were in a state of mind where I could appreciate the architecture and beauty, but I'm too nervous.

A pretty penny was definitely spent on this house. Tani explained how there were ten bedrooms, so we would have to double up. I was ecstatic when Moon came up to me asking if we could room. I totally thought that she would want to room with Sapphire, so I was pleasantly caught off guard. When the bus finally comes to a stop, we all unload, dragging our carry-ons to the elegant home.

Everyone is running, shoving each other out of the way as they rush for the door. It takes a couple of seconds before understanding sets in, and I break into a sprint. I'll be damned if Moon and I end up with the worst room in the house. My eyes search for her, but she's nowhere to be seen. I hope with all my might that the reason she isn't here means she's in the house.

Opting for a different route, I'm running full speed to the right of the house when I find a high stone wall, maybe six feet tall. I place my hand against it and will myself through. As I step through the wall, I enter an exterior bathroom.

Before I let myself enjoy, I dash into the bedroom, chucking myself on the bed right as the door barges open. I flip over to see Peri, and I stick my tongue out.

"Fuck you," he says, before disappearing back out of the room. I smile at myself as I lay back against the covers. I send Moon a quick text telling her I secured our room, before rolling off the bed. We weren't told to pack more than four days' worth of clothes, so I don't even bother putting them away.

The room I chose has a brown boho aesthetic. Everything is in a variety of neutral shades from the queen bed sheets to the wall décor. It isn't so much that it is overwhelming, but it has a nice balance and feels homier than a hotel. The doorway and wall I entered from are made completely of glass, obscured with frost in the shape of turtles. Tempered glass surrounds the sea turtles as if they are bubbles in water. Walking back to our outdoor bathroom, I take in the scenery. The bathtub is made of stone, matching the bathroom walls. Directly to the right of it, a few feet away, is a large shower head, parallel to the ground. Over both is nothing but the sky. To the right and left of where I'm standing are the toilet and sink, respectively. There is a slight overhang from the room upstairs, providing some type of shelter from the weather.

"Jackpot, Ruby." The voice makes me jump, and I whip my head. Moon is sitting in a fluffy papasan, taking in our room. Closing the door behind me, I walk back inside to sit cross-legged on the bed, facing her.

"Right?" I ask, running my fingers through the sheets. She nods, sliding her phone in her back pocket and looking at me curiously. I sigh internally, already knowing what's about to come.

"How are you?" Moon asks, playing with the ends of her white braids. Part of me wants to say that I'm fine and ready. That we are going to kick some familial ass and save the entire freaking world from . . . who knows what. But I know she's hoping I respond truthfully.

"I'm scared, Moon," I confess, uncrossing my legs and bringing my knees to my chest. "This is really it. Everything has been happening so fast, it just seems surreal." She nods along to my words, listening thoughtfully. "I just have this feeling in my stomach that something is going to go really, really wrong, and no matter how hard I try, the pit isn't being filled." I look at her, waiting for her input, but she's silent. She continues playing with her hair, staring up at the ceiling with her head leaning slightly to the right.

"Don't," she says, looking back at me.

"Don't what?"

"Don't fill the pit of dread. Use that fear and knowledge of BS to think objectively." She twists a braid around her finger. "I can't say that I understand where this feeling is coming from entirely, but, of course, I didn't see what you saw. And even though Pearl was very graphic with her description of what happened before, I couldn't help but think she may have been exaggerating a little. I know I'm not the only one." I open my mouth to tell her that everything that Pearl described was accurate, but when she sees me move, she holds a hand up. "Now, I'm not saying that didn't happen, but Garnet and Tani's optimism is addicting and spreading through us all like wildfire." She cocks her head again. "Well, all except you, Pearl, Tory, and Turq." My eyes shoot up to her.

"Turq?"

Moon nods.

"She was skeptical about us all coming here, remember?" I pause, thinking back to our family meeting from a few days ago. Her face flashes in my mind: crinkled eyebrows, tight lips, fear in her eyes. "There's not much we can do now. We have a solid plan, and we're all already here. We just have to be careful is all."

I fall back into our shared bed, pressing my palms to my eyes. Honestly, I don't know how to feel after this conversation. It just seems that a lot worse could come out of this than good. But, then again, Moon's right about the plan. It's solid. Maybe I'm just all in my head.

I make sure to shut my alarm off before it wakes Moon up and slip quietly out from under the covers. Heading to the bathroom, I grab black leggings, a black halter top, some underwear, and a bra before shutting the door behind me. Garnet is itching to get the plan in motion, so last night, during dinner, she told everyone they could enjoy the morning while the scouting team leaves at sunrise, which, unfortunately, means me. I drag my fingers through my twists as I sit on the toilet. *It'll be fine.* I wipe and flush, then get up to wash my hands. *The plan is foolproof.* I tie my hair up into a bun, open the linen closet adjacent to the sink, and head to the shower.

I hesitate before pulling off my pajamas. This is such a weird experience: showering outside. I feel as though anyone could just decide to look over, and they'd just see me. Cooter out and everything. *This is a Peeping Tom's fantasy bathroom, I swear.* I peel off the sweaty pj's.

Last night was restless. I'm glad I didn't have a nightmare or any sort of dream, but the night wasn't rejuvenating at all. In fact, I feel more tired than I did when I fell asleep the night before. I turn the shower on and brace myself, letting the cold water wake me up. Gasping, I fight the urge to step out of reach of the liquid icicles. I need to be at 110 percent today and tomorrow. I let the water pound against my lethargic body, letting the exhaustion and sleep wash down the drain.

After some intense soaping, I step out of the shower, wrapping my towel around my dripping limbs. Although the sun isn't up, the morning breeze isn't chilly. It's refreshing. I breathe in the scent of the ocean while dragging the towel across my skin. When I'm completely dry, I use the complementary vanilla coconut lotion, gently applying it.

Within minutes, I'm dressed and headed for the living room, my phone tucked in my back pocket. I puff out my cheeks when I realize I'm the last one of the scout team to be ready. Pulling out my phone, I check the time. The sun shouldn't rise for another fifteen minutes. With a sigh of relief, I take a seat next to Peri.

"How'd you sleep last night?" I ask. On the coffee table is a platter of fruit and granola bars. I reach for a chocolate chip one and pop a strawberry in my mouth.

"Like a baby," Peri says as he stretches his arm.

"Who'd you room with?" I ask, grabbing another strawberry.

"Emerald. Thank god he doesn't have a snore like Tani," Peri says, sending her a glare. She meets his gaze, flicking him off before returning to her . . . well, I'm not sure what it is.

"What are you eating, Tani?" She tilts what she's holding toward me, and I nod.

"It's cereal. I cracked a coconut, drained it, and put coconut milk and Honey Bunches of Oats inside," she explains before taking a spoonful. "It's quite good."

"Shame on you for wasting perfectly good coconut water," Peri teases, but she's ready for it.

"Actually," she starts, taking an exaggerated spoonful, "it's recommended to drink coconut water from a Sweet Young Coconut, which lacks the exterior husks these have." She holds up her brown natural bowl. "But I did save the water from this for later on today. It's chilling in the fridge," Tani says, nodding her head toward the fridge.

"Smart ass," Peri mumbles, his mouth full of peanut butter granola. Tani smirks at him, lifts the coconut to her lips, and drinks the remaining liquid, emphasizing a sigh. Peri opens his mouth to say something, but Garnet comes around the couch, rubbing her hands together. Her excitement is evident, and it makes sense. She remembers our parents better than any of us and probably even has some pictures she keeps hidden. Of course, we all want this: to be reunited. But for her, it's different.

"Alright, y'all. Sun's up, fun's up. You ready?" Garnet asks us, not even trying to hide the grin on her face. I know she's hoping she'll see mom today, but in the state that she was in when we saw her last time, maybe seeing her isn't a good idea. Pearl stands up, grabbing my hand on the way. I follow suit and hold onto Peri's. In seconds, we form a small circle around the coffee table, hand in each other's hand.

"Welcome to Pearl Express," Pearl says, giving us all a wink. "Prepare for nausea."

"Nausea?" Peri asks just as Pearl ports us all out of the house. Her skills have gotten better. She doesn't have to make as many stops before making it to the clearing. When we make it, Pearl and I wait for the others to gather their footing. Peri barely lasts two seconds before vomiting all over the ground. Tani and Garnet don't look so hot either. They both sink to the ground slowly, laying in the grass.

"Damn, girl." Garnet grunts, tucking her legs to her chest.

"No, 'cause for real," Tani says, a hand over her mouth. Pearl chuckles as she watches them gather their bearings.

"While y'all are . . . y'know . . . remember the plan." Pearl pops her iconic piece of gum. "We go in, we find the locations of his captives or whatever, and then we're out of there," she asserts.

"Bruh," Peri says as he wipes his mouth, "we know. We went over this so many times."

"Yeah," Pearl agrees, her voice full of attitude. "I'm just trying to make sure that we *stick* with it." She stares at Peri, and he matches her. But then his expression changes. I look at Pearl and see she's eyeing Garnet between her gazes with him. Peri gives a curt nod, eyeing his eldest sister too. She's on her feet now, jumping up and down, shaking the nausea off. She's talking quietly to herself, giving herself some inaudible motivational speech. Pearl tries to get Tani's attention, too, but a curt nod from her tells us she already knows what's up. It takes me a few seconds, but when I understand, I nibble my lip.

"Alright, we good to go?" Garnet says turning to face us.

"Yeah." I clear my throat as we move to stand in a circle again. "Phone ringers off?" Everyone nods. "Good. Remember, I can only make visual things disappear, not sound. I'll form a bubble around us, so just stay close. Communicate through text." I squeeze Pearl's hand to let her know I'm done with my spiel.

"And off we go."

CHAPTER 34

In less than a second, I'm back in the main room of his lair. Garnet and Peri take in the scene, mouth agape. Tani gazes thoughtfully, eyeing the structure and the space. I wave at them to get their attention and point up toward the office. We begin the climb up the stairs as memories come back in flashes. Anxiety and discomfort bubble in my stomach. *Will you be my mommy now?* The boy's voice rings in my ears, and the gunshots echo in my brain. No one should have that much power. I'm consumed with pain, so much so, that I didn't realize I stopped moving. Then, it flickers: my invisibility.

My lips part in silent surprise, and I take control of my power again. It was just a moment, nearly less than a second. But to the cameras that are sure to be hidden in this room, we were seen. I focus, remembering that this could be a repeat of last time too. I catch up to my siblings, only a few steps behind, as we make our way to our uncle's lair's office. Unsurprisingly, the door is unlocked, and we walk in with ease. Soundless gasps come from Peri, Tani, and Garnet as they see the blood-stained walls and floors. The chains that once held my mom captive are discarded in the corner of the room, forgotten.

Sensing the emotions and memories returning, I point toward the door where the boy and mom came from and try to usher my siblings to head for it. Pearl has no problem. She's already by the door. But the motions of my other siblings are slow. Tani and Garnet exchange some sort of weighted look, and

Peri drags his hands across his face. A pang of twisted hope shoots in my chest. Maybe they can snap out of their ridiculous optimism and confidence streak and realize what we are *actually* up against.

I lean toward Garnet and tug hard on her arm, pointing toward the door. She gives a stiff, curt nod and follows me, the others on her tail. Pearl turns the doorknob slowly, but the rotation is interrupted with a lock. A gaze at me lets me know it's my turn to shine, and I press my hand against the door, pushing my arm through. I unlock it from the other side, pull my arm back, and open the door. When I see Peri shake his head with irritation, I send him a wink. The power of claircognizance is only useful when approached by an unknown person, or with getting dirt to use against his siblings. It makes sense for him to be jealous of someone who can literally walk through walls.

We pass through the doorway, entering a long hallway that stops short with a dead end. Like our uncle's office, the walls are a deep red and the floors a gray concrete. On each side of the hall are three steel doors with bars as windows. We exchange slow glances and walk down the hall.

The first door is on our left. I peek inside and grimace. It's dimly lit, but I can make out the bodies and shadows of at least fifty people. Some of them are asleep. Others of them are whispering quietly. My eyes widen, and I dash to the next door, this time on my right. Again, fifty or so people, a variety of sizes. I'm zigzagging to the doors, my stomach filling with dread. I feel a pull on my power and look back at the others. They're still at the first door. Peri is taking pictures on his phone while Tani and Garnet type aggressively on their phones. Pearl is on the floor, her back against the wall, her eyes fixed on the ceiling.

Right, we're here to gather intel. I'm literally being useless right now. But when I reach the last door, my whole body freezes. This room is unlike the others. It's about the size of a small bedroom, and I see one body on the bed. It rolls over, facing toward me.

I whip away from the door and wave at the others aggressively, trying to capture their attention. They're on the second door now, repeating the same process as the first: pictures and typing. Peri sees me first and taps Tani's shoulder. Soon, they're all jogging toward me. I point to the door and step back, giving them all some space. Tani covers her mouth quietly, her eyes full of hope. Peri stumbles backward, holding on to the wall across from him for support. Before any of us can react, a loud, painful sob escapes Garnet as she clutches onto the bars.

I make a move toward her, but Pearl is faster, clamping a hand over her mouth. Mom's sitting up now, staring intently at the door. Garnet pulls at the bars, shaking the locked door violently.

"Who's there?" mom yells, fear in her eyes. She's standing up now, backing away to the corner. I rush over to help Pearl, trying to pry Garnet's fingers from the metal bars. But her grip is like stone. Muffled words come from under Pearl's clamped hands, but it's incoherent. Pearl whips her head toward Peri and Tani for help, and they immediately snap out of shock. Tani ducks underneath Garnet's arm, pushing her away from the door, while Peri and I tug at her shoulders. Garnet kicks back, hitting Peri on his upper thigh, and he stumbles back, falling into the wall loudly.

Pearl kicks Tani lightly, gathering her attention, then looking at me intently. No words need to be exchanged for us to understand. Tani moves from under Garnet and dives for Peri, linking her foot around Pearl's ankle. I move my hand from Garnet's shoulder to press the top of Pearl's hand covering Garnet's mouth. The familiar squeeze rips through my stomach, and when I open my eyes, we're back in the clearing. Pearl and I let go of Garnet, who falls on the grass sobbing and yelling.

"Mom!" she cries loudly. "Mom, I'm right here!" Pearl and I rush to check on Peri, now moaning in pain in Tani's arms. Within several moments, Garnet realizes we're out of the prison, and she turns to us slowly, angry.

"What the fuck was that?" shouts Pearl, getting up to stand in front of her.

"No. What the fuck is *this?*" she growls, pointing back toward Mauna Kea. "Mom was *right there*. We could have saved her now."

"That wasn't the plan," Tani says, her voice hard. She's staring at Garnet with an expression I've never seen before. Usually, the two of them are two peas in a pod, always in cahoots and planning. A spark of disappointment and distrust shines in Tani's glare. Garnet breaks eye contact with her to lock eyes on me.

"You could have saved her," she says, making her way toward me. I carefully step back, my hands up in innocence.

"Me?" I ask, continuing to walk backward. Pearl sidesteps in front of me, blocking Garnet's path. But Garnet doesn't even hesitate. In a smooth stride she whips off her glove and slams her palm into Pearl's chest. An expression of shock freezes on her face as ash slowly creeps up to her neck. She falls to the ground hard, paralyzed by Garnet's power. My eyes widen in horror. I've never seen Garnet's power in action, for obvious reasons. Although the paralysis is temporary, a chill is sent through my spine. She's gone too far. Looking at Pearl, I see her beautiful mocha skin covered in ash, as if she hasn't put lotion on in years. You can almost count every skin cell.

"Garnet!" Tani gasps, removing herself from under Peri to check on Pearl. I analyze his state. Besides some dizziness and pain in his leg, he looks fine. He crawls toward Tani awkwardly, attempting to help Pearl. Garnet still has her eyes set on me, every step purposeful to doing me some sort of harm, I'm sure.

"Yes, *you*." Garnet says. "You could have gone through the door and brought mama back to me. To *us*." I successfully dodge a palm to the chest but land directly into a trap. Her gloved hand grabs me by the throat, and she slams me up against a tree. Her eyes are a deep dark red, inflamed with hatred and failure. I squirm, but my hair gets caught on the bark, tugging tightly on my scalp.

"That . . . that wasn't what we . . ." I gasp, struggling to take in air. "We didn't . . . talk about it." Garnet squeezes tighter, and my vision clouds, fireworks of light erupting behind my closed lids.

"It doesn't matter," she spits out, pressing me harder into the tree. "We weren't expecting to find mom, so the plan should have changed. You all should have followed *my lead*." Before I start to lose consciousness, I latch onto my power, making myself invisible and slipping through and out of her grasp. Her hand clasps on empty air, and she lets out a growl, pounding her fist against the tree. With Pearl out of commission, we're all stuck here. And it doesn't look like Garnet is going to calm down any time soon. I stay on the ground silent, trying not to cough, trying to take in air.

"And then what!" This time it's Tani. She's standing about ten feet behind Garnet, her hands outstretched at her sides. "Then what, Garnet? You tell me." Tani's muscles in her jaw are tense, eyebrows furrowed.

"Then we go home, and we're done!" Garnet says, clearly blinded from reality.

"Wrong," Tani replies, her voice sharp. "Then, Bloodstone knows we're here, finds us, and we all get captured. Or maybe we do make it out, but what about all of those innocent people?"

"It's fine," Garnet says. She's pacing now, tugging at the glove in her hands. "Then we come back later. At least we have mom!"

"But what about dad?" Tani shouts, tears streaming down her face, her hands in fists. Garnet's head whips to meet her eyes, and she freezes, staring at her younger sister. "Bloodstone would have known we grabbed mom and would have moved everything. We don't even know if dad is down there!" Tani grits out, pointing toward the dormant volcano. The tension in Garnet's shoulders begins to ease slowly, and she looks around the clearing quietly. Sensing that things are safer, I release my invisibility, giving in to the coughs that overtake my lungs.

"We're on your side, Garnet. We all want the same thing: to save the world and be the family we were supposed to be," Tani confirms, her voice softer now. "We had a good plan, and it's *still* a good plan. We just need to stick to it." Quiet tears stream down Garnet's face, and she falls to her knees, giving in to the sobs of sorrow.

"I'm sorry. Fuck, I'm so sorry." She takes in the scene: two sisters, one paralyzed and one gasping, and a bruised brother. Tani walks over to her and bends down, clutching Garnet in her arms. The cries strengthen now, and Garnet curls into a ball, cradled in her younger sister's arms. Tani gently takes the crumpled glove from her fist and puts it back on her hand, stroking Garnet's hair and back with comfort. Tani calls to me softly.

"Ruby, call Tory." I slowly pull out my phone and do so.

"Is everything okay?" Tory asks, her voice filled with worry.

"Um, things didn't go as planned. We need you to pick us up at the clearing." I say, watching Garnet wail and Peri struggle to his feet.

"What about Pearl? Can't she—"

"Tory, please come now." She pauses, catching the severity in my tone.

"I'll be there soon," she replies before hanging up. In about five minutes, a wide-eyed Tory appears in the clearing. Her gaze lands on Peri and Pearl, and then Tani and Garnet before resting on me.

"Let's take Pearl and Peri back first. We'll come back for the other two." I say, walking over to Tory. I wrap my invisibility around the four of us, and Tory teleports us out. She isn't as skilled as Pearl and needs to make more pitstops. Thankfully, the final stop is in Pearl's room, away from the curious and sure to be concerned eyes of my siblings.

Tory and I carefully lift Pearl to rest on her bed before porting back for Garnet and Tani. Instead of the last stop being Pearl's room, this time it's Garnet's. Tani whispers something in Garnet's ears, and she slowly and silently walks toward the bathroom. Tani gestures to the door, and Tory and I follow her out.

"What happened?" Tory asks, tugging at her silver braid.

"We'll talk about it later," Tani says, running her hands through her hair.

"No, what hap—" Tory starts again, but Tani whirls her head around, glaring at the confused fourteen-year-old girl.

"I said, we'll talk about it later." Before anyone can add anything, Tani disappears down the hall, out of sight. Tory then looks at me, her eyes pleading with me to tell her what happened. I know I should respect what Tani wants, but I don't. Knowing the relationship that Tory has with Pearl, as well as everything that we went through together, leaving her in the dark is cruel. I grab her by the wrist and tug her down the hall, weaving my way through room after room until we reach the backyard.

As soon as we step onto the patio, we're met with a beautiful rectangular glass outdoor table, meant to seat twenty. Nine chairs lay along the long sides, with one on either short end. Shielding us from bad weather is a large overhang, keeping the table and outdoor appliances safe from Mother Nature's grasp. We walk past the patio, past the pool, and through the grass, headed to the beach. When I'm out of earshot from any curious ears, the words flow out in a hurricane. When I get to the part where Garnet paralyzes Pearl, Tory's face is full of shock, and she freezes before crumpling to the sand.

"G-Garnet did that to her?" Tory asks softly, and I nod, moving to crouch next to her. "I thought it was Bloodstone. I thought he found you guys. But it was Garnet." I tell her the rest of what happened quickly. How Garnet was so clouded with rage she didn't realize what she was doing. As I go through the retelling, she nods slowly, pushing herself to her feet and brushing sand off her.

"How long does it last? The paralysis?" Tory asks, her face somber. I grimace and shrug.

"I don't know; all I know is that it's temporary." Tory nods quietly at that and walks toward the house.

"I'm gonna stay with her until things clear up."

I spend the rest of the day in my room. So far, every time we've infiltrated Bloodstone's lair, the mission has gone to shit. I hope and pray that tomorrow, if we can even go, things are okay. At around noon, Tory texted me telling me that Pearl started to blink, and at around 1:30 p.m., she was able to move her facial muscles. She is critical to the mission, so if she isn't better by tonight, we might have to push it back a day.

My siblings came into my room, asking how the morning went. I tried not to be solemn, but I guess when they saw the look on my face, they knew it couldn't be good. At 5 p.m., a family text was sent out.

Tani: Dinner is ready! Come to the table to eat. We will also discuss how this morning went.

CHAPTER 35

I tug the covers off and make my way to the kitchen, stomach gurgling. On the table is a large bowl of what smells like Huli Huli chicken, a platter of fish and veggie tacos, garlic shrimp, a large salad bowl, grilled vegetables, and a platter of malasadas. My stomach grumbles at the aroma, and I take a seat eagerly. Already at the table are Tory, Pearl, and Emerald, all sitting together.

"How are you, Pearl?" I ask, my voice filled with concern. When I see her shrug, I am overcome with relief.

"As good as I can be. My legs are still fried, though," she explains, nodding her head toward Emerald. "He carried me down for dinner early. Didn't want all eyes on me, y'know?" I nod, reaching for my glass of water.

"I'm just glad you're okay."

"Hell, yeah. Me too." Pearl reaches for her own glass. She takes a long gulp before setting it down. "I'm just hoping this shit clears up by morning. I wanna go home." She eyes the food eagerly. "I fucking hate this place." At that, Emerald chuckles, laying his napkin across my lap.

"Hate it here? It's Hawaii. This is paradise," Emerald remarks, leaning back in his seat. Pearl reaches for a taco and takes a bite, before setting the rest on her plate.

"Talk again to me tomorrow night. We'll see if this place is still paradise to you," Pearl replies with her mouth full, her eyes glued to Emerald's. He shifts uncomfortably under her gaze before trying to break the tension.

"You aren't going to wait for everyone to get here before eating?" Emerald asks, gesturing toward Pearl's plate. She shakes her head.

"Naw, I'm hungry as fuck." Pearl plops her plate in his hand. The weight surprises him, and he sits up quickly, holding the plate steady. "You wanna grab that chicken for me. Ooo, and those grilled vegetables." I chuckle as Emerald scrunches up his eyebrows, standing to fix Pearl's plate. Tory lets out a giggle, too, lightly bumping shoulders with Pearl.

"I'm glad you're back." Within five minutes, the table is full of all my siblings, everyone eager to eat. The only one who followed Pearl's lead is Peri, for obvious reasons. To be honest, I'm about to call it quits and start making my plate, but Tani stands up, tapping a glass with a spoon to gather our attention. We all give it to her. Curious looks spread through Citrine, Sapphire, Moon, and others. Garnet is usually the one at the head of the table and the one giving the speeches. But tonight, it's Tani, Garnet quietly sitting to her right.

"I hope you all had a nice and relaxing day. I'm going to fill you in on how this morning went, but first, let's eat! We need everyone on their top game tomorrow, and we have no room for error. So that means a full stomach and lots of sleep tonight! We'll strike at noon!" Tani says, a broad smile on her face. "Cheers to all our hard work and to our family!" She extends her arm in the air proudly, and everyone follows suit with cheers and applause, the most enthusiastic from the ones who are unaware of this morning's events.

Trying not to look too eager, I quickly fill my plate with Huli Huli chicken, grilled vegetables, and two fish tacos, along with water as a beverage. Coolers are behind me, and I grab a strawberry soda before bowing my head silently. Right as I pick up my taco, Turq speaks to me.

"You're religious, Ruby?" she asks, sitting to the right of me.

"What do you mean?" I take a bite of my taco. I sigh as the flavors dance over my tongue, causing me to do my own little happy dance.

"You just prayed, didn't you?" asks Turq curiously, taking a bite of shrimp.

"Oh, I did. Yeah, uh," I place the taco back on the plate and shift to face her, "my adopted family is . . . was? I don't know. They're Jewish," I explain, taking a sip of the soda. "But like, I don't really know if I'm religious. Do I speak to God and pray to him sometimes? Yes. But I wouldn't say I practice Judaism."

"So you're spiritual," Tani chimes in. The conversations are hushed, everyone listening.

"Yeah, I guess I am." I take a bite of chicken. "I'm also Kosher. I never ate pork or shellfish and so on. Never really saw a reason to start either," I say, my mouth full. This chicken is so good, the sauce sends fireworks of delight to my brain. I keep forgetting that we all grew up differently. There's still so much more I need to learn about my siblings. Their favorite colors, music, food. What scares them and what makes them happy. *Have I been an awful sister?* I look at all of them, watching as they ease back into whatever conversation they were having. From being thrown to Tennessee and then Hawaii, I feel like I've lost valuable time getting to know them. That's why the day we spent together was so amazing. I can't wait to share more moments like that with them. And after tomorrow, when we are all *officially* reunited as a family again, that bond will only strengthen.

"What about you guys?" I ask quickly, before the gap between my previous statement extends. We go around the table, sharing our beliefs and our experiences practicing religion. Garnet, Diamond, Emerald, Alex, Moon, Sapphire, Jasper, and Citrine are all Christian. About half of them regularly attended church with their old families and explain that is one of the things they're looking forward to doing when we can finally go out into the world. Like me, Tory and Turquoise are spiritual, believing in some form of higher power or another. Topaz's eyes light up when she learns that Opal is Muslim, too, and I can tell she wants to talk to them more about it later.

Tani and Ziri are agnostic, while Pearl is atheist. For the rest of my siblings, they aren't exactly sure what they believe in. They shift uncomfortably in their seats, unsure of how to add to the conversation.

"Don't feel like you have to believe in something," Tani explains, trying to provide them comfort. "It's okay to not know, and it's okay to explore and do research."

"I think as long as you have faith," Ziri chimes in, smiling kindly, "that's all that matters. Whether you have faith in your friends and family, faith in yourself, faith in a higher power, or faith that everything will be okay, then there's something pushing you to live . . . to go through the world and progress in society."

"To be honest," Peri starts, and by his tone, I nearly begin to roll my eyes. "I feel like things, like the future and life or whatever, finna go to shit. Like, I'm so for real right now." The air that was once filled with hope and belonging begins filling with something else: agitation. "Like after this morning, I don't know about faith, man." He takes a long swig of his soda and places it down on the table. When he sees everyone eyeing him with either concern, worry, or irritation, he holds his hands up in defense.

"Now, I'm not telling y'all to stop having faith and shit. Hell, if y'alls beliefs and stuff finna make tomorrow go great, then praise Jesus! Yes, higher power! Do your thang!" he says encouragingly. "I just never believed in that type of shit before. Not that it's shit," Peri adds quickly, trying to be respectful while explaining his thoughts. "I tried to. Shit, I tried hard. But shit went down anyway . . ." He trails off, taking a long thoughtful bite of his taco.

"What *did* happen this morning?" Topaz asks. All eyes fall on Tani, and she takes a deep breath before going into today's retelling. Learning from Pearl's interruption from the last time someone attempted to omit mission details, she doesn't skip a beat. She tries to be as objective as possible. When she gets to the part when we make it to the cell hall, she asks Peri to airdrop the photos to everyone. He grumbles something about Topaz's Android before I feel my phone buzz in my hand. Tani explains how Team Red, the rescue team, will be teleported directly into the hall. Or, if it's better for Emerald, one of the rooms. Since he's an escapologist, getting out of the room may be easier than breaking i
n.

"I trust y'alls judgment for that. You're a team, and as a team, you can discuss what works best for you. After dinner, actually. Please do that." In response to Tani's words, Team Red nods. With another deep breath, Tani explains where the plan went awry. She doesn't even try to soften what happened for Garnet's sake. She explains how Garnet went rogue, overcome with emotion. Unable to control herself, we ported out of there. Blah, blah, blah. Tani is much more detailed, but since I lived the experience, I feel no need to pay attention to *everything* she says. Gasps erupt, jaws drop, and some siblings side-eye Garnet as she explains what happened to Pearl. Pearl throws up an awkward peace sign.

"Y'all, chill. I'm fine," Pearl voices reassuringly. After a short pause, Tani finishes the story. She tells us all that Pearl should be fine by later tonight.

Pearl chimes in, "I can already feel my toes!" With both Tani and Pearl confident in her recovery, positivity slips back into the atmosphere. Tani opens her mouth to talk more about tomorrow, but she's interrupted.

"I won't stand for this," Opal says, rising to their feet. They look frustrated and confused.

"Well, I literally can't stand for this. But go on." Pearl smirks, leaning back to look up at Opal across the table. They look down at her apologetically, some of the furiousness leaving their features.

"It's just that," they sigh, dragging their hands down their face, "how do we know for sure that our uncle is inherently bad? What if there are other factors at play? What ever happened to innocent until proven guilty?" they ask genuinely. We all look at them as if they've morphed into a horse with the body of a shark.

"The fuck?" Peri exclaims, eyes wide in disbelief.

"I see what you are saying," Emerald starts, leaning in. "I honestly get it. But you need to look at what we know he's done and—"

"He's guilty to me!" Citrine shouts, interrupting him. "You heard what he did! How can he be innocent?" It's barely there, but I can catch the glint of orange glowing in her eyes. Opal sighs and ruffles their silver curls.

"Look, all I'm saying is that maybe he has a reason for this. Maybe he's a good guy, and from where we're standing, it just doesn't look that way," they propose, playing the devil's advocate.

"Now if that ain't the most Hitler ass bullshit I've ever heard," Peri says, rubbing his wrists to calm himself. The arguing across the table erupts into incoherent throwing of ideas and words. Some people think Opal might be onto something, saying that our uncle is just misguided or tempted by the devil or money or something. Others retort saying that the devil can't tempt himself and that our uncle is pure evil.

"*Stop*!" says a strong voice, and we all go silent. I'm surprised to see who it's coming from. "Please stop," Topaz repeats, quietly this time. "I don't like when families fight . . . Please stop." A quiet tear rolls down her cheek, and everyone is speechless. Those who got up slowly take their seats, and we are all silent for a moment.

"Sorry," Opal mumbles, looking up to meet all our eyes. "Sorry I just . . . to be related to someone with *so* much *hate*. I didn't want to believe it. I *don't* want to believe it." Quiet apologies are exchanged, and the heavy weight of silence begins to lift.

"You're not wrong, Opal," Tani begins, providing comfort. "He may have intentions that he deems pure, but that doesn't change the fact that he is holding people against their will. Murdering people. So maybe you're right about the classic 'good guy doing the bad thing,' but that doesn't change the fact that what he's doing is, indeed, bad. It's cruel." She pauses, thinking about her next words carefully. "Now, what his reasoning may be . . . I don't know. But there is never only one way to do something. He *chose* to do this. If he truly was good and wanted to do something good, he would have found another way." At that, Opal nods, agreeing with Tani.

"But what if there isn't?" Jasper asks, a look of deep concern on his face as he glances between his triplet and his older sister. Tani shakes her head and throws up her hand.

"There's always another way."

CHAPTER 36

The rest of the night was spent discussing the strategy. We went over the plan, over and over, until everyone could recite it from memory. We have such an advantage in numbers and abilities that we should be fine. And it helps that Bloodstone doesn't know that we're all here for him. The only conflict is with my team's job. Since Tory, Pearl, and I were unable to watch his habits, we have no idea where he'll be. So the plan is to stake out the lair if he isn't already there. If so, then perfect.

Falling asleep last night was easily one of the hardest things I've ever had to do. I was so anxious that the night was filled with tosses and turns, and I wasn't the only one. Moon was restless right beside me. Luckily, the exhaustion that should have been there this morning was replaced with adrenaline. When my alarm went off, I shot out of bed, showered, and changed into some black athletic shorts and a cropped hoodie.

Slowly but surely, everyone is making their way to the living room. Everyone is wearing black, some in stylish clothes and others casual. When Citrine steps out of her room, I have to hold in a laugh. She's wearing a black leotard with fishnet leggings. A tutu rests on her hips turning from black to orange. Her hair is pulled back into a slick ponytail tied with an orange scrunchie, and her tiara sits atop her head. Under her eyes is black war paint; she looks like some fierce fire ballerina. From behind her, her twin walks in reluctantly. Topaz is in a near matching fit, except blue instead of orange.

"Let's fuck this shit up," Citrine announces, swinging her hips as she strides deeper into the room. Her palms are up and outstretched, tiny flames dancing in them.

"Badass as fuck, Citrine! *Purrr,*" exclaims Pearl. Ziri sighs, dragging a hand down her face.

"When you asked for the fit, this is not what I was expecting." She gestures toward the twins before elbowing Pearl. "And you, stop inciting that language from her!" Pearl lets out a hearty laugh before placing her elbow on Ziri's shoulder.

"In the future, I'll consider it." Pearl's eyes trace over all her siblings, most not paying her any attention. "But today, we need all the badass we can get."

We have a couple hours before the plan is to be put into action, so we spend the morning eating, training, and consulting. Tani reminds us not to train too hard and to save our energy for later. I peek over my shoulder at Garnet who's sitting at the counter alone, watching us all eat, laugh, and talk. Since she went rogue, she ostracized herself, leaving Tani to take the lead.

I excuse myself from the couch, grabbing my plate to sit next to her. I'm almost to her when a burst of laughter erupts behind me. I make sure not to look back, knowing Garnet is watching me, confused. Placing my plate on the counter, I jump onto the stool facing her.

"How did you sleep last night?" I try to ask casually. I feel like it's the best way to strike up a conversation. I don't usually talk to Garnet about "life things." It's always about mom or dad or mission this and that. I can sense the awkwardness in my tone, but I decide to ignore it.

"Fine," Garnet replies, on guard for reasons I don't know. I sigh and take a bite of pineapple.

"You know we aren't mad at you. We get it," I confide, hoping she already knows this. She stabs her fork in a melon angrily before shoving it in her mouth.

"That's the thing," she explains after swallowing. "You *should* be. I know I would be." She pauses before moving to take another bite of food. "I was being selfish and impulsive and . . . things could have gone really bad." I push out my lips slightly, nodding along.

"You're one hundred percent right," I agree. "But stop punishing yourself. You're not the enemy, so stop antagonizing." She's looking down at her plate in defeat. I tilt my head so I can meet her eyes. "Bring back the 'boss bitch' energy. That's what we need today." Before I give her a chance to respond, I grab her wrist, tugging her toward the couch.

"Ruby, what . . . ?"

"Room for two more?" I ask Opal as they deal out the Uno cards. They are a small octopus, all eight of their arms being used to deal. They hold a tentacle up to me, which I assume to be some cephalopod version of a thumbs-up, and I take a seat, tugging Garnet down with me. She's extremely tense, filled with guilt and shame, and she has to snap out of it.

Something I learned the last time I played cards with Opal is that they are ruthless and out for blood. Of course, we only played spoons, so I'm curious to see their behavior in a more strategic game. When they finish dealing, they morph back into a human, and I am pleasantly surprised by their appearance. Not the soft silver iridescent curls that lie atop their head, but what they're wearing.

"How are your clothes on?" I ask, eyeing the black material. Their head jerks toward Tani and Ziri before speaking.

"I was talking to them about how my power's great, but it sucks that I turn back naked. So they came up with this material." They tug at it and the black fabric easily expands. When they let go, it slingshots back to their body, skin tight. "I don't know what it's made out of, but it's infused with our stones."

"Nice," I say, noticing the people on either side of them are in similar material. The October triplets can all shape-shift in one shape or another, so it'd make sense for Tory and Jasper to be wearing it too. When the game starts, Opal doesn't prove me wrong. They're making alliances, coaxing different siblings to be antagonized or become allies, before betraying them, taking the win at the end. For each game, Opal asks to switch who we're sitting next to. They say it's "more fun" that way, but I think they want a chance to wrong as many of us as possible.

In the last game, Emerald takes their heat, falling into a five card "plus two" stack.

"Uno out," Opal quips, crossing their arms over their chest and smiling with pride. Everyone is laughing at Emerald's face, so full of defeat.

"How are you going to ask me to work together at the beginning of the game and then do me dirty like that?" Emerald complains, his hand heavy with cards.

"It be like that sometimes." Opal shrugs, and Garnet chuckles. Out of the corner of my eye, I see she's completely relaxed, almost her old self again, minus the authority.

"Betraying a sibling is the worst betrayal of all." Emerald agonizes, clutching a hand over his heart dramatically.

"If that's how the cookie crumbles . . ." Opal has a glint in their eyes. Emerald scoffs and pushes to his feet. "Don't hate the playa. Hate the—"

"Shut up," Emerald interrupts. "I need to go cope." He feigns pain, before walking toward the bathroom. Opal is about to deal out another set of cards when clapping flares up, catching our attention.

"Alright, y'all. It's about that time," Tani announces. She's standing in the middle of the room, like all of us, dressed in black. She has her hair pulled back into a tight ponytail which works nicely with her skintight jumpsuit. Her shoes are black wedge high-tops, with a bedazzled *T* right on the toe. Her face is set with love, determination, and confidence, one of which I don't feel at all. Immediately, nervous butterflies fill my stomach, bumping against the walls.

"Go pee, drink water, do what you gotta do. Then let's split into our teams." We all head off, the game discarded on the coffee table. As I'm about to walk to the bathroom, Emerald exits the closest one, chuckling at something on his phone. I slip in, lock the door, and plop on the toilet. I try to steady my leg, but it bounces, full of angst. After I flush, I take a step in front of the sink.

"It'll be okay," I say, scrubbing at my hands aggressively. "Things will be fine. We're gonna kick some butt and come back okay." I splash cold water on my face before jumping up and down, shaking my wrists. "We got this," I insist, hyping myself up. When I walk out of the bathroom, everyone is outside on the patio. I make my way to the door, noting the two groups that have formed. I walk over to where I see Pearl and Garnet.

"Alright, guys, remember, I just need to get close enough to inject him with this." Tani holds up the syringe. "Then it should be smooth sailing for us all." We all give curt nods in understanding. Team Red spent the majority of last night analyzing the videos and pictures Peri took and have a solid plan. Early this morning, when Pearl was able to walk again, she ported Tory to the hallway with the hostages so that she would be able to port to it later. Team Red will go straight there, before Tory ports one person into each of the rooms, providing comfort to those held captive.

While Emerald tries to unlock the doors, those who are ported inside the cells will assess the situation, gathering the people who may need medical attention so they can be teleported out first. Jasper and Alex will be in and out of the clearing, taking the wounded to the hospital. Jasper will shape-shift into a stretcher, if need be, and with Alex's super speed, they'll make trips back and forth. Everyone else will help when they can, a first aid fanny pack strapped to all their waists.

"Ready?" Tani calls over to Team Red. Tory gives a thumbs-up before her entire team disappears. I imitate her dutifully, wrapping my team with invisibility. I nod at Pearl, letting her know we can't be seen. Grinning devilishly, she rubs her hands together eagerly.

"Let's rock this shit."

When we appear in the lair, everyone is frozen. Thank goodness Pearl landed us along the wall because our uncle is in the center of the room. He's sitting in a gold chair lined with red velvet, scrolling on his phone lazily. He's wearing a neat dark red suit with a black shirt underneath. His hair is pulled back in six tight braids, gold charms sprinkling on them. Attached to his wrist is a metal leash, pooling on the floor. I trace its path to a pile of red fabric on the floor. When the pile moves, I see that it's mom. My hand tightens around whoever's hand I'm holding as I examine her.

She looks clean, dare I say, pampered. Her hair is styled in black knotless box braids that fall to her mid-back. The red fabric she's wrapped in is actually a dress. Her curves are pronounced, and the bodice is studded with rhinestones. Bloodstone tugs on the leash attached to a collar around her neck. She grunts at the pull, moving closer to him.

"Watch," he orders. In front of them are many bodies of people of a variety of ages, all of them also dressed well. Mom turns her tear-streaked face toward the people as they rise in unison. The men and boys bow to each other while the women and girls curtsy. Suddenly, "Waltz of the Flowers" rings from invisible speakers, and the people dance. Their movements are completely in sync, my uncle the puppeteer.

A tap on my shoulder makes me jump, and I whip my head around. Everyone else has huddled, facing one another. I grit my teeth, upset at myself for getting distracted, before focusing on Tani. She points at Bloodstone, and then her left finger, holding it up straight in the center of our huddle. With her right hand, she gestures toward all of us, moving her hand behind her left finger. With understanding, the plan clicks in my brain, and we move. We stay along the walls, making our way so we can be behind our uncle.

Laughs and cheers erupt from the dancers as their movements spread out. A new song is playing, something more upbeat than the waltz. Everyone grabs onto each other's hands, making a large chain of dancers. They dance around the room, grins plastered on their faces. I watch Peri press against the wall, just missing an outstretched hand of one of the puppet dancers. They wrap around Bloodstone and mom, dancing around them in three closed circles. The middle circle dances in the opposite direction from the outer and inner, making it nearly impossible for us to get through. I silently curse, wishing Moon was on our team. She could have flown over all of this and injected the serum. Speaking of, I turn to my right, leaning to get Aquamarine's attention. When we lock eyes, I raise my eyebrows, giving her a thumbs-up, and then I point it down. I hope the other team is doing fine. She nods in understanding and puts her walkie-talkie brain to action, locking her eyes somewhere behind me.

She seems to almost zone out, as if she's daydreaming or reminiscing. Within a few moments, she meets my eyes, giving me a thumbs-up. A sigh of relief escapes me, and I am thankful for the music. Her telepathic twin must have told her that everything is going well on their side. Suddenly, an idea rushes into my head, and I gather everyone's attention quickly.

Pointing at Aqua, I hold my hand in the shape of a finger gun in the air. I float it to my neck before sticking my pointer finger in my skin. My team's mouths form an *o* in understanding, and Tani takes out the syringe. Since Aqua is telekinetic, too, she can float the syringe and inject it in our uncle from here. We don't have to get close to him at all. I'm overcome with pride at the idea, patting myself on the back mentally.

We move back to the front of the room silently, getting a better view of him. He's mumbling something to mom, inaudible over the sound of the music. Once we're directly in front of him, I check on my invisibility. The familiar warmth pulsates through my body, and I rub my necklace for reassurance. With a nervous nod, my eleven-year-old sister focuses on the syringe, making it float over everyone's heads. When it reaches the height that my bubble can't reach, I have to make the syringe itself invisible. Aqua looks at me alarmed, but I nod for her to continue. Although she can't see it, hopefully she can get the needle past Bloodstone. I can make it visible again when it's out of his line of sight.

The dancer's movements slow as the music subsides. Without a sound, they take their seats again, sitting with perfect posture. Aqua pauses, looking at us with unease. A look from Tani tells her to continue, so she looks back up toward the ceiling, focused.

"You know . . ." Bloodstone starts, playing with one of mom's braids. He snags all our attention except Aqua's, whose eyes are now wide with fear.

"Guys . . ." she says so softly I can barely hear her. Tani and Garnet's head whips in her direction, eyes full of irritation. It's been drilled into our brains not to talk until he's been injected, so Aqua speaking fills us with angst. "Something's wrong."

What? Tani mouths, alarmed.

"I . . . I can't feel Jade anymore." A pit of dread fills my stomach, and with the next words said, the pit ices over.

"Being able to control bodies, I can always sense when new ones enter the room." We all freeze, our uncle's words capturing our attention. "And ten bodies . . ." He sighs, twirling the braid between his fingers. "Well, that's a whole lot of sensing."

CHAPTER 37

An eerie chill runs up my spine as he seems to look directly at where we are huddled. Tani holds a hand out, telling none of us to move.

"A valiant effort it was. Really. I'm impressed," Bloodstone says, waving his hand in the air. Next to him, mom's eyes glance around. Bloodstone watches as she strains her neck and he pats her on the head. "It appears your children have come for you, Rubes," he says in a comforting voice. "I'm really not the bad guy," he continues, now talking to us. "Well, I've done some god-awful things." He chuckles awkwardly, stroking the beard on his chin. "For a good reason, I pr omise."

We all exchange looks. This was *not* part of the plan. My head falls in shock when I realize: *If he can feel us now, he could feel Tory, Pearl, and I in his office. He knew we were there. Why not do something then?* Pearl taps Tani's shoulder, asking her if we should port out, but Tani shakes her head. She's right. We can't leave. Our cover's blown, and we've lost contact with Team Red. Leaving now could put them at risk.

"Ruby? I'm guessing you're here." My siblings' eyes latch on me as my heart falls to my stomach. "Seriously, I know how this thing works. Like mother, like daughter . . ." He trails off in thought. "Or did the invisibility ability fall to someone else? Alexandrite? Pearl? Sardonyx?" He laughs at himself. "I'm just listing off stones at this point."

We're all looking at each other, wondering what to do next. What makes this situation scarier is that even Tani is at a loss. Tani *always* knows what to do. I come to a decision suddenly, hesitation unseen in my movements. I get up, moving away from my brothers and sisters. Ignoring the flashes of alarm and concern in their expressions, I walk about fifty feet from them quickly and quietly before I decide to make myself visible, making sure to keep the others hidden.

"What do you want from us?" I shout, approaching him slowly. My heart is beating at the speed of light, and I pray that fear isn't written on my face.

"Ah, there you are." He taps his chin as he watches me curiously. "And . . . you are?" he asks, amused.

"You got it right the first time," I retort. The attitude and irritation in my tone is evident, surprising me. I pray to God that I look confident, intimidating would be even better. I step around the eerily still people sitting cross-legged on the ground. There is a clearing directly in front of him, as if the people left it open for an aisle. When I get there, I stand about ten feet from him, my back stiff as a needle. He cocks his head to the side, a smile spreading slowly on his face

.

"I like her," he tells my mom, holding her head by the chin. "I like you." He leans back, crossing his hands over his lap. My uncle looks me up and down before pursing his lips. "I can see how mama mistook you for Rubes. I thought she was having one of her moments, but," he pats mom's head, "you're almost a spitting image of her younger self." Unease roars through my veins, but I attempt to ignore it. Of course, Adelaide would tell her son about our visit.

"If you like me so much then can you explain all this?" I plead, gesturing to the people on the floor. "What is this? Who *are* you?" He gives me a soft smile, something filled with kindness and earnestness.

"I'm your mother's brother," he explains before throwing his thumbs back to point at his chest. "You can call me Uncle B." He grins, winking at me.

A wave of disgust rolls over me. When I feel something brush over the back pocket of my shorts, I nearly jump. As not to look suspicious, I readjust my position casually, leaning my weight on my back leg and sliding my hands in my back pockets. My left hand doesn't have to go all the way in for me to feel the syringe. Aqua must have put it in my pocket.

"And for your other question," Bloodstone says, pushing himself to his feet, "in due time, my niece. I promise." He gestures to where my siblings are gathered, invisible. "You all might as well come out too. I know where you are." I look back at the area I left them in and sigh, looking down in defeat. With my sigh comes the drop of invisibility, revealing my siblings.

"It's over, guys. I dropped the invisibility," I explain solemnly, holding up the facade of surrender. They come to stand with me quietly, exchanging frantic and worried glances. Bloodstone claps eagerly. He looks genuinely excited to see us, which maybe could be a good thing.

"This is the perfect pic for the family photo album." He giggles, taking his phone out and snapping a picture. "'Kid's First Overthrow!'" He makes air quotes. I shift uncomfortably, waiting for something bad to happen. *Is he going to take over our bodies? Torture us? Kill us? That is, if we can be killed.* "Well, overthrow attempt, but potato tomato." He plops down in his seat while pressing some buttons on his phone. I watch him carefully, trying to plan the best method for injecting him with the needle. With the powers that we have on standby, it's either me or Diamond. If they can distract him enough for me to get invisible, maybe I can run up behind him and jab it. *Shit, no. He would sense me there.* But he couldn't sense Diamond. With her prehensile hair, depending on how long it can stretch, she could inject him easily and he wouldn't realize the movement! He can only sense blood and muscle, and, technically, her hair is neither.

I inch closer to Diamond when I'm suddenly overcome with exhaustion. Metal bars surround us, shooting up from the ground as if out of nowhere.

"Hey!" Garnet yells, trying to jump the bar before it's too high. But she's too late. The bars stop her mid-jump, and she bounces back, screeching in pain.

"Garnet!" Ziri, Peri, and Tani yell, catching their eldest sister. Her skin that hit the bar is red and irritated, some of it even in welts. Tani's eyes widen, going back and forth between the bars and Garnet's wounds.

"Musgravite," she whispers, her voice full of fear. "He has musgravite."

"Yes, a silly little stone, isn't it?" he inquires, playing with another one of mom's braids. "Don't worry, you won't be trapped for long. I just need you all . . . a little dampened." A look of hatred floods Peri's face, and he stands up, shouting at our uncle.

"What the fuck do you want from us?" He trains his eyes on our uncle, trying to use his power to gain some sort of intel. But, with the effect of the musgravite, it just leaves him in pain. "Fuck." He groans, massaging his temples and falling to his knees. "Fuck, fuck, fuck . . ."

"Bring in the rest!" Bloodstone shouts. To our left, a garage door rolls open, and out comes a small golf cart pulling a large wagon. On the wagon is a large cage: Citrine, Emerald, Alex, Moon, and the others are inside, trapped in a cage laced with our kryptonite. The people surrounding us move to stand against the walls of the lair, ready to be used as puppets when needed. The wall-less wagon holding the cage is placed directly to our left. Suddenly, the man driving the golf cart exits through the same door, before it rolls closed behind him.

"Now that we're all here," Bloodstone begins, clasping his hands together, "let me explain something to you." He pushes himself to his feet, discarding the leash on his chair. He turns to mom, his tone serious. "Don't move," he threatens. "Or else . . ." He gestures toward us, not even bothering to finish his sentence.

"You see, kids," Bloodstone says, turning back to face us, "you've got it all wrong." He smiles at us all sincerely. "I'm not evil. I'm not the devil. I am God." Although the musgravite is filling me with exhaustion, my eyebrows shoot up. Of everything I thought he would say, this was *not it*. "At least, I am God on Earth. Of course, there is a real God. There is a greater good who gave me these powers to make me who I am. Make us who we are." He gestures again toward us, his eyes filled with a twisted pride. "And now it's time to pay our thanks. I am now . . . a new God. God has inhabited me; I am Him. He is *me*. Don't you understand? I am making the world better. I am making the world the way God wants." I exchange a glance with Moon who's in the other cage. Her eyebrows are squinted in confusion, and I'm glad I'm not the only one who thinks what he's saying is wild.

"That," Peri grunts, lifting his head from where it was resting on his knees, "is the shittiest excuse I've ever heard." Tani elbows him, hard, and I shoot him a glare. Why does that boy always have to instigate? Instead of being offended, our uncle just smiles, shaking his head, before continuing to explain.

"God wants kindness, yes? He wants everyone to treat others like the Golden Rule states: treat others the way you want to be treated. Isn't that something we all learned in kindergarten?" Not sure if this is some interactive monologue, I nod hesitantly, my siblings soon following suit. "It's an adapted phrase from the Bible you know?

"But there are bad people. Bad, horrible, cruel people in this world." Seth flashes into my mind, which sends a wave of disgust and discomfort through my body. I rub my left wrist anxiously. He isn't *wrong*. There are some terrible people in this world. I've had first-hand experience. But still, the logic behind his actions is hard to grasp. "And I am going to fix that . . . for Him. Because He made me, and I am thankful for that. Grateful. So I will help the world!" He throws his hands out. "I've taken upon myself the burden of evil. So then, there will only be good left. So that I am the only evil. Can't you see I'm doing good?" His eyes search ours for agreement, but all our faces are blank, confused, or disgusted. He sighs, pulling his beard again.

"If I take all that is evil from the world, all that's left is good. And of course, there must be evil to balance out the good, which is why I've burdened myself with it all. If I can control everyone, I can make everyone do the *right things*. Have I committed sins? Yes, I have. But I have to commit sins so that I can *be* evil. Because I will hold the burden of everyone's evils, so that no one else has to." In some weird, twisted way, I can see how it could make sense, but there's no way that would work.

"The woman you saw me, well, *Benji*, kill," Bloodstone begins while adjusting his suit, "was the leader of a sex trafficking ring that trafficked over one thousand men, women, and children over the past ten years." I nibble on my lip, shooting a glance at Pearl and Tory. Their lips are parted, faces filled with confusion and disbelief. "Don't worry, little Benji doesn't remember a thing.

That was just for dramatics." His smile is broad as he does jazz hands. He clears his throat, resting his hands on his lap before continuing his sick explanation.

"Think of what the world would be like. If I was the only thing bad, the only thing evil, there would be world peace. No more school shootings, no more rape, no more hate crimes. There would be no prisons because nobody would be committing any crimes. "

"What in the Thanos type shit?" I hear Pearl mumble, and I nearly burst into nervous chuckles before he continues preaching.

"They would know right from wrong," Bloodstone states, his eyes dazzling with the thought, "because I would show them the difference." My brows furrow with dismay, and I shake my head slightly. I can't hold back anymore.

"But who are you to decide what is right and wrong? What gives you that jurisdiction?" I interrupt, eyes blazing. It's evident that this thought has been in his mind for a long time. There isn't a hint of doubt in his tone or posture.

"Have you not been listening to anything I've been saying?" He sighs, dragging his hand down his face. "You'll be good, won't you?" he asks as he grabs his phone and presses a button. On both of our cages, the bars sink into the ground, freeing us from captivity. No one dares to move.

"Good, good. Now, when I was only twelve years old, God spoke to me. He spoke to me and told me, 'Bloodstone, you are now my disciple. Make the world what I want it to be.' He spoke to me in a dream, and ever since then, I've seen Him. He spoke to me in a dream, and I will make His dream come true. And I need your help to do so. Not only do I have the burden of holding all the evil, but it's all of us. We are the evil that the world needs to become good!" He clutches his hands to his chest, staring up toward the ceiling admiringly. After a thoughtful pause, he sighs, returning to his seat. "So, yes, I kidnapped your parents. I've planned for you all to come here thinking I am the bad guy. Because really, I am the bad guy. I am the bad guy doing the good things that nobody else will do. But I can't do it without you. Yes, I'm powerful, but with us together, we will be undefeated. So I ask you to come willingly. Please understand this."

We are all quiet for a moment, exchanging glances. No one knows what to do. I can understand how a person who is missing a couple of brain cells can think this is a viable plan, but I like to think that all my brain cells are present. Something is seriously wrong with my uncle. If only someone could have gotten to him early, squashed this theory before it could develop to this. When no one responds, Bloodstone sighs again, rubbing his fingertips against his eyebrows. When he looks up, he no longer looks disappointed. His face is filled with hope and promise.

"Emerald understands. Come here, son."

Everyone's jaws drop as Emerald pushes himself to his feet, jumps down to the ground, and walks over to our uncle. Bloodstone daps up Emerald before tossing an arm around his shoulder. When they turn to face us, the smile on Emerald's face wavers, a flash of guilt crawling against his features.

"I found Emerald coincidentally when he was a kid on a . . . what do you guys call them? A *Gem hunt*," Bloodstone says, squeezing his nephew into his chest. Rage boils in my veins, the steam attempting to bubble out of my mouth in a flood of vulgar cusses and cries. I whip around to look at Peri. His jaw is slack, eyes glazed over. If anyone should have known Emerald would betray us, it would be Peri. Guilt washes over his features before his face hardens. Similar expressions arise on my siblings' faces. Citrine's eyes are blazing, staring into Emerald's soul, or should I say, lack thereof.

"If that's how the cookie crumbles . . . too soon?" Emerald asks, a genuine smile on his face. "I thought it might be, but—" Pearl interrupts him.

"No," she grits out, her voice hard as stone. The smile on his face falls, and he looks between us.

"But—"

"You better shut the fuck up," she snarls, her hands clenched in fists. I'm glad I'm not the only one with murder on my mind.

"Just listen," Emerald pleads as guilt rings his eyes. "I'm sorry, okay? I'm sorry I didn't tell you what was going on, but y'all's minds were already set on what you wanted to do," he claims. His eyes search everyone else's before locking on mine. I don't break our gaze. I try to put as much pain and furiousness into my eyes as I can, portraying my emotions wordlessly. "I tried. I tested the waters, to see if you could understand!" he confesses, his eyes still locked on mine. I think to the one time we got to talk freely: the walk. He was *testing* me; he was testing us all. He wanted to see what we thought of good and evil and what we could do if we had the power to change it. My eyes widen with the memory, and he breaks contact with me, looking at my other siblings. "Just think of what the world would be like! We'd be unsung heroes, creating a world of peace."

"Doesn't it just sound perfect?" asks a voice from the shadows. We all whip our heads to the back corner where the female voice is coming from. When she's engulfed in light, my mouth goes slack, eyes filled with disbelief. Corallina comes around to the other side of Bloodstone and gives him a kiss on the cheek before holding onto his hand. "Hi, Daddy," she says sweetly. I look away, clamping my hand over my mouth. Corallina from Tennessee is the daughter of a psychopath. She's my *cousin.*

Her eyes find mine, and the smile she flashes me is as sweet as an ant trap. "I told you about the family reunion, didn't I?"

CHAPTER 38

My entire body goes slack as I am filled with humiliation, regret, and disbelief. We were never going to win. Every great plan and thought we had, Bloodstone already knew. Every acknowledgement hits me like a bag of rocks, and I have to put my head in my hands to stay oriented. He knows *everything*: our powers, the syringe, musgravite, where we *live*. We never stood a chance. Sorrow overtakes me, and I want to give up. In fact, I'm ready. I look up slowly, defeat written in my features. Corallina sees it and smirks.

"Shouldn't be long now," she says softly to her dad and cousin. Before I have time to react, a girl's voice rips through the room.

"You think we're gonna give up that easy?" Citrine says, standing on her feet. "Bitch, the *fuck?*" she asks, face scrunched in disgust. The anger and pain in her voice adds to her determination, causing the small girl's voice to boom throughout the room. "We've trained like hell for this, and if you think we won't go down fighting, you're dead wrong!" Before any of us can react, flames erupt from Citrine's fists and hair, her eyes blazing deep orange.

"Yes, Citrine, the fire girl," Bloodstone coos. "Which most likely means you," he points at Topaz, "are the twin." Suddenly, Topaz stands up and walks over to our uncle. He doesn't even break a sweat as he manipulates her limbs.

"*No!*" Citrine shouts as she makes a move for Topaz. Before she can get far, strangers' hands grab her arms, holding her back. Citrine is breathing rapidly, her eyes locked on her twin who is now standing in front of Bloodstone. The flames begin to creep up her arms toward the civilian's hands, and I'm snapped back into reality.

"No, Citrine! They're innocent!" I yell, urging her to stop. She looks at me, realizing what she almost did. The flames fizzle back into her fists, her hands now only red with heat.

"Perfect," Bloodstone sings, grabbing Topaz by the neck. "Let's do a little trade, shall we? Your sister for your allegiance." He tilts Topaz's neck to the side. "As you know, I can easily control all of you, and this could have been over with by now. But you coming on your own volition would make things *much* easier for me." He releases his hold on Topaz, giving her back control of her body. She struggles in his grasp before looking at us with determination.

"Don't do it." She strains. "Don't give in!" We're all silent. Unable to communicate with one another, we don't know what to do. After a few more minutes of exchanged worried glances and silence, Bloodstone exhales, cocking his head to the side.

"I'll do you one better. Let me sweeten the deal for you, a nice two for one." With a glance at Corallina, she nods and heads up the stairs and toward her dad's office. She's only there for a few minutes before she returns down to us, tugging another person on a leash. I lean forward, confused, pushing my glasses up to make sure I'm seeing things correctly. When I recognize the person, a sob escapes my mouth. I run over, not caring if I get in trouble, pulling him into my arms.

"How-how did this happen?" I ask, caressing Zach's perfect face. Corallina rolls her eyes, letting the leash sag.

"How do you think?" she retorts. I ignore her, examining Zach instead. I'm thankful to not see a single cut or bruise on him.

"Ruby," he whispers with longing, pulling me into a hug. I hug him back tightly, tears streaming down my face. "Don't worry, Zach. I'm going to get you out of here. It's going to be okay." Before I'm ready to let go, a rough tug on my hair pulls me away. I thrash and shout, kick and claw, but the grip is strong. Corallina yanks me back to where I was sitting before, leaving me with my siblings.

"Keep her here if you know what's good for you," she says, but I pay her no attention. I lunge back to Zach who's kneeling next to Emerald, but hands grab me from behind, keeping me there.

"*No!*" I scream, thrashing against my siblings. "No please . . . *please.*" I break into a fit of sobs, leaning onto someone's lap. They rub my back, whispering inaudibly into my ear. I know Topaz is my sister; I should have reacted the same way or more for her. With Zach, it's something different. I've known Zach all my life. He's been my rock since forever. Of course, I love Topaz. Watching her and Citrine and spending time with her over this past week has really built the sister connection that we were deprived of. It did that with us all. Peri, Tani, Opal . . . If any of them were in Topaz's position, of course I would be afraid: for them and myself. I know I love my siblings. We've bonded through trauma and humor and a concrete goal. But I *love* Zach. This isn't his fight. This is mine. *Ours.* Garnet and Peri were right. I shouldn't have gotten him involved.

"How's the deal sounding now?" Bloodstone asks eagerly, tapping his fingers contemplatively. A heavy weight seems to fog the room, filled with distrust, vengeance, and defeat.

"Fuck you!" Citrine spits out, her voice filled with hate. "You're just some ignorant son of a bitch who wants some excuse to be cruel to people. It's pathetic!" Her words are like acid sizzling in the air. The soft, cocky smile that was on Bloodstone's face dissolves into a sneer. The people holding Citrine pick her up and move her closer to him, and she lets them, not putting up a fight.

"What's wrong with you?" she teases sourly in his face. "Mommy didn't give you enough attention as a kid?" The majority of us shoot to our feet, standing, just as a loud slap lands on her face.

"Stop it!" Tani shouts, moving to the front. "Get your hands off of her!"

"You're lying to yourself. This isn't some *burden.* You like it!" Citrine challenges, tears stinging her eye. "Admit it." Citrine spits in his face. He wipes it away, a smile attempting to return to his features.

"It is my duty—"

"Lies," Citrine interrupts him. "You're fucking lying."

"Citrine!" Garnet calls out, but she ignores her. Clearly, she has some things she needs to get off her chest, and it doesn't look like any of us will be able to stop her.

"You're just some big bully who gets a kick out of this," Citrine growls. She grabs our uncle's suit jacket, attempting to pull him down to her height. But he stands tall, and her attempt is in vain.

"It is my—" Bloodstone starts again, the expression on his face amused. But suddenly, he jumps back, shoving Citrine off him. "Fuck," he grunts, patting at his suit. Where Citrine's hand was is a burned handprint, ruining his deep red suit.

"Little bitch," he growls, rushing toward her. His hand wraps around her neck, and he lifts her off the ground, her legs dangling. "Fine. I'll admit it. I do enjoy the cruelty that must be done. But it didn't start off that way." Citrine gags, prying and pulling at his hands. A quick glance at Garnet, and I already know the plan. We all rush at him, screaming and pleading for him to put her down, when a wall of puppet people stop us in our tracks, holding us back.

"You . . . you can't kill me . . . anyway," Citrine chokes out, gasping for air. At that, he lets her go and Citrine falls to the floor, coughing wildly.

"That's right . . ." Bloodstone looks at us all thoughtfully. We're still trying to break through the wall of people but failing miserably. "You are 'immortal.' I forgot about that little unique tweak of the gene that happens every hundred years." I try not to react and hope the others don't either. Bloodstone doesn't know it, but he just gave us a chance to win. We had all thought that everyone in our family had the ability for the cells to regenerate at our speed, creating the facade of immortality. But maybe not.

"Let's put that little gene to the test, shall we?" he asks, walking back to his seat calmly, where Emerald and Corallina are on either side. While I was focused on Citrine, Zach and Topaz had been chained to the ground a good twenty feet from us and Bloodstone. Zach's holding Topaz, who's crying uncontrollably. I can't hear what he's saying, but it's clear he's trying to comfort her. "I'm sorry you have to see this, sister," Bloodstone says to my mom, wiping the tears off her face. She looks like she's about to speak but doesn't. It looks as though she physically can't. I watch as her throat moves and mouth opens, her throat constricting as if she is trying to use her vocal cords but struggling. All she can do is plead with her eyes, trying to convey unspoken words.

With his back still turned, Citrine moves fast. Within seconds, her arms and legs are combusting with flames, her hair a blazing orange, white, and blue. She dashes at him, a powerful roar full of emotion escaping her when she's mere inches away.

"Dad!" Corallina shouts, just as Tani yells, "Citrine don't!"

I whip my head toward her for a split-second. All my siblings who entered on the wagon had gotten off a while ago, joining us on the floor shortly after Emerald's betrayal came to light. Tani is standing right next to Sapphire who is looking straight at the minion in front of her, lips moving fast as she talks under her breath. Before Citrine can touch him, she freezes in her spot, hand outstretched.

"Such a hot head," Bloodstone notes, flourishing into his chair, legs crossed. The only thing that Bloodstone isn't controlling is her face.

"Ah." She gasps, her head facing away from us. "I can't move. Guys, I can't move." Her voice is dripping with fear, causing panic to well in me. My head aches with tension, and I feel the pain emanating from the others. Citrine rotates to her left, taking three steps forward. The flames on her further ignite, her fists no longer red with heat, but blue, like the hottest part of a fire.

"I'll ask you again—" Bloodstone starts.

"Guys! I can't stop! Help me!" Tears stream down Citrine's face as she takes another step toward Topaz and Zach, body ablaze. I try to lock eyes with Emerald, but he's looking down, shame flickering across his features.

"Bloodstone, stop!" Garnet yells as Citrine takes another step. She's sobbing now, arms outstretched and pointed toward her twin. Bloodstone stands and takes off his ruined jacket, tossing it on his seat, as he walks to stand a couple of feet behind Citrine. Bloodstone looks through the wall of people, unsure who called out.

"I said, call me Uncle B.," he purrs, before turning his attention back to Citrine. When she's forced to take another step, a scream rips through the air, sending goosebumps up my arm. Citrine is maybe seven feet away from them. A few more steps and they'll feel the lick of her flames. Zach tries to scoot away, but his leash has been shortened, giving him nowhere to go.

Topaz's face is filled with determination as she looks at her twin. Her hands are in an open circle, as if she's holding a small animal. When she begins to pull them apart, a large water droplet begins to build.

"Nice try," Bloodstone says before the water splashes to the ground. "Concede, and this can all be over. Help me make the world *good*." He's controlling Topaz now, too, keeping her from extinguishing Citrine's flames. I look around frantically; there has got to be something I can do. "Or, y'know, one less mouth to feed is always a plus." He winks.

Turning invisible is useless. Bloodstone can still feel my body, so I have to be quick. But first, I need to get past this human wall. A feeling of unease rips through me as I realize what I must do. I place my hand on the person in front of me but hesitate. I've never walked or passed through a person besides when Garnet was choking me yesterday. But this is my whole body. I'd probably be fine, but what about this woman? Will she be okay?

"No!" yells Topaz. "Don't give up! Don't let him win!" Tears leave a path on her face as she directs her next words toward Citrine. "It's okay, Citrine." Garnet, Peri, and everyone else is throwing themselves at the human wall, trying not to hurt them but trying to break through. Sapphire is still whispering urgently to the person in front of her, fixated on them.

"No!" Citrine chokes out, struggling to speak through her sobs. Another step, and a shriek of fear erupts from her body.

"Citrine, it's not your fault," Topaz comforts, unable to move from her spot. Zach holds onto her tightly, shifting his weight so he can shield her from her sister when the time comes. No, *if* the time comes; I close my eyes, making myself invisible and focusing on the woman in front of me.

"It is." Citrine sobs. Another step. Another scream.

"You aren't doing this, Citrine. It's okay. We'll be okay." Zach's lie is so smooth that I almost believe him. I want to believe him. Gritting my teeth, I push my hand through. It passes through skin and muscle, and I almost gag at the sensation. The woman's heart is beating at a calm pace, the vibrations evident in my fingertips. I have to be fast, fast enough to get to Bloodstone in time, but not too fast that passing through will ruin this woman's body.

"I love you." I hear Topaz weep, causing a much louder eruption of sobs from her twin. A sharp intake of breath and small cries of pain notify me that I'm out of time. I have to push through. I slam myself into the woman, passing through her veins and bones. It's different from the feeling of passing through the wall, more slime-like. When I pass through the woman, I hear a loud thump followed by a chilling shriek of pain. I'm too late. My eyes shoot open, head whipping toward the flaming girl, but she's not where I expect her to be. She's on the floor about ten feet or so from where she was before, wrapped around a screeching body, covered in flames. Topaz and Zach watch, wide-eyed and unharmed.

"Nooo!" Ziri screeches in horrified realization. In front of her, the wall of people is broken, my siblings rushing through. Ahead of the pack is Sapphire, her face full of terror. The screeching is bone rattling and soon, the smell of burning flesh is evident. I freeze, my hand covering my face to ease the wretched stench. Bloodstone throws a hand out, and my siblings who broke through the human wall stop in their tracks, all under his control. He sighs, waving a hand in front of his nose, face scrunched in disgust.

"Now, look what you made me do." The two flaming bodies are rolling on the floor, both screeching: one with grief and one in suffering. I squint, looking closely, then my heart plummets. I catch sight of a shoe that makes my blood run cold. Before I can grasp what I'm doing, I'm leaning forward, running full speed at my uncle, still invisible. When I'm about a foot away, I reach into my back pocket, yanking out the syringe. I roar as I jump on Bloodstone's back, jabbing the needle into his neck. My nose is filled with the scent of leather and fermented grapes, but I press hard, injecting him with the syringe. Wailing in agony, he throws me off him, and I land on my side. Pain shoots up my hip, and I hiss, clutching the area.

"Daddy!" Corallina shouts, rushing over to him. Bloodstone rips the now empty syringe from his neck, tossing it aside, before turning to look at me. The shock of pain made me forget my invisibility, and he shoots toward me, grabbing me by the hair, yanking me to my feet. I wince in pain.

"You little bitch!" he spits, saliva splashing my face. He moves to cause me some sort of harm but then doubles over in pain, releasing me. His hold on my siblings vanishes, and they race over to our now extinguished sister, sobbing over a charred body. I stumble out of his reach, glancing back over my shoulder at the woman who acted as my doorway. My hand rushes to my mouth, and I hold back a shriek. She's on the floor, shaking violently. The floor surrounding her is covered in bloody vomit, coating her hair as she seizes over it. I take a step in her direction, but the jerking subsides. Then it stops altogether. Her head rolls back so that her cheek lays in her bile. Lifeless eyes stare back at me.

"Oh . . . I didn't—" I bite down on my knuckles, swallowing an ache of guilt and disgust, not at the scene, but at myself. At what *I did*. A screech full of loss makes the hairs on the back of my neck stand at attention, and I turn my head slowly in that direction. I half run, half trip to my siblings, holding my hand over my hip. Thoughts of the woman I killed slip my mind with each step.

"I'm sorry," Citrine whispers, reaching out her hand to touch the person in front of her, but the body isn't even a body. All that's left of Tani are her broken round glasses and her shoes, liquefied and morphed, small flames still on the melted aglets.

Everything seems to freeze. I can't think. I can't move. I . . . can't. Citrine is staring at the body, wrapping her arms around her knees. She rocks back and forth, mumbling apology after apology, eyes wide. Garnet reaches out to touch Tani, but she crumbles under the light brush of her thumb, leaving ash on Garnet's fingertips. Shocked tears stream down Ziri's and Peri's faces, heavy with the weight they'll never see her again.

There had to have been another way. There's *always* another way. Tani's the smart one. *Why didn't she think! Why didn't she use that amazing ability of hers to come up with another way! Why didn't she . . . ?*

"I'm sorry." Citrine sobs, clamping her hand over her lips. With her mouth covered, she seems short of breath, her nose clogged with grief and remorse. Topaz rushes over, enveloping Citrine in a hug. But Citrine doesn't hug back. Her eyes are latched to the sister she just murdered, her face filled with shame and regret. I reach out to try to comfort the sibling nearest to me, Sapphire, but my hand trembles so terribly that I pull it back to my chest. Silent tears fall as I stare at the charred bones and scorched flesh that sticks to the floor.

Peri pushes himself out from all of us, only making it a few steps before vomiting on the floor. The smell of bile and burnt tissue is so overwhelming that I feel my own nausea rising. I struggle to my feet and stumble away, seeking fresh air. Ziri's silent tears are no longer muted. I look back to see her lying against the concrete, weeping uncontrollably. Garnet extends a hand of comfort, but Ziri throws it back at her and curls into a ball, her arm next to her triplet's ashes. The other triplet falls onto her knees, clutching her chest, mouth agape.

I know what she feels because I feel it too. It roars through my blood and radiates from my tears and sweat, burning a trail of despair in its tracks. Maybe it's the relationship we were building, or maybe it's something more. The gene? The legend? The supposed *magic?* But something from me is missing. I felt it fizzling the moment Tani sacrificed herself. But with the pressure of reality, the emptiness inside became evident. With Tani's death, a piece of me died too—a piece of all of us did.

I turn around stiffly, unable to witness the sorrow emanating from Citrine and Ziri. As I turn, my eyes lock on the vomit-soaked woman. I feel another gasp bubble up, and I turn again quickly to the only direction where death does not overshadow my view. There, I see my uncle on the floor curled in a fetal position, and I see mom leaning over the chair, hand covering her mouth, tears streaming down her face.

"Mom," I cry out, stumbling toward her. I want to be held and caressed. I need my mother to calm me, tell me this is all a bad dream and I will wake up soon. I need her to do what mothers do, save me from my nightmares. *Wake me up, Mom.* "What—" A punch lands on my jaw, making me bite my tongue, and knocks me off my feet.

"You selfish bitch!" Corallina yells before kicking me in the gut. I groan, clutching my stomach. She pulls her leg back to kick me again, but a figure zooms into her, knocking her on the floor. Alex speeds back to me, her face stained with tears. She helps me to my feet, and I grimace.

"You okay?" Alex asks softly. Her usual soft girl makeup is interrupted with a trail of mascara-stained tears. One of her heart earrings is missing, and her blondish lace wig is in disarray. I open my mouth to tell her that I'm anything but fine when a yelp erupts from behind us. Alex speeds back to where everyone else sits, surrounding Tani's ashes. I hobble over there slowly, squinting my eyes to see where the sound came from, when I notice Topaz scooching away from her twin. Citrine's skin is a deep red, and her hair is on fire. I pause, watching everyone stumble away from her and what's left of Tani.

She's kneeling now, her forehead resting on the smooth concrete floor as she begins to scream, roaring uncontrollably. Mouths move, Garnet's, Ziri's, and Topaz's, as they try to calm and comfort the nine-year-old, but her grief is consuming her, causing her to turn into a human torch. Topaz has her hands open, ready to throw water on Citrine, or anyone else, if things get too out of control. She hesitates, letting her sister sort through grief that no one should ever have to deal with.

Feeling a soft tug on my shoulder, I turn around into a slap that stings my cheek. I take a couple of steps back as does Corallina, her arms outstretched at her hips. Blood drips from her nose, and she wipes at it aggressively before extending her fingers by her thighs. I watch as her pink nails elongate, slightly curling inward. When she sees my face, she laughs, holding up her hands for me to get a better look.

"You didn't think you guys were the only ones with powers, did you? It runs in my veins too!" And on *too*, she jumps forward, slashing me in the neck with her claws. I gasp, holding my hand to my neck as blood gushes out of the wound. It burns, like alcohol on a paper cut.

"Ruby!" I hear Zach shout from where he's still locked on the ground. I hiss as the stinging worsens.

"You like that?" She pants, admiring her fingernails. "It's bubblegum pink with a hint of musgravite!" She moves to slash at me again, but someone grabs her, yanking her back by her arm.

"Stop," Emerald says, tugging her away from me.

"Fuck no. Get off of me." She tries to shake herself out of his grasp, but his hold is strong. I apply pressure to the right side of my neck, hoping my wounds can still heal even though I was sliced with musgravite. I turn back to Citrine, who's still howling on the floor. The flames are bigger now, engulfing both her body and Tani's ashes. The flames lick her body, roaring over her skin with an unspoken urgency. I can feel the heat from where I'm standing faintly, and I can only imagine how much hotter it is where the others are.

"This was wrong. We were wrong," he confesses, and I turn my head to face him. Tears of guilt stream down his face, as they should. "I'm sorry." Corallina whips her head toward him in disgust before digging the nails of her free hand into his upper right arm. He yelps, letting her go, and she dashes back toward me. Although it's much harder, I muster my power, turning invisible and taking a step to my right. She runs right past me, claws out.

"Where are you, little miss—?" The punch I throw is the hardest one I've ever thrown in my life, square in her face. She cries out, stumbling back with her hand over her nose. I take a step forward and punch her again in the same spot. This time, she falls to the ground, hard and unconscious. I make myself visible again, shaking the soreness out of my hand.

"Ruby, I'm so sorry," Emerald apologizes, coming to me. "I really thought—" Turning to face him, I hold a hand up, cutting him off.

I gesture toward my mom and Zach before saying hoarsely, "Get them out of here." And I turn to walk back to my family. When I finally make it to Moon, I gesture to the first aid kit at her hip, then my neck.

"Oh, shit." She helps me lay on the floor. "We can't hear much over the flames and Citrine's cries," Moon says, opening a piece of gauze.

"What's wrong with Citrine?" I ask, my voice scratchy. If Corallina had struck slightly more to her left, I would have bled out by now probably.

"I don't know. Denial? Grief? It's only getting worse." Moon applies the piece of gauze to my neck, holding it firmly, before wrapping my entire neck with a medical cohesive bandage, securing the gauze in place. I wipe the blood off on my shorts, looking at Citrine. Topaz is in front of her splashing water onto her, but it does nothing, evaporating almost instantaneously. Suddenly, the ground begins to rumble and everyone standing falls to the floor.

"What the fuck?" asks Pearl, looking all around us. I am, too, trying to figure out if there's someone else we have to fight. My eyes land on Bloodstone immediately, and I'm filled with relief to see him still curled into a ball on the floor. Another rumble, this time even more powerful. Rocks from the ceiling fall, and I watch Alex dodge them. She zips throughout the room, seeing the danger before we can and tugging my siblings out of the way.

"What's going on?" Jasper shouts, just barely audible over the flames and Citrine's cries.

"Guys!" I hear Peri yell over our mourning sister. He's pointing out of the window. Everyone jogs over to him except Topaz, still trying to get through to Citrine. When I see what Peri is pointing at, my jaw goes slack.

"I thought the volcano was dormant, Ziri!" exclaims Garnet, looking through the window at the bubbling magma, maybe fifty feet below us and rising quickly.

"It was!" Ziri shouts back. A howl from Citrine and the magma splashes up, landing on the inner walls of the volcano and darkening. Another cry from Citrine, and the liquid pops up again. Understanding, we all turn our heads toward Citrine, a mixture of fear, amazement, and alarm on our faces. Pushing off the window, we run back to our flaming sister.

"Tory, Jasper, Alex, help Topaz put out Citrine. Everyone else, we gotta get everyone out of here. *Now*!" Garnet yells as we race toward the twins.

"What's going on!" cries Topaz, splashing Citrine with water. She's using much more water than before, but it's still barely making a dent. Steam arises, filling the room with a foggy essence. Peri pushes his way to the front, just as the pressure from inside the volcano builds, shattering the window. We all fall forward to the ground as the room shakes violently. A rock falls, just barely missing Opal's head.

As the rumbling briefly stops, Peri is the first to scramble to his feet and shouts to Topaz. "Citrine is gonna make the fucking volcano erupt!"

CHAPTER 39

With the room heating up quickly, we all divide and conquer. Garnet gathers a group to help finish freeing all the people who are still locked in the cells, while me and a couple of other people stay in the larger room. First thing's first, we have to put out the bonfire that is Citrine. My powers are no help for that, so I watch Topaz, Jasper, Alex, and Tory do their thing while helping the innocent people move under the metal overhang, away from the falling rocks.

In all the previous commotion, a handful of Bloodstone's former puppets were hit with falling rocks. The others, forgetting how to use their bodies, are unable to move. Emerald, Zach, Amethyst, my mom, and I are moving the people as fast as we can to safety, while Moon, Jade, and Aqua stop as many falling rocks as they can. The rocks float softly to a pile in the corner of the room.

My brother and sisters who are working on stopping Citrine are huddling along the wall, stumbling over when another large rumble strikes them. Unexpectedly, Jasper crumples into a pile of clothes, which Alex puts on quickly. As I carry a little girl in my arms, I squint my eyes, trying to figure out what it is. A fire suit. With her super speed, she dashes toward Citrine, moving her away from Tani's charred corpse, now even more crumpled by Citrine's heat.

"I found one!" Ziri calls out, dropping something over the balcony. Tory catches the ceramic vase before it shatters to the floor. She and Topaz begin to break down the charred clumps immediately, which easily wither under their touch. Without warning, Pearl ports in the room a couple feet from me, her eyes roaming around for a target.

"I need you!" she shouts to Emerald. She doesn't give him time to speak before she runs to him, grabs his arm, and they both disappear in an electric blue spark. With one less person with us, we immediately start to struggle. Mom and I have managed to get all the kids and most of the teens to safety, but she is so malnourished, she's too weak to help the adults.

"I'll handle my brother," she says, walking over to me and grabbing my hand. She looks into my eyes, giving my hand a tight squeeze, before letting go and heading to my uncle. So much was exchanged in our gaze: grief, hope, pride. I grab a woman from under her arms, dragging her to the overhang. When the vase is full, Tory teleports away. Sweat and silent tears drip down Topaz's face as she dusts off her hands, dusts *Tani* off her hands. Her face sets on her twin, and she puts her palms together, pulling them apart slowly. A small water droplet quickly grows in volume, doubling in size every second. After a few minutes, she raises her arms above her head, the ball of water about the size of a semi-truck.

"Hold on to something!" she yells, and I look around me. The only thing I'm holding onto is the shoulders of this grown man. We'll both be washed away by the tsunami of her powers. I'm maybe twenty feet from the overhang where Amethyst has stretched her body, acting as a small fence around the people, keeping them from flowing away.

"Wait!" I shout, pushing up my glasses and looking around me quickly. Jade and Aqua are on top of the metal hall-like balcony that leads to our uncle's office and also creates the overhang. Their focus is on the rocks, falling at double speed now. My mom is holding the leash my uncle had, but instead of her neck within the collar, it's his. Corallina is matching him, in Zach's old leash and collar. Mom's tugging on both of their arms, but they're going nowhere.

"Moon!" I shout, pointing over to our mom. Her braids whip when she turns to where I'm pointing. With an outstretched arm and furrowed brows, she lets out a groan, lifting them to safety and placing them next to the telekinetic twins. At this point, there are only a few people left on the floor.

"Hurry! It's heavy, and I can't hold on for much longer!" Topaz groans. Zach rushes over to me, taking the man from my arms.

"I've got him! Get behind your sister," he tells me, gesturing to Amethyst. Her face is squeezed tight as she holds her outstretched position. I look over my shoulder at the last two innocent people on the floor.

"Let me just grab them real quick . . ." I dash toward the people. Zach groans as he tugs the man toward Amethyst. Just as I make it to the two women, the room rumbles violently, knocking us all off our feet.

"No!" Topaz yells as she falls forward, the water splashing down onto Citrine, drowning her and the flames. Alex sprints up the steps, still wearing Jasper on her back, just avoiding the water. Moon levitates off the ground, her attention on the crumbling ceiling. The water is rushing toward me and the women, and I don't have time to hesitate. I grip onto the women's arms, focusing on my feet sinking through the floor. When I'm shin deep in the concrete, I stop sinking, just as the water rushes into me. It threatens to yank the women from my grasp, but I hold on, pulling their heads above the water.

The sizzling of water in magma is overpowering as it flows through the broken window, dripping onto the now visible orange-red liquid. Citrine's unconscious body floats in the water, rushing toward the broken window. I'm rooted in place, hands full, unable to get to her.

"Topaz!" I scream, but she's already on it. She's running for Citrine, tutu heavy from the weight of water, hands outstretched. She yanks them back, causing the water around Citrine's body to lift rapidly, slinging her limp body through the air and toward the other twins.

"Alex!" Topaz cries, unable to help much more. Alex speeds over to where Citrine is about to land, quickly taking off the fire suit that is Jasper. He morphs back into a human just as Citrine is flying at them. They both catch her, falling back from the force. I let out a sigh of relief and put my focus back on my situation. With most of the water through the window, it's safe for me to move. I work one leg at a time out of the ground, planting each one on the solid floor. Tory ports back, eyes wide with confusion and concern as she takes in the scene.

"We need to get out of here." Amethyst pants, still holding all the ex-puppets together.

"No kidding." Tory breathes as she dashes toward her sister. She grabs onto ten people, porting them out. Moments later, she's back, taking another group. Tugging the women to the others, I let out a sigh of relief, seeing Zach disappear in the second group that leaves the demolishing lair. She's fast, but Pearl is faster, joining her after a minute or so.

As magma pools into the room, the acrid sulfuric smell is overwhelming, and those who are left start to cough. With Pearl and Tory working together, we're all out of the lair in about half a minute, and I breathe in the fresh air eagerly, letting go of the women I'm holding and falling on the floor.

The relief I feel is short-lived when the ground shakes again. I hear a siren in the distance, its eerie tone ringing through the sky over and over. Puffs of smoke spurt from the volcano's mouth, a light gray that is sure to darken soon. The clearing is a couple hundred meters or so away from the volcano's lips. We'll be fine for now, but not for long.

The clearing is filled with people, most having to lie inside of the forest since there isn't much room. I spot Zach near a little girl, rocking her softly. Those of my siblings who were teleported out first are all gathered in the middle. I leave the two people I saved and head to them. I peek between Garnet and Peri's shoulders and see my mom and a man, Citrine on their laps.

"I am just . . . words can't describe how thankful and proud I am . . ." Mom looks at all of us while stroking Citrine's hair. The man puts his arm around mom, pulling her into him. Just like all of us, his almond skin is dirty, his hair and beard overgrown. His hazel eyes mirror Peri's, and my heart seems to thump out of my chest while examining the once handsome, tattered man. *My dad.* The sentimental family reunion is interrupted by another set of rumbles. I widen my legs, grabbing onto Peri to keep my balance.

"What do we do now?" Jasper asks, seeking guidance not from our parents but our leader siblings: Garnet, Ziri, Pearl, and surprisingly, me.

"We have to stop the volcano," Garnet says, running her hands through her hair. What is usually an intricate pattern of finger waves is in complete disarray, filled with ash and dirt.

"We can't just stop a fucking volcano," Peri responds, mirroring Garnet in her actions.

"But we can redirect it." We turn to Turq as she pushes her way to the front. Our family circle widens, mom, dad, and Citrine in the center of it. "I can make a path with the ground and trees, steering the lava straight toward the ocean. Away from the town." Turq's hands casually rest in the pockets of her black cargo pants, her hair frizzing out of her low ponytail.

"What would you need from us?" Ziri asks, impressed at her last surviving triplet. The grief is still heavy in her eyes. Really, it's heavy in all our eyes. Tani's absence is evident, her always having an idea or something to say within a family huddle.

"We gotta get these people out of here. If my idea fails, they'll be the first to burn. I'd also need Tory and Citrine."

"Me?" asks Tory, surprised to hear her name. "Shouldn't I be teleporting people out of here?"

"I need your help directing the lava. If you can help guide it into the path I make, it will make things go smoother, and keep me safe too," Turq explains, glancing a look at Citrine, now lying awake and still in our parents' arms, eyes wide. "I think it'll take both of you, but I don't know if she's up for it . . ." Citrine makes no acknowledgement to the plan or her name, simply staring off into space.

"She can do it," acknowledges Topaz, a couple siblings down to my right. "Let me talk with her. She can do it." Topaz is confident in her words, shivering in the early evening breeze.

"Then it's settled," Turq says with a nod.

"Guys—" Emerald starts, but Pearl interrupts him.

"Now to get these people out of here . . ." Pearl thinks aloud, tapping her chin.

"All we need to do is get them to the side of a road. Passersby will see and stop to help them," Ziri offers, gesturing toward the one hundred plus people surrounding us.

"I can form some type of wagon that we can pack the people in," Jasper suggests.

"Nice, I can port everyone out easily like that," Pearl says, impressed.

"And I can be a horse, carrying the most lucid people on my back," Opal adds willingly. Garnet nods at them, and they grin, happy to be more useful.

"Guys—" Emerald tries again, but it's like he's an annoying fly on the wall, soon to be swat.

"The Tele-Twins and I can walk; as long as the road isn't far, we can carry people," Moon says, wrapping her arms around Jade and Aqua.

"I'll take the kids," Alex chimes, referring to her superhuman speed.

"Me too," Diamond adds, her hair in her notorious pigtails.

"And I'll be by the road, siren singing for people to come help." Sapphire tucks her hand around her blue locs to bring them around her shoulder. "I would siren sing these people, but they've been controlled enough." We all nod, turning to look at the people around us, now rustling and whispering. A loud and extreme rumble shakes the ground beneath us, causing shouts of terror from the hostages.

"Okay!" Garnet shouts over the volcano, arms outstretched to keep her balance. "Alex and Diamond take the kids. Opal, Jasper, Moon, Tele-Twins, and Pearl take the adults. The rest of us will be on first aid."

"*Guys!*" Emerald yells, catching all our attention.

"What do you want?" Pearl's voice is acid, and the scowl on her face burns even more.

"I messed up," Emerald starts, pulling at one of his braids. "I know that now. And I'm really sorry."

"Yeah, well, no amount of your 'sorrys' will bring Tani back," Garnet spits.

"Yes, but—"

"So just grab one of these." Garnet chucks a first aid fanny pack at him. "And make yourself useful."

"I'm trying, but I have to tell you something." He looks nervous, like he's about to vomit all over the floor. All of us are staring at him with faces of distrust, disgust, and betrayal.

"Spit it out! We have things to do." Peri glowers. Emerald tugs at his braids again, looking down at the ground in shame. *He's wasting our time.* I'm about to leave and find my own fanny pack to help these people, but his words send ice through my veins.

"I swapped out the serum," he says, biting the inside of his cheek. "I emptied the syringe and filled it with something else." I feel myself go numb as I meet his eyes. "I know I should have told you earlier, but everything was happening so fast! I forgot . . ." At that, everything seems to happen in slow motion. I look over my shoulder at the tree where our uncle is supposed to be lying, but I only see Corallina.

"I've been planning this for years, and you little *fucks* ruined it." Bloodstone's voice is scratchy and full of hate. All our heads whip in his direction, and my heart leaps into my throat. Bloodstone has Ziri in a chokehold, a broken piece of glass to her throat.

CHAPTER 40

Someone to my left takes a step forward, but Bloodstone tightens his grip on Ziri. She's clawing at him, drawing trails of blood down his arm.

"Let her go," Garnet says, hands ready to paralyze him. Our uncle lets out a heartful chuckle before narrowing his eyes at her. She gasps and her hands are brought to her sides by Bloodstone's control.

"It's over. You lost. Just let—" Peri halts when he loses control of his body. Each one of my siblings who attempts to speak or take a step are stopped by Bloodstone's manipulation. I don't dare move, and no one else seems to either.

"Now, you'll let me and my daughter go, or else you'll be down another sister." He pulls his arm tighter, and Ziri wheezes for air. This doesn't make sense. I held that syringe. I felt the weight of musgravite in it. So if Emerald swapped serums, he must have just drained the real serum replacing it with a placebo. Meaning there must have been traces of the inhibiting stone still in the syringe.

I eye my uncle carefully, and a small piece of reassurance surges through me. His face is ashen, and he's breathing heavily. His dramatics from earlier weren't entirely an act; musgravite is coursing through his veins. I look around at my siblings and parents, and it seems that no one else has caught on. *What do I do?*

"Uncle B., *please,*" Emerald begs, but Bloodstone continues to take slow steps backward, heading toward his unconscious daughter. My eyes search for anything I can do. I can tell my other siblings are trying to plot a plan, too, and I'm just hoping they figure out what I have. Maybe I can throw something at him? He wouldn't be able to stop it, but I could hit Ziri. A rumble from the volcano and gasps from the former hostages remind me just how urgent it is. Whatever happens, one of us has to do it now. The longer we wait, the more he's getting accustomed to the musgravite in his bloodstream. If we all attack at once, it should work.

My eyes meet Jade's and Aqua's causing their own eyes to widen. I feel my thoughts go fuzzy, then jump when I hear a voice.

The syringe had traces of musgravite in it still. His powers are weakened. It's Aqua's soft voice, but in my head. The siblings who still have control over their bodies and my parents snap their heads toward the Tele-Twins, and my eyebrows raise in realization: *they're casting.* Another rumble from the volcano nearly makes my knees buckle, and I look back at our uncle quickly. He's getting away. The next voice I hear is Jade's.

If we all attack now, Ziri can have a chance to get away. He won't be able to control us all. The girls must have been reading my thoughts. On any other occasion, I would have felt violated, but now, I'm thankful. Before, they were only able to read their twin's thoughts. With the stress of this situation, they must have pushed themselves, casting themselves into our minds to figure out what to do.

Count down, I think, staring at the twins as they both nod.

Three.

Two.

One.

The sixteen of us that are still capable of moving charge at him, and a surge of pleasure courses through me when his eyes widen in horror. He starts to pull his arm back, slicing the glass across Ziri's neck, but his jaw goes slack. We all slow down, only a couple of feet from him. Our uncle's arms drop from around Ziri and she gasps for air, stumbling toward us. Moon catches her in her arms, but her eyes are fixed on Bloodstone. All of our's are. He's choking on something, his arms limp against his sides and legs wobbly. Blood trickles from his mouth, and his breathing becomes shallow. He lets out a strangled cry of pain before falling to his knees and landing on his face. My lips part when I understand why.

Behind him stands mom, eyes full of anger, staring at something in her bloodied hand: a beating heart. Blood coats her arm all the way to her elbow, and she scrunches her face in disgust, tossing Bloodstone's heart aside before looking at all of us slowly.

"I wasn't going to let it happen again."

CHAPTER 41

For a moment, all we do is stare in shock. Her arm shakes violently as she looks between her bloodied hand and the discarded organ. She wipes her arm on her dress carefully, the blood nearly blending in with the fancy fabric. My lips are still parted as I take in the woman who is my mother. The woman who gave up her life, spent years being tortured, and murdered her younger brother to protect her children and the world. Until this moment, I thought we were saving our mom. Our parents. But in reality, she was always saving us.

Another thundering of the volcano reminds us the threat isn't over, and we still have a job to do.

"Let's get these people out of here," mom says solemnly, gesturing at the injured people still scattered across the clearing. At that, Tory mimics Pearl's power, wordlessly teleporting herself and Turq to the top of the volcano. Most of the people here still don't have control over their bodies, but others are staring at us with a mixture of fear and hope. Nodding and mumbling in agreement, we all break off to do our parts that we decided before everything went to chaos, shaking the bloody scene from our minds.

Those with first aid fanny packs who are on evacuation duty take them off, discarding them on the floor for those of us on first aid. I grab Moon's, clamping it around my waist before finding someone who needs help. I blink, and mom's bloodied hand flashes in my brain. Another blink and the seizing woman flashes behind my eyelids. I blink again. Gone. I spy Zach with some of the victims before Garnet approaches him. With a quick glance over his shoulder, he mouths "stay safe" before helping the little girl out of the clearing. A weak smile tickles my lips as I turn to help someone in need. The first person I approach is a young boy with a gash down his arm. I muster as much cheeriness as I can and crouch to meet his height.

"Hi, my name is Ruby. What's your name?" I ask, speaking kindly. He doesn't notice how my hands shake as I open the fanny pack and pull out alcohol wipes and a bandage wrap. When I bring them close to him, he flinches away, hiding his arm behind his back. "Hey, hey, I'm not here to hurt you. I'm here to help," I say comfortingly. His eyes are full of fear, and I hope that when he looks into mine, he sees kindness and trust. Eventually, he takes his arm from behind his back and outstretches it to me hesitantly.

"I don't know," he says, his voice small.

"Hmm?" I ask, peeling back the paper that encapsulates the alcohol wipe.

"I don't know my name." My head whips up to his face, but his eyes are focused on my hands, and he's ready to snatch his arm away in case of any danger. My heart breaks, and I wonder how long the boy must have been held captive for him not to know his name.

I choose to not make a big deal of the situation, casually asking, "Well, do you want one?" I grab onto his wrist gently, pulling his arm closer to me. "This might sting and hurt a little bit. It hurts because it's cleaning your cut, okay?" The boy nods slowly, and I wipe the gash. He hisses as the alcohol coats his wound. I gently hush him, cooing to him that it will be okay and that it's almost over.

"I do." He grits his teeth, clinging his eyes shut. "I do want a name." I'm almost done when he tilts his head back, opening his eyes. His mouth falls open slightly as he stares at the clouds. The setting sun reflects in his eyes, and there's a small tug on his lips. When the ground begins to rumble again, he looks at me, alarmed.

"We're going to get you out of here soon, okay. Did you like that?" I ask, wrapping his arm, the blood slowing.

"No, it was scary! What was that?" he asks, nearly shaking from the scare.

"That was the mountain." I point behind us. "It's called a volcano." I continue to wrap his arm, talking to him softly and calmly, trying to distract him from the terror. "Sometimes, this fire liquid called 'lava' will come out of it. And unfortunately, that's happening now. But don't worry, we're going to get you somewhere safe." His eyes are back on my hands, and he is watching them circle around his arms. "That wasn't what I meant though. Did you like what you were looking at?" I ask, pointing up at the sky. He nods slowly, lifting his head back up.

"It's *so blue*," he says, his eyes sparkling again. "I don't think I've ever seen anything like it." My heart breaks for the second time in a span of five minutes. The boy can't be more than five or six years old. He must have learned how to talk from the other hostages. I pray that Bloodstone never used him for any of his semantics.

"That's called the *sky*," I tell him, cutting the wrap with small scissors.

"Sky," he whispers, his eyes blinking slowly as he takes in the clouds and birds flying. When the ground rumbles again, he isn't as scared, but his head yanks down to meet my eyes, seeking comfort. "Can that be my name? Sky?" I look up at him and smile.

"If that's what you want." Glancing over his shoulder, I see Diamond has returned, and I wave her over.

"It is . . . .what I want." He examines his completely bandaged arm.

"He's ready," I tell Diamond, putting everything back in the fanny pack and getting ready to stand up. She nods and bends down to the boy. She opens her mouth to say something, but he speaks first.

"My name is Sky," he chimes, waving up at her. My whole body warms when I see his smile, a missing tooth on the right side.

"Hi, Sky! My name's Diamond. Let's get you someplace safe." Diamond bends down and scoops him up into her arms. As she does, her pigtails thicken and lengthen to the floor. Instead of bending her knees to stand, her hair extends, pushing her off the ground. She takes a large step with her hair, using them as extra limbs. It looks like giant black muscle fibers acting as two enormous legs, leaving her real legs dangling a foot or so off the ground. Then, she breaks into a sprint, dashing through the woods with massive strides, expertly and rapidly.

I continue to make my rounds, checking if people need bandages or ointment. As I help them, I ask if they remember anything from *before*. A lot of adults and teens say they do. Some remember everything, being taken and the whole time being held captive. Other's memories are spotty and inconsistent. While I wrap a large gash on a man, he tells me how he remembers before, but barely anything after. A woman taps me, tugging me close.

"They took him a lot," she whispers before going back to lying on the grass, waiting for her turn to be saved. My mind sweeps me into a memory, filling my brain with Bloodstone's reasoning. Are all of them like Benji's mom? *Why did my uncle take these people over others*? I straighten my back, choosing to focus on the present situation. The time between each rumble is getting shorter and shorter, and I pray that Tory and Turq are working on changing the lava's course. As I'm holding an instant ice pack over a woman's dark bruise, I look around the clearing. Not including the Gems, there are about fifty people left. Diamond and the others are working fast. Mom and dad are walking around, also with fanny packs, Citrine nowhere to be seen.

Topaz must have been able to get through to her. Now she's probably at the lips of the volcano, holding the lava back for Turq. In about thirty more minutes, the ground rumbling is near constant, the sky a gray hue. The area is clear of all but family members and Zach. Corallina still lays unconscious by the t ree.

"The people should be fine." Sapphire pants, sticks and grass poking out of her locs, her face smeared with dirt. "They're getting a lot of help down there."

"What about Citrine and Tory and Turq?" Topaz asks, biting her lip.

"I'll check on them," Pearl replies, disappearing in thin air. We're all standing quietly, waiting for her to return. I look at my siblings: cuts and scratches litter their bodies, their clothes are torn, and their hair amiss. They're whispering quietly to one another, but I'm not close enough to hear. The awkwardness between us and our parents is evident. I watch the Tele-Twins eye mom and dad, exchanging unspoken thoughts.

None of us really know how to react. Yes, they are our parents, but they didn't raise us. We don't know them, and they don't know us. Hell, they probably don't know which kid is which. But there's a newfound respect for them, especially mom. Although our parents are strangers to us, the want for that feeling to end is loud in the air from all of us. Pearl pops back into the clearing, eyes blazing and soot sprinkling her features.

"Turq says it's safe. Do you guys want to see?" Pearl asks.

"Yeah!" exclaims Topaz, running over to grab Pearl's hand.

"For sure, heading toward the danger sounds like a *brilliant* idea," Peri muses sarcastically, reluctantly approaching the chain of hands holding each other that has formed. It's not his usual sarcasm though. The annoying prick that normally comes with his comments is not there. In less than a second, we're all on a tall rock, looking down into Mauna Kea. It's significantly hotter here than it was in the clearing, and I start sweating almost immediately. It's tolerable for now, but it will be overwhelming soon.

Tory and Citrine are lower than us, standing right on the edge of the volcano. Their hands are outstretched over the volcano's mouth, eyes focused on pushing the magma down as much as they can.

"Are you ready?" grits out Tory, shouting over the pops of the boiling liquid.

"Yes! Get ready!" Turq calls down to them. Then she turns her attention to Moon. "Can you lift them up fast?"

"Of course," she replies, shifting her weight to focus on her fire manipulating sisters.

"Now!" Turq yells. Moon sets her jaw, lifting Tory and Citrine from Mauna Kea's lips quickly. She sets them down beside our parents who are at the end of the line. Moments later, the magma is bubbling out of the volcano, slowly oozing its way down the path Turq created. The path starts like a spiral, walled in by the tall rocks we're standing on. It guides the lava around the volcano's crater directing it away from civilization. Although it's hot and the air is smoking, causing the scene to be filled with coughing, it's beautiful. Turq's elevated ground works, the magma calmly continuing down its path.

Every now and then, the lava pops into the air. When it does, Citrine and Tory make sure to guide the sparks away from us. Our arms are all wrapped around each other, some heads resting on each other's shoulders. A movement on my left catches my eye, and I watch mom take a step near the edge. When she lifts her hand from her sides, my stomach churns. She opens her palm, letting our uncle's heart roll off her fingertips. It topples down the side of the rock before falling into the lava with a splash. Embers and sparks bubble up as the organ is enveloped with a sizzle.

As Earth's natural beauty erupts in front of our eyes, the aesthetics can't be ignored, even with the loss and torture that came with it. Pain leaves a shadowy aura over what would have been a divine conclusion to our quest. But now that the chaos has died down, the reality of Tani's death weighs heavily on us, and I let it overwhelm me.

Not including Moon, Tani was the first sibling I met, and I really cared for her, even before I knew the truth. She had a beauty that dazzled both inside and out. And her brain . . . She's easily the smartest person ever met. Sure, her social abilities were sometimes questionable, but it also added to her charm. Her smile flashes in my memories, and her laughter rings in my ears. I finally let myself feel the grief, taking it in all at once. The tears are hot and ready, dripping off my eyelashes like a leaky faucet. I feel them fall down my cheek and roll slowly to my chin. Other drops fall on my temple, my arms, and the ground. I tip my head up to the sky, letting the incoming rain mix with my tears. The raindrops soon come down in gentle sheets, drenching our bodies before sizzling into the lava below.

CHAPTER 42

When my alarm goes off, I roll over, dragging myself out of my bed. This isn't my first time getting up today. I've been in and out of sleep all day, distracting myself from this evening's scheduled events. After taking a shower and brushing my teeth, I sit on the end of my bed, untwisting my hair silently. It's been nearly a week since we returned from Hawaii, and I haven't found the energy to wash my hair. When I'm done untwisting, I push myself to my feet tiredly, walk over to my closet, and choose a black dress with sheer polka-dotted sleeves and a matching tulle skirt that ends just above my knees. I pull the dress on, looking in the mirror as I flatten it against my skin. I style my hair, too, making my twist-out look as if they're bangs in front of my face. Pushing up my glasses, I walk to the door, flicking off the light switch on the way down.

A couple of us are ready, waiting for our other siblings to be dressed and downstairs. We're all sitting in the living room, silent in grief and thought. All except Emerald. For three days, we tried to forgive him. Put all the blame on our uncle. But Garnet couldn't. Peri couldn't. Ziri couldn't. *I couldn't.* This morning he left, an apology letter placed carefully on his bed. I would be lying if I said I was sad to see him go. The moment I heard he was gone, an invisible weight lifted from my shoulders.

Ziri sits across from me, holding the vase that contains Tani's ashes. Within ten more minutes, everyone else is ready, and with a few exchanged words, we load the bus, Garnet driving.

Ziri planned everything, knowing Tani for the longest. One thing that she made sure to do was talk to everyone. Since we all have different beliefs and practice different religions, she wanted to create a custom ceremony, something that would allow everyone to feel comfortable. And although cremation was against some of our beliefs, that wasn't a factor in our control.

When we get to the destination, Ziri asks us to follow her. The path she takes isn't a path at all, some invisible steps she must have taken many times. I watch my step, making sure to not trip over fallen trees and jutting roots hidden in the late evening. Soon, the trees become uncrowded, and we approach a clearing that looks over Lake Erie. We stop a few steps out, but Ziri continues, almost to the edge of the cliff, before turning around.

"Tani found this place a little over a year ago," Ziri begins, clutching the vase to her chest. A cold wind breezes by, and I shiver, tightening my coat around me. "She liked to come here to clear her mind and look at the stars." She lifts her head up to the sky. "She dreamed about getting up there." She is choking on her words, silent tears running down her face. The next statements she directs toward our parents. "She was really smart. *So smart.* She could touch anything and know about its properties and chemical makeup. School was child's play to her. She never had the opportunity to learn because she knew everything already. She described it as intuition." She looks back up to the stars, and I do too. The light pollution is weak here, so the stars are evident, sprinkling the night sky.

"What she didn't know about was space. Stars and galaxies . . . Because she couldn't touch it, the intuition would never come." Ziri bites her lip, squeezing her eyes shut. "'After all this is over, I'm gonna get up there,'" Ziri quotes, squeezing the vase tighter. "I'm sorry you never got to. So, Tani, this is the best I can do." Turning away from us, Ziri scoops her hand into the vase, taking out the ashes. She holds her hand up and opens her palm. The night wind blows it out of her hand, carrying it into the dusk sky. Ziri puts the vase down, dusting off her hands respectfully, then turns back to face us.

"I know a lot of you didn't know her as I did. Some of you, not at all," she adds, referring to our parents. "But us being all together, being a family, that was another one of Tani's dreams." Ziri sniffs, holding back sobs. "So I ask, if you are comfortable, to help me put Tani to peace." She reaches back down to pick up the vase and steps slightly to her left. Without hesitation, Garnet steps forward slowly. When she makes it to Ziri, she nods to her solemnly. "Thank you," Ziri whispers as Garnet dips her hand into the vase. She turns to the lake, raising her full hand out in front of her.

"Go to the stars," Garnet says softly as she opens her palm, ashes flowing into the wind. Like Ziri, she softly brushes the remaining ashes off her hands and turns to walk back to her place. Before she makes it, Peri is next, walking forward to Ziri. He puts his hand in the vase and turns to the edge of the cliff.

"Go learn something new for once . . . smart ass." Peri sniffs, a small smile of sadness written on his face. He opens his hand, shaking the ashes gently from his fingertips before coming back to the crowd. We all take turns going up and scattering her ashes. The ones who don't know her as well do so quietly, silently paying their respects. As each sibling finishes their turn, I think about what I will say. *Should I say anything?* I've only known her for a little over a month, but so much has happened since then. Although most of our time was spent trying to save our parents, when we did have fun, I got to see more than her intelligence and leadership. After Moon's turn, I take a step forward, walking to Ziri. The ashes are cool to the touch, and my fingertips scrape the bottom of the nearly empty vase. Holding out my hand, I ponder my next words carefully.

"Thank you for bringing me to my family and being the sister I never knew I needed." The wind spreads the ashes through my fingers, covering my hand in a thin layer of gray. Dusting off the excess ashes, I turn back to my family, walking back to my place silently. Mom and dad are next, their steps in sync, arm in arm. Together, they dip their hands in her ashes.

"You were such a beautiful baby, and there wasn't a day that went by where I didn't think of you," mom says softly, before looking over her shoulder at us, her face stained with tears, "any of you." She turns back to the lake. "I'm sorry

I never was able to meet the amazing woman that you became, but I am so, *so* proud of you."

"Reciting your name . . . all of your names, was the one thing that kept me going," my dad says. He's clean-shaven and in a black suit. When he stands next to mom, his head rests about a foot higher than hers. "'I'm gonna meet my babies soon,'" he stammers, squeezing my mom's hand. "You were taken from us too soon, Tanzanite." Simultaneously, they release her ashes. The wind seems to roar as they do, spreading the ashes in the air rapidly.

Citrine is the last one to go. Although Topaz and Opal didn't sprinkle ashes, they walked to the front, saying nice words. As Citrine walks to the cliff, her movements are slow, and her head is down. She reaches into the vase, grabbing the last of Tani's ashes, and for the first time in a week, I hear her speak.

"I'm sorry," Citrine whispers, tears streaming down her face as she opens her hand. Before the ashes are scattered completely, she falls to her knees in a fit of sobs. "I'm sorry!" she wails, gripping the grass. Ziri places down the vase quickly and rubs Citrine's back, trying to comfort her.

"Citrine, you—"

"*I'm sorry!*" The pain and guilt in Citrine's screeching wails stab me in the chest, and the tears that flow down my face are unstoppable. I watch as dad walks up to her, pulls the nine-year-old off the ground, and holds her tightly. She sobs into his shoulder while he carries her back to where we all stand. Ziri walks back with us, too, vase in arms, and stands next to Garnet. When Citrine's weeps begin to calm, Turq takes a couple steps forward.

"If you all could just take a few steps back . . ." Turq trails off. We do as she says, giving her more space. When we are far enough back, she kneels, holding something in her hand and pressing it into the ground. We watch in awe as a tree begins to sprout in front of our eyes, the trunk unfolding. When it reaches about waist height, Turq steps back, giving the tree more room to grow. The branches flourish, growing at a rapid speed, pine needles poking out. Turq grows the tree, letting it reach a height taller than all the others surrounding it. When the trunk is wide and the tree is sturdy, she backs up even more, hands on her hips, admiring her work. The giant spruce rests comfortably near the cliff, the evergreen to stay standing for eternity in Tani's memory.

EPILOGUE

I lie outside by the pool in the summer's heat, eyes closed as the sun rolls over my skin. As I play with my braids, I clink the red and brown beads that lie on the ends. My phone dings, and I reach for it. When I see it's just an email from a retail store, I sigh, opening a browser to scroll aimlessly through news articles and recent journalist stories. I stop when I see something that catches my eye, falling for the clickbait. At the top of the news website is a picture of my uncle and cousin.

Father of Father-Daughter Serial Killer Duo Found Dead-Daughter in Custody. I don't bother reading the article, already knowing the story that we decided on. Ziri fabricated evidence she couldn't find in his cloud account. She listed nearly every person that we knew he murdered, knowing full well that it's most likely an underestimate. One hundred and two people: women, men, kids.

We left an anonymous tip that criminals were spotted at some run-down motel in Cleveland. There, we left Bloodstone's body and a sedated Corallina for the police to handle. We had to be sure that Corallina wouldn't use her powers wherever she was taken. With a lot of brainstorming, one of the Tele-Twins joked about a tattoo. So, with some research, courtesy of Ziri, we were able to put musgravite dust into tattoo ink, give the ink to a tattoo parlor, and have her tattooed. Sapphire's siren song made the whole process smooth. Although we wanted to pick what that tattoo was, mom convinced us not to.

"She's going to be losing a piece of herself forever," my mom said, referring to the feeling of wholeness when using our power. "And yes, it's well deserved, but let her pick." Corallina chose a sea turtle, having grown up surrounded by Hawaiian culture. Scenes at the volcano flash in my mind, but they're not as vibrant as they once were. I touch my neck, my fingers tracing the scar that she gave me as I reflect.

"The scar makes you look a little rugged," Zach notes, carrying two glasses of lemonade. He hands me mine and takes a seat next to me. "I like it." He leans over, kissing me on the lips. I smile as he pulls away, reaching for the drink and taking a sip.

"Oh, do you?" I laugh, looking out at the yard. Garnet, Peri, Diamond, and Amethyst are playing volleyball in the grass against Moon, Sapphire, Turq, and Alex. "Who do you think is gonna win?" I ask Zach, taking another sip of lemonade. Zach leans forward, examining the game.

"Team Garnet for sure. Hair power? Elasticity?" He chuckles, leaning back in the seat. "The teams aren't balanced at all."

"But," I object, "Team Moon can levitate and has super speed."

"Still, no match." Zach shrugs, taking a swig of the lemonade. Everyone is outside. Topaz, Sapphire, the October triplets, and the Tele-Twins are in the pool. Zircon is on her laptop on the patio while mom and dad are cooking on the outdoor grill. Citrine is sitting quietly, a couple of lounge chairs away from me, book in hand. She hasn't been the same since all the events and trauma we endured. When we told mom and dad, they put her in therapy. But she can't exactly tell the truth of what happened, so I don't know if it's much help. Mainly, though, she does not speak. She gestures for the most part, and Sapphire teaches her some sign language. But mostly, she communicates through nods, gestures, and writing.

Emerald is also alone, sitting on a hammock on his phone. I know my uncle manipulated him, getting into his head, but it's hard to forgive him. Mom reminds us that he did the right thing in the end, and that no blood is on his hands. So I've been trying—we all have. We include him when we can, but he's like a constant reminder of betrayal and Tani's death. Even though his actions didn't pull the trigger, they loaded the gun.

When my phone buzzes, I pick it up, smiling when I see a text from Maria. As the months went by, our communication dwindled, but not in a bad way. Maria is *living*. Lisa has signed her up for after-school activities, and she's even allowed to have friends over. The text is a picture of her and her friend in her room. Getting Zach's attention, I take my own selfie to send back to her. I silently remind myself to get my bunny, Snowball, some more food. A little bit after my return from Hawaii, I secretly met up with Maria. While I gave her my gift from the beautiful island and explained to her that I was safe and everything would be okay, she returned Snowball to me, along with all of her supplies.

"Food's ready!" Dad yells as mom sets the long outdoor dinner table, fit to sit twenty-six. Starving, I grab onto Zach and pull him to his feet. He chuckles as I steer him to the table and we take a seat. In a few minutes, we're all at the table, laughing and making our plates. Even Grandma Adelaide is here with her at-home caretaker, having moved in with us soon after mom and dad fell into their societal roles as parents, a lawyer and a doctor.

"Ruby, have you picked a school yet?" Ziri asks, filling her plate with grilled vegetables. I sigh.

"That's all anybody asks me, I swear," I say, using tongs to grab a hamburger patty.

"Well, yeah," Garnet admonishes filling her plate. "Decision day was like a month ago."

"I can get you in *anywhere*," Ziri sings before taking a bite of her hot dog. "All you gotta do is pick. And soon too. The longer you wait, the slightly more irritating it is to hack the system."

"Yeah, I know," I respond, sitting back in my seat. I push the vegetables around on my plate. "I just have been trying to live in the moment, you know? Make memories and stuff." I sigh and put my fork back. "We worked so hard and lost so much to get to this point," I point out, sagging in my seat. "I'm just not ready to give it up."

"You're not giving this up," dad says, crossing his arms over his chest. "You're continuing on with your life. We'll always be right here." He gestures to the house.

"You'll see us for summers, and winters too," Topaz chimes in, taking a bite of her burger.

"Yeah, but . . . I don't know." I take a bite of my food, ketchup catching at the corner of my mouth.

"Yo, guys, hear me out," Peri says, leaning forward. "We all go to the same school," he declares, referring to the college ready siblings. Garnet scoffs at him.

"What?"

"Listen, listen. We further our education or whatever, but also bond. We can make up for all those years we missed." Peri shrugs, a grin on his face.

"Your breaks would line up . . ." adds mom, smiling softly as she looks at us. Garnet bites her lip, giving Peri's idea more thought.

"We all don't even want to go to the same school." Garnet sighs.

"Then we compromise, eh?" Peri asks, hands outstretched. "C'mon it's not even a bad idea." I stare between Peri, Garnet, Sapphire, Amethyst, Alex, Moon, Pearl, and lastly Emerald. I give him a small smile.

"*All* of us," I say, nodding my head at Emerald. Nearly nine months after Emerald left, he came back, knocking on our door, pleading for forgiveness. Of course, mom and dad wouldn't turn him away. Although it's been only a week, I feel a smog of distrust coating the air. His attempt of apology has not been in vain. He's holding himself accountable, explaining his reasons and actions, but not justifying them. I appreciate the effort, and with mom and dad begging us to try to understand, maybe he deserves a second chance. Peri visibly tries to keep his face from turning to disgust, so I guess that's progress. The others hesitate, but don't disagree. With a sigh of defeat, Peri puts a forkful of potato salad in hi s mouth.

"So where are we going?" For the next hour, we debate on what school we should enroll in. Since Ziri has one more year of high school left, picking a school based on major isn't a large concern. However, Pearl and Sapphire want a diverse and work-hard-play-hard school. Moon says she doesn't care where we go as long as it's not in California.

"I'm done with shaking grounds," she admits, and we all chuckle lightly at that, relating to the want to be as far from the tectonic plates as we can. Narrowing down our choices of schools on the East Coast, we agree it should be a big-name school. Since we saved the world, we deserve some prestige. After a lot of back and forth, the decision we make has me tugging on Zach's arm with excitement. Ziri types rapidly on her keyboard, hacking into the university's database to enroll us. I'm surprised that I don't flinch.

Before *this*, before the *Gems*, college was my way out. An escape from Lisa, but also, it would be proof of all my hard work meaning something. At first, I was against Ziri enrolling me. But after surviving sexual violence, saving my parents, rescuing hostages, escaping an erupting volcano, and honoring my sister, I don't need proof of all my efforts. I see it every time I look in my mirror. I feel it with every step and breath I take. And yeah, maybe these efforts aren't academic, but if I am capable of all of that, I am capable of anything.

After a couple of minutes, she lets out a satisfying sigh before closing her laptop and leaning back in her chair, arms folded across her chest.

"Congrats, Blue Devils. Y'all are going to college."

PREVIEW OF - THE GEMS: EMERALD EYES (A NOVELLA)

It's not my fault. He said we were doing good. Saving the world. It was so convincing . . . I believed him. Anyone would have. He's my uncle.

I pace the room anxiously. This was never my intention. I tug at a braid, letting out a roar of shame. Ruby and my other siblings weren't telling me "useless propaganda." They were telling me the truth. *I take back what I said. This is my fault. All my fault.* Bloodstone knew about everything: everyone's abilities, where they lived, when they were coming, and the plan for defeating him. I told him everything. Uncle B. tossed the bone, and I chased it, returning with it entrapped in my teeth, slick with drool, tail wagging.

"Idiot, of course this is your fault!"

"Leave me alone!" I shout, pounding my fist against the motel wall. "I said I was sorry. I tried!" Tears of agony stream down my face. "I tried, but they cast me out!"

"Of course, they did! You killed their sister. Your *sister. Her blood is on your hands!"*

The voices started in the volcano, sometime after Tani's first bloodcurdling screech and when I threw Corallina off Ruby.

I tried for days: apologizing, groveling, pleading. But of course, none of it would bring our sister back. Eventually, the hateful looks and negligence from my siblings became too much to bear, and I left. That was three days ago.

I tiptoed down the stairs, hair begging to be washed and bags in tow. I froze when I saw Ziri sitting in the living room, typing away aggressively, headphones on. There was no way to avoid her. I woke up at dawn believing no one would be awake, or at least no one would be downstairs. I wanted to sneak out smoothly, only leaving a note on my bed as a way of goodbye. With Ziri there, things had become more complicated. I had hoped that if I was quiet, staying close to the wall, she would pay me no attention. I was gravely mistaken.

"Where are you going?" she asked, words slick with acid-like disgust. I froze, surprised to be acknowledged, unsurprised by the tone.

"I'm leaving," I responded softly, my voice as delicate as a white dandelion.

"Took you long enough," she mumbled, never giving me her eyes. I hesitated. One second. Two seconds. Three. *Should I say something? Apologize for the betrayal that had cost Tani her life?* Instead, I made a smart decision. Probably the smartest I had in a while. I started to leave. "How?" Ziri asked, stopping me in my tracks.

"What?"

"How are you leaving? With what funds?" She sat back, looking at me from over her glasses, the first time she had looked at me in days. Her eyes bored into mine, taking in my sand-colored sweatshirt and black joggers. I looked at her awkwardly, slowly taking my duffle bag off my shoulder.

"I emptied my account before coming here," I said, tugging at my braid. "I have a couple thousand from my magician gig." At that, Ziri scoffed and put her headphones back on her ears.

"Not enough." She stared at her laptop, not speaking. I thought she would say more.

"She hates you. They all do." I shook my head and plugged my ears subtly, before reaching down to pick back up my bag.

"Because I respect mom and dad, set up a new bank account and send me the routing info. They will send you a weekly allowance," Ziri said, eyes glued to her screen once again.

Then I left. And now, I'm here: a cheap hotel somewhere near Cleveland Hopkins International Airport. I haven't decided where I want to go yet. Tennessee is out of the question. With my magician act, I was a local celebrity. The farthest I've ever driven for a show was two hours; the pay that day was glorious. And the farthest anyone had come to see me was from Hawaii. That was the first time I met my uncle and Corallina.

"What are you going to do now, traitor?" It's never the same voice. Sometimes, it's high-pitched. Other times, it's low. Once, it was a little kid's voice. A boy, maybe?

"Please, leave me alone!" I press my hands over my ears, gritting my teeth in frustration.

"He was groomed. Take pity on him," says a soothing woman's voice. It drips like honey in warm chamomile tea.

"He should have known better." This woman's voice is harder, as ragged as the nails that slashed Ruby's neck. I let out a scream, taking big strides to the pillow on my bed. I pick it up, slam it on the covers. Over and over again. Roaring with guilt and fear and pain. I need the voices to stop. I need everything to stop. The next hit with the pillow is lighter, distracted in thought.

I need everything to stop.

I never wanted to kill myself before. Before, I had a purpose. Something to live for. But now? My family hates me. My sister's blood is on my hands. My nine-year-old sister's voice silenced by trauma—nonverbal forever maybe. There's nothing for me now.

No purpose.

No love.

No will.

Nothing.

I don't wait another second. I grab my wallet and keys, darting to the door and locking it behind me. Walmart is only a ten-minute walk away from the hotel, but I make it there in seven. I don't need to think about the means in which I should take my life; it's already been decided. I walk straight to aisle fourteen, grab the cheapest item of the selection, and jog toward the self-checkout.

Twelve minutes later, I'm in my hotel bathroom, leaning in front of the mirror. The Walmart bag is on my left, making the air in the room heavy. With a deep breath, I lean into the shower-bath combo, turning on the faucet and plugging the drain.

"The best decision you've made in a while," a voice hisses at me.

"I know," I reply, filled with determined grief. As the tub fills, I shake the anxiety from my fingertips. Grabbing the shopping bag, I take out my purchase, open the box, and take the toaster out. I lean over, checking the water height, and sigh. It's filling too slowly. I plug the toaster in before pacing in and out of the bathroom.

About two days after the voices started, I began doing research. I *knew* this wasn't normal. Hearing your inner monologue, that's one thing. Hearing different voices with different beliefs and personalities, that's a whole other thing.

It wasn't like I was going to ask my parents or siblings for help. I don't deserve their aid. So after scrolling through Wikipedia and the CDC website, as well as Googling my symptoms, I deduced that it's psychosis. It made the most sense. The trauma of realizing my uncle's manipulation combined with his and Tani's death would result in this.

I stop pacing, standing in front of the mirror solemnly. When I look up, my eyes lock on the foggy person in the reflection. *Right.*

I haven't just been hearing voices. I've been seeing things too.

Yesterday, it was a little girl chasing after a cat at the end of the bed. The day before, it was an old man reading a newspaper. The day before that, a woman was eating a plate of food. They would focus on their actions, but eventually, they looked at me. Some had pity in their eyes, others disgust. I hated it.

I check the water level again. Perfect. Before I lose any confidence and determination, I rip off my clothes, settling into the water. The hallucination is gone now, only visible in the mirror. I reach up, grab the toaster from its place on the counter, and hold it above the water.

One deep breath.

Another.

I shut my eyes, ready to let go.

Three.

Two.

One—

"What do you think you're doing?" My head shoots up. This voice is unlike the others. It's less echoey, as if someone is in the room with me.

"Leave me alone! I'm doing what I have to do. What I *deserve*." Now I have to start the process again.

Deep breath.

Another.

Three—

"Don't fucking kill yourself, you coward!" the same voice says, now directly in my ear. I jump.

"What do you want me to do? What is there *to* do?" I move the toaster higher above the water, annoyed by the voice's interruptions, but interested in what it has to say.

"*Idiot*, make it up to them!"

"Tani is gone!" I shout, choking on the last word. "Citrine isn't talking anymore. And so many innocent people have died. *How* do I make that up?" The voice is silent.

One minute.

Two minutes.

Three minutes.

Nothing.

I readjust my position in the tub, prepping my hands to drop the appliance.

"I can't tell you," the voice says softly. "This is a journey *you* need to take. Something *you* need to conquer. I can help lead you down the path, though. However, you have to take the steps that lead you to your destination."

"And what's that? My *destination?*" I spit, irritated that this hallucination keeps stopping me right when I'm about to gather my bearings.

"Forgiveness." Sparkles and fog start to fill a spot outside of the tub. I blink. Then I blink again. They're still there. The glimmery mist begins to form a body, and soon, it materializes in the air. The grip of the toaster in my hands goes slack, and I gasp, eyes widening at the figure in front of me.

Tani.

Ending
Author's Note

In many ways, Ruby is the person I wish I was. She takes risks and stands for what's right, even if it may not be in the most direct way. There were many times in my life where I ran from my trauma, coping by building walls I thought would never come down. However, while writing this book, the walls fell. This book was a journey of me coming to love myself and the beautiful skin I was born in, as well as coping with some unfortunate events I had to experience.

My writing journey started in the fourth grade, when my teacher gave an assignment requiring us to write our own story. At the time, I was extremely invested in rocks and birthstones, even having my own collection of rhinestone gems. But when I began to write the idea, I realized it could be something more than just a short story. Every year since then, I wrote.

As I grew, Ruby did. When I was twelve, she was twelve. When I was fourteen, she was fourteen. At seventeen, she finally stopped growing with me, and I was able to really dive into the person I wanted her to be. This is when I reevaluated what I wanted my book to stand for. Growing up in a predominantly white community, seeing people like me in my classes was rare. From this, I developed some internalized racism. I used to imagine showering in white paint so I could fit in at school. So that I could validate my crushes on the boys in my class.

Because of this need to "fit in," all my characters started off white, and they wouldn't change to represent my community and others until my last year of high school.

SEXUAL VIOLENCE:

Sexual violence and assault is never the fault of the victim. As a victim, it took me a long time to come to terms with this. The scene in Chapter 18 between Ruby and her perpetrator was written in a time of need for me, when I was finding ways to cope with my own experience of sexual violence. What happened to Ruby is similar but different from what happened to me. At the time, I thought I was alone. I didn't know who I could talk to or who I could relate to. So I *made* someone who would understand. Doing so helped me not blame myself for what happened, which was something I had been doing for about a year.

For a long time, I contemplated if I wanted to include this scene. What happened to Ruby was not essential to her story, just as what happened to me was not essential to my life. To my readers, I ask you not to narrow down Ruby's story to her sexual assault, as that is not the big take away of the novel.

The National Sexual Assault Hotline is a confidential hotline that provides 24/7 support.

For more information, chat online at: online.rainn.org or call: 1-800-656-4673

ACKNOWLEDGEMENTS

Completing this novel wasn't something that I ever thought I would do. Thank you Mrs. Piazza for giving us the assignment to write a short story. I remember sitting at one of the three computers in our trailer classroom, excited for the idea that sprouted in my fourth-grade head. If it wasn't for you and your excellent teaching, I wouldn't be where I am today. You have really impacted my life, and continue to do so to this day. Thank you for inspiring me.

To my parents. Thank you for all of the sacrifices that you have made for me. I strive to make you both proud with everything that I do. This book has been my dream for a very long time, and thank you for being there to support me in this new journey. Mommy and Daddy, I love you so much. Even though I'm getting older and growing up, I will always be your Mimibear.

To my sisters. We may have had our handfuls of sibling bickering, but thank you for being such wonderful sisters and supporting me constantly. Talya and Rayna, you're always able to keep it real with me, and I really appreciate that. Thanks for putting up with me for most/all of your life. Talya, thank you for being my proofreader. Something I will probably remember for the rest of my life is the moment you said "M. C., your book is *actually* good!" Rayna, thank you for letting me spoil my book to you during the writing process. I appreciate our late night talks and am looking forward to reading the writing you'll put forth into the world. I could not ask for better sisters and I love you guys so much.

To my Market District Gang, Chloe Chen, Michelle Xiao, and Ayah Aldosari, thank you. You all have been my ride or dies for over five years now, and I wouldn't be the person I am today if it weren't for you three. Thank you for laughing with me, and crying with me. Thank you for supporting me, and challenging me. I love you three so much!

Finally, I would like to thank everyone else who has helped support me on the path of publishing this novel:

Thank you Jessica Berry for being an amazing editor. The first copy I sent you was complete trash in the grammar department, and I appreciate you indirectly teaching me how to write. Your communication and editing is absolutely stellar and I hope that we can continue to work together in the future.

Thank you K. Yan for designing my beautiful cover and Juliet Campbell for creating an amazing book trailer for me. You are both amazing artists and I hope we can continue to work together in the future. I am so excited to see the work you will put forth in this world.

Thank you Ellie Guyton for being my beta reader. Your comments were extraordinarily helpful and I wish you the best in your future endeavors.

Thank you Booktok for all of your amazing support! I have met so many amazing authors and people through Tiktok, and I appreciate each and everyone of you. The community has been so uplifting and inspiring and I am very thankful for everything you all have given me. To all the authors I've met on Booktok, I am excited to read your books.

Thank you to my high school and middle school friends Kari Adkins, Ashley Butcher, Megan Watkins, and Samantha Thomas for the support you have given me, both directly and indirectly. Some of my favorite memories of my primary education are because of you four. Thank you and I love you all.

Thank you to my roommates Phoenix Lee, Amber Dowd, and Kay Merill. Your support and encouragement means the world to me. Phoenix, thank you for being my roommate since freshman year at OSU and putting up with my craziness. I enjoy all the times we laugh together and our movie nights. Amber, thank you for being my rock when I needed you most Summer 2022, and for beta reading my novel. I don't know what I would have done without you.

And Chef KRD, thank you for cooking amazing food that powered my brain to work on my homework and my writing. I cherish our game nights and all the moments we spend together. I love you all.

Thank you Christian Coulibaly for putting up with me and being my first beta reader. Editing my novel with you would sometimes be the highlight of my day. Watching your reactions and listening to your heartfelt laughter always brought a gasp or smile to my face. Thank you for using your techno-wizardry to build my website. I could have never done it myself. I love you so much and thank you for supporting me.

Thank you to Author F. K. Davis for your mentorship. Being able to talk to another Black woman fantasy writer was so helpful and enlightening to me. This is entirely new territory for me and you helped me feel more confident in tackling the self-publishing process.

Thank you Dr. Swindle Reilly and everyone in the lab who has supported me. Thank you so much Dr. Swindle Reilly for connecting me with Author F. K. Davis. Without your support and help, I would feel so lost in my journey. Thank you for providing me direction. You are the crosslinker that stabilized my process, and for that, I will forever be thankful. Not only have you provided me the resources to help me pursue my passion, but your lab has also inspired other book ideas that I am excited to write about. An extra special thank you to Vedshree Deshmukh, Peter Jansen, Mimi Ghosh, and Raima Puri, thank you for letting me geek out about my book with you. Whether it be via text or in the lab, your support, advice, and encouragement provided me much needed confidence, and I appreciate each and everyone of you.

Thank you LSAMP Gang and OSU friends for all your encouragement. Your excitement is addicting and has helped me power through my edits.

Finally, thank you to my aunt, Auntie Tami, for encouraging me to stick to my January 31st deadline to finish writing the book. I beat it by four days.

About the Author

M. C. Jeter is an American writer from Northeast Ohio. A current student at the Ohio State University, she is studying neuroscience with a minor in American Sign Language. She is set to graduate in May 2024 and intends to apply to medical school and continue her education there. She will continue to write as it is one of her passions and a means of self care. *The Gems* is her first novel and she plans to continue the trilogy with two novellas *The Gems: Emerald Eyes* and *The Gems: Sapphire Secrets*.

Scan here for access to my website, newsletter, Instagram, Tiktok, Spotify profile, Goodreads profile, and more!

Who ~~am~~ I?   Who are we?

most importantly...
What can we do

Note to self: Leave space to add more information
later on!

Take / print more pictures of everyone !!!

SIBLINGS	AGE	MONTH BORN IN	POWERS
Garnet	20	January	Petrification
Amethyst	18	February	Elasticity
Aquamarine	11	March	Telekinetic Telepaths
Jade	11	March	Telekinetic Telepaths
Diamond	16	April	Prehensile hair
Emerald	17	May	Escape Artistry
Pearl	17	June	Teleportation
Moonstone	17	June	Levitation/gliding
Alexandrite	17	June	Super Speed
Ruby	17	July	Invisibility
Peridot	18	August	Claircognizance
Sapphire	17	September	Siren Song
Opal	~~13~~ 14	October	Animal Morphing
Tourmaline	~~13~~ 14	October	Power replication
Jasper	~~13~~ 14	October	Shape Shifting
Citrine	9	November	Fire manipulation
Topaz	9	November	Water manipulation
Turquoise	16	December	Ecological Empathy
Tanzanite	16	December	Enhanced Intelligence
Zircon	16	December	Technopathy

Tuesday September 13th 2022

The Legend of the Twelve

Know	Don't Know
• Atlantic Slave Trade	• True Origin
• First Twelve	• Genetic mutation or Gifted from Ancestors?
↳ Twelve slaves with amazing abilities	• Magic

The Legend:
~ 12 slaves took over a ship turning it back to Africa
~ Healed & helped those who were sick
~ 12 magical hands, 12 slaves disappeared when the ship landed
↓
invisibility? my power?

★* How the heck do I find out more?
• College?

I'mma Dukie now

Monday September 12th 2022
Ruby ~~Dent~~ Gem (me)   she/her
Birthday: 7/1/2005   Age: 17
Power: Invisibility (so cool!) (ツ)
   • fast cell regeneration
   ↳ I'm immortal ???
   • can't mask sound   ↑ no... none of
   • walk through walls   us are
        ↳ manipulation of matter?

Call me Casper bitch

• Jewish? Spiritual? Kosher ☑
   • What do I believe in
   ★ I should go to therapy :)

Garnet Gem   she/her
Birthday: 1/1/2002   Age: 20
Power: Petrification
   • Temporary Paralysis
      • ungloved hand to the heart

Other info: + Stubborn   + Gloves
+ Condescending   + "The Boss"   + red finger waves
+ Scary   + light skin   + Christian

Sapphire Grem — She/her
Birthday: 9/1/2005 — Age: 17
Power: Siren Song
    • compels others with her tone of voice

Other Info:
- Blue Butterfly locs
- Bohemian aesthetic
- Super sweet and pretty
- fluent in ASL
- Christian

Citrine Grem — She/her
Birthday: 11/1/2012 — Age: 9
Power: X Fire manipulation
    • linked to emotion   • fire power
    • magma controlling

Other Info:
- Sassy
- Hot head
- SO MUCH HAIR
- attitude
- Bullies me (ㅠ.ㅠ)
- Potty Mouth
- Loud
- Zach's #2 fan
- Christian
- non verbal
- → Therapy?
    ↳ She needs help managing her trauma
        ↳ who could help?

Zircon (Ziri) Gem   She/her
Birthday: 12/1/2005   Age: 16
Power: Technopathy
• Computer whiz   • electricity too?

Other info: she is very cool
• Bantu Knots   • Big glasses   • nice I guess?
• Agnostic   ✳ Also needs therapy
                    ↳ we ALL need therapy
                        ↳ Gem therapist? Doctors Mom &
                    Dad trusted?
                            Ask them

Tanzanite (Tani) Gem   She/her
Birthday: 12/1/2005   Age: 16
Power: Enhanced Intelligence
• Super smart I guess
• A walking Google

Other info:
• a little socially awkward   • Big Glasses   • Wavy lace
• a little condescending   • Agnostic
↰ mental note: thoroughly   • Death Date: 10/23/2022
think so you don't sound   ✳ Rest in Peace in the stars
like an idiot when you speak   ✳

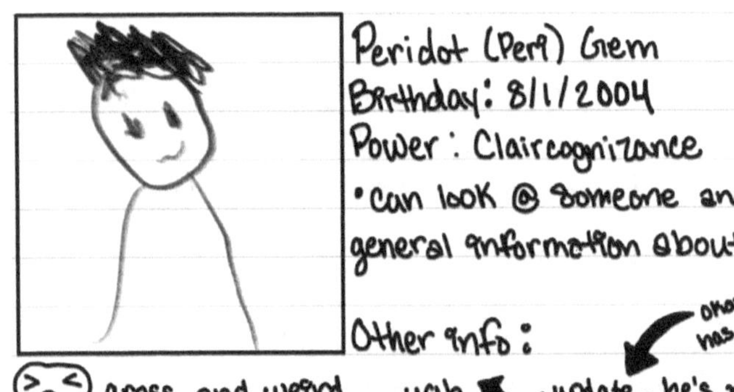

Peridot (Peri) Gem — he/him
Birthday: 8/1/2004 — Age: 18
Power: Claircognizance
• Can look @ someone and know some general information about them

Other info:
okay he has passed the vibe check now ✓
gross and weird... ugh ← update, he's not that bad
• Curly hair   • Fuck-boy Face   • light skin   • Stylish   • annoying
• Comedian   • dependable

Moonstone (Moon) Gem — she/her
Birthday: 6/1/2005 — Age: 17
Power: ✗ Levitation
• manipulates gravity
• Can float!

Other info:
no more secrets ↙
+ Bestie and sister   • Kanekalon white Box Braids!
ICONIC
♀ Goddess energy
✝ Christian

Monday September 26th 2022

Turqoise (Turq) Gem — She/her
Birthday: 12/1/2005 — Age: 16
Power: Ecological Empathy
- Cries when people step on grass
- Can cast herself into nature

(Damn)

She can control her power now so not so much anymore

Other info:
- Depressed

Tani is Dead

- Sensitive topic: adoptive parents
- loose curls
- Soft girl and modern vibe aesthetic
- Spiritual

Aquamarine (Aqua) Gem — She/her
Birthday: 3/1/2011 — Age: 11
Power: Telekinesis & Telepathy
- read her twin's mind
- Can move things w/ mind

and other people now too

Other Info:
- Identical twins (They look so similar >.<)
- The quiet one
- Dark skin
- Curly kinky hair

Jade Gem | She/her
Birthday: 3/1/2011
Power: Telekinesis and Telepathy
• Same as Aqua

Other Info:
• refer to Aqua's entry   • The loud one (well, loudER)
                          • I'm not a bad sister, I'm just lazy

Emerald (Emmy) Gem | he/him
Birthday: 5/1/2005 | Age: 17
Power: Escape Artistry
   • modern day Houdini

Other Info:
• hazel green eyes   • dangly braids   • Band nerd!   • Magician
• Christian   ★ Emmy? More like enEMY   • COWARD
   why did he do it?

Topaz Gem   She/her
Birthday: 11/1/2012   Age: 9
Power: Water Manipulation
  • waterbender   #atla
#SouthernWaterTribe #otterpenguins

Other Info: She prefers cool
                     colors though

• Citrine's twin! → polar opposite • NOT BLUE TOPAZ
• Quiet & calculated   • Dependable • So sweet
• Muslim   • Citrine's crutch
          ↳ Does Citrine talk to Topaz?

Opal Gem   They/Them
Birthday: 10/1/2008   Age: 13 14
• Can communicate and morph into now
any animal

Other Info:

• Gender fluid   • High fade iridescent curls • light skin
• Competitive   • Muslim

✻ Mental note: hang out w/ the October triplets more!

Tourmaline (Tory) Gem   She/her

Birthday: 10/1/2008   Age: ~~18~~ 14

Power: Power mimicry
- Basically a copy cat
- leaches power from other's stones

Other info:

- Super Kind   • Quiet   • Close to Pearl   • Spiritual
  ↳ has an angry side

Jasper Gem   he/him

Birthday: 10/1/2008   Age: ~~18~~ 14

Power: Shapeshift
- Can shape shift into inanimate objects
  ↳ takes their properties

Other info:

- Basketball   • Short   • apparantly super cool
- Christian   ↳ I want to find out on my
- fav. player is Kobe Bryant... I think   own
  ↳ screensaver on phone

Alexandrite (Alex) Gem   she/her
Birthday: 6/1/2005   Age: 17
Power: Super speed
  • pretty self explanatory

Other Info:
- pinkalicious soft girl vibes   • Grew up with Pearl
- a little impatient   • Christian

Pearl Gem   she/her
Birthday: 6/1/2005   Age: 17
Power: Teleportation
  • Can go anywhere
    ↳ within a given distance

Other Info:
- Bossy   • Goth/edgy aesthetic   • Always chewing gum
- piercing galore   • Honest   • Bad Bitch energy
    ↳ The coolest Gem of them all

Pictures 📷

Saturday
        December 3rd 2022
We couldn't find the Switch one weekend. We were looking for it Everywhere. Alex was hiding in the Training Room playing Animal Crossing. She's a hard core cozy gamer!

Thursday November 24th 2022
For our first ever thanksgiving, Perl INSISTED that he choose everyone's outfits. I have to admit, we looked great, but I just wish I could wipe that smug smirk off his face

Pictures Cont!

Saturday May 13th 2023
Mom would CONSTANTLY
tell us all about how she
always wished she had
a vegetable and flower
garden, but she didn't have
a green thumb. Tung
started growing a beautiful
garden in the backyard,
all while for Mom's Mother's
Day gift, all while sipping
a lemonade!

Thursday October 6th
2022
The picture Peri
snapped of me while
my foot was still
stuck in the wall
of the training
room. I was so not
in the mood LOL